The Kiss
That Saved Me

Kristy Nicolle

Kristy Nicolle
x

The Tidal Kiss Trilogy – Book 2

TRILOGY ONE IN
THE QUEENS OF FANTASY SAGA

First published by Kristy Nicolle, United Kingdom, June 2016

QUEENS OF FANTASY EDITION (1ˢᵗ EDITION)
Published June 2016 by: Sapphire Press
Copyright © 2016 Kristy Nicolle

Edited by: Jaimie Cordall and Kristine Schwartz
Cover by Red Umbrella Graphic Designs

Adult Paranormal/Fantasy Romance

ISBN: 978-1-911395-02-7

www.kristynicolle.com

For Ali and Juanita

Most people talk about the harshest Winters they can remember.
I want to talk about the kindest.

Prologue

ORION

I watch her sleeping beside me. I want to wake her, shatter her dreams and give her a waking experience better than anything running through her beautiful mind. My heart breaks at the fragility of it all as I remind myself that I must be patient and let her find consciousness on her own. My father taught me to be patient. Or at least he tried. My father taught me to be a gentleman. Or I thought he had. The problem is, you see, he didn't teach me how to love. Where are the boundaries? How do you possess someone without imprisoning them? How do you hold a heart in the palm of your hand without crushing it? If only he had taught me these things. She did not want patience, for she was the speed of light. Nor a gentleman for she was coarser than volcanic sand. What she wanted was to be free. Free to die. To martyr herself in the name of love. I do not, cannot understand this, for my father did not teach me, and can no longer teach me, for he is entropy. A sweeping fine entropy. Waiting patiently for me to slip through the waist of the hourglass in the Ocean of time. Waiting until we meet again.

1

Rose-Tinted Haze

CALLIE

I collapse back onto the dusky, rose coloured silk sheets of the finely crafted, mahogany, four poster bed. My chest rises and falls, rises and falls, rises and falls as the silk drapes over my goose-pimpled flesh like water, cooling the ravenous blood that courses around my circuitry. My hair is spread out around me and it tickles my ears in that all too familiar way as a bead of sweat runs from the dip in my collar bone, between my breasts and settles on my stomach before dissipating in the heated air of the ornate room. My mind is in a rosy haze, foggy and delighted by passionate sex that could have lasted hours for all I know. My legs are like jelly and my arms are splayed out, feeling beneath the sheets like a skin seeking missile.

"Orion?" I call into the darkness, and I hear a stir from the bathroom, the door is open a crack and the tiniest beam of stark white light is falling onto my face as I prop myself up, allowing the silken sheets to slip, leaving my chest bared to the night air.

"I'm coming hold on." I hear him reply, so serious after all the fun we've just had. I want to frown but my forehead can't find the will to crease. He emerges from the bathroom, silhouetted against the light in all his glory, a Greek demi-god in every sense of the word. His ripped abdominals, moving fluidly into the seductive triangle that frames his groin, ripples as he turns off the light and moves to relight the candles that have long since burned dim. His eyes are set on me like a hawk, watching terrified, but I choose to ignore this and focus on his ass which is now turned toward me.

"You okay?" he asks, catching the longing look in my eyes.

1

"Of course." I reply automatically in answer to his new favourite question. He sits down on the bed and pulls the sheets over his legs, coming to lay beside me in my dusky tinted field of vision. He draws the net curtains of the bed, so only dim candlelight penetrates the space. I curl into his chest, kissing the smooth surface and nuzzling the lines of definition over his heart.

"Mmmm" I murmur, breathing him in.

"Shhhh." He demands, knotting his hands in my hair and pulling my head back so my eyes meet his dominating stare. My eyes water.

"Kiss me." He commands. It is not a question, it is not a plea, but rather something that has sprung from terror. I watch the new fear dance lightly behind his irises, it is something born from the very moment I decided to die. I obey him and his tongue possesses me slowly, assaulting my senses and I let him take me. This is not like the first time we made love, it is different, animal and desperate, a need to possess above all else. Something that he craves to repeat over and over. Perhaps then this is madness. His hand glides down to the apex of my thighs and I let them fall apart, surrendering to his control, letting him love me, if that's what this really is. I could ponder that question forever, but instead I choose to stay lost, lost in a rose-tinted haze, from which, I really could not give a damn.

The warm ocean waters beckon in the dim light of the morning, their call pulling at me from within my blood.

"Come on Callie!" Orion calls to me from the edge of the shore. I have no idea where we are, a beach somewhere in California but the exact location I'm not quite sure of. *Jeez he's so impatient*, I think to myself as I jog quickly across the sand to catch up to him.

"Ready?" He asks me, taking firm grip of my hand in his smooth palm.

"As ever." I say the two words breathlessly as my calves' burn from lack of use. He places an arm around the back of me, ushering me into the waves. I pull the floor length cotton night dress over my head and stand nude in the lavender hues of dawn. Orion pulls off his jeans and wades in after me, I stop to stare at his ripped silhouette, anxious that we still have two more nights together before the full moon leaves us.

"You are so beautiful Callie Pierce." He compliments me, I've heard him say these words a million times, but recently they've become pained. Desperate like everything else between us.

"And you are so handsome Orion Fischer." I return and his eyes blaze, the flame behind them all-consuming. He towers above me, swooping down as we stand waist deep in the cool waves, cupping my face and allowing his fingers to tangle through my curls. His mouth meets mine leaving me gasping for air as I feel the change take me back to what I am at my core.

Underneath the warm ocean surface we spend the day travelling.

"Are you nervous?" I ask him half-heartedly as I watch an Emperor Tang circle my tailfin playfully.

"About?" Orion looks withdrawn, as is a usual state for him since the death of his father.

"You know what I'm talking about," I smile at him slyly, trying to coax a response.

"Yes I do, and I don't want to talk about it." He sighs as we continue to journey through the sea, coral and sand passing below us, silently teeming.

"Ignoring it isn't going to make it go away you know," I pry further and watch his brow crease in distaste of the subject.

"All we've done for the past four months is talk about it, Callie. Aren't you sick of talking about it? I would have thought you would have been sick of small council meetings, grand council meetings, and all the other stupid irrelevant shit we've been dealing with ever since my father..." He trails off, crumpling under the weight of his own memories.

"Left you his Kingdom?" I finish for him, trying to turn Atlas' death into something positive. Something it really isn't.

"I don't want it, I've never wanted it." Orion bites the words out as though they pain him.

"It isn't your choice. The votes have been cast. Your people *want* you Orion... more than that, they *need* you."

"I'm a warrior. Not a politician and certainly not a ruler."

"Neither am I," I remind him gently. He's stopped stroking against the current with his long body and is allowing the water to carry him as he lies on his back looking up at the sun through the barrier that separates us from the air. I push myself forward, taking thick breaths of water and lie myself on his chest, looking down into his eyes with my palm over his heart. "Look, I know you're scared about being the one everyone turns to. It's a dangerous time right now. But it's in your blood. I know you'll be great, and Atlas knew it too." Orion melts slightly under my touch and his eyes fill with fear.

"I'm sorry about the last few months. This isn't what I wanted. I didn't want this for us. I wanted to show you the world. Not have you stand on ceremony while I lead an army to war." He runs his hand through his hair, resting it on the back of his neck in the way he does when he's worried.

"You don't know that there'll be a war, Orion. No one knows that, not even Starlet and she can see the future."

"I know she hasn't said anything, but I can tell something's bothering her. She's barely been able to sit across from me in the small council meetings, other than that I haven't seen her at all," Orion responds and I can't say he's wrong. I've noticed Starlet's discomfort around us too. I guess I'd just figured it was because she didn't like me that much.

"No matter what happens, I'll be by your side. You aren't in this alone." I wrap my arms around his thick body and nuzzle his chest. The water is fairly still around us and I find a peace I had been seeking since leaving the hotel room this morning.

"I... I know," he falters and I raise my head.

"I'm serious, Orion. No matter how many boring ceremonies I have to stand through I'm not going to run. As long as we still make time for us."

"That's what I want to ensure. I think you and I need somewhere to go that isn't a sanctum. Somewhere that's ours. Where we aren't crowned rulers... just us." Orion muses and I smile.

"And where do you suggest... we had enough trouble finding a hotel to stay in last night after you so quickly decided we just had to take off yesterday," I ask remembering being pulled through the water and away from the city so hard I thought my arm would come out of its socket.

"I needed to get away. The Alcazar Oceania is making me feel like a caged animal." Orion admits and I do understand, after the last few months

4

we had barely found any time to get out into the open ocean. Everyone was too worried about the Psirens' increasing numbers to leave the city alone and they were looking to us to keep it protected. We had found ourselves trapped as Orion had sent the Knights of Atargatis to the coastline, trying to prevent what Azure had informed us was a large recruitment of 'lost souls' by Psirens. She had finally revealed that Psirens could make more of their kind through a transfer of blood with humans. It was a decision we had to make, but it didn't make having the guardians as the only form of protection for the city any easier. Especially now that the Psirens had once been inside, showing a hole in the city's glimmer of defence which was upheld by Saturnus. His red hair and green eyes float into my mind.

"I know. Did you tell Saturnus you were leaving?" I ask and watch his expression turn incredulous.

"Are you kidding? Mr Grumpy Gills? Mr *You are the beacon of shining hope to our people in a time of encroaching darkness?*"

"So that's a no then?" I giggle, remembering the hideously angry expression Saturnus tried to hide when the votes were counted and he lost by an alarming differential to Orion. "I still don't understand why Saturnus got so angry about having to stay hand to the crown." I bite my lip, feeling uncomfortable as we continue to glide slowly across the ocean floor, allowing ourselves to fall to the depths of the ocean in lazy momentum.

"I don't understand why he wanted to be Crowned Ruler. It's a ridiculous job," Orion sighs again and I laugh at him.

"Well, I still don't understand why everyone voted for us."

"I do." Orion looks at me, adoring me so much in that second I feel slightly sick.

"You do?" I ask him curiously and he nods as we finally hit the sand and it billows up around us in the water. The conversation has dominated everything, stopping our journey. I stare into Orion's glacial gaze as I lay on top of him, flicking my tail behind me playfully.

"It's you, Callie."

"What the hell did I do?" I ask accusatorily.

"You're a hero to the people of the Occulta Mirum, I mean surely you've noticed…"

"My million and one new best mermaid friends?" I cock my brow and he nods fighting the urge to laugh. Things have certainly changed ever since that night, I admit to myself. I'm now the centre of attention at parties among the other mer after I sacrificed myself to save them.

"But what about you? You're the real hero. Sophia told me about how you made that giant tidal wave and blew the army out of the city. All I did was hold on to the scythe and..." I stop, unable to admit to myself what has passed.

"Die." Orion bites out the word like a curse and his gaze is feral. He looks angry and suddenly I can't think of anything to say. I don't want another argument. It seems that's all we do these days, argue about my death and maul each other in a passionate frenzy. It's exhausting and pointless, it's not like I stayed dead.

"Yeah." The silence engulfs us as we disentangle from each other, beginning our momentum again.

"Hey... why don't you use your powers more often? I mean, I didn't know you were that powerful." I ask him, fluttering my eyelashes slightly.

"I dunno... I guess I don't like using them, I want to beat my enemies on fair ground. With the Psirens, it's hard to explain, but it's not like with demons, it's like a family feud. I don't want to be accused of winning by cheating." He shrugs and my brow creases.

"Titus didn't seem to care about using his powers. That tidal wave thingy must have been amazing. You could protect the city indefinitely with that..." I muse. He frowns.

"I can't perform this stuff on que, Callie. They were special circumstances." He looks miserable at the thought of losing me, watching me fall still under the moonlight once more. This grates at me a little. I wish he would just let it go.

"We still have tonight free anyway, unless you want to head back. The coronation isn't until tomorrow night after all." I break the silence after a few moments of swimming side by side.

"I actually have a gift for you. I thought we could take a look tonight." Orion looks at me and I can't quite tell what he's feeling. His jaw is hard set but his eyes have softened slightly.

"You know I don't need any more gifts. You already had my dress made for tomorrow night's ceremony," I remind him, the image of the gown flashing across my mind as he nods.

"This is something I bought with the money Shaniqua gave to me, you know, from my father. I didn't want to say anything until the details were finalised. Besides, I have more money than I need and I like being able to buy you things." He pouts, his royal blue facial scales glimmering, and I instantly feel bad.

"You didn't have to buy me anything with that money, Orion. That was your father's, he would want you to spend it on yourself," I say feeling guilty. I remember only too well my disgust over how the mer remain wealthy, selling their sorrow in the form of their tears which turn to diamond in sea water.

"This is for us, not just you." He bites out the words again, still clenching his jaw. I could ask him what's wrong, but it would just lead to another argument and I just don't have the energy. The fight in me has gone. It's been lost ever since the night I returned to this world.

We pass the day in denial. Escaping our prospective responsibilities and losing ourselves in the magic of the sea. A pod of Commerson dolphins befriend us as the sun reaches its full height in the sky, Orion and I take to playing with them, creating a makeshift ball out of a buoy we fish from the surface. Orion uses his ability over air to cause the buoy to sink and we devote our afternoon to pure fun, so sick of all the meetings and the formalities that have taken over our lives. The dolphins, a hearty party of six, enjoy this immensely, nudging me and Orion with excitement as we pass the ball between us, trying to get it over the dolphins as they race, batting the ball off course whenever they can. We race them too, speeding through the water and jumping out of its cooling clutches at regular intervals, pulling somersaults and corkscrews as the dolphins match our height and agility stroke for stroke. We don't really talk, because that's dangerous right now, but we do enjoy one another's company, laughing and splashing loudly, forgetting the weight of the world which in no time will once again be lying on our shoulders.

"It's getting late," Orion says as the dolphins depart off to find some dinner, taking the buoy with them and nudging it along the top of the water in the cutest fashion ever.

"So where to?" I ask as I note the sun lowering in the sky.

"Not far, we're just off the coast of L.A"

"We've come that far north?" I ask feeling surprised at the distance we've covered in one afternoon.

"It goes by quickly when you're racing a dolphin pod, doesn't it?" For the first time in a while, Orion's expression is like it used to be, when he was showing me his world but viewing it through my eyes. He looks joyous and proud of the seas which he protects and all that they hold. In this look I see the Crowned Ruler he can be. That I want him to be.

"Yeah, it's been a great afternoon." I smile, hugging myself as I feel a little tension that I didn't even realise was in my gut unknot.

"I know you're going to love what I got you."

"I thought it wasn't *for* me." I say rolling my eyes at him incredulously.

"Hey I'm just saying... I would have been happy with another hotel room." Orion winks and I slap his arm playfully through the water.

"You mean you got us somewhere to stay?" I ask looking at him with wide eyes.

"Not just any place to stay, Callie. *Our* place to stay. A place where, as promised, there are no crowned rulers... just you and me. Callie and Orion."

"Thank you," I gush reaching forward to stroke the side of his face, he grabs my hand.

"Don't thank me yet. You might hate it." He smiles and places a hand on my back, ushering me forward as we begin to undulate against the current racing against the setting sun.

"I doubt that, you have impeccable taste, it's actually really annoying."

"How's that?" He asks, his brow cocked and his mouth twisted at one side.

"Did you ever even contemplate being slightly imperfect?" I ask him with a sly smile. He returns and runs his hand through his tousled locks, knowing it turns me on, as he turns to swim on his side next to me. He flashes me a Hollywood smile and I feel my heart flutter unwillingly. Goddamn him and his eternal beauty.

"Nope. Not a drop." He grins wickedly and races forward. I pout as bubbles fly up in my face, tickling my skin and enticing me to accept his speed challenge as always. I pick up my pace, a grinding, gruelling rhythm that isn't even half as fast as his, though being quicker than any dolphin or whale in these waters I still couldn't match his speed, and it wasn't for a lack of trying either. I catch up to him eventually, but it's only because we reach the shoreline and he slows to a halt grinning. I never question how he knows where we are going in the hundreds of miles of ocean that all look similar to me, but without fail he always gets me where we're supposed to go.

"Ready?" He asks, holding a hand out to me. I nod in acknowledgement and his expression remains beautifully passive. We wait in the shallows for the last dying embers of sunlight to flicker out on the horizon, sat in the shallow sand with our tails concealed by the waterline and our bodies out in the dry air. If you walked by we would look like any other couple.

"Aren't you worried about people seeing us?" I ask him and he laughs.

"Nope."

"Because...."

"Because I own this beach and everything on it." Orion looks at me with a deliciously satisfied smile as my mouth pops open.

"You know what most guys get their girlfriends Orion? Jewellery, maybe a bunch of flowers?"

"Yes, but you make two assumptions. That I am both a guy and normal. Which I thought you would have figured out by now is false at best." I scowl at him but he chuckles again, laughing at me.

"You're right... and I said that you were my boyfriend which implies you're a boy. Not an old man." I quip back at him and he splashes me with faux offence plastered over his porcelain features. "Seriously Orion, you didn't have to do this." I look at the beach behind us, it isn't miles long but it's still pretty big and I wonder... exactly how much money did Atlas leave his son?

"Nonsense, this is a good investment, and we can't put a price on discretion when it comes to our comings and goings at odd hours." What he says makes sense and I roll my eyes.

"True. I hate it when you make your extravagant spending seem logical."

"I know." He pokes his tongue out at me and he's almost carefree.

"So there's somewhere for us to hang our hats around here right?" I ask, turning back from the beach to look out at the horizon.

"Of course. Turn around." I turn as Orion commands and I notice that perched on a climbing outcrop of the rising cliffs that cup the beach into a beautiful semi-circle is a lone house. My mouth pops open in awe. Okay... so house is underselling it.

Orion's gift to me, is more decadent than any Cartier watch or Gucci handbag. Nuzzled on a low hanging clifftop, among beachy flora and under the cries of departing gulls, it sits. As we embrace the change together and emerge from the water, once again human, I can't help but be distracted from my nakedness.

"Come." Orion beckons to me and up the shore in a wicker basket are two large white fluffy robes. I pull one over my shoulders and wrap it around myself.

"Always prepared," I mutter and Orion smiles to himself.

"Thank Georgia, she moved in all the furniture and drove your car up here. It's in the driveway."

"Good ol' Georgia," I mumble to myself, not allowing my hostility against the image of her mentally undressing Orion to ruin my mood. At least we have robes and I don't have worry about being arrested for indecency. Though with the lusting part of being a mermaid, I'd probably have the cops drooling over their shoes, giving me a chance to bang them over the head with something.

Orion and I creep once more, as is becoming habit to us, over the sand of a beach semi clad and dripping wet. I kind of understand why Orion didn't bother coming ashore so much before I existed for him, seeing as even with someone like Georgia to organise everything it can be a pain. *He came ashore to have sex with other women though,* my subconscious snarls at me. I banish this thought from my mind once more as we begin to climb the sand dunes that lead to the incline of the cliff which holds the house. Twilight opens above us, weeping vanilla, lavender and periwinkle down as a birth of new stars hang dimly in the dying light. The house stands, modern in its design, a single story.

"It looks so cosy," I comment as Orion and I climb across the sand and up towards where the cliff begins to climb horizontal to the sea.

"I'm almost wounded you would use the word cosy to describe this place." He looks at me seriously.

"Why?"

"This house is far more than it seems." He gesticulates downward.

"You mean it goes into the cliff?" I look at him incredulously.

"Yes. This isn't just any house, Callie."

"Meaning?" I feel excitement rise within me as he smiles.

"I designed it," he acknowledges.

"You did?" He nods vigorously, his tousled locks glowing slightly auburn in the warm dying light of the sun just below the horizon.

"Of course. I'm not just going to buy us any old place. If I wanted to do that I'd have bought one of the houses on the beach where we first met." He looks at me with a gaze full of soft sentimentality.

"Well, can we go inside?" I beg him, unable to keep the joy out of my words at the extravagance of the gift.

"After you, Princess." He whispers his pet name and I feel myself choke up a little, it's a word I haven't heard in a while, something he's refrained from using ever since it had become a real possibility that we would rule. I run up the remainder of the cliff, my feet pounding against the ebbing heat of the concrete as the cliff rises away from sea level and then twists into a jutting edge on which the house is perched. The moon is rising right before my eyes, enormous and magnificent, kissing the sea with its glowing curves. The house on closer inspection is clearly brand new, untouched. The cliff opens up into the platform which forms the houses foundation and a white picket fence separates the front garden.

"A white picket fence?" I query aloud.

"What can I say, I'm a traditionalist." Orion catches my sentiment as it is swept up in the cool salty breeze and I turn to him.

"I love it." I kiss him on the cheek, his rough stubble tickling my lips.

"You haven't even stepped inside the fence yet!" He exclaims.

"What can I say, I'm easy to please." I shrug and he ushers me forward. I move toward the fence and open the matching gate, it swings forward with a creak of new wood and unused hinges. I feel Orion at my back and step into the front garden, which reminds me of a Zen Garden from Japan. There are tiny water fountains, and fairy lights hang, dangled from something invisible to the eye, twinkling intermittently. The floor is covered in smooth pebbles that roughly caress my bare feet. Potted palm trees tower in each corner of the fence perimeter, swaying slightly. I step along the pebble clad path, taking in the neutral beiges and greys that calm me. Orion overtakes me, taking a gold key out of the pocket of his robe and moving toward the glass panelled white French doors. The glass has a pattern scored into it that I recognise.

"Hey that's my tattoo!" I comment and he nods smiling.

"I want this house to reflect us, and I love that tattoo." He winks at me cheekily.

"You're impossible." I breathe and he grabs my hands, pulls me into his arms and carries me through the door.

The inner space I'm carried forward into is unbelievable. The whole space is stark white and onyx black. The floor is white tile, but the individual tiles have fibre optic lights that glimmer intermittently, making the floor look like an alabaster milky-way. The walls are white too, with similar fibre optics but these are coloured and move progressively around the outside of the walls, swirling and curling repeatedly in a wave like pattern. The ceiling is black and shiny, reflecting the light specks back at me.

"Holy crap," is all I can manage as Orion places me down on my feet.

"You like?" Orion asks me, his lips are quirked, pleased with himself.

"Orion... it's..." I begin but he runs across my sentiment with his own excitable babble.

"There's more." He slides his fingers through mine and pulls me out of the hall and forward into the living area. This space really is cosy, despite the extravagances within the walls and floors. The centre of the room is home to four ice blue corner sofa's, each upholstered in fleece and scattered with aqua throw pillows. They look luxuriously soft and I can't help but skip forward on the balls of my feet and jump onto the closest sofa, laughing as I fall backward, hair splayed out in a halo of curls against the softness that surrounds me. I curl onto my side and look at the colour. It reminds me of Orion's eyes. I close my own and bury myself into the depths of the seat, letting the fleecy embrace hold me. I hear Orion move around to sit next to me. I sit up, snapping my eyes open as he places an arm around my shoulders.

"Let me show you something." He smiles at me, pulling a small black remote out from his robe pocket.

"That robe is like Mary Poppins' handbag. Seriously... you'll pull out a flat screen next." I joust him and his forehead divot appears.

"Mary who...?" He asks... Damn I seriously need to get him some lessons in movies.

"Pop culture thing..." I mumble and he smiles again calmly. I wonder if he thinks I'm crazy. Well, I suppose if he does it just proves how well he knows me.

"I don't have a flat screen in my pocket... but," he clicks a button and part of the wall panel opposite the sofas slides away. A seventy-five inch, flat screen is revealed.

"You like TV?" I ask him with a smile.

"No... But you do," he returns and I nod slightly.

"Maybe we can watch some movies together?" I suggest and he kisses me on the forehead.

"Whatever you want," he whispers.

"So that's the TV remote?" I ask him and he shakes his head.

"No. This is the house remote. I have one for you too." He hands me one out of the mystical pocket of his robe. I take it in my palm, power ebbing through me at the possession of so many buttons.

"FP?" I ask looking at a big red button at the top of the rectangular plastic console.

"Press it," he commands and so I do. Much to my astonishment, the ceiling falls down soundlessly, bringing with it a square fire pit.

"A fire place in the ceiling?" I ask him and he smiles.

"I've always wanted to make love in front of a fire place. Something about heat on my bare back." He gives me a hungry stare and I look down at the remote again, trying to distract myself.

"What's this one?" I look at him again, pointing to the lilac, blue, green, and red options underneath the FP button.

"Press them. It's more fun getting to see the surprised look on your face." I indulge him and press the lilac option down. The fireplace erupts into hearty flame, but this flame burns with a beautiful purple haze.

"Purple fire?" I ask him and he nods with a smile on his face. "You want me to get some money so we can use it for kindling, or is there a button for that too?" I tease him and he pouts.

"If I'm building a house and going to the trouble of buying the land, getting damn human planning permission, and hiring a team of construction workers, I'll have whatever colour fire I damn well please," he growls in an authorative tone. He claims he doesn't have the capacity for leadership, but with every stroke of his dextrous hands, every step of his purposeful stride, and every order barked from his lips, I know he is wrong.

"So where's the kitchen?" I query, changing the subject.

"Turn around." I notice now that the great room is an L-Shape and as I look back over my shoulder I notice an expansive kitchen. I rise from the couch and pad over to behind the square kitchen island. Everything in this culinary oasis is black chrome and stark white granite which is speckled with silver flecks. The double doors of the fridge are cold as I pull them open and find the fridge full of food.

"Wow. There's so much junk food in here." I say to him with a concerned look.

"Don't look so worried, it's not like we can get fat. We only eat three nights a month... why not eat something that doesn't taste like processed grass." Orion smiles.

"You like junk food?" I ask him feeling surprised.

"When I was a human, all I had to eat was olives, salad, fish, and this oatmeal grain crap. The way I see it the Goddess blessed me with a long life so I could experience the Twinkie." As this sentence hits the air a bubble of high pitched laughter escapes my lips.

"You like Twinkies? You just wait until I order you Dominos. Or even better, In-N-Out burger." I say to him and he raises his eyebrows.

"Dominoes? Like the game?" As I stand in the state of art kitchen I see a certain naivety rise in him and I love him just a little bit more.

"No… it's pizza," I explain and he smiles.

"I like pizza," he reveals. I am reminded in this simple admittance that even after four months there's still a lot I don't know about him.

"Me too. My favourite is pepperoni feast."

"That sounds good."

"You're not the only one who's a traditionalist." I shut the fridge door.

"Do you want to see the rest of the house?" He inquires, holding a hand out to me. I skip to him, slip my palm into his, and smile.

"Yes… Where's the bedroom?" I inquire as innocently as I can but as the final word falls between Orion and me, something within him switches on and a sense of urgency visibly clutches him.

"Come." He commands the one word. Leaving no room for argument.

2
Breathless

CALLIE

In the bowels of the house I expect the décor to become less staggering. However, i'm completely off base. A transparent spiral staircase leads down into the lower levels, which have been carved out of the supposedly immovable rock.

"This is the lower level, which holds a game room, a library, and the master suite."

"Can I see the master suite first?" I ask him, once again feigning innocence with my thick lashes, fluttering them like the wings of butterflies, thrumming with sexual anticipation.

"Of course. Patience." We reach the bottom of the staircase and Orion watches as I get my first look at the room in front of us. The floor is no longer white tile, but has been replaced by cool milk chocolate coloured stone, that's chilly on my feet. We are standing on a platform elevated by a few inches which lowers into a colossally deep swimming pool. A bridge towers above it, built from the same stone, transitioning seamlessly from the floor and rising in a gentle arc over the water, creating dry passage.

"This pool is deep enough that there is an exit at the bottom, an exit which will take us back to the sea," he acknowledges the moon which is dangling low in the sky out of a glass panel which has been inserted into the side of the rock. I wonder how I hadn't noticed it before. I listen for a moment hearing the cool sound of rushing water. A sound I sometimes missed as it was something you didn't really hear beneath the ocean's surface.

Orion glides across the cold floor, still wrapped in his white robe, and leads me across the bridge to the source of the insistent splashing. Across the entirety of one wall is a waterfall, covering the bare rock face in a rush of white spray and transparent curtains of fluid.

"A waterfall?" I look at him incredulously and he laughs again.

"I already told you... If I'm going to be going to the trouble..."

"Of building a house from scratch you'll have what you want yada yada yada..." I dismiss him with a wave of my hand and he grins, wielding his magic house remote from the depths of his robe pocket.

"What are you doing?" I ask him, wondering what he could possibly control in a room with walls made of bare rock.

"You said you wanted to see the master suite," he purrs, sliding an arm around my fluffy waist. I curl into him, his solidness as always a comfort to me. He bends to kiss me and presses a button on the remote and as I open my eyes I see the waterfall part, falling away from the centre of the wall in two sweeping curtains as double doors that are fashioned from the rock itself swing toward me.

"Oh my Goddess." I bring my hands up to my mouth.

"I believe you wanted privacy."

"So you got us a waterfall?" I ask him with a raised eyebrow and he nods smugly.

"You are mad." I shake my head, ringlets tickling my ears as I step cautiously into the master bedroom. Orion steps in behind me and the doors swing shut, the sound of the waterfall eclipsed completely. The silence takes me away from the troubles of the impending war, the responsibilities of the Occulta Mirum, and to where I want to be. With Orion.

Before me spreads pure decadence, the floor is a deep mahogany with white fur rugs placed, straight edged, parallel to the walls. The walls, now I mention it, show what the room once was or has been modified to look like, which is a cave. This however is not the most magnificent show of nature within the room. A panoramic glass window looks out of the cliff face in which I am encased, onto the sea and the giant white orb which is kissing its sparkling surface tenderly. In the centre of the room is the bed, glazed in a beam of dim light from the scattered candles and fairy lights that cling to the crevices in the wall's natural formation. It is circular and stands on an elevated platform, a sensual stage that I can see can be closed off from the rest of the room by a white gossamer curtain that hangs limply from a curved iron rod. Above the bed is more glass, a skylight of wide proportions opening up to the velvet blanket of the night which is scattered with diamond like stars. The sheets on the bed are scarlets and plums, warm colours, the colours I flush when Orion is undressing me under his burning gaze.

"Scarlet silk?" I question him and he looks at me oddly.

"You don't like the colour?" He asks and I shrug my shoulders.

"I'm just surprised. I never figured you for liking scarlet. It's so blatant." I admit to him and he comes towards me.

"So are you."

"You think I'm blatant?" I ask him and he smiles at me.

"Of course. There's no mistaking what you want, Callie. You're headstrong." He removes his robe and stands in the light of a hundred flickering flames, unveiling his glory to me in a brash yanking of the robe from his form.

"I don't think that's true," I comment, biting my lip as I step up onto the raised platform and towards the bed.

"You don't? You're a pretty insistent little thing in bed," he quirks a smile and one breaks across my lips unwillingly.

"You don't seem to mind."

"I relish your demands, Miss Pierce," he purrs, eyes set on me like a jungle cat readying himself to take down his prey. I roll back the white fleece of my robe from my shoulders and let it fall, pooling thickly at my feet. I watch Orion move swiftly around the bed, as though my barren flesh has called to him, as though the space between us is painful.

"You're pretty demanding yourself," I mutter as he reaches me and pulls me toward him, yanking my head back with one hand and pulling one of my knees to his hip with the other. I break the kiss, looking into his frenzied expression. I know I've been flirting, but I can't help myself. I know he needs to talk, scream, maybe have a good cry. I'm so conflicted in this moment between what I want and I what I know he needs I can't help but sigh, "Orion I..."

"Shh," he places a finger to my lips and looks at me with a ferocity I had thought reserved for feral beasts.

"But..." I begin and he kisses me again, shoving his hands into my hair, yanking my waist forward, and clutching at my back. I break away, gasping, my lips red and tender.

"I..." I begin again but he pulls me in closer.

"I need this. Here. Now. Just let me love you, Princess. Please." He pleads with me in a guttural breathless torrent of truncated longing. He traces a finger up my bare spine. I shiver and relinquish, giving into my selfish desires. He pulls me down to the bed with him and takes me, aggressively and without mercy, into a place of thoughtless, submissive ecstasy on top of blatant, bloody, scarlet sheets.

ORION

I lay next to her and watch her, sleeping soundlessly. She's been doing that a lot lately. Sleeping. I wonder why. Is it because she's noticed I'm impenetrable? I wonder when I became like this, so desperately hungry and yet empty... I wonder if it was because I had waited such an eternity for her to arrive, that the dam of unrequited passion had finally burst and had taken my sweet sensibility with it. Her lips match the sheets, scarlet and raw after my possession of them. She stirs beneath, alabaster skin paler than ever by contrast to the 'blatant' folds. Had I thought about the colour of the sheets when I'd designed this room? Probably not, but it seems now to be fitting, fitting that I'm devouring her one limb at a time atop them... fitting that she looks so fragile, so porcelain, lying out naked against them. I rise out of the bed, leaving her alone under the soft fusion of moon and candle light and sweeping my robe off the floor. The pockets are heavy. Maybe that's what's really weighing on my mind. I step across the soft rugs that I had picked to warm her cold feet, they're always so damn cold.

I stand in front of the motion activated doors to the walk in closet I had installed for her shoes and clothes... she had mentioned something about loving shoes and clothes once, I suppose that's a female thing. Whatever she wears, she looks beautiful, but I know she looks most beautiful when she's wearing nothing but a smile. I grin foolishly. The closet stretches out and the doors sweep together behind me, reconstituting the appearance of the rock face. I turn a sharp right and move into the depths of the space, pulling a pair of jeans over my ass and a white shirt over my shoulders, after dumping my heavy robe onto the corner of the chaise longue I had upholstered in red silk too. I look at it and imagine spreading Callie out over the arch of the seat spread eagled.

I look back at the robe lying over the arm rest and internally slap myself. What the hell am I doing? I'm acting like she's a common prostitute... like the women before. Goddess, am I that perverse? She's eighteen for the love of all that's holy. I look at the robe again, unable to draw my eyes away. I walk over to it, palming the fabric and feel the weight. I sit back into the chaise longue and let it hold me. Goddess knows I need it. I rummage through the pocket and pull out my remote. But that isn't the weight that's been weighing heavily on me. I dig deeper and feel it hit the tips of my fingers. Velvet. I grasp it, wondering if by holding it tightly enough I can wrangle it. Make it bend to my will. Take the power it holds over me away. I pull it up, facing the beast. Of course I've seen it before. But this is the first time I've really held it. Had it in the palm of my hand with Callie sleeping next door no less. I examine it. It's so small. I pop the lid and my breath is rushed away on a wind of anticipation and fear. I haven't been this nervous since I waited for her to open her eyes after that night. It winks back at me in the light. All two carats, glinting in the stark florescent of the closet, nestled against the tiny ice blue tinted pearls and aquamarines. It's a beautiful ring. The conversation with Saturnus still haunts me now. I remember, leaning back against the red silk.

One fortnight ago...

20

"Orion, you have to understand. You're going to be crowned ruler, Callie needs to be at your side, supporting you."

"She will be," I bite out at him, angry as per usual.

"Yes, but for how long Orion? She's stubborn, she's restless. She wants to fight. You can't allow that."

"And what do you want me to do, Saturnus? Collar her? Tie her to something? She's a grown woman for Goddess' sake!" I exclaim looking at him.

"The stunt she pulled, not telling you about her role as 'The vessel' was reckless, we both know that Orion. She's a risk. She's dangerous."

"She's also my soulmate," I remind him, breathing in and out thoroughly, trying to extinguish the anger that flares within by consuming as much water as possible.

"Exactly." He looks at me blankly and unfeeling.

"What do you mean?" I ask him with a cocked brow.

"I mean you need to get her under control. It's your responsibility. You two are an example to us all. You need to show unity, especially now."

"Callie doesn't like being dressed up like a pony and paraded around. I don't blame her and you can't make me force her to do anything. She's her own person," I remind him again.

"I was thinking about that. Have you thought about marriage?" He pulls the word out of thin air and I feel my chest expand in surprise.

"You want me to propose to Callie? She's only eighteen, Saturnus. I've only known her five months. People usually wait years now. It's not like it was before." I feel as though he needs a book dictating my relationship history to him. It's like he lives in some kind of fantasy world.

"Women don't care about that Orion. She's expecting it from you. She told me so herself. I've heard her talking about it with the other mermaids too," he reveals and I recoil slightly. Callie wants me to propose? My heart palpitates. I love her so much. Could it be she wants to make it legal so soon?

"You did?" I cock my eyebrow, hope pooling in my stomach slightly as fear clutches at my heart. I wonder if it's normal to be excited and terrified all at once.

"Yes." He looks me straight in the eye and I nod slightly.

"Well then. I suppose I better find a ring." I look at him and rub the back of my neck awkwardly. He beams proudly.

"Your father would be so proud, Orion. He would want to be here to see this," he says clasping at my shoulder with a comforting smile.

I think back to this conversation and look down at the platinum band that is nuzzled in icy blue velvet. The centre diamond is a Princess cut, my nickname for her resounding through each of the fractal surfaces that sparkle. The icy blue pearls have been retrieved from the oyster fields of my people, a twin set, lucky some would say, and the aquamarines I had chosen as they reminded me of her eyes. I look down at the band for a long time until its design and pattern lose meaning. I was going to get it inscribed- but there isn't a sentiment to express my feeling that would be short enough. I get to my feet and pull out my phone. I put the ring back into my robe and dial the oh-so familiar number. She answers on the first ring.

"Georgia," I snap.

"Yes, Mr Fischer." I can hear the liquidity of her tongue through the crackles and pops of the line. The service isn't good, but what do I expect, I'm inside a cliff.

"I'm leaving this ring in our walk in closet in my robe pocket. You'll take it to the Lunar Sanctum and hang the robe in my closet, understood?" I'm barking orders like a drill sergeant these days, but today I'm not in the mood to soften for her. She probably hasn't even noticed, too transfixed by the idea of me to care.

"Yes, Mr Fischer. I'll come at sunrise."

"Good." I hang up the phone bluntly and run my fingers through my tousles. I hang the robe up again, feeling the weight of it, and walk from the closet.

CALLIE

I stir from the depths of forced sleep. My hands reach out, gliding over the sheets, searching for him.

"Orion?" I murmur looking around me. He's gone. He usually waits until I'm awake before leaving. I wonder if maybe watching me sleep reminds him of how I looked when I was in my mystical coma. Technically dead.

"Yes?" I hear him before I see him as he exits the left wall.

"Where did you go?" I ask, pushing myself back and kneeling up, wrapping the sheets around me like the petals of a rose.

"Just checking out the closet," he murmurs. He's wearing jeans and a white shirt now.

"Closet?" My ears prick at the word.

"Want to come see?" He asks and I nod. I move off the mattress, gliding forward, pulling the sheets around me tighter at the front but letting them hang loosely down my back. They reach just above my buttocks, low enough to reveal the ribbon tattoo Orion is fond of. I move over to him and he walks me through the sliding panel in the rock face and turns a quick right. The closet is long and narrow but expansive. A red chaise longue sits propped in front of a dressing table and tall mirror. I move toward it and sit. Orion's eyes blaze.

"What?" I query nervously. He looks like he might take me right here. His mouth contorts.

"Nothing." He replies as I stand and kiss his cheek, distracting him from whatever images are running through his mind.

"Thank you for this. Everything. It's beautiful."

"Would you like to see the rest?" He asks.

"Can I get dressed first?" I ask him, eyeing the racks of untouched clothes still in transparent dry cleaning bags.

"Sure." He leaves the room quickly. Like he can't stand my proximity all of a sudden. I sit back into the chaise longue again, letting the curve of the seat hug my spine. I wonder what Orion's problem is. He's switching between two personas. The first is fevered with a passion unlike anything I have ever seen within him before. The second is as cold as the ice blue of his eyes. I stand to dress, deep in thought, trying to discern how he must be feeling. I know his father's death has affected him, but this runs deeper. Is it something to do with me? I wonder this to myself as I run my fingertips down the long rack of clothes. Silks, velvet, and satin prickle the pads of my fingers and I hesitantly pick out a floor length silk night gown. *Orion really likes me in these, he relishes pulling the skirt up to my waist* I remember, noting that he hasn't actually ever provided me with any night gowns that come above the knee. The sheets I leave discarded in a pool on the floor as I brush past them. I step out into the bedroom and Orion takes my hand, admiring my plunging neckline appreciatively. I say nothing but he eyes me hungrily once more as he leads me from the room, to continue the tour of the rest of the house which he has built for us.

We stand in the kitchen together, leaning against the white graphite of the kitchen island. I'm chopping bacon, preparing to make Orion my famous mac n cheese and bacon. He's got his hand on my belly, arms around me, his fingers interlock over my navel with his head on my shoulder. He kisses the side of my neck, fingering my curls.

"I'm trying to cook," I comment and he laughs huskily.

"I can see that."

"Well then you should know I'm not great at multitasking," I comment.

"I am," he whispers into my neck.

"Please, Orion. I'm hungry," I whine at him.

"Me too."

"I meant for food."

"I didn't." I can't see his face but I feel the lions smile spread across his lips as they pull back, baring his teeth. He sucks at the flesh of my neck.

"Look... Orion...." I try to worm out of his arms.

"Stop wriggling. I can't devour you if you wriggle."

"I don't want you to devour me," I pant, finding his arms immovable as stone. I feel something dig in at my back. My mouth pops open.

"Please tell me that you are poking me in the back with a rolling pin." I turn back over my shoulder and he flips me, using my change in

24

weight to leverage me, trapping me between his body and the counter.

"Nope. You don't need a rolling pin for mac'n'cheese." He purrs, kissing me.

"Orion! Stop!" I squeal. I really am hungry. I really don't want to placate him with sex and if I were a normal woman I'd be putting up a stronger front of defence. As it stands if I don't let him take me now he won't have his hands on me for potentially another month and I just can't stand that thought. He growls, a deep sound escaping him desperately and in one flail swoop knocks the knife, chopping board, and meat to the floor with a clatter. *Holy crap.* I think to myself as he starts to kiss me. *This is getting out of hand.* He leans me back over the white granite, holding me to him and lifting my ass so it tops the counter. He pulls up my skirt with two hands, predictably sliding them over my legs as he climbs in a graceful leg motion on top of me. I could push him back. Reject him. Tell him we need to talk. But we can talk tomorrow. We can talk after the sun rises. For now I let my denial overtake me once more, let it roll over me in a sensuous wave of momentum. I let Orion make love to me on the kitchen counter. Then on the floor. The icy blue sofas. On the rug next to the fire place which burns lavender. I lose track of time and before I know it I am truly and utterly lost in the ever present rose-tinted haze of his glacial blue and burning gaze.

Sometime later we descend into the depths of the house. I am naked and so is Orion, but it matters little as the sun is rising and we know what we must do. I slip from the chocolate stone steps into the pool beneath the bridge that leads to the master suite. Orion follows in after me as I turn to look back at him. He gets a guilty look on his face.

"What's wrong?" I ask him and he looks hesitant.

"I may have… left you slightly love bitten." He coughs, plunging into the water as to avoid my shocked expression. I look down at myself and notice he's right. Red flecked areas of my flesh show the shadow of where his mouth has been on me. *Oh for craps sake!* I snap internally. *It's not bad enough he has to sex me to death, I've got to go around sporting battle scars now?* He surfaces and I stare at him, unamused.

"I'm sorry."

"This," I gesture to the three or four love bites above my breasts, "Is not cool." I don't yell. I just stare at him, slightly disgusted.

"You think that's bad. You should see your neck. I'm sorry. I just got carried away," he apologises. My hands move up to my neck as I keep myself afloat effortlessly. The thin veil of skin above my carotid is tender. When he said 'devour' he wasn't wrong.

"I'm going to look real classy at the coronation sporting these," I mutter and he looks instantly mortified.

"Oh Goddess, I didn't think about that."

"Yeah well, now I can be the slutty Queen. Great," I snap again and he winces. I stay silent as I feel the change take me. I look up and see the burning sun rising and then I'm back to my usual self. Tail and all. I look down, hoping my breast scales will cover the love bites. They don't.

I turn back to Orion and I see the familiar royal blue facial scales that surround his eyes have returned.

"I really am sorry about these," he murmurs and I nod. Not an acceptance but I'm not going to cause another argument either. Together we plunge to the bottom of the pool and through a small opening. It narrows but I power through, ignoring the encroaching sensations of the inner tube of the slide and the feeling of falling through the remaining height of the cliff. The bottom of the tube comes out into the sea. Orion and I head back to the Occulta Mirum, to all our problems and our new responsibilities.

The Alcazar Oceania towers before us as we reach the centre of the city. Eyes bare down on our undulations as the blackness of my shadow falls over the bottle bases that line the streets, dulling their shine.

"You know what I really hate?" I turn my head to Orion, my back is tickled by a slight warmth from the surface.

"What?" Orion asks me looking worried.

"I really hate it when people watch me like I'm an animal in a zoo," I say to him and he looks apologetic.

"I'm sorry. I wish I could stop them. It'll get better once the coronation is over," he promises, but I wonder if it's really Orion's crowned ruler status that's making me so popular, or if it's actually the events that led to my death.

"I hope you're right," I mumble. We reach the gates of the palace and Cole is guarding the door as usual.

"Oh there you are." He looks concerned and I smile sheepishly into his blue eyes.

"Yes. We've returned," Orion says firmly, pursing his lips.

"I gathered. Saturnus isn't pleased," he warns, his expression strained and stormy. It's clear he's had to deal with more than one or two complaints because of our sudden departure.

"I'll handle Saturnus," Orion vows and Cole nods his head placing his right fist across his chest, leaving it to rest over his heart in a sign of respect, a sign of brotherhood. Orion does not return, he is the superior and merely waves a hand to indicate he wants Cole to stand down. Within moments Cole has allowed us to move past him and Orion is pushing his hands into the tall arching double doors. I swim past him and as Cole shuts the doors behind me I hear a voice call out from behind one of the crystal pillars of the main entrance room of the palace.

"You're back brother." A long black and azure marked tail fin wraps itself around the crystal column, pulling the pale body of Azure into the morning light.

"Azure," I breathe her name even though she hasn't called to me. Our relationship is strained for sure, she murdered me after all, but I am none-the-less fascinated by her, unable to look away from her. Even I cannot deny she is beautiful, especially since the powers of darkness have receded within her ever so slightly. Her eyes are no longer the diluted black pits they once were, returning to a polluted blue which shine against her inky torrent of hair that falls like a blade in a poker straight curtain of darkness. Her tailfin is still like that of a thick black eel, sparked with sapphire lighting. Her eye mask is still missing, but the azure veins of dark magic that once mapped across her forehead and cheeks are fading slowly into the past.

"Callie," the word slithers from her lips. I don't know what to respond with now so I just smile at her. It's odd, I know she's kind of evil, but I can't help but like her more than her sister. I laugh internally. *Hell, I like pissed off piranha better than Starlet.* I feel something move within me suddenly, a shift as my heart feels like ice for a split second as I look at her and a desperate anger appears from nowhere. *Pity,* I think, snapping like a bear trap. I blink, confused as to why I would think such a thing, I may have messed up feelings for her but I certainly don't pity her. I shrug it off and wonder what came over me as I feel Orion at my back, protective as always.

"Yes. Are you alright?" He asks her, I feel his hand move to the edge of my skin, ready to pull me out of the way of a confrontation.

"Yes. Of course. I'm trying to decide what dress to wear to the ball. I'm thinking... black? Like my soul. My colour don't you think?" She laughs in a hollow exhalation and I feel Orion relax next to me, shifting by mere millimetres in the water.

"I'm sure you'll look beautiful whatever you wear." Orion compliments her and she smiles a little too wide.

"You always were a terrible liar. I should know, you came in runner up to myself." The whites of her teeth actually hurt me, but it isn't the whiteness which pains I muse, but the extreme falsity of the expression itself. She skulks away from us in a split second, her tail slicing through the water seamlessly. I breathe out, not having realised I was holding my breath at all.

"She's... having a bad day today," I note.

"Yes. You know withdrawal from the darkness isn't easy. She's the only one... the only one I've ever known strong enough to stop once consumed."

"I wish we knew a way to help her. She saved us all, Orion," I speak the words out of loyalty to my soulmate, but I feel the truth of them ring out as they fall from my tongue.

"We will," he sighs.

"I think Starlet could be the key," I say aloud, moving across the foyer of the Alcazar slowly.

"I think you're right, but that means that helping her will be harder than I thought. Fixing their relationship isn't exactly an instant cure type situation." He agrees with me, frowning as we move to the cylinder of clear water. It runs through the middle of the tallest shard of crystal which makes up the giant structure we float within, allowing for movement between each of the levels to be achieved momentarily.

"Do you think Saturnus is gonna yell?" I ask Orion as we move past the throne room and up toward our suite at the top of the tallest spire.

"I should think I am." A chilling tone reaches my ears as Orion spins in the water next to me, creating a flurry of bubbles. I turn, a split second behind him, until my eyes rest on the one outline that always brings an awe inspired fear to me as of late. Especially since Orion started disobeying his every order.

"Saturnus," Orion lets the name roll out from him calmly.

"Do you mind telling me where you thought it wise to disappear to, two days before you are anointed Crowned Ruler?" He looks really pissed, *so pissed in fact that his red hair could be flames and his head could be on fire with all the pissed-ness,* I muse to myself.

"I had to get away from here. Callie and I needed some time to be together." I watch the two men move closer to one another, challenging each other with their stances.

"And you couldn't possibly have told someone where you were going?" Saturnus asks, arching one red eyebrow and folding his arms.

"I didn't think I needed to. You're not my mommy. I'm Crowned Ruler, remember?" Orion looks cocky in his manliness and I stiffen as Saturnus narrows his eyes.

"Not yet you're not, and if something had happened? If the Psirens or a demon had attacked? What then? You left us with no protection. The Knights are gone. What if they'd taken you or Callie and tortured you until you let them into the city?" He looks at Orion seriously and Orion shrugs, as though in the act of physically moving his shoulders his responsibilities will disappear as well.

"You know Orion, after all these years I never really understood what people meant when they said you were just like your father. But now I know, because I see you are just like him; Arrogant, stubborn, and careless." I watch as Orion goes from calm to violent in under two seconds. He pulls his arm back and does what I've only ever seen him do once. To Daryl. He pulls his fist back and punches Saturnus straight in the jaw. The crack is horrifying and I watch Saturnus fall abruptly through the water as Orion clutches his knuckles in one hand. I rush to Saturnus, wanting to help. I understand he crossed a line insulting Atlas, but hitting someone so close to our Goddess is not okay. I move quickly to Saturnus' side and place my hands on him as he reels backward from Orion's primal unleashing of force. A split second passes and instantaneously I am seeing Saturnus but in a totally different way. His eyes are yellow slits. Terrifying like that of a feral cat. I blink, moving backward momentarily as his eyes bulge, with fear in their now emerald depths. *What the hell was that?* I think. The same insistently familiar and bitter voice in the back of my mind whispers *Truth,* before I silence it again. I don't have time for this crap. I have a man in bits, the Goddess' soulmate with a cracked jaw, and one half of a prophet team going out of her mind with withdrawal from the darkness that has consumed her for centuries. Since when did things get so wickedly complicated?

"WHAT THE HELL WAS THAT?" I roar, feeling a violent fury unleash within. We're afloat in the waters of the royal suite after Saturnus has skulked off to lick his wounds.

"You heard what he said about my father, Callie!" Orion tries to justify his violence.

"Yes, I did, and you know what, you're proving him right by acting this way, Orion." I bite out the sentiment and he looks wildly offended.

"You're saying my father was arrogant? Careless?" He accuses me.

"No. I'm saying *you* are! You can't just go around hitting people! Particularly not Saturnus. You're shaming yourself, you're shaming the Goddess, and more importantly, you're shaming me. You think I want people thinking I love someone so violent? You think I want people thinking I'm the other half of someone who can't control themselves?" I spit the words angrily, realising instantly that I'm not just talking about the violence. My mind wanders back to him grinding against me next to the fire place.

"I'm just..." His chest expands and then he turns, moving beyond the clam shell bed that sits central to the room at great speed and slamming his fists into the wall. I watch him pound, cracking the crystal but unable to move it, bloodying his beautiful knuckles. I stand with arms crossed, realising he's really not interested in being angry at me anymore, more content with taking out his frustrations on the inanimate objects that don't talk back. I move to the crystal chair of the vanity and pick up my conch shell comb, a parting gift from Shaniqua. I brush through my hair, ignoring the pained thuds. I turn as I hear them stop, watching Orion sink to the floor, spent. I place the comb back on the vanity and go to him. At my touch he begins to sob.

"I can't do this," he cries, his manly tears more beautiful than any diamond they could crystallise into.

"Yes. You can," I whisper, sitting next to him against the now fractured wall.

"I'm just... so angry," he mutters as I kiss his cheek.

"I know, but it isn't Saturnus' fault. I know he said horrible things about your father. But..."

"I shouldn't have hit him."

"No," I admit, placing my hand on his scales that lay out in front of me. His tailfin is spread before him. Weary.

"I'll apologise." He turns to me and I wipe the diamonds from my tailfin where his tears have fallen.

"I think that's a very grown up decision."

"You'd think I'd be grown up by now. I am over five hundred." he comments smiling slightly and I nod.

"I think age is just a number. Maybe you're still young up here," I point to his head and he nods slightly. I run my fingers through his locks again. It seems to soothe him.

"We had better get ready for the coronation," I say, "I'm getting ready with the other mermaids."

"I'll miss you," he kisses my fingers as I lower them out of his hair.

"Don't. It'll only be for an hour. You'll get to be surprised by how not ugly I am." I smile at him cheekily and he rolls his eyes. I think about the mermaids who have overtaken my personal grooming habits since I became the other half of The Crowned Ruler. Many of them have come from pre-feminist time-periods and self-maintenance is their only skill. It amazes me how they fill their time with creating underwater fashions and pearl hair pieces. I mean, don't they know we're here to do a job? I often think they'd be better off learning to fashion armour, or weapons, but then I'm reminded they're the only ones who could transform me into the transcendent being I must be for the night's events, and I find myself grateful for the shallow depth of their obsession.

"I'm going to go and find Saturnus," Orion says and moves from the floor.

"Don't forget I'll be travelling with the mermaids to the sanctum," I say to him and he nods.

"I've got to be escorted by a collection of Knights." He sighs at the security measure that I know Saturnus must have insisted upon.

"I'll see you later?" He asks me almost at the door now, having moved seamlessly.

"Yes," I reply, "See you later." I'm still sat against the wall where the crystal has been crunched into a cracked dent at the hand of Orion's grief built rage. I move upward and trace the fissures with my fingers gently, wincing at the pain it must have inflicted on his fists. It seems like things are as unstable as ever. Like I can't quite catch my breath for a moment before something else starts to crack and disintegrate beneath me.

The voice that I've silenced twice already tonight snarls. *Your descent will be glorious.* I startle, looking back at the fractured jade and stroking it for comfort. A black cloud moves across my vision and I feel rage curdle in my blood at events beyond my control. I move to leave the room, but catch something out of the corner of my eye as I fume about Orion's rage and Saturnus' over controlling spite. I turn my head but before I can catch a proper look it's gone. The seed of a shadow behind my aquamarine eyes fades as quickly as it came.

3

Maiden

ORION

Down in my father's old study, I hang upside down in the water, blood rushing to my skull, creating a pleasant calming numbness. I clench my taut abdominals, biting down to stop myself from grunting in pain as I haul my lower half upward, crunching toward the iron bar that is held up by two coral stands. I relinquish at the shock of eyes looking back at me, losing control of my muscles and feeling my scales slip against the metal bar. I fall to the floor, upheaving sand and debris.

"Real slick." I hear the familiar sarcasm dipped tones exclaim lazily.

"What are you doing here Starlet?" I push myself away from the floor with aching but angry muscles.

"I just saw Callie leave. I heard her yelling at you," she admits.

"Well. I deserved it." I flex my fist as I feel the wounds on my knuckles start to heal up. They're sticky with dried blood that won't wash away.

"I know. I saw Saturnus a few seconds after he apparently saw your fist," she informs me as her eyes flick to my knuckles and then back to my face in a movement so small anyone who didn't know her wouldn't notice. Her magenta scales are shimmering wildly and her long white blonde hair flips over one shoulder as she moves her head slightly in disapproval.

"I shouldn't have hit him," I relinquish despite feeling satisfaction at the memory of Saturnus' stunned expression.

"No. This isn't like you. I know father's death has been hard on you but…" She starts to go off on a spiel about repressed grief but I cut her off with a wave of one hand. I sit back into the clutches of the armchair pressed

33

against the left wall.

"It isn't father," I admit. It's the first time I've said it aloud.

"Oh?" Starlet corrects her position in the water, waving her tail in delicate minute movements and moving so she is suspended in front of me.

"It's Callie." The images come at me again, her limp form, porcelain face, and empty eyes.

"I don't understand." Starlet looks at me with a reserved expression and I wonder what she's thinking.

"She just... died and I stood there. I let her. I let it happen." The words drop from my lips like lead. Heavy with self-doubt.

"Yes, but she came back," Starlet says with her eyebrows raised in surprise.

"What if she hadn't?" I ask her and she shrugs her shoulders.

"I don't like Callie, but what she did... what she did was heroic, Orion."

"Dying is a lot of things, Starlet. Heroic is not one of them," I bite out, feeling anger rise within me again, a tidal wave waiting to crest.

"Callie looked at the situation and realised that the needs of the many outweighed what she wanted. She didn't want to leave you Orion. She chose what was right, not what was easy. I'd call that heroism." Starlet looks, for the first time in a long time, calm with an unbreakable resolve.

"You hate Callie. You don't even know her," I remind her, spiteful in my intent but she, regardless, disarms me as she crosses her arms and narrows her eyes.

"True, but hate is a strong word and I don't have to like her to respect her." She doesn't deny anything and it leaves me off balance. She continues, "You know it's funny. I don't like Callie, but right now I can see that she is prepared to do what you are not. She is prepared to put the needs of this city before her own. That's why I voted for you as Crowned Ruler. We need someone like her now more than ever." Starlet makes this spiel and my stomach falls in horror.

"You voted for me?" I ask her rising from the chair.

"Yes." She bats her eyelids.

"You knew I didn't want this job."

"Yes, but suggesting Callie as crowned ruler wasn't going to fly. No-one around here is going to vote for a maiden." She locks eyes with me.

"That doesn't make you trapping me in this stupid regal façade okay, Starlet. You know I didn't want this job!" I whine at her. I may sound like a small child but I'm so enraged I lack the ability to care.

"You need to calm down. Whether or not you wanted the job, it's yours now. There's nothing you can do." Starlet looks at me and sighs, turning towards the door. "I'll see you later," she says wistfully, leaving in a flurry of sickly sweet pink sparkle. I run my fingers through my tousles trying to calm my nerves and move back over to the bar where I was hanging before. I start to take out my frustrations on my body, sculpting each muscle to the point where I am unbeatable. To the place where, finally, nothing and nobody but me can touch my maiden.

CALLIE

As I descend through the Alcazar Oceania I see the bloody red mane of Saturnus beneath me. I let myself fall through the central column of the shard like building until I am before him. He has a lovely fist shaped bruise on the side of his face. I cringe.

"That looks painful," I say reaching up to touch, trying to take on the caring maternal role everyone expects of me. He brushes my hand sideways like it's dangerous with a curious look in the grassy pastures that lay in green behind the surface of his eyes.

"I'm sure I'll be fine," he mutters, looking angrier that I've mentioned it.

"Did Orion find you? I told him to apologise." Saturnus shakes his head in response and I curse internally.

Dammit Orion, do I have to take responsibility for everything around here!

"I'm sorry. I know he is too. He's just busy I guess." I make the excuse but I hear how unconvinced I sound.

"I don't need you to apologise. You didn't do anything wrong and you are a woman. You do not speak for Orion." I watch his expression and I can see that he's deadly serious. Since when did being a woman become such a damn ball and chain around here? *He didn't mind me being a woman when he asked me to die to save his sorry ass.* I become irritated and he just looks bored.

"Don't you have somewhere to be?" he asks me and I am instantly transported back to a duck egg blue kitchen. My step-father asking me the very same question, a similar feeling of absurd offence taking over me. I swallow hard and feel my mind clear with a certain and sudden tranquillity.

"Yes. I'll be going to meet the mermaids for the pre-coronation preparations now," I say to him and he nods. I'm glad he won't be there tonight. I'm glad he has to stay in this stupid palace. *Rat bastard.* I cuss at his back as he moves away from me with a slight, and now I'm sure entirely fake, smile. I descend further through the palace and see Azure skulking in the hall again.

"There are mermaids outside looking for you," she says wistfully. Her eyes are diluted again and I brush past her, not wanting to deal with any more insanity.

"Thanks, I'll see you later," I mutter and she skulks away with a distracted nod. I knock on the jade crystal of the doors lightly and they swing open. I'm greeted by something like a scene out of a Greek Musical, plus of course the tailfins, as the doors swing open and mermaids move forward in a flurry of dreamy pastels.

I move outward, sighing internally.

Great... more people.

I'm not an introvert by any standard but I feel momentarily claustrophobic by the amount of sparkling gemstone eyes staring at me.

"Hey guys," I mumble and they all come forward at once. A babbling, rambling, overly-excitable mess of mermaids headed right for me like a gossip seeking missile. It's hardly surprising they're so excited, the coronation is the kind of event that's only ever happened once before, and they didn't even have curling irons back then. I can't understand what they're saying so I put up a hand and they silence instantly. Putty in my hands.

"Whoa! One at a time!" I exclaim and a girl named Alannah starts back up with her babble. She has ink black hair and pale green eyes. Her tail is mint green with splashes of coral and baby pink on the tips of her fins.

"Orion left you a gift." She is moving up and down in tiny hop like movements. I remember her from before but I don't ever think I've really talked to her in depth. I think she kept asking me about Orion's courting skills.

The mermaids move back, there's around thirty of them in total and they disperse haphazardly around me, rounding on me, so they're at my back in force pushing me forward. Standing, puffing, and padding from hoof to hoof at the end of the palace garden's path stands Philippe. I sigh inwardly at the magnificence of the Equinox, standing with leathery-scaled wings and eye scale blinkers in royal blue. I knew this was Orion's way of keeping me safe, being here when he could not physically be. I smile to myself, giddy.

"Philippe," I whisper the animals name like a magic spell and I hear a stir from behind me.

"Is that really an Equinox?" I hear the beguiled voice. It belongs to a stunned young mermaid called Skye. Her hair is a chestnut brown waterfall of thickness and her facial scales match her tail in a pale lemon.

"Yes. Haven't you guys ever seen Philippe before?" I ask them feeling confused. They've been alive so much longer than I have. How is it none of them have ever seen Orion's steed.

"No! Oh! Isn't he darling? My other half, Jeremiah, he told me but I never believed him." Skye cannot keep her gaze on me any longer as she becomes overtaken by tears. "He's just so beautiful!" She sobs. *Oh for the love of the Goddess.* I snap internally. *Why is she crying? It's just a kickass, magical, aquatically immortal pony!* Something inside me realises how I'm severely underwhelmed after the last few months and so I lead the flock of mermaids behind me, trying to be patient and kind, to live up to what they expect.

"You guys can pet him if you'd like. Just don't get behind him and stay where he can see you," I warn them and they dart past me in a cloud of calm, graceful tailfins, and long lustrous hair. They make movement look effortless, even more so than the faster mer I've been around. They move with a kind of ethereal invisibility, whereby nothing can displace the things that make them beautiful; their hair is never out of place and their garments never skewed, I wonder how they do it. I hear them squeal as Philippe snorts and shakes his head.

"You're going to make a fine Queen," I hear the whisper in my left ear and I swivel, turning my back on Philippe and his admirers.

"Marina!" I squeal, throwing my arms around her.

"Hey," she breathes with a sweet smile.

"How are you and Christian?" I ask her and she nods.

"Very well, thank you. He's wrapped in research as usual. Trying to find a scientific explanation as to how our magic works. Silly man." She shakes her head and looks me in the eyes. "You're a bundle of emotion aren't you?" She exclaims with enthusiasm.

"You have no idea," I reply putting my hand on my hip.

"Actually, I do. I'm vibrating right now at how much is going on with you emotionally, darling." She reminds me of her empathic perceptions and I shake my head.

"I'm sorry…" I begin to apologise but she cuts me off in her usual Italian way.

"Don't you apologise for one single bit of what you're feeling, Callie. You have a lot going on."

"Ain't that the truth," I admit and she laughs slightly at the expression, her red scales shining.

"Don't you worry, darling," she whispers to me. Placing her hands on my shoulders she turns me back toward the Equinox, "My Claude will unravel you in a single moment. I promise."

Marina's Claude, as it turns out, is an extremely blonde, Swedish masseuse who works in the spa, housed in the right wing of the Lunar Sanctum. I lay out on his table under a towel, after my underwater horseback ride to the sanctum, surrounded by excited, gossiping mermaids. Marina feeling my need to be alone, had swept me away to the spa and to Claude the second my feet had hit dry land, telling my gaggle of groupies that we would meet them in the salon in a few hours. I am splayed out naked, but for the first time totally at ease under the hands of a man. I think back to the sex from last night and then banish it away, not wanting to relive the desperation of it all. It wasn't that the sex was bad. No that wasn't it at all. I suppose it was just the fact that Orion was using it to replace the talking in our relationship. As evidenced this afternoon when he was more than willing to resort to violence in the face of having sex become an inviable option. I want to worry about him, but I feel those worries fall away as Claude starts to work on my shoulders.

"Oh my God, how did I not know we had a spa..." I moan as Marina sits back in a white love seat, watching me. The spa is coated in beautiful aqua and white décor. The colours of purity and wellbeing alone make me feel slightly better. I look up at her from the hole where my face has been laid the last few minutes.

"You've been getting your massages from the Spa of Orion I would imagine." She winks at me but I pout back. "What no massages?" She asks me and I shake my head.

"Not lately."

"Trouble in paradise?" The sentiment is one I've heard used in a bitchy tone before, but I can sense she's genuinely concerned.

"He's just messed up. His Dad died and then I died all in one night. I figure he's allowed to be messed up. If sexing me to death is how he chooses to deal then who am I to tell him he's wrong," I admit.

"Oh darling, no. That's not good for anyone." She shakes her head and I put my face back into the massage table.

"I know, but what can I do? He won't talk to me. I try to talk and he just starts... you know." I am speaking to the immaculate white floor and actively ignoring the fact that the masseuse who is rubbing me is listening to my every word.

"Men are so tricky darling. If you could feel what I do coming off them, you would know why. They've got the weight of the world on their shoulders, but it's like they think they're not allowed to admit it, or it will crush them flat," Marina sighs to herself and I wonder what it is like for her being in a relationship where you can constantly empathise with what the other person is feeling.

"I know. He's just struggling. I'm trying to let him ride it out, but I don't know how much longer I can deal with him being so angry. It's madness," I confess and I can feel the empathy roll off her.

"I understand sweetie but he's still very much a self-contained creature. He was alone for a long time, remember." She reminds of the fact that everyone always brings to my attention at the idea of Orion.

"Yeah I know. He doesn't let me forget it." I bite down on my lip as Claude reaches the base of my spine with his thumbs, releasing any tension that could be mounting. He jumps slightly.

"You okay back there?" I ask him over my shoulder.

"Yes Miss. Is just small electric shock." He kisses his thumb, his accent rolling out as thickly Swedish and continues to rub me.

"I won't lie to you, I felt him earlier, I swam past the window of Atlas' old study and I could feel it coming off him in waves." Marina looks at me and frowns as I raise my head again in surprise.

"What did you feel?" I ask her and she contorts the redness of her lips into a grimace.

"Pretty much what you'd expect. Rage, sexual frustration, regular frustration… but more than that: fear. He's carrying around a lot of fear." Marina looks me square in the eye.

"He's scared," I repeat and she nods.

"Yes darling and I think we can guess why. He waited with one goal in mind. Finally getting to have you, be with you, and love you. Now he has you…" She stops and I finish the sentence for her with a sigh.

"He's afraid to lose me."

"Yes and he did lose you. You didn't see him carrying your body through the streets, Callie. I have never felt such despair. It was like there was a hole in him."

"But mermen have lost their soulmates before. They live through it," I muse, trying to shed the familiar guilt that's settling over me.

"Yes. But those mermen have had hundreds of years of memories with their maidens. In some ways, that makes it harder yes. But for Orion, it's like giving a giant plateful of spaghetti and meatballs to a starving man and then taking it away after he's had a single bite." She uses the analogy of food and

I raise one eyebrow to hide the palpitations in my heart.

"I know I hurt him, but I did what I thought was best for everyone," I spit out the words, they taste sour in my mouth.

"In saying these things you're assuming Orion sees this from your point of view. He doesn't." She reminds me and I drop my head so it hangs as I prop myself up on my elbows.

"So what do I do?" I ask her and she shrugs.

"Keep him happy, but don't let him do anything insensible. This isn't the time for him to make drastic changes. He is not thinking clearly."

"I wish he hadn't been voted in as Crowned Ruler," I admit to her, she does not look surprised.

"I think you'd be surprised at how many people feel the same way, Callie." She smiles and I pinch my brow, confused as to what she is implying.

"He won the vote by a landslide, Marina. It can't be that many," I think aloud and she gets up from the sofa.

"You forget, Callie, behind every great man is an even greater woman. Surely you do not believe those votes were *only* for Orion?" She smiles at me and exits the room silently, leaving me to think under the waves of relaxation that Claude continues to create as I relinquish to denial once more, letting them pull me under.

"Girls! The irons, stat!" I wince as Alannah pulls on my hair with a paddle brush and I ponder if she's asking for hot irons or the kind pirates were once clad in to stop them escaping. *Well she does keep telling me to stop fidgeting,* I note, as I fear for my freedom with a half-hearted smile at the thought.

I'm sitting in the 'salon', or so this is what the maiden's call the gargantuan room walled by mirrors and stuffed full of plush seating. It's all very pink, very girly. Powders and pastes are scattered around the metre-long boudoir that lines the walls of the room and behind me is a colossal wardrobe filled with corsets and undergarments that fit under specific dresses. There are women everywhere, elegantly limbed, shiny skinned, long-haired women, each as beautiful as the next in their own unique way. They're all clad in corsets and panties running around with faces half made and hair falling out of rollers. I watch them flurry about, caught up in a self-made energy and excitement.

"OW!" I scold as Alannah snags another knot. I am so not cut out for this high maintenance crap.

"I know it hurts, Princess. Just sit still and it won't pull so much." A maiden called Rose who stands behind me with long, muddy blonde hair rolls her eyes, she thinks I can't see her.

"I can see you rolling your eyes, Rose." She looks instantly confused and mortified. "In the mirror..." I enlighten her pointing toward the reflective surface before me with an unimpressed sigh and watch her blue eyes dart from left to right guiltily before she scurries away. I hear a cacophony of girlish chatter behind me as Alannah begins to straighten my hair with irons before she intends to start re-curling it. I personally don't understand why she can't just leave it naturally curly, but when I suggested this she rolled her eyes too. Apparently I'm an eye roll inducer. I hear a familiar tone and then a large amount of successive gasps. I crane my neck and Alannah tuts as she quickly has to turn with me, continuing to straighten my hair and beginning to pull them up into those big rollers you see on women who were born in the fifties. I turn to see what the gasps were regarding. Marina has entered the room with my dress, the one Orion paid for, the one I've been waiting to see for months with relish.

"Oh my Goddess..." I hear one of the mermaids breathe as they glance through the clear panels of the garment bag. I stand and Alannah sighs at my lack of cooperation in playing Barbie for her, ignoring her I step across the plush plum carpet and walk toward the gathering of mermaids.

"Hey back up girls, let the Princess through." Marina makes the request and I wonder when everyone started calling me Princess.

"It's Callie, Marina," I say to her and she bows her head, lustrous black hair falling forward.

"Of course. Now come see this dress, darling. It's perfect." The maiden's part and I move past envious and admiring eyes. Marina takes the bag down and pulls the zip over metal teeth, pulling out the dress and hanging it on the curtain rail that lines the top of the room's walls. I step back and admire the work of the seamstress, this dress is nothing like the gown I wore to my initiation ceremony, nothing like the dress I was murdered in. This is not a Princess dress, but rather a dress fit for a Queen.

ORION

I stand at the foot of the staircase of the Lunar Sanctum on the jade green runner, I never liked the colour personally, thought it looked like mould, but today it's particularly bothering me. Mainly because I've been staring at it for longer than I should be. I'm the man of the hour and for some reason, after everything that it's taken to get here, I feel calmer than I thought. Well mostly calm anyway, except for the fact that I can't quite understand why women are always late. It can't take that long to get ready, can it? She's beautiful anyway. It'd be like asking an art student to recreate the Mona Lisa. Pointless and completely unnecessary. The other maidens have been gathering in the ballroom for hours... where the hell is she?

I noticed the maidens watching me beneath blushes I had not seen from them before. Did they know something I didn't? Had Callie even turned up? I wonder if I can blame her if she runs. Probably not. I've had half a millennium to prepare and I'm still not ready. I sigh and look down at my watch. Not one for ever wearing watches before, I had found it in the pocket of the robe I had asked Georgia to deposit, a gift for the coronation from a human. I remember the inscription on the underside of the face now. 'A show of thanks for your sacrifice. The sacrifice for all time.' I tap the face again. Can that really be the time? It's so late? Why isn't she here? I wonder if this is similar to how I'll feel waiting for her to come down the aisle. God I hope not.

I hear a cough as I'm absorbed in the ticking hands on the dark blue face and my head snaps up. I back away from the railing and stand in the centre of the moss runner as Marina stands at the head of the staircase in a torrent of scarlet silk with a knowing smile and flushed cheeks. What the hell is everyone so flustered about?

"Your Highness... Your Queen," she says the words in a simple breathless gush, stepping aside as the two double doors at the top of the staircase which lead to the salon open wide. Callie steps forward out of the dim light and into the glare of the chandelier. I do a double take and feel the hairs rise on the back of my head. Oh... my...Goddess.

She stands, a sparkling, shining, shimmering edifice of beauty. Everything I have waited for. The dress, worth every penny, is a ball-gown like no other. Midnight blue silk makes up a sleeveless, diamond embedded bustier bodice before pinching in at her miniscule waist. The skirt poofs outward in a waterfall of light, each of the gossamer layers of dark weightless net are covered in hand-sewn diamonds, hundreds if not thousands of diamonds at every layer, the very embodiment of the weight which she is about to bear with me. The weight of the sorrow of our people. She does not seem phased by such responsibility, but rather wears it as her crowning glory covering her from head to foot in a galaxy of tear shine. She is beaming, her blonde hair falling in angel curls around her shoulders, pinched back into a thick curled cascade with more diamonds clinging to each ringlet subtly. Her arms are clad in white silk elbow length gloves that make her skin glow like the moon and the aquamarines of her eyes shine. I sigh outward. It is no wonder she was destined to be a Goddess. She is too good for this world.

She descends the staircase, not walking but gliding beneath the layers of fabric, her bedazzled high-heeled shoes peeping from the skirt at playful intervals.

"Hey. Sorry I'm late," she whispers to me, looking through thick black lashes.

"You look..." The words fail me under the thrall of her perfection.

"Yes?" She looks at me too seriously. As if I could possibly utter a marring remark. The dark red of her lips making me want to possess her, wade through a galaxy of diamonds to find her bare and waiting.

"Transcendent." The word is not enough. I am stunned and shocked to my core. Any man may call me shallow but that was because he had never seen such a godly beauty walking toward him, reaching out to touch his mere mortal flesh.

"It's just make up. I'm still me underneath." She giggles touching her white gloved hand to her red lips self-consciously. I don't have a response. I just stand watching her. I kiss her cheek.

"That dress… worth every penny." I find myself having trouble putting my words in order. Pull it together man!

"You still haven't told me exactly how many pennies though."

"Well… real diamonds cost." I look her in the eye and she gasps slightly.

"Real? These are real diamonds? I thought these were like… diamantes. Are you nuts!?" She looks at me with horror and I shrug. It's hard for me to even think about arguing against her. Her looks have reduced my brain power to nil.

"It's a special night," I reply and she narrows her eyes.

"I'm going to be having words with you about this later." She rolls her eyes and kisses me on the cheek, wiping away the lipstick residue as Marina descends behind her. Poor Marina, I had forgotten she was even there. Callie completely overtook my field of vision.

"Come on you two. We have a coronation to get to. Wait until you see what I've done with the décor!" She sounds upbeat and excitable, just like everyone else. I wonder if it's novelty, or the spectacle and the grandeur. Then again, what do I know about grandeur, I just spent six figures on a ring the size of a quarter. "It's time," Marina nods with a large smile as we move toward the double doors and I hear our names being announced behind the thick mahogany. I shuffle in my midnight blue suit and correct my aqua silk tie, shaking out my legs as I feel nerves clutch at me. I take Callie on my arm, push my back poker straight so it strains across the tapering of my suit and breathe, standing tall like a male peacock in mating season. The doors open and, with a Goddess on one arm, I step forward into the light.

4
Become
CALLIE

The double doors swing forward and Orion and I move into the light. My feet step onto an icy blue runner, speckled with silver, and mer stand on either side of me, lining our path. Orion is holding my hand, which is looped through his arm, like his life depends on it. I know deep down he's scared, I am too.

Marina wasn't wrong when she had told me, while binding me into my dress that, much like my attire, no expense had been spared when it came to the ceremony. The ballroom has been stripped of its usual burgundy and gold trim and replaced with platinum and glacial pastel blues, the colour of Orion's eyes. I can't help but wonder if that's why she chose the colour. Maybe I'm not the only one who has noticed how distinctive they are. Eyes follow us as an eerie hush settles over the room before, in a stroke of pure elegance, a half orchestra begins to play some song I've never heard before. As the song progresses we move, step by painful step, along the frosty velvet path, heading toward the stage at the head of the large dancefloor. Two silver thrones sit, side by side, the arched tops looking like they've been constructed from silver coral. Behind them comes a familiar face, one I had not expected to see and I turn to Orion, wide eyed with a gentle comforting happiness. He smiles back as Shaniqua stands before us in robes of lime green, beaming and genteel.

"Shaniqua is here?" I whisper to him and he nods slightly, acting ventriloquist to an invisible dummy, trying to keep his lips unmoving.

"Yes. She's performing the ceremony."

"I'm glad she came," I whisper again, pretending to cough to cover my mouth, meeting the eyes of the vast crowds that fill the entire room. I hadn't realised there were so many mer I hadn't met before. I guess some only come on land for special occasions. I look past a man with violet eyes and silver hair slicked back against his skull like an eighties rocker, his cheekbones defiantly protrusive against his pale white skin, trying to spot Sophia but I can't see her. She said she would try to be here, but I guess she couldn't talk Oscar into leaving the ocean. We reach the stage and climb as Shaniqua bows to me and I return, pulling the sparkling tresses of my skirt up slightly and crossing my ankles. Orion lifts his right fist over his heart and she curtsies back, her lime robes unmoving in stiff silk.

"Please... kneel," she commands us and so I bend my knees beneath me, my skirt pooling around me in a puddle of crystal droplets.

"We gather here today to anoint these two people in the salt of the sea. To place on their shoulders, the weight of its beating waves, and the pleasures of the life held within. To charge to them the sole responsibility of the protection of this realm from within the depths of the ocean, an ancient responsibility and one which is not bestowed lightly," Shaniqua speaks clearly and I can tell she's broken. Her voice lacks the lustre it had once spilled. My knees are beginning to ache as I keep my head bowed toward the ice blue of the carpet and feel eyes in their hundreds baring into my spine. I see Shaniqua's feet move briskly and then feel her sprinkling what I assume to be salt water. I shudder as the droplets trickle over me.

"Please rise," I hear her command and so I get to my feet. In her hands she holds an orb and a sceptre. The objects are new to me, I have never seen them before but they call to me, dying to be held in my hands. The orb is a giant moon-like white pearl, surrounded in a spherical cage of platinum and diamonds. The sceptre is platinum too, with hundreds of pearls spiralling around its length. Orion lets go of my hand, letting my silken clad fingers fall through his and takes the objects in his palms, clutching them clumsily. I watch him stumble and something within me sighs, wondering what they would feel like in my palms. I shake my head subtly, trying to disband the thought. I am not power hungry. Shaniqua nods and we turn to face the crowd.

"Repeat after me, Orion," she whispers, breathless and husky behind us. I wonder if she's tearing up. "I, Orion, the Hunter."

"I, Orion, the Hunter," Orion repeats and I wonder about the title. Since when had he been a hunter?

"Solemnly vow to uphold the values and protection of the people of this world and any other whom may look to those blessed by the Goddess for help. To place those needs of my people before those of myself and to understand that my life and death belong to the service and wellbeing of my Goddess and her mission on earth." I look over at Orion after hearing the part about death. I wonder if he's thinking about me. I place my gloved hands on top of my skirt and look down. In the crowd I spot Sophia's eyes, finally, watching me widely. In front of her is the silver haired man I had seen on my entrance. His eyes are burning an intense lilac and he's staring at me like he's fighting internally about something. His cheek bones are prominent as his mouth twists and he sucks in air. His left eyebrow sports a slash on the outer side and I wonder why I haven't seen him before. Surely I would remember such a face. Orion has finished repeating his vow and I stand, a spare part to the Crowned Ruler, but not spared the scrutiny of his people. We both have been walked through this ceremony a hundred times before in the small council meetings so I know what comes next.

We turn in unison and take our seats in the two silver thrones in the centre of the stage. The throne isn't as comfortable as you'd expect, it's hard and cold, requiring me to sit up at an acute angle, pushing my spine straight. Shaniqua comes forward with something ornate between her long elegant fingers. My tiara. It's small and threaded with shells, diamonds, and pearls intricately. She bows slightly and nestles it between the curls that were so lovingly placed, diamonds clinging to them, into a braid which pulls them to the base of my neck where they fall down over my shoulders and back. Shaniqua rises and smiles at me, a knowing look of something sentimental flashing behind the limes of her irises. I smile back at her and look over to Orion. His eyes ground me, making me appreciate how far I've come. From just an American teen struggling to pass chemistry, I'm now being crowned Queen over an aquatic city of merfolk. Not bad for less than six months when you think about it. Orion is crowned, the platinum crown of faux seaweed metal curling through his tousles, interrupting their steady wildness. Shaniqua bows to us as Orion holds the orb and sceptre in both hands and sits, head back against the substantial height of his throne, legs crossed in cocky reserve. I slant my lips in disapproval but then look at him, really look at him, before realising he has relaxed. I relax slightly too as Shaniqua turns.

"I present to you, blessed ones, his Highness, King Orion the Hunter, and his other half, Queen Callie, the vessel." Shaniqua practically sings these words and we rise together to our titles, to our obligations. Orion still holding his symbols of power and me folding my hands daintily in my skirt. The room bows before us, a tidal wave of humble abandon. Holy crap. They're bowing to me? I watch the man with silvery grey hair stumble as he moves to bow later than everyone else. Someone hadn't taught him the protocol, clearly. He must have been sick the day they taught Coronation 101 at merfolk etiquette school. We stand, becoming what we supposedly are, becoming the rumours on the wind, becoming the myths of ancient times gone past. We watch, surveying the humbled crowd as a large crash breaks the eerie, respectful silence. A hundred well-groomed heads turn in alarm and I feel my heart quicken. Azure stands in the doorway, wrapped from head to toe in a black silken ball gown that is speckled with rubies the colour of blood. She is revealed, hair whipped back from her face in an elegant knot, eyes an old and familiar icy blue, with skin the colour of bone.

"Sorry I'm late," she breathes.

AZURE

Everyone is staring. I wish they'd stop. Or maybe I should make them stop. They're standing looking at me like I'm the crypt keeper. I glide forward, transcending their disapproving and shocked stares. My black heels click against the floor in monochromatic rhythm, like a funeral march. I walk down the aisle, watching fear rise in each of the individuals that line it. They should be scared of me. I'm scared of me. I watch them shift their eyes tentatively as they rise from their humbled state on bended knee. Pathetic. I bow to nobody. I see Star in the crowd, dressed in blue. Well, at least it's not pink, she's worn the colour to death and it really doesn't suit her. Now black, there's a colour that never goes out of style. As I move I notice a pair of eyes on me, though I am not surprised, there are hundreds. However, these in particular I notice, because these eyes aren't filled with fear. I turn suddenly and the line of people I am facing dimples, trying to move away from me. The unpredictable harbinger of darkness. God I hate them. They will never understand what I've been through, and the irony of the fact that I saved them all. I feel the darkness stir within my gut.

No, keep it cool, don't play into their hands. Be strong. Focus now.

I mutter this internal mantra, trying not to allow the shadows to take me, dilate my eyes, and spider web a map of power across my flesh once more. Containment, containment is the key. I turn and spot what I'm seeking in the crowd. Orion is coming down the stairs, his dress shoes padding like the paws of a jungle cat, soft yet ready to pounce into action at any moment. I narrow my eyes and zoom in on my target, lilac eyes, silver hair pushed back against his skull, a slashed eyebrow, and cheekbones that protrude at acute angles. I look at him and he stares right back, unwavering, intense and fearless. Psiren.

"What the hell are you doing here?" I shout abruptly and he looks at me and shrugs to the people surrounding him, confused. They turn back to me looking increasingly unnerved.

Okay, not going to come right out with it then, rookie mistake boy.

I guess I'll have to force him.

I launch myself, pushing forward on the balls of my feet and hoisting my skirt up around my haunches. The crowd parts, stumbling back into one another and quickly regaining composure. I reach out, fingers splayed, red nails claw-like and feel my expression turn feral as a map of azure darkness fades back into existence over my translucent flesh shell. I tackle him to the floor, no easy feat for someone my size as he's taut with tightly packed, but minimal muscle. He looks short and therefore light, but he isn't and it takes me by surprise as I knock him down into the cold hardness of the floor beneath. I'm straddling him and he looks up at me blazing.

"Love, if you wanted a shag we could have gone outside. Bit public don't you think?" He pulls out a thick, rough English accent which leaves me surprised. He smiles up at me with a cocky reverence that pisses me off.

"You shouldn't be here," I growl at him, clutching his white tuxedo shirt in my balled fists.

"I'd say underneath any woman willing to tackle me for my body is exactly where I should be, Love." He laughs throatily and lies back, putting his hands behind his head, relaxing into the spectacle.

"Pig. Psirens aren't welcome here. I should know," I bite out and shove his chest into the floor angrily.

"Psiren?" My slow brother comes up behind me and looks down at the specimen beneath us.

"Yes. I can tell." I look at him intensely and I know my pupils have dilated. I know I must look like a Psiren myself. The crowd around is backing away. The silver haired man jumps to his feet in good spirit.

"I must say. You guys know how to show a man a good time. I can see what mother meant about you. Really. Bravo. I've had four glasses of champagne already. That's good shit you're peddling there. But I do have one question... does anyone in here..." he turns, surveying shocked faces, "know where I can get a light?" He is pacing, arms loose at his side with an evil smile spreading across his bony features.

"I'll take care of him," I say to my brother and he opens his mouth to argue. "I'll take a guard of two Knights if you've got them. I need to make sure this piece of shit gets back to where he belongs," I mutter and Orion relaxes at the mention of guards. Callie is standing at his side, watching in slight shock. I note that she can't take her eyes off this guy.

What? Has she never seen a dumbass before? I know I have. I hear the mystery Psiren.

"You wound me Love." He looks at my gown and licks his lips. "But just so we're clear Pet, the name's Vex. You'll need to know that when you're screaming it later." I snort as a sinister twinkle passes beneath the dusky lavender of his irises and wonder if he's referring to torture or sex, or both. What the hell kind of Psiren is this guy? This is what you get when you recruit children. Poseidon should be ashamed. I think back to Callie, outfitted

51

like some bejewelled icon of hope and snort to myself. Atargatis is no better.

"Don't test me boy. I've been dancing with darkness since before you were a speck in your daddy's eye," I snarl at him as Orion beckons on two of the Knights that are in charge of security. I look at them, at their incompetent and embarrassed expressions. *Stellar job guys, you've officially reached pointless in your roles as protector. Bravo indeed.* I muse to myself about how easy it was for me to just walk in here. What the hell was my brother playing at being so lax with security? The two burly knights pull Vex's arms behind his back, restraining him and place one hand on the back of his head. I walk behind them back up the length of the ballroom, eyes following my every move and out into the main entrance hall. My heels hit the floor hard, like a hammer hitting iron and the sound rings out like a bell. Warning everyone that trouble is imminent.

On the top of a moonlit cliff where Lunar Sanctum stands, I walk behind the guards, my dress trailing in the dirt behind me. We reach the top of the rock which juts out from the land and stand, wind whipping around us on its sheer edge that leads to a vertical fall. My black hair flies out like tendrils of shadow in the breeze.

"Thank you," I nod to the guards and they look hesitant to leave, but I assume my still dilated pupils scare them so they do. Vex stands, squat and tightly packed in his suit, back to the ocean which froths at the mouth like an angry dog below.

"Go back to Solustus. Go back and tell him to call off whatever crap you're trying to pull. We've had enough." I tell him straight and he puts his hands in his pockets.

"We... or you? I didn't take you for a damsel in distress Love."

"I'm not. Whatever it is you want, it isn't good for anyone. Go home. If I see you again I'll slit your throat and let you choke on your own dying breaths," I bite out and try to push him backward. I know the fall won't kill him, but I figure he deserves a spank at the hands of surface tension regardless.

"Uh, uh, uh," he shakes his head with objective guttural sounds and pulls me close to him. I struggle looking down. We're close to the edge, teetering fatally close to oblivion. "You push me away, but I know you're ripe and ready to be picked... picked like the dark, sweet plum you are," he whispers in my ear. I want to shove him backward but realise it'll only lead him to pull me with him.

"You're sick," I spit and he laughs huskily.

"Aren't we all Love?" He pushes me back and falls, arms spread like Christ back off the cliff, I hear him splash into the cold depths below and hope he hit his head hard.

CALLIE

Orion's expression is strained as I watch him looking at the last traces of Azure's dress as it disappears around the corner. For a woman clad in something so stunning, she's terrifying.

"Did you see her eyes when she walked in here? She almost looked normal," I whisper. He looks around us at the scared faces and puts his hands in his pockets. He opens his mouth to speak but Shaniqua beats him to it.

"I think that's enough drama for one evening. Back to the celebrations," she beckons over to the half orchestra and they begin to play again as people start to relax, turning to each other and gossiping. No doubt expressing their shock and laughing off their fear.

"Callie!" I hear the squeak travel from somewhere behind me and I turn, now standing in the middle of the room, to Sophia's tear stained cheeks.

"Sophia! You made it." I sigh and hold out my arms as she hugs me. If I hadn't had her voice, which to me speaks reason and understanding above all else, I don't know how I would have survived these last few months.

"Yes. Oscar..." She trails off looking guilty but I understand. Oscar never leaves the ocean if he can help it.

"I understand, don't worry. I'm just happy to see you. I can't believe there's so many people here I don't know!" I exclaim and she nods.

"Yes, this kind of event doesn't come around that often. There are people here I know haven't been on land for centuries." She nods and turns as the crowd begins to disperse and waiters descend. She grabs a champagne flute off a silver tray and takes a slug.

"Who was that guy?" she asks me and I shake my head.

"Vex, apparently."

"I wonder what he wanted." She looks scared and I place a gloved hand onto her alabaster shoulder.

"Nothing good I'm sure. I love your dress by the way," I distract her, changing the subject. She looks down at the halter necked, lilac silk sheath that covers her slim figure.

"Thanks...it's a little more subtle than yours though." She twists her mouth and I laugh.

"Tell me about it." I can feel Orion reach out from behind me and grab my hand.

"Hey, Sophia. It's so nice to see you here." Sophia bows her head and curtsies.

"Oh, no need for that," he says and puts his hand out to pull up her chin. She blushes scarlet and I laugh silently to myself. Good God Sophia, could you be more obvious?

"Callie, there are people who want to congratulate us." He puts his hand around my corseted waist and I look apologetically at Sophia.

"Sorry... duty calls."

"It's okay, I've monopolised enough of the Crowned Ruler's time." She smiles back at me and winks, turning away. I watch her beehive of auburn hair disappear and I wonder if she's leaving already. It must be uncomfortable for her, being here alone. I'm grateful she came for me and vow to send her a bouquet of sea flowers when I return to the city. Orion walks me across the room and over to a woman with caramel coloured skin and shiny black hair. He moves his head towards mine.

"Take your gloves off," he whispers and I furrow my brow.

"Why?" I ask him and he sighs.

"Just do it, you'll see why." I slip my gloves off as he asked and look at the woman before me. She's in a yellow floor length dress and has large, beautiful brown eyes. She moves forward and grips my hand.

Hello Callie. It's lovely to finally meet you. I hear her voice ring clear in my mind but her lips remain closed.

"Hello," I reply back, slightly shell shocked.

"This is Fahima. Ghazi's wife," Orion elaborates and I understand why he wanted me to touch her directly. He wanted me to absorb her telepathic ability so we could talk.

"It's lovely to meet you!" I exclaim and she nods, her hand still in mine. *You look very beautiful.* She compliments and I smile at her.

"So do you," I reply. I watch Fahima examine my face for a moment. She looks slightly worried as she says finally.

You'll look after my husband. He is in your service now.

"Of course, but as you know Ghazi can take care of himself. Your husband truly is a skilled warrior," I acknowledge, remembering Ghazi ripping apart Psirens as they overtook the city.

Thank you Your Highness.

"Please, it's just Callie," I remind her and she nods. Marina is moving toward us, a scarlet tornado of excitement.

"It's time for your first dance as Rulers," she reminds us as Fahima turns and moves away toward the back of the room.

"Okay. Did you get my selection?" I ask her and she nods.

"Yes, Gabriel's Oboe?" she replies questioning me and I smile.

"Yes. That's what we decided in the end."

"Very well," she moves past me, grabbing a glass off a passing waiter's tray and ascending onto the height of the stage. She clinks her glass against the edge of the throne in an impatient flurry and stands before the room which has now fallen into silence.

"Please clear the dance floor for our new King and Queen," she beams with a wide smile. The mer start to move outward, clearing the dance floor and turning to face Orion and I, who are left standing together alone, the centre of attention. The half orchestra starts to play and Marina downs the glass of champagne in her hand in one masculine glug. Orion steps toward me and places his hand around my waist. I rest my hands on the tops of his arms, careful not to step into the frame he has constructed with his body. Marina opens her lips and starts to belt out the lyrics of the translated Italian aria and Orion moves me in calculated rhythm, twirling me in choreographed time to the music. This is so far from our first dance across this floor. This is duty.

After a three-course meal, more dancing, too much champagne, and a quick change of clothes, Orion and I are ushered down to the beach where Philippe is waiting on the sand. No longer clad in the heavy ball gown, I'm now scantily dressed in the outfit I will be wearing to the underwater segment of the celebration. We mount the Equinox, Orion rising behind me, to cheers from the crowd who are wrapped in white terry cloth robes, ready to embrace the change. As the sun begins to peak above the horizon Philippe whinnies, a harsh and brutal battle cry, and gallops back into the sea. The change overtakes us all, changing legs to tail and surrounding my eyes with scales. Orion's arm slide around me, holding me as leathery wings spread out in front of me once more and the Equinox starts to plough through the water at epic speed. I turn my head and see the rest of the mer plunge into the depths with us, following in a trail of multihued glisten.

Back within the Occulta Mirum I sense unrest within Orion. The crown of platinum seaweed like shapes is still on his head, just as my tiara is still on mine. I wonder if it's bothering him as he keeps going to run his hand through his hair but stops himself, knowing he will dislodge his new accessory. I'm sat, gathering my bearings with him, alone in our suite at the top of the Alcazar Oceania when a knock on the porthole in the floor alerts us that we aren't alone.

"I'll get it," Orion says quickly as I brush through my hair rhythmically with my conch comb, readjusting my tiara. He moves in one fluid movement with a flick of his tailfin, lifting the hatch and disappearing beneath. I stare at myself, my eyelashes thick and my scaly chest heaving. I'm still wearing the teardrop diamond necklace from my father and I wonder where he is now. Will we ever meet? I hear the hatch open behind me and Orion re-enter.

"Who was it?" I ask him and he shakes his head looking disarmed.

"Uh just... Marina," he's holding a single white clam shell in his palm.

"What's that?" I ask him innocently. He looks instantly panicked.

"Uh... nothing. Some kind of coronation gift. It's just a shell." He tucks it into a pouch on the white belt hanging around the top of his tailfin, it's studded with sapphires.

"You're gonna carry it around?"

"Who knows, could be lucky," he gives me a boyish grin and for the first time since we left the beach house I feel the need to be close to him. I swim forward and move to kiss him. He recoils, his skin covered in goose pimples.

"Oh my Goddess, you're an emotional wreck. What's wrong?" I look up into his worried gaze and he crosses his arms defensively, biceps pulsating.

"It's been a long night. There's a lot going on. It's nothing," he smiles and moves toward the hatch again to exit the room.

"You're going downstairs?" I question.

"Yes. I'll see you in a moment," he moves, not looking me in the eye and descends out of the suite. I turn my back to the mirror, facing the room but looking back over my shoulder at my face in the reflective glass. I wonder why Orion's being so distant. Have I done something wrong? I thought I'd been the perfect companion so far tonight. I'd laughed at his jokes, I kept him from drinking too much, I'd danced and curtseyed, and been kissed for display. I had been perfect. I feel something stir within me, something resembling anger. I push it back down as far as it will go. Now was no time for petty insecurities or anger over something I had no control. I try to remain serene, allowing the rose tinted haze to fall over my field of vision once more.

I descend through the water that fills the palace, moving my tail gently and allowing the weight of my body to carry me downward. I know where I'm headed as I feel the pearls in my hair stir with my movement against my ears. I look down at my body and take a moment to appreciate the nautical attire. I'm wearing traditional pearl studded fish netting up my arms and around my tailfin and a gossamer lightweight halter crop top in lilac over my breast scales. It's stylish and as much as I loved my ball gown, I'm glad I'm not carrying the weight of it any longer. I reach the throne room and find it filled with mer who have come straight from the Lunar Sanctum. They're dressed in aquatic finery, fish-netting, pearls, and metal plating used in the most unusual designs you could imagine. As I emerge through the jade crystal archway eyes turn to me and a kind of familiar hush falls, I know this kind of hush, because as an ex high school student of America I know when people have just been talking about me. I look around and mermaids place their hands over their mouths, blushing. I turn around me and at my back is Saturnus staring right at me. *What the hell are you looking at?* I snarl internally at his smugly serene expression. The bruise on his jaw is gone from earlier, healed in a flash just like so many other mer injuries. I look back across the stained glass image of Atargatis that makes up the floor, the early rising sun causing spectacular kaleidoscopic light to bounce around the room, leaving rainbows in its wake. Orion sits in the place of Atlas, in the throne made from the Olive tree of his origin island, somewhere off the coast of Cyprus. I look at his face, and in all honesty he looks a little green. *Can mermen get sick? God I hope he doesn't puke in water that's going to be a nightmare.* I think to myself as he rises. Skye comes up behind me, wrapped in decorative netting and with sea stars clinging to her tresses.

"Go to him. Go on," she pushes me forward and I scowl back at her, rushing to get away from her.

"Geez, okay. God, stop manhandling me!" I snap. She frowns at me and rolls her eyes.

I look back around and Orion has risen from his throne, crown multihued in the light. His eyes are wide, like he's seen a ghost and I watch his fumbling fingers.

"Callie…" He breathes, shaking slightly. He takes both my hands and we rise until we are around six feet above the floor. The crowd stares up at me. *What the hell is going on? Did someone die or something?* I look into the eyes of Saturnus curiously and notice the mermaids around the room blushing insanely. Oh Goddess… What on earth? Then it clicks and something inside me realises what's happening before, only God knows why, Orion pushes back from me and lowers himself so the tip of his tail is touching the floor. He pulls the shell from his belt and before I can say a single word he's opening it and speaking the words I had thought were years away. My heart falls through my chest as they hit the air, smashing my rose tinted haze so completely I feel faint.

"Callie Pierce, you are the woman I've waited for, the woman I've longed for, and the woman I want to spend the rest of my life with. Will you marry me?"

5
Rise
SOLUSTUS

It trembles. I can hear the susurrations of its blood, coursing in frantic folly around its spindled skeleton. I raise my rapier, my beautiful Scarlette, so named for the litres of blood she has spilled, the marks she has left on another, her long slender length sharper than the wit of any woman I've ever known. The seahorse, pitiful creature that it is, moves again as I block its path, the power of Scarlette exerting itself over its meaningless existence. I could kill it, but that would be too easy. Torture, pain, stamina; those are the real challenges. My tail is cocked over the edge of the throne in which I sit, a throne of death, a throne of bone. More comfortable than you might think, especially when one drapes themselves across it like a relished victory flag. I look out over the room, surveying all it holds, blackness, roughness, the structure having been formed out of the sea's hot rage. It's fuming tumult and carnivorous appetite. The floor is scattered with the remains of things once alive and the walls are clad with calcified teeth that snag and tear. I look up into the darkness and recall once more a time in which I stared up into a different darkness, into hopelessness.

The stars blink out one by one, extinguished, dead already. I am cold and the floor is hard. My ankle is swollen and so is my eye. It hurts so much and is weeping plasma. I hear something stir in the next room. It's him. My brother lies in the corner, red hair muddy with dirt and dust, sleeping, whimpering as nightmares tear at him. I don't sleep anymore, or at least I try not to, I

60

learned that trick long ago. I hear the thud, the metal tankard fall to the floor and spill its precious nectar and the reactive cuss words, travelling through the wood of the door. I tremble, cornered by thick stone walls that chill my emaciated body to the bone. I stretch out my hands, I can see the veins ebbing beneath my translucent skin. I hear the sound of his heavy tread come louder, like that of an ancient monster of myth. I watch the light under the door disappear and hear the keys jangle on their iron chain. The familiar eerie wail of the door hinges as they complain under the friction of heavy wood. The light falls on me in a sheet, laying me bare to his scrutiny. My father stands in the doorway, tall as a mountain and thick as an oak, immovable and terrifying, his balding head dripping with sweat, with taboo need.

"Get up boy. I need you... now."

No! I snap, sitting bolt upright across the throne. Enough is enough. I comfort myself, remembering the look on the old man's face when I returned with the power of Poseidon behind me, the terror that filled his eyes as I tore out his throat and let the blood run down me like holy water, a purifying entity. I hated him, but he had made me what I was today, impenetrable. He had let them take my younger brother, let them hang him after months of leaving him tied to a bed in a straw hut on the edge of the village with no food or water. Possessed they had said, but I knew different. I knew my father's torment had left him mad. He had already killed our oldest brother in a drunken stupor, a glass bottle to the throat for his eldest, who was ready to wed. I had gotten out, charging the wooden door when he was at his most intoxicated once I was old enough, but I couldn't save Caedes. I was the only one left to get revenge for all three of us. I was the one who had sunk my teeth into my brother who had risen a mer, but still quite mad. I saved him from the judgement of those who did not understand. I did what needed to be done.

It catches the corner of my eye, glinting, heavy with mystery and power. The Scythe of Atargatis, the thing that had left me trapped, waiting for the opportune moment once more. I look at its length, not a particularly powerful weapon to behold, but then this was not like Titus' trident, which stands next to the scythe. He had rarely used it, who needs a weapon when you personally qualify.

I think of his pathetic attempt to raise a power like the Necrimad, my lip curling upward, *what a fool*. All that power and not enough control over his rage to see through the poor acting skills of Azure. I will not make that mistake. I will not be blinded by rage. I am fuelled by something far more powerful. Hate and the love of the one person I know should be ruling these godforsaken depths: Me. I am glad, of course, that Azure was stupid enough to cross the likes of Titus. Without her I never could have performed the role I had been waiting centuries for: supplantor.

I move over to the window, slicing through the water and sucking it down my gullet, sniffing it like an opiate gas. I wonder what it must be like, getting high and communing with the Necrimad, I feel anger rise at my impotence. I suppose I will never know. It bothers me, crawling beneath my skin like scarabs, my inability to communicate with the beast. I reach the window and survey the shadowy beauty of my Kingdom under the clouds of pulse electricity, jellyfish swarming like a thick layer of neon above the crushed bone and dust of the streets. I look over the Cryptopolis. It is mine, all mine, but it is too small. I want the high shard of the Alcazar Oceania above me, I want to sit in the throne room, the mer at my fin, terror running behind a heady aura of respect and love for yours truly. Below the army teems, seethes like scum and I feel joy bubble up within me, the number of bodies exciting me at the thought of each of their glorious sacrifices. A sacrifice so I, their King, can cast my shadow on their bones as I pass over them and rise to my rightful place. Their lives will slip from them, bleed out into nothingness.

I turn away from the light, smiling contentedly, looking back over the scythe. I run my hand through my slick hair slowly, feeling my nails bite into my scalp as my forehead furrows. I have obstacles, of course, between the Necrimad and myself, between ultimate power and myself. I need to find out more, know more about the scythe in order to possess it fully. I am sure, sure it can be mine. I run my tongue over the points of my teeth, feeling the jagged serrations pulling across the flesh of my tongue, releasing the blood into my mouth like syrup, thick and sweet.

The scythe glints in the light. It's the key, or should I say the lock. I need to find the key to unlock it, release all that delicious lunar energy that it absorbed. It's clever to say the least, the Goddess creating a vessel to bind such power within the weapon and prevent it from being used by those who would sacrifice her. That blonde haired, doe eyed harpy. For who would sacrifice a mere child if they were in her service? I muse the predetermined calculations of those who have put us into slavery, running my nails across the skin of my chest, the pain giving me clarity of thought. I am sure there has to be some hoop to jump through, some insanely cliché condition, a next step to unlocking it, something laughable just like happily ever after. I feel my anger simmering, a consistent feature within me at the thought of the Goddess. That bitch. Playing with her chess pieces and manipulating us all. They said Poseidon was bad? At least his appointment of power was honest, he knew he needed those who had suffered, because that's what we were in for in the service of the Gods: Suffering.

I let the shadows fall over me as it flickers in and out of being, like a light on the fritz. I look down at my pale skin and silver scales, the sight of my body both disgusting and arousing me instantaneously. I need to find the key, but when I say I- I mean the fodder that was teeming below. I had ordered them, in my infinite wisdom to raid the chapels, sanctums, temples, and anywhere else we may find a clue to unlocking the power of the scythe. I can't deny it. I'm stuck. But a man like me is never stuck for long.

The light in the room is scarlet, coating everything in a crimson hue. I can't tell whether it's from the blood of the fodder I've sliced for their incompetence, or because of the Erenna, trapped and squirming helplessly inside a mesh cage that has been haphazardly strung from the stalactites that hang, broken, from the ceiling. I hear something stir behind me and turn, pulling my rapier beside me. Scarlette vibrates, slicing through the water with deadly vigour.

"It's only me, Solustus. Relax," the purring vibrations of Alyssa's voice penetrate me and I shudder. Her femininity and sexual allure make me sick, the harlot reeks of humanity.

"Alyssa, would you detest not invading one's personal space

unannounced?" I roll my eyes, sheathing Scarlette and she moves forward, the tentacles stemming from her waist pulsing with her momentum.

"Why? Getting naughty were we?" She looks me in the eyes, her black hair trailing across her breasts, the rusty coloured scales look like she's bleeding, rotting through her pale skin.

"I was looking over your children. They disappoint me," I say the words disinterested in her already, keeping my sharp features impassive.

"I don't think it's your approval they're craving baby," she wraps her tentacle around my tail, or attempts to but I flex and slash, moving away from her suckered clutch.

"My approval is what they need. Remember what happened to the last child you brought me who didn't respect his elders?" I flex my bony fingers, feeling the absence of my rapier.

"I liked Samuel," she pouts at me and I cock an eyebrow.

"So did Scarlette." I watch her tentacles undulate where her tail used to reside. The octomaid sends shivers through me, this new breed of psiren quite the perversion of nature. "How is the boy?" I ask her, thinking back to the night I turned him, sunk my teeth into the sinew of his pectoral.

"Darius? He is a fine warrior. He is not one of my babies, but he is a fine warrior none the less."

"None the less?" I bite out, anger rising.

"I didn't mean…" I cut her apology off, uninterested, unamused. I pull Scarlette up to her gills, imagining widening them into smiling, gaping mouths gasping for air.

"He's more than merely fodder. He knows the girl. He has hurt her, loved her. He may be of use," I muse aloud, unsure of the reason for allowing her into my thought process.

"Of course, your plan was genius… Your Highness." She bows her head.

Ahh at last, a little respect. Why are fear and violence the only ways to gain such subservience? I wonder, irritated.

"I have observed them, your children from above. They are weak. They are divided. We must unite them. I assume you have explained to them our position?" I query her, feeling empowered at the prospect of my army, lowering the sword once again but enjoying its light weight in my palm.

"I have explained to them about the Necrimad, how we need its power to take our rightful place as defenders of the sea. About how the mer live in luxury whilst we live in the darkness, shunned. They are seething with the resentment that I hoped would infect them post indoctrination. It's easy when they feel so robbed of life, poor babies." She moves her tentacles, stirring the sand around her, the only remnants of her insolent children.

"They need training, you should have seen them the night Titus perished, they need proper instruction. They need to be strong."

"Regus would be a suitable candidate," Alyssa muses and I nod, thinking about the bulk of the half-shark half-man concoction. I hear a crash come from the arched door and turn, a movement so pointed and fluid no man could ever perform it.

"Bloody hell!" The voice is British and coarse. I assume him to be from England. Alyssa's eyes sparkle.

"Vexus, sweet child, what has happened to you?" She pulls her spawn forward, arms stroking his slender face. He has crashed into the wall, unable to halt in time from the immense speed of his violet and black tentacles. His lavender eyes are slits, his cheeks hollow.

"What is this incompetent doing here? Don't we have any security?" I bark at Alyssa and Vexus laughs from the very back of this throat.

"I wouldn't worry about that, I mean the mer don't seem to give a rats arse. I just walked straight into that coronation you sent me off to... no invitation necessary," he straightens himself.

"You... went to the coronation?" I look at him surprised, his gall is alarming.

"Yeah. Quite the uh, shindig too. Lots of pretty doilies and... well...the ladies...." He trails off and examines his stubby nails casually. He angers me, does he not know who I am?

"Orion is now Crowned Ruler," I smile, the child will be out of his depth. This pleases me. I continue, "And the girl? Any other announcements?" I ask him thinking back to the conversation I had held with my brother not one hour ago via the looking glass at my back.

"I dunno mate. I got mounted and kicked out by this... spitfire. Seriously... that bird..." His eyes cloud over and I wonder who would be ballsy enough to mount a stranger.

"Was her name Azure by any chance?" I ask him, floating seamlessly within the water stroking my fingers back through my hair again.

"Maybe. Dark hair, yay tall, quite the black beauty," Vexus muses and I nod.

"Yes. You say she's still infected with the darkness? How interesting," I remember her abilities to see the future, the advantage they gave us... it's tempting... I mentally slap myself. She cannot be trusted. She is too strong willed to be used. Azure was lost to the cause. For now. "Did you find anything?" I ask him, looking into his gaze with an intensity that demands honesty.

"Unfortunately not. The Sanctum seems to be nothing but a fancy bollocks hotel to me. Besides, why would they keep anything of true value there? It's not like they're frequent guests." Vex looks back at me, eyes baring into my face. His retort makes sense, he's smarter than he appears. It enrages me.

"So you've failed," I bait him.

"I prefer to think of it as eliminated another dead avenue, mate," his reply catalyses a calculated, concisely controlled rise of malice within me. I strike instantaneously, moving my tail with all the muscle it can possesses. I head to hit him head on in the gut, but seconds before contact he moves upward through the water with one mighty contraction of his tentacles, leaving me to smash into the wall. *He used my speed against me,* is all I can think as my face meets with wall in a deafening crunch of impact. I hear him laugh and push myself upward, twisting and corkscrewing through the water as I draw Scarlette once more.

"I am not, your mate," I remind him, eyes slits now. He laughs again, careless. He is... *Perfectly Wicked.* I muse with a smile to myself, I need fodder like him. So I let him live. For now. He rolls his eyes over my form as I turn away, I feel them continue to stare, settling on my back and hear him sucking water up under his pointed cheekbones. Alyssa is watching us, amused and unmoving as I dart back over to the throne, using it to assert my dominance. I turn and drape myself over it again lazily, casually, erasing my humiliation. Vex slinks out of the room slowly. With a smirk of victory my eyes find Alyssa's dark eyes once more.

"I like him. He's smart. We need more of that around here. I can't be the only one," she nods to me, not dismayed as to the inclination that she's as stupid as I know she is. You'd have to be to put up with that human loving ex of hers, Gideon.

"I'll go and find Regus."

"No. Not Regus," I muse, I think about the simple intelligence in how Vexus had bested me, not using his emotions but allowing logic to rule all. Like all great rulers I speak my mind, unafraid of the opinions of those submissive challengers. "I don't just want raw strength. I want tactics, I want wit, I want skill and unity," I command her, feeling the regality of my destiny bearing down upon me.

"Then who?" Alyssa queries.

"I will command my own army," I make the gesture, selfless and generous, quite unlike me. It is time to start paying my debt, toiling to achieve the greatness I know I am destined for. It is true, if you want something done right. Do it yourself.

"Very well Your Highness," Alyssa purrs, moving to touch me. I flinch away from her, fearing her touch like poison.

"Gather them," I bark. It is time to make the gaggle of cursed children into an army of men. It is time to rise.

6
Alone

CALLIE

I'm staring at Orion, mouth hanging open, my heart thudding so loudly it's the only thing I can hear. I can feel the eyes of the anxious onlookers bearing into me, waiting for the answer. My answer.

"I..." I begin, my voice a squeak. Orion is beginning to look stony faced as we hang there, suspended in an answerless void. I look at the ring, nuzzled inside the shell he's still holding open. A giant sparkling diamond, cushioned by tiny ice blue pearls and aquamarines. It's beautiful. I can't move though. Can't move to take it, can't move to answer. I am suspended, the silence and my blood rushing around my body, the only actualities within the awkward bubble. A voice within me says only one word. *Flee.*

I turn, past the gasping figures and swim as fast as I can from the room, past a smirking Saturnus. *What the hell are you looking at?* I snap internally, working my tail against the surrounding water, moving from the room at a speed I have never reached in my life. *Oh my Goddess, am I actually doing this?* I ask myself, but I don't have time to think it through, I just know I can't answer him. I can't humiliate him by refusing, but I can't say yes! Who the hell ever heard of an eighteen-year-old marrying someone she's known for just six months! What was he thinking?!

I swim, out the double doors of the Alcazar Oceania and out into the city streets. They're deserted except for the odd patrolling Knight, everyone else is inside. I move up under the heat of the morning sun, the water protecting me from its rays. I long for its heat on my skin, something familiar and comfortable but know that's suicide. I move up through the sea, getting as close to the surface as I can, skimming in thoughtless rhythm away from the city. Away from the crushing pressure that has been mounting. Apparently proposal is my breaking point. *Who knew?*

I move with increasing speed away from my problems, until I see a Commerson dolphin in the distance. It stops me in my watery tracks. The memories come at me like a tidal wave of arctic proportions, chilling me to the bone. Orion filling the buoy with air, Orion smiling, Orion laughing. Orion bending me over the kitchen counter in our beach house, Orion kissing me, Orion loving me, Orion needing me.

"No!" I cry out, trying to stop the flood of nostalgia that is making me short of breath. I move my hands up to my throat, clutching at my gills which are rapidly opening and closing, pulling in water which floods my gullet, but still can't quench my thirst for air. I start moving again, fleeing from the memories, the cascade of horror that is making my heart ache with the uncertainty of my return to the other half of my soul. I say I don't believe it's true, that I think it is all crap, but swimming out, roaming the water and the barren expanses of sand, I have never felt my longing for him more. I have never felt him so necessary and yet I cannot give him my vow of eternity. I have never felt so alone.

The sun falls from the sky as I feel my muscles clenching, enjoying the pain of each stroke that my tailfin makes, pushing me through the water. My mind is racing wearily, struggling to put the jumbled pieces of the puzzle together. Orion getting down on bended fin, Orion looking at me, Orion asking me to marry him. It just doesn't make sense. Or does it?

I'm starting to wonder whether I've missed something, whether that's what his aggressive desperation since Atlas' death has been leading up to. I feel myself wilt slightly. Looking at the fish stirring around me, darting in hues of yellows, greens, and blues. I watch the moon rise over a bloody horizon and continue to ponder.

ORION

"I don't care if she's not in the city! Find her!!!! I want every stone upturned, every inch of every cave searched. I want her found!" I bellow, slamming my fist down onto the wooden armrest of my father's throne; or should I say my throne now. It sounds wrong no matter how many times I think it. Ghazi is kneeling before me, nodding with a look of puzzled pity knitting his brow together. Cole is beside him, his eyes darting between myself and Saturnus who is floating next to me, unmoving and inexpressive. The water is stirring, vibrations of displaced air rippling in my surroundings. They look too afraid to move, afraid of what I might do. "Well? What the hell are you waiting for? GO!" I feel rage move up through me. They don't bow in respect but instead bolt for the exit.

"Might I suggest you calm down?" Saturnus comes before me in an effortless momentum.

"May I suggest that you shut up?" I bite out. He looks surprised, but then the mask of calm falls over his features once more.

"It is not my fault the girl was not as pliable as expected, Your Highness." He takes a formal approach and I find myself unreceptive.

"The 'girl' was just cornered in front of the entire city's population on a piece of advice YOU gave me Saturnus," I accuse him, suddenly realising with whom this fault belongs.

"I swear to you; I have heard her speak of engagement. I have heard her long for such a vow," Saturnus runs his hand through his hair, looking concerned but I see that it is a faux gesture. I cock my head, looking at him, suspicious. I feel my eyes narrow.

"Yes. Well. I suppose these women can be temperamental. She is young," I speak the words and watch him with careful intent.

"Indeed Your Highness. Of course it is no surprise she has swum out into the open ocean. She is not a creature with much regard for her own safety, I'm sure you'd agree," Saturnus smiles slightly, almost sympathetically toward me. I nod.

"Agreed. I want her found," I mutter.

"Let your men do their job. It's what they're there for," Saturnus reminds me.

"Will you go and watch over them. Make sure they are taking necessary precautions for mobilisation?" I request and he nods. Slamming his fist into his heart.

"Of course. It would be my honour," he responds, bowing his feathered mane of bloody hair and turning swiftly, leaving a trail of refracted rainbows in the wake of his diamond encrusted tailfin. I rise from the throne, moving to suspend myself inches from the panoramic glass window, surveying the city.

I watch the horizon as the moon rises, light falling over everything, dulling it by comparison to sunlight. How can Callie not want to be here beside me? I wonder, feeling my heart fragment.

I watch the Knights of Atargatis, few in number now, depart the city to find her. I wonder if she'll come back willingly. Then I think to myself about the notion of marrying her. I can't help but know now, despite my nerves about asking her, that I need her to be my wife. Is that unreasonable? Perhaps. But what is there to stop us? She may only be eighteen years old, but when you know someone is who you want to spend eternity with, why should that matter? I know she feels the connection, the pairing of our souls, so why would she run? I let a sense of foreboding ambivalence settle over me.

The emotions within pull in different directions so I silence them, stopping them from pulling me apart. I need her. Physically, emotionally, and soulfully and I always will. Does it matter if we are wed? *Yes. She must be mine and mine alone.* I whisper internally, this confession of need so sacred I shudder at the vulnerability it sets loose within.

I feel my shoulders hunch as the prospect of her absence, anger and pain looms like a dark cloud over me. My own anger simmers beneath my slouched exterior as I curse all women. What the hell are they playing at, being so fragile but refusing protection? So loveable and yet so unwilling to be loved? So coveted and yet so unattainable? Why won't she just let me love her for Goddesses sake?

Then I feel my own pride vanquished as I wonder if it's not her at all, but instead me. Am I worth marrying? Has my sordid past been bothering her again? I wish she would talk to me. I want to read her as an open book, splay out her pages and study all her intricate calligraphy. Trace my fingers across her inky curves and study her intricate gliding lines. As I look out over the horizon, into the stormy shadows, I cannot help but wonder if she can be found. If she will return to me. I am still, suspended in a state of waiting, my back to the throne I have just taken and as onyx dusted clouds begin to swirl overhead, a single diamond falls in pitted silence.

CALLIE

The dark clouds above puff out like the chests of peacocks, asserting their majesty. I watch the waning moon disappear behind them and continue to move through the waves, breaking the surface every now and then, letting the water carry me wherever it wills. I find clarity above the surface, the dryness of the air clinging to me and encasing me in a blanket of acute thought. The situation begins to become transparent in my mind, easily foreseeable. I wonder why I didn't see this coming. It is in fact the single most logical way for Orion to assert absolute ownership over me, and that in its entirety is why I could not say yes.

The next problem I am faced with is the fact that I have just left him standing in front of his people without an answer. I wonder if I have made the right choice as my tailfin flicks upward, sending salt spray up around me and I feel the first drops of rain begin to fall on my back. *Can I go back now? Will he be contented us being together as just Orion and Callie, not man and wife?* The word wife makes me irrationally angry and I clench my teeth, riding through the increasingly tumultuous waves, enjoying each bite of the ocean's white capped surface, stinging my skin as I bury myself within it once more. *What the hell was he thinking? I'm eighteen for goddess' sake!* My own internal monologue reminds me of his motives. *He thinks we're destined.* I want to spit the word, slam down on it hard with my fist. I hear an inward sneer, a cajoling bite that whispers to me, stirring my anger.

I feel my blood boil as I break the surface again, without direction or reason, riding the waves of a growing storm and enjoying my insignificance against the trembling waves, the beating of the rain against my scales, the darkness of the depths beneath. I watch the fish stirring, moving in time with their frantic, fearful heartbeats. *Pitiful.* I think a thought that isn't my own and shake it off. Eventually I find myself looking upon a shoreline I hadn't even realised I had been heading for. It was the root of my problem, so it was no wonder really, but I had returned once more to the beach where Orion and I had first kissed. Where I had died in his arms.

I bob up and out of the water at increasing intervals of nearness to the line of the sand. I feel the wicked currents pulling at disjointed angles beneath me so I continually move my tailfin, left then right, correcting my position. I can see the light from where I am, even though the rain is coming down in sheets.

The beach house. The life I've left behind. I wonder if my friends are inside. If they're giggling, laughing, watching a movie without me. I miss them now more than I can say I have since I died and was reborn. I miss the warmth of their bedrooms, the simplicity of quilted bedspreads and bowls of popcorn. I long for their company, for the simplicity of their lives. A simplicity I had all but taken for granted once. I had thought my life was so hard. Had I known what was to come, I can't help but wonder if I would have been slightly more grateful for Carl and all his bullying. I'm not saying he wasn't a bastard, of course he made my life difficult, but he was nothing compared to the armies of Psirens and the demons I had seen rise from the depths of the ocean. I longed for his critique. I longed for my mother. I longed, for just a moment, to be human.

I move forward, sloshing water up my back in a cold cascade, allowing my head to immerse itself once more in the ocean. I swim, desperately, quickly and wanton toward the shore. I climb up on my haunches, moving my slickened scales against the grain of drenched sand. I haul myself, the weight of my tail immense now on land, toward the life I had once lived. I find myself out of breath quickly, heart hammering, waves lapping over me in a chilling realisation that I cannot go back. I look up at the lights of Chloe's beach house, the place where I once had so many human problems and collapse onto the sand, letting it catch me and the waves climb over me like a sodden blanket. I roll onto my back and let my tears fall, exasperation and grief overcoming me like a tsunami. The rain continues to fall down over me and lightning illuminates my broken form as the storm washes my tears back to the sea, hardening them into something eternally cold. I lay there, under the intermittent sparks of the raging storm, stuck in the place between my old life and new. Wanting to go back.

I slowly curl up, pulling my tail up to my chest and place my chin on the aquamarine scales. I let the waves pull me back to where I've come, back into the ocean's depths. I surrender to the movement of the storm, surrender to the idea of being alone, surrender to my inner tumult and let myself be taken by the rage of the water.

Falling through the waves so deep, I close my eyes and beckon sleep.

I hear something stir beneath the earth. It is hot to touch underneath my fleshy mass. I can hear it, whispers crawling over me with arachnid softness, a tingle moving across me with wicked intent. Tremors are moving through the dense rock and heat is breathing in and out of all the fissures of the ocean's bedrock. I close my eyes, scared to know what is encased in a timeless coffin. I see black slashes, symbols flash across the back of my eyelids. Something I've seen before but cannot quite remember. I hear a cackle as I writhe with terror in a place unknown to me. I know not what surrounds me but only what lies beneath, the jaws of something old, something dark, stretching open in a grin, a grin that will swallow me whole. I don't think this is a memory... or at least... it's not my memory.

I wake with a start, curled up on the ocean floor, alone. Or not, as I look up into the eyes of Cole.

"Callie... what are you doing here?" He looks at me, something unmistakably horrified in his eyes.

"I... I ran away," I stutter, shaking off the dream that had not belonged to me. I wonder if it was a reaction to the stress of everything that's going on around me. But then again, mermaids aren't supposed to dream, we are only meant to consolidate our memories into a flawlessness that time cannot erode.

"I don't think you ran... more like swam," Cole presents a hand to me, helping me up from the sand. His onyx tail is moving impatiently and it aggravates me slightly. I don't wonder why he is here. I know Orion has sent him.

"So exactly how much trouble am I in?" I ask him and he shakes his head.

"I don't know. It seems to me like Orion is pretty worried. I think he'll be glad you're safe." His armour is shimmering around him. I turn from him, feeling the pressure of his presence. "Let's go back to the city. I can call off the search and the rest of the Knights can return to their proper duties. Keeping everyone safe," Cole speaks the words and I can't help but feel they're directed at me. Like I'm causing some huge inconvenience for everyone. My heart is stony in my chest, emotion from the night before, much like the storm in the midst of which I had sobbed, is clearing, vaporising into nothing.

"I don't know if I want to go back," I whisper. Faux weakness sounds throughout my tone. I want him to pity me, but I no longer feel sorry for myself. This wasn't my fault and I'm not going to deal with it on anyone's timescale but my own. Cole opens his mouth to retort but I turn and start to swim away from him. He follows me insistently.

"I cannot go without you. If I have to stay here I will. It's not safe to be out here alone. You need protection," he implores my fear to engage an understanding of his logic within me. This only makes my anger grow.

"No. I need to be alone. I can protect myself. I died and came back to life remember?" I continue to move away from him, something catches my eye and an abhorrent feeling of rising vomit follows. We are still close to the shore and I can see its proximity to the human world now more than ever. A turtle is caught in a plastic bag, throttling itself within the rungs one would use to carry groceries home. Next to the poor creature is a discarded soda can and several candy wrappers. The remnants of a sugar binge. I move down through the water and rip away the plastic bag. The turtle's brown leathery flippers beat against my arms as I free it, desperate to be back, swimming free. As I pull the tacky plastic loop from its neck the big beautiful black eyes connect with mine in a moment of thanks, a second of mutual respect. It swims away, slowly, gracefully through the azure hue of the water and into the distant morning light. I realise Cole is now beside me.

"Must have thought it was a Jellyfish. They eat them you know. It's good this one got caught up in the bag and didn't eat it. That can kill them," he speaks like this is common knowledge. I feel bile rise up within my throat, thick and sweet.

"You've seen this before?" I query him, horrified.

"Near the coasts, yes. We try to help wherever we can. But sometimes it's not enough." His royal blue eyes fill with a kind of melancholy knowing. I wonder why it is Orion and I are working so hard to save a world full of people who are so goddamn ignorant and disrespectful to the needs of their own planet. I feel something stir within me, that tiny voice at the back of my skull, growing louder with each instance. *Exactly.*

"Humans suck," I exhale and Cole nods.

"They are... young even still I suppose. Evolution takes time."

"This isn't evolution, its common sense and a lack of care," I shake my head, the anger not fading but reverberating through my every thought. I clench my fingers into my palms.

"I think we should go back, Callie. I can tell you're stressed out. Maybe you need to talk things out with Orion. It isn't safe out here," he reminds me once again of the Psirens and my anger crests. I roll my eyes and he frowns.

"It's not my fault you know, that he's like this with you."

"So I'm not overreacting about him being so overprotective?" I ask him and he looks deeply uncomfortable.

"Look... I shouldn't really be talking to you about this stuff, it's not my place to..." He trails off and I glare at him, erect as a poker in the body of the sea and determined to know another sees my point of view.

"Cole. Spit it out."

"Well... My soulmate, Jack, he's with the Knights of Atargatis all the time, and I love him. But, I can't stop him from going out there and doing his duty. He'd kick my ass." He looks at me and his mouth twists into a smile at the thought. I can see the love there instantly.

"So you're saying Orion should suck it up and let me fight if I want?" I look at him hopeful, warming to him slightly.

"I'm saying if you weren't a woman, he wouldn't have much of a choice. You may look small and dainty, but I saw you that night over the city. You're stronger than he thinks. You're stronger than even you, yourself, realise," he smiles at me and I feel confidence grow within my chest, blooming outward from my sternum and crawling around my ribs like vines, reinforcing my bones, protecting my heart.

"Thank you," I smile at him and he nods, an expression crossing his face that I can't quite read.

"Don't mention it. As in, actually don't mention it. I don't fancy pissing off the new Crowned Ruler," he shrugs and I nod.

"I think we should go back now. You're right," I do this to show my gratitude and smile gratefully. I know I'm doing him a favour by not putting up too much of a fight, but I also know that I do need to go back to the city. I need to go and talk to Orion. I need to go and tell him how I feel. I need to fix things between us. After all, what other choice do I have?

7
Salt

CALLIE

The surface of the water rolls, unrestrained and boundless above as I move through the city. I can feel eyes peering through glassless windows and watching my return in the bioluminescent dim. My body feels strong, my views definite, my heart encased in my ribs, no longer trapped like a bird but rather using the alabaster bars as a kind of armour. I wasn't going to be distracted, I was going to put my fin down.

Looking back over the past few months it's been easy to be swept away with the huge current of Orion's love, the passion we share. But I needed to be able to swim in the current, enjoy it and not get pulled under by its intensity. I look around me at the city and its great height, the towering turrets of surface scrapers looming like huge bollards above me, trapping me within their streets. Cole and I are moving toward the Alcazar Oceania, which does not yet feel like home, accompanied by a small guard of Knights who had aided him in his search for me.

I can't quite bring myself to feel bad at the inconvenience to them. Rather I choose to feel irritated at Orion for making such a fuss. It is getting embarrassing for him, how desperate he appears all the time when trying to keep me caged in next to him. He doesn't look like the ruler I know he can be. He looks like a lovesick schoolboy with an edge of overbearing father.

I sigh, running my fingers through my hair, feeling the tiara that still clings within the thick, stiff locks of my mermaid tresses. It feels heavy on my head, its claws digging into my scalp ferociously.

"You can go now, Cole. I don't need an escort. I know my way to the

Alcazar Oceania," I turn to him and he throws his fist against his chest, hard and unwavering in its trajectory.

"Of course," he looks worried.

"I'll be okay. Go home to Jack. That's an order," I smile at him kindly and he looks surprised, a tiny flame of thanks flickering into life behind his royally blue eyes. He turns from me wordlessly, taking the rest of the mermen with him. I watch him interlock his fingers with one of the other Knights who had been following us and I wonder if Jack had in fact been accompanying us the whole time. I shrug it off, feeling the weight of the fight ahead of me. *Maybe there won't be a fight. Maybe it's all a big misunderstanding.* The naivety of my own thought surprises me. Of course there is going to be a fight. I left the man hanging there without an answer to a proposal of marriage. More than that, I can't even claim that I want to get married. Because I don't.

Within the Alcazar Oceania I feel the weight of the porthole shift as I open it, rising up into our chamber. The jade crystal walls shimmer dully with memories in the wake of our pre-proposal domesticity.

"You came back." I hear the voice, cracked, like a mirror reflecting back the consequences of what I had done straight at me, full force.

"You didn't exactly give me much choice," I mutter and Orion comes into view. He glides toward me. His face is impassive but his eyes are scared. There is fear in them. Fear I've never seen before.

"If you hadn't run off in the first place then it wouldn't be an issue," he doesn't snap. He just sounds tired. I take off the tiara that's still digging into my skull and move over to my vanity, placing it in front of the conch comb. The diamonds glitter coldly.

"I needed some time," I admit, turning and meeting his eyes. They're dead.

"Why?" He asks me, I can tell every muscle in his body is tense as even his tail moves in calculated and measured momentum.

"To think," I reply honestly, earnestly. Not whispering but speaking clearly. I do not want there to be any mistake of my intent.

"That's funny. I thought you had your mind all made up."

"What's that supposed to mean," I rise slightly so my eyes meet his. I suck down thick salty mouthfuls of water, letting it quench my thirsty lungs and give me the confidence that I need to get myself heard.

"I asked you to marry me." He puts his hand through his hair in that way he does when he's stressed, fingers bristling against the metal of his crown. I know what would calm him, stroking his hands through my hair, over my body, but I cannot let him seek comfort in me any longer.

"And I said no." His head snaps up only moments after his eyes have fallen to the floor as my words reach him.

"You didn't. You just fled. You always flee. So you're saying no?" He narrows his eyes. I inhale. My heart begins to hammer but I have to confirm his claim, I have to put myself first.

"I'm saying no," I nod and he turns for a moment, as though I've physically slapped him. "Are you mad I'm saying no?" I ask him, wondering what to do as I hang, limp in the water.

"Not angry. Humiliated maybe…" He mutters, waving a hand, back still to me, dismissing my existence almost.

"You chose to ask me in front of everyone. It isn't my fault. I was kind of humiliated too," I remind him and he still doesn't turn around, robbing me of his gaze, like a small child refusing to kiss his mother after he's thrown his toys out of the pram.

"Yeah, I can see how."

"Orion, please don't be like this…" He turns on me, finally deciding to square up to the problems that have come to a head after months of denial.

"I waited for you," he snarls. I straighten my back and cross my arms.

"I didn't ask you to," I remind him, glaring.

"You're my soulmate. Would you rather I be in love with someone else?" He asks me the question and I contemplate my response carefully.

"Maybe you should have been, I mean, I don't like you being like this, Orion. There's too much pressure," I admit to him and in the confession I feel lighter. I feel my heart begin to swell with truth. Orion looks confused.

"We were made for each other, Callie. That's the opposite of pressure." He snorts, then looks at me like I'm crazy. Like what I'm saying is in some kind of foreign language.

"Not to me," I say the simplest answer I can think of. I don't rise, I don't bite. I just go for what I know will infuriate him most, acting like I don't care what he thinks. Acting like my thoughts are completely cleaved from his own.

"I don't understand you!" He exclaims, throwing his arms up in a flurry of disturbed bubbles.

"Please don't yell at me," I say calmly. My lack of retort makes his expression turn nasty. An Orion who is not a white knight. Not a prince charming. Not a crowned ruler. An Orion who is distinctly human.

"NO! I am a calm person Callie, but I've had enough! I waited, I did my part. I suffered! I paid my dues! Then you DIED CALLIE! YOU KNEW YOU WERE INVOLVED IN THAT GODDAMN PROPHECY AND YOU LIED TO ME! I GOT YOU BACK FROM THE DEAD! DO YOU KNOW WHAT THAT'S LIKE? DO YOU?" He stops for breath, his muscled pectorals rising and falling like twin peaks of masculine assertion. I stand, facing his rage, his anger and grief like the storm I've just ridden into the dusk. "So I'm sorry if I proposed to soon! Maybe I jumped the gun! But is it so much to ask that I just get to have you for a little while? Just for me? Is it so wrong that I want to lock you away from the world after everything you've been through?" His eyes have gone from burning with rage to imploring me to see his point of view in a few seconds. I find his intensity tiring, he's so invested. I'm just exhausted.

"I'm eighteen, Orion. Yes, I died, but I chose to come back to be with you, over being a Goddess! What you're doing is just like you say, it's locking me away, so I can't escape even if I want to. That sure as hell isn't a good enough reason to get married... I mean you need trust for a start!" I feel my emotion getting a little loose, I check myself internally. Distance is the key to getting through this. To getting what I want. If I let myself feel, I'll crumble into his arms and be back at square one all over again.

"Can you blame me for not trusting you, Callie?" Orion's expression is deadpan and the water around us is tremor-less.

"Okay, so I lied to you, I get it. You have a point. But I'm not marrying you because we're 'destined' either," I bite out and he looks affronted once more, in spite of my generous acknowledgement that I might have given him some reasons to distrust.

"You met Atargatis! You can't tell me you don't believe..." I cut him off mid-sentence. Feeling myself becoming angry. I don't like to talk about my experience with the Goddess and I certainly wasn't going to bring it up in a shouting match.

"It's not about that! I'm not happy like this! Can't you see that?" Now it is me who is imploring him. His sense of reason, which seemingly departed along with Atlas' soul. His look quickly turns sullen as his eyes glass over, the frost within them creeping across his field of vision like a window pane.

"I thought you loved me." His chiselled jaw bulges as he presses his lips, those same lips that could be so incredibly soft against the nape of my neck, into a cold hard line. A line incapable of caress.

"It's not a question of that," I realise that this is true. My mind spilling its thoughts out, untarnished, like the first draft of a poem onto a blank page.

"Then what?" We are both suspended. Hanging like the questions we ask in the water between us, still, facing off. Cutting each other, edging around the subject of our imminent destruction. We could both see it coming, but neither wanted to move.

"It's about trust, letting me go and knowing I'll come back. Not chaining me down with passionate possession and praying I won't break free."

"You could be a poet," he quips, raising his chin, looking down over me in my youth and stupidity. *How dare he.* I think to myself. *He took me away from everything I've ever known. He was the selfish one. He let me die and did nothing to save my human life. He let me be taken away from my mom, my sister. How dare he look at me like that!* The venom of the sentiment crossing my mind shocks me. It is no longer the voice in the back of my mind implying such things. This is my voice. My anger. My hate. I recoil. Trying to calm myself.

"I'm trying to be honest," I admit to him. Trying to retract my anemone like spikes. Trying to work through it, trying to reach a conclusion.

"Fine. What do you want then if not marriage?" He looks at me and I realise, I don't know. I don't know what I want. I don't know who I am. I used to be Callie Pierce, San Diegan teenager. But now... now I was The vessel? Failed Goddess? Orion's soulmate? The revelation strikes me and I feel ashamed of myself. I feel humiliation and weakness envelope me.

I can tell you what I am to the people of this city, what I am to the people who wanted to sacrifice me and leave me for dead. I can tell you what I am to my Goddess, and to Orion, but what am I to myself. Who am I?

"Maybe we need some time apart," I hear myself say the words and know instantly that I'm craving to remove my constraints. To swim the oceans, to spread my wings. I want to fly. I want to become whoever the hell it is I'm supposed to be. Without Orion.

"You're leaving me," Orion turns away from me and I shake my head. Desperate for him still.

"No. I said time, a lot has happened. I'm not sure what I want. Who I am," I move toward him, taking a stroke forward, closing the distance between us. For this to work, I need his patience. Unfortunately, I think that's already worn far too thin.

"I think we both know that isn't me," he says it in a childish, self-pitying whimper. *Oh for Goddess' sake!* After all this time. He still doesn't know. I wonder, for a moment, if I can show him. Take him into my arms on my terms and kiss him in a way that will resonate with both my flittering body and my needy soul. I flick my tail, taking him by surprise, moving my hands up to his head and feeling my rage at his stubbornness rise. Something happens I don't expect. Orion cries out, a harrowing, scorching scream that could shatter glass. He collapses.

"What the hell, Callie? Are you trying to kill me?! Do you hate me that much? Do I make you that unhappy?" He bursts out, his tongue an unholstered weapon, shooting vocal bullets of devastation with each word.

"What? No... I..." I reach out to touch him but he flinches away. I feel my insistence grow and I move closer to his slumped figure, touching him gingerly with one hand. As my skin touches his, I feel something pass to me as he grabs my hand hard. He tries to pull me toward him, tries to subdue me again, suddenly with an assault of his own, trying to possess my mouth with his tongue as he rises over me like a mountain, immovable, solid. I struggle as he grasps my upper arms in his palms, gripping me like he wants to shake sense into me. *I don't want this. I don't want this.* I repeat internally, almost screaming. I don't want him to turn this into another overly enamoured cover up of the problems he's been ignoring all these months. I try to say no but his lips are clutching mine. I'm stiff in the water, unmoving. I struggle but he holds me still. I've had enough.

"ENOUGH!" I scream out in a muffled exclamation against his lips. As the sound escapes, something else does too. I create a tidal wave of air, displacing Orion and knocking him back against the wall of our chamber with a dull crunch. He hits the crystal, smacking his head and collapsing against the floor below the crack he recently made with his fist.

"You.... You took my power," he looks at me with a wicked grin on his face. Like he knows something I don't.

"I..." I begin and turn, exiting and fleeing into the castle below. I hear him call after me with a laugh.

"What a surprise... You leave... like you always do! Well this time, don't even think about coming back!" His words pain me, fear cresting within me, crashing down over me and drenching me. Leaving me sodden, naked, and cold.

ORION

"Well you handled that nicely," The surly tones of Starlet reach me as her magenta length rises through the porthole, entering our... I mean my chamber.

"Go away Star," I bite out. Why is she always around when I'm angry? My heart is pounding against the inside of my rib cage, longing to escape and follow Callie, but the throbbing of my spine is preventing me from moving. The impact of having my own power used against me still reverberating within my skull.

"I personally liked that 'don't even think about coming back' add-on at the end there. Nice touch," she moves over to the vanity made of jade glass and picks up Callie's tiara, fingering the diamonds.

"I said go away." I slump against the wall. Starlet perches on the vanity across from the wall and looks at me with a cocked brow.

"Unlike Callie, I don't listen to every word you say with baited breath, Orion. I think you need to get over yourself."

"She'll come back. She always does," I relinquish my own personal assurance, the one that lives in the back of my consciousness, making me feel safe.

"I think you're over estimating the power of her ability to deal with your crap." Starlet puts the tiara back on the vanity and shifts, crossing her arms.

"You don't understand. She's so difficult." I crick my neck from left to right, rubbing the back of it half-heartedly.

"She's a person, Orion. It's not her job to do whatever you ask without question. That's called slavery," Starlet looks at me with her head tilted, running her fingers through her long white blonde hair and letting them snag.

"I know that."

"Do you, though? Really? People feel so sorry for me..."

"No they don't, where you getting that from?" I look at her surprised at the confession.

"You think I don't see the pity in people's eyes at every goddamn formal event? You think I'm imagining people avoiding me?" She looks at me seriously and I wonder. I guess I hadn't noticed before, but maybe she was right, I had never seen her with the other mermaids.

"You don't think that's because you're, you know..."

"A bitch?" She finishes with a smile and I laugh back with an almost cruel edge.

"Well... you can be," I admit.

"Maybe I am a bitch... but the point is... I walk around with everyone pitying me for being alone. But it's not so bad. I don't have anyone to answer to but me." I still don't get what she's insinuating.

"And this has what to do with me and Callie?"

"Oh come on, I wasn't one of the two people involved in the argument and even I can guess what her issue is," Starlet rolls her eyes at me and I wonder when Star and Callie became a team. I wonder if Callie is even aware of what Starlet is saying right now.

"This isn't any of your business," I remind her, rising up from the floor of the chamber. Straightening my spine is painful, but the pain quickly recedes as my accelerated healing begins.

"Yeah, well it will be my business when Callie takes your advice and doesn't come back and you're miserable for the rest of eternity. It'll be all 'poor me I'm so alone and brooding' again. Not a good look on you by the way." The words have an unexpected effect on me. I think back to those years of moving alone through the ocean. The emptiness. The touch of other women who were not and never would be her.

"She'll come back," I repeat.

"I wouldn't be so sure. You're caging her in, Orion. Freedom is probably looking pretty good right now."

"I didn't do anything of the sort," I laugh, a kind of sneer at the implication that my love is anything but endearing.

"Seriously? Really? After everything that girl is telling you, you're still not gonna listen?" Starlet looks at me, incredulous, as I turn to face the window that looks out over the city.

"I haven't done anything wrong, Star," I say the words, the truth in them assuring me I'm doing the right thing. Callie needs to know I won't stand for her putting her own safety at risk. She means too much to me.

"You proposed to her with no warning in front of a room of people," Starlet frowns at what I assume is her remembering the giant fiasco after Callie left me standing there.

"She wants to marry me, Star. She just doesn't know it yet. She always does this. She always needs a little push. Then later she thanks me for it," I nod and she frowns deeper still.

"She became a Queen for you yesterday. Took on a Kingdom at eighteen. What more do you want? I can't see her getting any more committed than that."

"She's always known what the deal was. This bond… it's forever. A ring doesn't change anything," I rationalise the situation, letting my sister's words roll off me.

"Okay. You keep believing that," she rises and moves, tailfin swaying from side to side, reeking with feminine allure. The kind too obvious for even me, as her brother, to ignore.

She descends through the floor of the chamber and I move, wondering if

I do, in fact, need some perspective. I look over to the clamshell bed and it beckons my weariness, like a pill for all my waking pain. I move the porthole lid closed and lock it, spinning the wheel so it's as tight as it will go. I flick my tail, displacing the water around me and move, diving and collapsing onto the shell bed. I knock the prop holding the hood of the clam away with the end of my tailfin and let it close around me. Shutting me away in darkness, where my lids slowly droop, and I call back to me the argument in a detail crystal clear like tropical waters.

AZURE

Crustaceans crawl through the sand, laboured, slow, and pitiful in their existence. Something catches the corner of my eye, an aquamarine glimmer that shouldn't be there, writhing, scurrying through the water to get away. I move around the edge of the surface scraper with its round walls that line the alley I am skulking in. I like this alley, it is comforting to me, after all the Occulta Mirum isn't like Cryptopolis, there aren't many dark spots where one can escape amongst the banal glimmer and the mundane sparkle of the surface world. I scratch against the sandstone of the building, leaving claw marks in my wake as I use the tower to leverage myself forwards, still encased in shadow like it's a child's blanket, comforting and safe as my tail lashes out behind me haphazardly.

I see Callie, swimming like her life depends on it, moving away from the Alcazar Oceania. *What, is she taking off again?* I'd heard about the scene in the throne room. My brother proposing. *Well, good for her, saying no to that whole bullshit dog and pony show.* I sneer internally. The idea of a forever bond with a man makes my inside furl and snarl like thorny vines, thirsty for blood, for death.

I move closer, deciding to follow her, stalk her like prey, good practice seeing as I haven't had a good stalk in a while. My tail waves sensuously, undulating, shimmering black and electric blue. I see Callie bump into Saturnus, who is hurriedly leaving the building in which his study resides. He flinches back, red hair floating innocuous in the water around him, like she's red hot and dangerous.

I never liked that man, even when I was a mermaid, all innocent and pure. There's something about him that's unsettling to me, so I enjoy watching him carefully manoeuvre around the girl. Now I think about it, it was probably some innate repulsion from the Goddess that lies at the heart of why he makes me so uneasy. The beginnings of my first touch with darkness maybe. Who knows? I've given up trying to understand it all, for who am I? Powerful yes, but on the grand scale I am but a pawn in a game of Gods.

"Yes, I think it's best if you leave. If Orion doesn't want you here... it won't be long before the rest of the city start to turn against you Callie... You need to get away," Saturnus' words look like they've physically pained the girl as I rise up the side of the tower, toward the light, eavesdropping on them mid-conversation. Her blonde hair is moving in cascades of fairness and her pert figure is dainty and weak looking. Her expression is crumpled, like a fallen angel, her tiny waist and arms look frail, pale... but that's not what catches my attention. It's something in her eyes. A sudden flash of rage, protruding through her anguish. I've seen that look before but can't quite place it.

"Fine," Saturnus' chest deflates slightly at her short but clearly agitated sentiment. She swims away and he looks around, slightly aware he is being watched, but not aware of the source... or is he? He moves back into the building from which he has come, at the other side of the courtyard. As he moves, I see him pull something reflective from a satchel around his shoulder before disappearing around the corner. Saturnus gone, I decide to follow a feeling of gut instinct and tail Callie for a while. After all, I have nothing better to do. Maybe the open ocean will do me good.

I've been hunting her for a while, keeping a distance so she won't realise it's me. She's crying, as a trail of diamonds in the sand below will attest to. I feel sick at the thought of all that emotion, all those leaking fluids. *Humanity is so gross.*

The open water is cooling over my skin, liquid serenity, clearing the darkness from my mind. *I should come for long swims more often* I vow to myself. It makes the darkness feel more manageable, less a part of who I am and more something that has happened to me.

Callie is still within my view but suddenly stops and turns, as though she's aware of me. I watch her, dropping back a little.

"Orion if that's you, I swear I'm going to..." I hear the call, angrier than I've ever heard her. She sounds fierce, like a mouse in a dragon costume. I writhe, undulating through the water, like the current itself my body takes on a fluidity that I adore. Sexy as hell but fast, too. Titus had taught me once upon a time.

"It's not Orion. It's me," I feel the darkness recoil as her petite features soften, her white skin glowing. Our eyes meet and she erects herself in the water. Her body is tense.

"What... what are you doing here? Did he send you?" She asks me, eyes full of fear, like a caged animal fleeing for her life. Does she know that I can beat her in a physical confrontation? She looks upset and her aquamarine eyes are rimmed red. I feel something I haven't in a while. Empathy. She and I aren't so different, we both sacrificed for the mer.

"No...I'm not here for him," I don't know what to say and I feel my pupil's contract, the blackness of them receding.

"That thing with your eyes... do you know that happens or..." She looks like a small child as she lifts a hand to her nose and itches awkwardly. I frown slightly, she's forward.

"Um... yes. The darkness, when I get angry it comes out," I reply, she smiles slightly.

"That sucks, you should be allowed to get angry without going all Morticia Queen of darkness," she sniffs and I cock my eyebrow, no idea what she's babbling about.

"Yes. It's not so bad. Stops people bothering me." She cocks an eyebrow at my explanation and I can't help but smile, she looks so young and naive.

"You look pretty when you smile, you should do it more often," she compliments me and my mouth instantly drops back into the sullen line it preferentially forms.

"So what happened? You don't want to marry my brother?" I ask her, changing the subject onto something that will make her uncomfortable.

"No. I don't," she sounds sure of herself. She realises we are suspended in the open sea and gestures to me. "Do you mind if we keep moving. I don't like floating like this," she admits the simple fact to me and I wonder why.

"Why?" I ask her, surprised at my own lack of self-containment.

"I don't like just floating out here, moving helps take my mind off things."

"Are you stupid? Not that, why don't you want to marry my brother?" I snap, and she recoils slightly but then narrows her eyes.

"You don't scare me you know," I snort at her transparency.

"Maybe not, but I make you uncomfortable." I snarl.

"No. Not uncomfortable." She doesn't look at me, skimming the water with the edge of her tailfin in an amateur stroke. I wonder how she beat Titus with so little knowledge of her own anatomy, what she was truly capable of.

"Well?" I tut impatiently, yearning for her opinion against my own better judgement.

"I feel bad for you," she looks at me with a pain in her face.

"Great, I love pity," I roll my eyes.

"Not like you think. I just mean, you lost your father, and Titus. I know it's not conventional... but, you and he had a connection. I think. I mean from what you've said he must have gotten pretty close to turn you into what you are... and well, so I sort of assumed that you and he... you know..." She is rambling, the truth of her words slays me. Shock of my emotion at the thought of Titus, after everything he had done to me, dying causes red mist to fog my vision. The black rose of my heart, blooms, vulnerable to its own thorns.

"Stop," I say the single syllable and she silences immediately, the only sound for miles is the muted sloshing of the surface.

In the distance I see the outline of a shark and several shoals of fish, I know what will happen next, they're minding their own business, will they become like I did, victim to circumstance. Something inside me snaps slightly, I wasn't the goddamn fish, I was the shark.

"I'm glad you didn't say yes," I whisper.

"What?" She says, not hearing my dull set tone.

"I said I'm glad you didn't say yes to my brother. You're better than

90

that." She looks confused.

"What do you mean?"

"Men make you soft. You don't need that. Don't let the Occulta Mirum fool you, don't let the doe eyes of the other mermaids fool you. There is something coming, something dark and being the sideshow to a man isn't going to save you," I look at her and she cocks her head.

"You've seen it haven't you?"

"I don't need to have seen it to know, Callie. Atargatis didn't make the mer immortal and practically un-killable for no reason. We need to be strong." Callie looks startled, brushing her blonde hair behind one ear.

"I don't know. I don't really think I'll be around for all that. I'm leaving actually." I raise my eyebrows. She wasn't taking Saturnus seriously was she?

"Don't be pathetic, don't listen to Saturnus!" I snap at her again and feel disgust at her weak sensibility.

"It's not Saturnus. Though I'm glad you were eavesdropping. Do you know how creepy that is?" She looks exasperated.

"Why are you leaving?" I demand of her.

"Orion... he doesn't want me anymore. I'm not sure I want him," she looks deeply fragmented by this statement, the anguish obvious on her elven features. She stops suddenly in the water and sinks, placing her head in her hands and allowing her shoulders to shake with uncontrollably pathetic sobs. *Oh crap.* I think to myself. I really don't have the capacity to deal with a crying girl... *can I leave?* I wonder internally as she hits the ocean floor and splays out, curling herself around the scales of her fluke.

"Callie..." I swim down to her with one slash of my eel like tail, moving toward her at a speed quicker than that of my inner workings. I reach out to touch her shoulder. "You don't need him," I say and she turns on me, face contorted, leaning up in a fluid movement and manipulating her features into an expression of wicked fury.

"How the fuck would you know. You're just a MURDERING, INSOLENT BITCH!" She shouts, her voice echoing in the emptiness of the water around us, reverberating off the flat plains of sand that spread for miles. What I notice as her expression drains of colour is that her eyes are familiar, because they're like mine. They're black as sin and diluted to a state of delirious abyss.

"Callie," I breathe her name like it's a curse word. What the hell is going on with this girl?

"Oh my... Azure I..." She begins, slapping a hand over her mouth but I put my hand on her shoulder, a slight electric shock hits the edge of my fingertip and I withdraw it... *It's almost as if... No it can't be...*

"Hey it's okay. Breathe," I recite my personal mantra to her aloud.

"What's happening to me? I'm up and down and all over the place." She sobs again, diamonds falling into her lap.

"You're just having a hard time. My brother can be an asshole," I smile at her, she liked that before, I remember. She looks calm again, the dark fog fading as quickly as it came from her irises.

"I hurt him I think. I touched him and I stole his power," she admits to me and I listen intently for any hint of *him*.

"Maybe. He probably deserved it."

"You asked me before... why I said no? Well, I guess I can tell you," she bites her bottom lip and sniffs a few times. I inhale water deeply; God this emotional confession stuff is enough to make anyone feel nauseous. I prefer my people nice and shallow.

"I don't know who I am, I know I'm Orion's soulmate. I know I'm the vessel and all that other destiny crap. But in all this change, my old self is gone. I don't know who I am without him."

"Well...what about your father?" I reply, wanting a quick fix, wanting this emotional geyser of a girl to disappear. I do not like the effect she's having on me, it is sickly sweet, like treacle being poured down my throat, globules sticking in my gullet, making me choke.

Her eyes light up even though she should be surprised that I know about her father at all, it was so long ago that I last saw him.

"But... I don't know where he is."

"Can't you ask Saturnus?" I say the answer, knowing it's obvious but wondering about the level of intelligence of the girl floating before me. I mean you have to have a certain level of stupid to fall for my brother's corny ass routine. I'd seen their courtship among the fog of visions, I knew the kind of mushy crap that had made her melt, like only too pliable putty in his hands.

Callie frowns, leaning back in the sand and unfurling her aqua scaled fluke, it's short compared to mine but stocky, too pretty almost. This girl should seriously consider pairing that aqua with black, she needs the edge. I mean, let's be honest, no one ever takes a fairy Princess seriously.

"No. He wouldn't tell me even if he knew. He hates my father," she breathes and I nod. Wanting more than anything to high tail it out of here. Suddenly, she looks like a wave of inspiration has hit her, she straightens her spine, letting her hair tumble back over her shoulders.

"I do know someone I could ask. But I don't know how to find him. He's a Psiren."

"A Psiren?" I look at her, shocked at the audacity of the idea.

"Yes, Solustus," she answers and my shock deepens. Is she stupid? What the hell is she thinking? Is she thinking she can get Solustus to sit down and take her to tea, gab about good old dad when his first instinct is going to be to slit her throat?

"I don't think that's such a good idea... Solustus is more than you can handle. Trust me," I snort, unable to hold back the absurdity of her trying to negotiate with the likes of Solustus alone.

"Tell me where he is. I don't need your approval. I can handle myself." I watch her rage snowball as I falter in my response and roll my eyes. Her independent woman routine is almost as believable as a Christmas pantomime dame, no wonder my brother has problems trusting her. I think back to my eavesdropping on their arguments through the thick crystal floor of the upper turrets of the palace. Orion will kill me if I get her hurt. I mean with actual beheading.

"Callie... you really don't want to be going in there..."

"I said TELL ME!" She screams out again, flying forward and placing her hands around my throat. She knocks me back into the sand and I cry out, feeling her weight crushing me.

Oh Hell NO! I scream internally, flipping her onto her back using my weight and years of experience to out-manoeuvre her. She's beneath me then, laughing and cackling as her eyes turn black once more.

What the hell is this girl's deal? Seriously? She's not a Psiren... and when the hell did she get so violent... she's acting like, well, my ex.

The questions make me stare at her, creating a moment where my arms slacken their hold and Callie wriggles free. She gets up, turning around and hissing like a pissed off cat.

"Fine! I don't need you! I don't need anybody. I'll find them on my own, and tell your asshole brother that I approve his request. I'm never coming back." She turns and moves away with a speed that she didn't seem to possess not twenty minutes ago. I am knocked back by the force of the water displacement and watch her disappear. I could follow her, but somehow it seems like too much effort to invest in someone I a) don't like that much and b) don't really want to piss off.

I watch the speck of her, insignificant in the azure hugeness and wonder if she really will find the Cryptopolis. Something tells me that she will, and that something was a tiny spark of recognition, of severed connection in the back of her ocular darkness.

8
Potential

CALLIE

I'm thrumming, vibrating with rage that overcomes like nothing I've ever known, addictive and jagged like broken glass, grating within me, and its edge is providing a clarity unlike anything I've experienced. What the hell was up with my life? What the hell was up with Orion and his screwed up family? When had I become a pawn in the plans of a Goddess I had never believed in? When had I started being the one that everyone looked to for hope, comfort, and reassurance? Where the hell is my hope, comfort, and reassurance? Why is it always me that gets the shit end of the oar? *Ugh, I am so sick of this crap.* I mutter internally whilst gritting my teeth. I wonder now whether I am naïve, thinking Orion and I were going to ride off into the sunset on Philippe and never have so much as a harsh word. Well maybe I am naïve, but he was also stubborn, overbearing, and controlling. I am not about to put up with that for eternity. I realise soon that I'm swimming with no end destination in mind, I seem to be doing that a lot lately so I slow, closing my eyes.

Hello Callie. The voice echoes in a flash across the backs of my eyelids. I snap them open in fright. *What the hell was that?* I stop, turning around. I wonder if Azure has been stupid enough to follow me in my current mood. She's not there. I am alone. So I haven't been imagining the voice speaking wicked nothings in my ear? Or have I? I close my eyelids again.

Sssstupid girl. Don't you know what you are? The voice is there, I hear it. I decide to try answering, feeling impatient. "No! I don't know who I am! Who are you?" I speak the words aloud feeling incredulous. A few moments

95

fade into the past as fish pass me, moving through the invisible rat race of evolutionary purpose. I shake it off, it's hardly surprising that all the stress of the last few days is getting to me, making me imagine things.

I think about the loss of Orion, the man I thought I would spend the rest of my days with. It infuriates me even further. I wonder if I would have hated being married to him. *No of course not,* I remind myself of the fact that it wasn't what he'd asked that had infuriated me, of course I was flattered. It was rather the way in which he asked, and how little time we'd known each other. This makes me even angrier and I wish I had someone to yell at.

I think about my father, about my identity and the longing I've always felt toward the idea of meeting him. I know now that I need to find him, I need to meet him. I need to find somewhere in this ocean to call home. Somewhere I belong.

I find a small reef to rest by, letting the ebbing fractures of my heart pulsate like they're infected with misery. Mortally wounded and bleeding.

The fish provide little comfort as wrasse and flame angel fish scurry, leaving streams of red and orange in their wake. My anger is still there, behind it all, seething and writhing, growing with each moment that I go over the argument with Orion in my mind. My anger morphs and I feel suddenly restless again, I need to find Solustus, I need to find the Psirens.

Let me help you with that.

The voice creeps from within the shadow of my psyche, like it's stepped through a locked door, using my anger and impatience as the key to gain access to the forefront of my mind.

Suddenly I see images flash by, like a mental map to a city I couldn't have imagined in my deepest nightmares. I don't know where it's come from. Maybe it's something I picked up from Starlet when I stole her visions at the masked ball all those many months ago, or maybe something I absorbed from Azure when I had tackled her to the ground.

I let the images continue to flow, a graveyard of sunken ships and submarines, doomed before they had even begun, and a giant crack in the bedrock of the earth. These are the things I need to seek out.

I'm instantly grateful to the voice inside my head, for giving me my next step, giving me an aim, a destination, anything to take my mind off the absence of Orion. I need to funnel my energy into something productive, I need to heal, be free and have fun. Find myself again.

I'm smiling to myself wildly as I feel the images begin to ingrain into memory, like they're my own. I turn to begin my journey, not knowing the path I'm taking will even lead me where I want to go. Rising from the ocean floor I begin to undulate against the waves once more, in search of sunken ships and a crevasse to abyss. I hear the voice calling to me in an eerie whisper.

You're welcome.

Once I know where I'm headed it doesn't take long before I start to find more and more traces of Psiren behaviour. Scattered along the dusty ocean floor are remnants of human sailors and transportation that have met a grisly end. I swim, more cautiously than I have before in these new and continually shadowy waters as I keep myself parallel to the sloping sand. As I pass a ship that is half buried in sand and consumed with crustaceans and algae I notice a hammerhead shark, teeth bared with its odd shaped head moving from left to right. I move away from it, feeling anxious as the hairs on the back of my neck rise, wondering why I hadn't thought to bring a weapon of some kind or at least some armour.

Because you were pissed and careless, that's why! I remind myself, wondering what it is about my whole relationship with Orion that made it almost impossible for me to think clearly. I mean, isn't that what had gotten me into this mess? Falling in love with a man I'd known a matter of days, knew nothing about, and who I couldn't stay away from? As I move over the increasingly sparse sea-life, consisting of bottom feeding plecos and sharks, I wonder what my life would be like now if I hadn't given Orion the time of day, if I hadn't returned to the beach as we'd agreed. Would I be happier? Would I be watching Kayla grow up and fixing my relationship with my mom? I push these thoughts aside as I come to what I've been seeking.

It lies next to a sunken submarine, one that looks as though it's left over from one of the world wars. The sub has been severed in half by whatever sunk it and is stuck out of the sand like some kind of statement about the killing nature of these waters. The sub though, with its water filled bow and jagged, metal protrusions, is not what I have been looking for. What I've been looking for is the crevasse, which it teeters next to.

I move forward, no longer worried about the hammerhead that, I can see now, has turned back on itself and is going back the way it came.

Huh. I think, *guess it must be bad down there if even a shark's swimming away scared.*

I hover above the edge of the fissure in the seabed and can see the monstrosity of its size. It is around a hundred metres across, and a mile long. I wonder how deep it goes, floating above the almost impenetrable darkness that hangs, as I continue to push myself through the water, directly beneath me. I let myself be suspended for a few minutes, looking up at the sun, which is high in the sky above the surface. Even from this depth its rays struggle to reach, so I wonder what it'll be like down inside the fissure. I look down into the blackness and the blackness looks back into me, I feel a chill run through me and I gulp, trying to calm myself. I wonder momentarily about turning back, but I can't quite bring myself, after everything I've been through and with the rage still burning in my chest, to go swimming home to Orion. I take one final look up above, at the silvery undulations of the water's surface tension, refracting the light from the human world above and I turn myself so I'm facing downward, away from the brightness and the day. I grit my teeth and squeeze my hands into fists, ready to lash out at anyone or thing that may try to take advantage of me in the dark and slowly but surely, begin my descent into the shadows.

As I begin to swim downward through the crack in the earth I feel eyes on me, but from where they originate I don't know. As I delve deeper I feel my ribs struggling to expand and my lungs becoming constricted. My ears pop with the increasing pressure, leaving me with an ache in my jaw that only increases my irritability. The darkness is making me anxious too, and I keep staring back up from where I came, trying to make out anything that could possibly be out to bite me, or worse, against the dying light of the surface. It isn't long before I notice other changes in the water too, like a slight smell of rotten egg, a taste of ash and metal in the normally tasteless water and a chill that is seeping into my bones.

Among the darkness further down, not all light is lost as a pyrotechnic display of sudden and fleeting flashes are created by wildlife trying to lure in their next meal. After around twenty minutes I begin to see a glow from beneath me and I move toward it, perhaps just as helpless as the tiny pulsating fish being lured in by local anglers.

As I get closer I realise it's too large to be a single animal.

Maybe I'm finally finding the bottom, I think to myself, relieved for a moment before realising that if I am near the bottom, then what next? Where is this supposed hidden city?

I begin to panic as I feel something brush up beside me and turn, catching a glimmer of some kind of huge shark with brown velvety skin and a large black eye before it moves away into the darkness again. I continue to move toward the light, my skin crawling, sure that if I can get some visibility I may be able to calm myself. Instead find myself repulsed as I move even closer, discovering that the glow is coming from large clusters of deep sea, bioluminescent jellyfish, crammed into a thin crack at the base of the crevasse.

I move backward, panicking as I have always been slightly disgusted and scared of jellyfish. These jellyfish in particular look rather predatory, as I watch fish become tangled in their absurdly long tentacle nets, helpless and doomed.

I float for a moment, suspended above the crack of natural light, wondering what to do. I can move into the darkness to my right or I can return upward and try to scan the sides of the trench for caves and possible entrances to the city, but neither of these options seem very appealing. After all, I don't really fancy groping around in the dark if this really is close to the Psiren city.

Well, you can't just float here. I think to myself angrily.

Then it catches my eye, something scoured into the wall in front of me, only just illuminated by the momentum of the jellyfish beneath. It's an arrow, carved into the rock primitively and it's pointing downwards. I look down into the tangled mass of jellies.

Oh that is so not happening. I think to myself, feeling my stomach turn.

I know that the ocean is supposed to be beautiful and majestic, but there's just something about jellyfish that makes me want to hurl. Whether it's their ability to make you have to pee on yourself to cure their stings, or the fact they're immortal and see-through, I just can't bring myself to appreciate them.

Then I remember something, a memory which stings far worse than any jellyfish. His voice travels through the recesses of time and into the forefront of my memory, rolling out like all too familiar silk sheets.

They kind of tickle actually. Orion's voice, reaches me and my heart falls through my chest.

I still miss him. I still need him.

No you don't! My subconscious snaps at me angrily.

I sigh again and look at the arrow and then the cloud of jellies beneath.

Oh for craps sake. I think to myself before reluctantly turning so I am once again facing downward into their white, pale glow. I close my eyes, trying to banish my melancholy at the thought of Orion's absence, wanting so badly to forget about him that I grit my teeth and plunge myself, head first into the dense clouds of jellyfish.

I fall, tumbling through the web of bioluminescent, charged tentacles and into the unknown below. The cloud isn't as thick as is looks from above and as Orion once told me, the brushing of the translucent, unseemly limbs does tickle ever so slightly. I keep my eyes wide as I come out the other side of the mass of light and below me see the outline of shapes I can't quite make out. It appears I've come into a cave, but I can't see anything as the floor is too deep beneath me.

Oh for craps sake! How the hell am I supposed to see anything down here? I cuss internally, angry that I've dived head first into a cluster of electrically charged tentacles for nothing, even if they did nothing more than tickle they still creep me out.

Let me shed some light on the subject.

The voice moves in and out of the forefront of my psyche like a wisp of smoke, having come and gone in a matter of seconds, untraceable and fleeting. I blink for a moment, unsure of what to expect, of whether I'm crazy or not. As I open my lids again it's like someone has placed contact lenses in front of my pupils, giving me some kind of night vision I wasn't aware I was capable of. I don't have time to be shocked by the immense relief I feel at being able to see again, because what I can see as I look down makes my heart stop.

Below me, over a hundred black pupils stare up at me.

Well, I sigh internally, *I guess I found the city.*

SOLUSTUS

I tilt my head upward at the sudden break in the light that pours down on my city. I feel myself surprised at the scene in front of me. The girl, the vessel, hovering high above, still and suspended, looking confused. Without warning, the subjects I'm talking through basic hand to hand with, fly upward without so much as a command from me and encircle her. Irritation rises, anger welling like a storm.

How dare they move without my command.

"STOP," I bark and they turn back, looking surprised as I rise above the ring within seconds. "What do you think you're doing?" I ask them, purposefully ignoring the blonde twiglet. I will tend to her when I'm ready. They look at me, half man, half monstrosity, black pupils blinking in confusion and slight fear, young and stupid. "Did I command you to go after her?" One of them pipes up.

"No, Sir!" I look daggers at him, asserting my masculinity.

"Then why do you ingrates insist on using your brains? Do you think you should be leading? Do you think you can do a better job than I?" I ask them, circling their assembly like a shark. They look horrified.

"No, Sir!" I hear them mumble.

"I want you to remember this lesson, remember whom you serve. It is not your job to lead, but to follow without question. Should I ask you to kill your mother, you do it, and you do it with a smile on your face," I pause...

"As it is, your quick actions have cornered this here intruder, you should be proud, but know that it should have been on my order. Understood?"

"Yes, Sir!" They respond, a mass of writhing tails and tentacles.

I turn finally, resting my eyes on the girl. Her face shocks me, the blackness in her pupils surprising to say the least.

"Solustus," she says, straightening herself, trying to appear less than the meek, infantile creature that she is.

"Callie," I reply, trying to give nothing away and hating the way her sickly sweet nomenclature feels rolling off my literate tongue.

I look at her, brushing away my nausea at the purity of the way she looks. There is something different this time though. Her eyes, for a start, hold the black pupils that the rest of the Psiren possess and her mouth is set into a hard line that before I hadn't noticed. She looks serious.

"I wish to speak with you," she says, conviction in her voice, as though she thinks she has some kind of authority here.

"Go ahead," I offer her this kindness, curious as to her intent. I wonder momentarily why I'm not killing her, but then remember she might be useful. If nothing else, she's the crowned ruler's soulmate. I'm not letting her leave here alive if I can help it.

"I was thinking somewhere more private," she looks irritable and my patience flits away as quickly as it came.

"I was thinking you talk to me here or I kill you," I cross my arms, ready to draw Scarlette and make an example of her in front of my fodder, slice her up real nice and watch her bleed.

"You're forgetting that I took down your predecessor with just these," she holds out her hands and I smirk. Young *and* stupid. What a mix.

"You're forgetting I don't have any powers for you to steal. My speed and cunning aren't something that you can get from any bitch Goddess," I snarl and I feel the young Psirens smirking at my smart mouth. My heart lifts slightly, shrivelled as it may be in my chest, yearning for their undying loyalty. Her face falls slightly, realising the fault in her tenuous logic.

"Got yourself in too deep, Princess?" I snarl at her, flicking my tailfin and lurching so I'm behind her in a matter of seconds. She puts out her hands and I feel her fingers catch me in mid stroke, clutching around my neck.

Then, something I hadn't felt in a while possesses me. Agonising pain, the kind you only get from someone manipulating the electric currents in your body.

I writhe, feeling the eyes of Alyssa's children on me, unimpressed. The blonde twiglet looks shocked as she takes her hands off me, letting me fall slightly through the water before I can regain my composure and snap my tailfin back into rhythm quickly. I rise to her eye level.

"Your argument is compelling. Maybe we should take this into the Necrocazar," I don't want to appear weak, but I don't want to continue the conversation with this girl, who suddenly has the power to incapacitate me, in front of them either.

I shake off the pain that clutched at my nervous system, brushing it away like I do with my emotions.

"Two of you! Escort The vessel to the Necrocazar," I bark and they move to touch her. Her eyes narrow.

"I can swim myself. Lead on," she flutters a hand forward, waving each of her individual fingers in succession and holding my eye contact.

"As you wish," I glare at the soldiers as they hover there, looking dumbstruck.

I really need to start giving Alyssa stricter guidelines about who she makes into her children, I muse.

I am sick of them being so stupid, so young. I want educated, cunning, subservient warriors. Not this gaggle of clueless, teenage angst.

"Go find Regus, he will give you something to do," I wave them away and they pivot, looking afraid under my scorching contempt for each and every one of them.

Callie looks to me and I move forward, silent as she follows, pitiful with each un-practiced stroke from her hideously bright tailfin. That aquamarine is so gaudy.

We travel together, mercifully, in silence. I am around twenty metres in front of the girl for the majority of the journey. I can tell she's struggling to keep up but, I wonder how she's even coping with the depth of the city at all as it's something any normal mer would be succumbing to like an asthmatic snail.

I reach the throne room at the height of the Necrocazar, my palace built into the immense dead vents, quickly and I realise she's still keeping pace.

Within the dark recesses and red lighting of the room I move forward, deciding I want to look regal. I drape myself leisurely across the bone construct of the throne as Callie enters behind me a few moments later. I watch her, curious, as she takes a few slow moments to take in her surroundings like a bewildered animal in a trap.

"So, what brings you to my little Kingdom?" I question her as she folds her arms defensively over her breast scales.

"I want to find my father. You implied, the last time we met, that you know where he is," she looks me directly in the eye and I wonder when she got so bold.

The last time I'd met her she'd been desperately in love with Orion, offering her own life to save his, a pathetic act in itself, yet here she is again risking her life for her father who had abandoned her. I wonder instantly if this girl has some kind of a death wish.

"No. I implied I knew what he looked like, if you can recall. Also, you misunderstand my question. How did you find this place?" I ask her pointedly. No mer before her had ever come here of their own will, they'd only ever been down here after being kidnapped, and even then they were unconscious.

"What do you mean?"

"No mer before you have ever found the Cryptopolis. How, I ask, did you? You don't seem particularly intelligent…" I pause with a smile, allowing my lips to pull back over my razor sharp teeth. She frowns.

"You have a whole graveyard of ships around the entrance to the city. It didn't take a lot to deduce that was a Psiren's doing. Besides, you're evil, mythical creatures, I just thought of the darkest, dankest place for a city and BAM. I mean, could you guys be anymore cliché?" She cocks her head and purses her lips. I ascend with a tiny minute flick of my tailfin, feeling the spines on my tail rise against the base of my back. Who does she think she's talking to?

"I would remind you, Miss Pierce, that you aren't among friends any longer. You aren't royalty here. You're just a poor, lonely, lost girl, far from home and in too deep," I annunciate clearly and move around the back of her stilled form. I watch her long, blonde locks stir with my presence. I brush them back from her shoulder and whisper in her ear. "You don't belong here, Callie," I do it to unnerve her, but as I move around to face her, I can tell I have hit a nerve that runs far deeper. Her black eyes get round and her mouth falls into a grim line.

"That's why I need to find my father," she relinquishes the information, a mistake, as it enables me to realise she's emotionally vulnerable. Her eyes shift and I watch as she becomes transfixed by something behind me. I follow her gaze to the weapon against the wall. She raises her hand and the scythe jumps through the water and lands solidly in her palm. She smiles knowingly and I wonder what she's feeling, is it a kind of power she alone can wield?

Something inside me shifts as I watch her. I wonder if perhaps she could be the key to unlocking it. I need to keep her around for longer and I wonder if perhaps this darkness within her can be used, manipulated. I watch her silently and play with the possibility of locking her up in the dungeon below, but rather than subduing her by force, which Titus once attempted to do and failed, I decide against it, instead using my real power; my cunning.

"I suppose I could look into finding your father's location. One does not become as old as I without amassing a certain amount of power." She looks hopeful at these words, before I continue. "But... I'd need you to stay here while I obtain the location. I'm not gallivanting after you." She looks uncertain as to my obliging her request with such ease.

"What's the catch?" She asks and I opt for a half truth.

"You go to your father, you leave Orion miserable and the Occulta Mirum without a Queen. What more motivation do I need than that?" She looks suspicious but shrugs.

"Fine, I'll play. But I don't want any of your Psiren buddies bothering me," she says with a cocked brow and I laugh internally. If she really does have the power to inflict pain like I think she does, she shouldn't worry.

"Fine. I'll issue the order but I can't promise you anything," I bend and watch her play with the scythe, passing it between her hands. She throws it to one side and it clatters to the ashen, bone strewn floor of the throne room. I give her a questioning look.

"Not really my style anymore. I don't think I'm cut out for it." I wonder what she means by this, but am glad I won't have to take the weapon from her.

"There are caves on the outer walls of the city, you can choose one that's empty and stay there. Just keep out of the way of my men, I won't be held responsible for whatever reactions you provoke out of them. We are no honourable breed," I bark at her, this isn't a hotel and she isn't a guest. There's no room service here.

"Fine, but hurry. I don't plan on staying down here for longer than I have to. Besides, who knows what Orion will do if he finds out where I am. As you may recall he can be VERY protective and I won't be the one stopping him from destroying the lot of you with a tsunami," she looks cocky but shudders at the chill in the water. I don't even feel it anymore.

"It'll take as long as I want it to. You have no power here, so don't try threatening me. It won't end well for you. Or the other mer. Need I remind you that we outnumber you quite substantially?" I remind her of our enormity, looking at the scythe out of the corner of my eye.

I need to work out how to unleash the power within. If it does have something to do with Callie, then my window is closing fast with the girl's naïve and grating impatience. She moves away from me and I relax ever so slightly.

She looks back over her shoulder and the darkness of her eyes crackles with aquamarine lightning sparking in their depths.

"Fine. It's your funeral."

9
Deep

CALLIE

I exit the Necrocazar through the many blackened rock corridors within its ancient looking construct. I think back to my negotiations with Solustus and wonder why he was so willing to help someone he would have happily killed a few months ago. I know he said that sending me off to my father would be detrimental to the Occulta Mirum's hierarchy, but I can't help but consider the fact that his motivations for keeping me here probably run deeper. Still, what was I going to do about it? It isn't like I could just waltz out of here. I know that my threatening Solustus with Orion's powers and The Knights of Atargatis is empty. I mean even if Orion knows where I am and cares enough to come after me, which at this point I highly doubt, how would he even find this place? I'm pretty sure if Azure wasn't telling me then she wasn't going to tell her brother, but then again what do I even know about Azure? Not a lot, and by attacking her in a red-mist fuelled rage, I am pretty sure that I'd slammed that door abruptly shut.

I sigh out, bubbles cloudy in the dark depths of the vents that make up the palace. I wonder what it must have been like when these main vents were active, I look at the walls as I pass through the narrow and winding passages, blood coloured tubules and mussels cling to them, encrusted and grimy.

I manage to find my way back out into the courtyard where the Psirens had been training, but once I get here I realise I don't have anywhere to go. I suppose there is the cave that Solustus had so generously offered, but I don't really fancy being alone with my own thoughts.

I hover for a second, too bright in the surrounding dim, my scales causing me to stick out like a sore and very sparkly thumb. I turn around, swirling my body in the water and come eye to eye with another Psiren, Caedes.

I had always been too alarmed whenever I had been around him to take in the details of his form. His tail is that of a Lionfish. I had never looked closely enough before, but now the resemblance is clear to me. He has long spines that he holds close to his body and the tail is cream, marred with bloody red stripes.

"Poor little lamb. Lied down in a bed of thorns and now her wool's all bloody," he exhales, almost dreamily, his blackened wide pupils crackling with scarlet lightning. He is terrifying and I'm not sure he's psychologically stable at this moment. He reaches up with a sharp, jagged fingernail to touch my cheek. I flinch backward, smelling the blood on his breath as my stomach heaves.

"Caedes," I breathe, trying to look stern but feeling like a small, lost child.

"That's my name, little lamb. Not yours," he smiles deep, his too dark lips pulling back over jagged teeth. His white skin is so pale I swear I can see and feel his veins beneath as I move away from him, afraid.

He moves closer, the spines fanning out from his body in a way that implies his arousal at the challenge I present. I've been in battle with him before, been clouded by his inky illusions and I don't really want to provoke him again.

I'm not in the mood for a fight, I feel vulnerable, not surprising seeing as how I've been resting in soft beds and surrounded by guards for months now. I move once more and he extends out his hands, ready to clutch them around my windpipe and rip me apart. His jagged teeth part into a sneer.

I'm turning to flee as I hear a crack, like that of bone on bone. My head snaps back around, blonde hair cascading around me. I'm expecting to see the one person who I relate with such an exertion of manly protection, Orion, but it isn't.

"Oi! Mate! Why don't you go crawl back into that hole you slithered out of? The lady's mine," the voice comes from a Psiren. Or at least I think he's a Psiren. I've been wondering about these Octomen, about when the Psirens started sprouting tentacles. As if they couldn't get any more repulsive. I look away from the undulating mass of black *things*, their undersides a slimy lilac, stemming from a waist of ripped abdominals and wide but stocky pectorals, pale as sin. I look up into his face and instantly recognise him.

"Hey! I know you!" I blurt, unable to stop myself. *Smooth. You look like a real badass now.* I snarl internally.

"Well, yeah!" He looks at me as Caedes rises from the crushed bones that line the city's floor, looking pissed. He rights himself again, spines fanned out, his black eyes scouring the body of his opponent. I try to think of his name....

Vex? Yes! That's it, I remember, realising that I had thought it sounded like sex at the time.

Vex sucks in air and I call to Caedes, not wanting to see the two scrap over me. I can defend myself, I don't need a white knight. I am already fleeing the so-called 'protection' of another.

"Hey. I don't need you to save me. If the creepy guy wants to tussle, I'm game!" I yell and Caedes looks at me surprised, no longer the poor innocent lamb led to the slaughter he keeps claiming me to be. I'm not playing anymore, I am a lion.

Vex looks at me, surprised as he hears me pipe up. His eyebrow cocks and I watch as his lips contort into a smirk.

What are you looking at? I snap internally as I watch the will of my words act itself out. Caedes turns away from Vex and towards me.

Vex folds his arms across his chest and floats back, nodding to me. *He's going to let me take on this psycho?* I think to myself flabbergasted. Then it hits me, *He's going to let me take on this psycho!*

Isn't that what I've been wanting, someone to let me prove myself? Even if Vex doesn't care if I am torn limb from limb, at least he is happy to let me do it on my own terms.

Finally! Someone without an egotistical, misogynistic complex.

I smile at him and he points, laughing slightly, reminding me I've now got to take down Caedes. I grit my teeth and clench my fists. I want to summon the ability I hadn't known I had, but I don't know how to control it. The only thing I know is what brought it out in me, and that was uncontrollable rage.

Caedes turns, twitching from side to side and then launches at me. I see Vex out of the corner of my eye, watching us with amusement as I move too, pushing myself through the water, hands outstretched. They land on Caedes skull and I watch as agony passes behind the blacks of his eyes. His mouth contorts into a little 'o' shape and I feel him falter a few seconds before he begins to smile.

"Lamby thinks she can play with my nerves and make me squirm? Little Lamby clearly hasn't harnessed the rage of her victim," he spits out the words and lunges for my throat, pushing me backward into the floor. I feel the bones and spines of dead things pushing into the back of my head and watch the fanned, spiny tail of Caedes flick as he prepares to strike. Before he can get his clawed nails around my gills something large and metallic smashes him across the back of the head. He collapses in a heap and Vex moves in from the shadows behind him.

Whilst I'd been trying to inflict pain Vex had moved in behind Caedes, taking the opportunity to use his tentacles to strike from afar. I wonder about being in a fight with Vex, those tentacles must be hard to get a handle on to say the least.

"Need a hand?" He asks me, offering me his. It has stubby, rough pale fingers and a wide palm. I move backward.

"NO! Why did you do that?! I had him!" I yell out and he smirks again.

"Yeah, looked like you were just about to rip out his heart and eat it for breakfast," he cocks his slashed eyebrow and his violet eyes bare into mine. The sleek silver hair is no longer sleek, but floating innocuous against the glow of overhead jelly clouds.

"God! What is it with you?" I exclaim.

"Me? We only just met?" He looks confused and that only stirs my anger further.

"Not you, idiot! MEN! Why is it you can't just let a girl…"

"Get herself killed?" He cocks his brow again and purses his pale lips in an amused scowl.

"Yes! If I want to get myself killed, why I can't I? What damn business is it of yours? With your stupid ripped abs and giant bulging arms. Why can't you just let a girl be in distress?"

"You seem pretty distressed, Love. If that was the aim, I'd say keeping you alive was definitely the right way to go. Though I can't say I'm not regretting it after realising that means I have to continue to listen to you whine."

"Well maybe you should have butt the hell out then!" I look at him.

"Well maybe I should have!" He counters coming in close to me.

"Fine!" I yell, unable to think of a witty retort.

"Fine!" He says, looking exasperated. I can't help but notice the look of hilarity behind his lilac irises. God he makes me furious.

"So, do you wanna go to a party?" He looks me in the eyes and I bust out laughing.

"Oh my God! I just told you to butt out. Are you deaf? What are you like two hundred? Your hearing going, grandpa tentacles??" I blurt out, feeling a catharsis I didn't know I'd needed at bantering with him...and as of now, winning.

"I'm actually twenty-one and my hearing is just fine," he snorts and my mouth pops open a little.

"You're twenty-one?" I look up at him shocked. I thought all the Psiren's were old.

"Yeah. So?"

"I thought all the Psiren's were old. How long have you been like this?" I ask him and he shrugs.

"Couple of months, Love. No big deal." I look at him, surprised. His tentacles move slowly, eerily in the water.

I still can't get my head around how odd it must feel for him. He is just like me in a way, from the modern world, ripped out of his normal life.

Suddenly the thought of finding someone to relate to has great appeal, even if he is evil. I scrunch up my forehead in thought.

"Don't hurt yourself." he jokes and I look at him and roll my eyes.

"Oh shut up. You said there was a party?" I ask him and he nods.

"Yeah. A rave."

"Okay. I'll go, but only because I want to de-stress. Not because you asked," I snap.

"Fine by me, Love, and don't worry, if you get tackled to the ground by Cthulhu himself I'll let him suck your face off and kill you. Won't be making the mistake of saving you again."

ORION

I wake up slowly, bringing myself back to consciousness willingly. None the less, I can't deny that I'm feeling less than inclined to deal with what is waiting for me outside the confines of the clamshell bed.

I reach over for her, wanting so badly to run my fingers over her lithe back and pull her close to me. I want to wrap myself up in her skin, her scent, in that way that calms me. I want to run my fingers through her cascades of blonde hair. I move my hands further across in the darkness, provided by the closed hood of the bed, realising she isn't there.

I meet the feel of velvet beneath my fingers from the white blankets, but no skin, no scent, no blonde curtain of hair. No Callie. My eyes widen as I remember that she's gone. I told her to go. Go and not come back.

I push the lid up from the bed suddenly with both my palms, the sprung mechanism responding as the clam opens, revealing the emptiness of our suite in the too bright light of sunset. I get up from the mattress, feeling panic clutch at my gut.

What the hell have I done? I think momentarily.

Starlet was right. What was I thinking? I take a few breaths before musing that I am probably panicking for nothing, Callie is probably back by now, she's probably sorted through her feelings and come back, just like she always does. I accused her of fleeing too often, but it is a fact that she always returns.

I calm myself, straightening my spine and slowing the tense movement of my tailfin, before descending through the porthole entrance to the royal suite and down into the Alcazar in search of my Queen.

She's not in the throne room, she's not in the entrance hall either, or the library. I feel my heart turn icy every time I round a corner and don't find her there. I wonder if I've gone too far. No of course not. It was just a misunderstanding, wasn't it?

Callie has to want to marry me, because I know she feels the same way I do. After all, our souls are one. How can she not?

I breathe out again, huffing and puffing like a whale coming up from great depth. I wonder if it is too optimistic for me to believe she would be in the palace at all. I know she has friends, mermaids who she can go and have a chat to if she needs it. I hope, in a way, that she is with another mermaid, because I know that the mermaids would be all for her marrying me. I decide to go and see the one mermaid I know she's closest to, above anyone else.

With the idea immediately striking me as the best course of action, I move from the Alcazar quickly and head across the courtyard and into the city, searching for the thing I need most.

I knock on the door of the apartment, remembering myself leaving here stunned a few months ago. I was with Callie then and she had in her hands the scythe that would prove to be the judge, jury, and executioner of her story.

The door falls back and a pale face and wide chocolate brown eyes look surprised to see me hovering in the doorway.

"Your Highness. What are you doing here?" Sophia asks me, bowing her head slightly.

"I need to talk to you," I announce, using my regal claim to force myself past her and into the room full of old fashioned looking furniture and stacked with books on weaponry. The room that holds Oscar's anvil, and his workspace is curtained off. "Is Oscar here?" I ask her impatiently.

"No, he's at the forge. I just like to come here sometimes. It's quieter than our other place. The couple downstairs have a tendency to serenade one another," she smiles shyly and I want to remove it from her lips. I want to make everyone feel the pain I'm feeling, make them realise how important finding my soulmate truly is.

"Is Callie here?" I ask her, my pectorals rising and falling dramatically.

"No. I haven't seen her," Sophia replies, closing the door slowly. "What's this about Orion?" She looks at me suspiciously, having dropped the formalities as she can clearly see that I'm distressed.

"She's gone. We had a fight about getting married... I proposed after the coronation and then she ran off. She came back and told me she didn't want to get married, that it was too soon and that I was doing it for the wrong reasons and..." I stop, feeling out of breath, which is ridiculous considering how fit I am physically. It's like my chest has constricted at the loss of my girl. "I told her to leave and never come back." Sophia, at these words, looks at me and frowns.

"Well, then why are you looking for her here?" She looks confused.

"You two, well, I know she comes to you for advice and to talk sometimes. I was hoping she hadn't listened to me and come to you instead," I look at her and she looks back at me, I can tell she's almost disappointed.

"I can't speak for Callie, but I can say that if I had just become a Queen at eighteen years old, after only having been a part of this world for a few months, I'd probably be wondering why that wasn't enough of a commitment for you? Becoming a sovereign is slightly more of a legal bind than marriage, Orion." I look at her dumbly. She's right, but that's so not the point of this conversation. I don't want a scolding. I want to know where Callie is.

"That's not the point. We're destined. She should want to marry me," I say it like a small child and Sophia suddenly looks bolder than I have ever seen her before.

"Marriage to Callie isn't like marriage to you. We come from a different world Orion. Marriage when we were alive, becoming a wife wasn't a choice. It was circumstance. If you didn't get married you couldn't survive, you ended up on the streets. Women can work now. Everything is different. Callie loves you. But she also comes from a place where marriage is a choice. If you ask me, it's something she feels is a big choice. She wants to know more about you before she commits to, let's be honest, what is slightly longer than the average nuptials."

"You're saying she thinks she doesn't know me?" I ask her looking incredulously at her. I wonder when she got so bold. Maybe it was Callie rubbing off on her, she used to be so much meeker.

"She's told me that you won't talk to her about your past. She's also told me, or as much implied, that you won't open up to her about your grief." She looks serious now, and slightly uncomfortable. I feel slightly shocked. I didn't realise Callie still had a problem with my past.

"Why should I open up to her about my grief? She can't fix anything. She can't bring my father back," I stiffen at the mention of his name, feeling it like a stab to the gut.

"It's not about her fixing something. It's about her letting you rely on her. Have a safe place to go and talk about things that bother you. You were alone for so long, Orion. I can honestly see why that's tough, but Callie is there to protect you and support you too. It's not just about her. There has to be a balance of power in a relationship. You do everything for her, I've seen you, how protective and loving you are. But she wants to do the same for you and you push her away," Sophia shakes her head and I feel slightly shocked, who knew she was so observant.

"So you're saying she won't marry me because..." I ask the question, not knowing whether I want to hear the answer or not.

"I think she feels like you're trapping her a little. You became Crowned Ruler and so she took the role of Queen in her stride. She wants to do things on her own terms."

"But the last time she took things into her own hands she got herself killed," I remind Sophia and she shakes her head.

"I can see why you want to stop that happening again, but I wonder why you think putting a ring on her finger is going to change anything. She comes from a different time, as I've already said, marriage doesn't mean she'll bend to you and act like a wife. It means she'll be Callie with a ring on her finger. That's about it. I wonder if that's what she means when she says you're doing it for the wrong reasons," Sophia moves toward me, closing the gap across which we've been exchanging words.

"I just want to protect her."

"I want to protect Oscar, but I can't do anything to stop him getting hurt." She reminds me and I look into her chocolate irises. She looks like she really cares about Callie and me. I soften slightly.

"That's true," I admit, wondering how Callie must feel, knowing I could be called away to fight at any second.

"I also think you may have a big problem on your hands. Callie takes what you say to heart. So if you've told her to leave and not come back. I'm pretty sure that's what she will do."

"I really fucked this up," I say cussing, the word doesn't usually pass my lips, but since I've heard her use it in bed when I'm teasing her, I can't think of anything else that would express the frustration I'm feeling.

"It's your first ever, serious relationship. You're going to make mistakes." Sophia floats absentmindedly. I look at her and realise that I don't deserve her kindness.

"I should go. If Callie really has taken my advice, I need to fix it. I need to find out where she is and go after her. It's not safe out there."

"Okay, well, if you need to talk again… don't come to me. Talk to Callie. She's the only person who can really tell you what she is feeling. Just make sure if you ask her, you listen to what she says. Not just hear her response. Really listen," she ushers me back out the door. I haven't moved to sit the entire time I've been in her apartment.

"Sorry for the intrusion," I mumble, but she smiles.

"You are quite welcome, Your Highness. Now please, go and find our girl, make sure she's safe." My eyes jump up to find hers before she closes the door softly. She really cares for Callie. I don't know why I'm surprised to find such affection for her in another, after all, she is one of those people you can't help but fall a little bit in love with.

"Orion!!!!" I hear my name bellowed once I'm back inside the Alcazar, ready to mobilise search parties to find my Callie. I turn and Starlet swims up to me, a flash of magenta moving so quickly that she nearly bowls me over with an inability to quell her own momentum.

"Callie…" She pants. Her eyes are bloodshot through. She only gets like this when she's had a vision. My stomach drops immediately and terror clutches at me.

"What? What did you see?" I shake her and she clutches my arms with her sharp fingernails.

"I saw her, through Azure, I saw her…" She pants again, looking like she may pass out. I look into her face, I know that the visions from the Goddess are hard on her, but I also know that the visions she sees through the eyes of her twin are the worst. Journeying into the darkness of Azure's psyche constantly causes her pain and grief. It's an extension of a soulmate's ability to share memories, and I also know it's how she and Azure had been communicating while our sister was with the Psirens and with Titus. I give her a moment, but only a moment, impatient.

"What? Where is she?" I ask her and her face contorts slightly, as though she doesn't want to tell me. "Tell me Star!" I bark at her and she flinches, actually flinches in my grip.

"I don't know... where they were... they were in the middle of the sea somewhere, no landmarks that I could make out. She attacked Azure..."

"Then what good is that to me? I need to find her!" I look at her and she breathes in, calming herself as her gills open and close in quick succession.

"I don't know where she was when she attacked Azure, but I know why she attacked Azure and where she's going," she rubs her head.

"Why did she attack her?" I ask, feeling surprised. Callie isn't violent. Or at least she hasn't ever shown any violence until our fight earlier, when she sent me writhing in agony with one touch. I still don't understand how she'd done that. Or for that matter, stolen my ability to manipulate air, which before today had been impossible.

"She wanted information and Azure wouldn't share."

"What information could Callie possibly want from Azure?" I interrupt her and her eyes widen with slight fear.

"She wanted to know where the Psiren city was, and something tells me she's going to find it, Orion. She's going to see Solustus."

117

10
Rave

CALLIE

"So, where is this party?" I ask Vex as we swim past the square in front of the Necrocazar.

I take a moment to examine my surroundings. Crushed bones and the remnants of crustaceans' shells line the city streets and eels trapped in jars flicker and illuminate the city at intermittent moments of electrical excitement. The Necrocazar towers high above the ground level of the rest of the city, blackened and charred, revealing its ancient purpose as a deep undersea vent, spewing out molten rock and boiling sulphur into the surrounding water. It feels odd, calling it a city, mostly because it's almost barren and the only other visible architecture in the dim is the expansive square in front of the towering cylindrical constructs of the dark, charred palace.

The square is filled with pieces of equipment, anvils, weapons, and obstacle courses built in the remains of enormous whale carcasses. I can't see homes anywhere, let alone the kind of venue suitable for a party. In fact, now that I look around I can't see any Psirens either... *where have they all gone?*

I feel the hairs rise on the back of my neck and goose pimples climb up my spine at the prospect of them watching me. I wonder why I'm down here, why I haven't gone running for the hills. I can't exactly trust Solustus to keep his word about finding my father, can I?

Even beyond that, I can't believe I've been invited to party by a Psiren. I'd thought they were nothing more than primal killing machines and before I'd come down here I'd wondered if any of them even had enough humanity left to hold a half descent, non-violent conversation.

I look up at Vex shyly, observe his smooth jawline and muscled pectorals, his gills that open and close just like mine. He lacks a scaled eye mask, he lacks any kind of shine and glimmer at all now I really look at him. He wasn't even remotely beautiful, he was something else all together and the confidence he exudes is both terrifying and attractive all at once. He catches me staring and answers my question with a smirk.

"Party implies ice cream and cake, love... this is more of a rave. I'll let you blow out my candle though..." Vex doesn't give away the location but smiles salaciously at his innuendo. I choose to ignore him and attempt further stubborn questioning instead.

"So where is it?" I ask, looking up at his broad pale chest and acute features. His lilac eyes have darkened now that we're away from the streetlights and moving into the shadow at the edge of the cavern, their pupils have fully dilated, leaving only blackness streaked by the occasional flash of lilac lightning.

"Patience, pet," he shakes his head, a smile creeping across his lips. He would look kind of attractive if it weren't for the jagged edges of his teeth and the dark pits of his eyes.

"Or you could just tell me now," I huff, feeling impatient. Why is everything always on someone else's time scale? What is with all the secrets?

"Where would the fun be in that?" He cocks his slashed brow yet again but his expression below his eyes stays stony as his thick, pale lips press into a line. We move close to the side of the crevasse and my gut clenches, suddenly uncomfortable.

"You better not be trying to corner me," I say fiercely, feeling the hairs on my arms rise at the thought of being alone with him in the darkness.

"Love, don't flatter yourself. You aren't that hot," he bites out the words and the corner of his dark eyes twitch. I watch him lick his bottom lip as his eyes roll over the side of my body.

He leads me upward as we meet with one of the curved rock faces that make up the deep cave and soon afterward he is pulling me hard through the entrance of a dark hole in the rock face. It plummets down, like a tunnel into hell.

"Where are we going?" I ask him, irritable at his silence.

"Do you want to go to a rave or not?" He turns on me looking exasperated, running his hands through his hair, smooth and slick to touch, it frames his skull in a cap of silver.

"Yes, but I at least expect…" I begin, but he places a finger to my lips and furrows his brow looking pissed off.

"That's the problem then. Stop expecting. This isn't your Kingdom. You aren't a Princess and I'm not here to serve you. Alright? I asked you if you wanted to tag along, so if you could do me a favour and shut the bloody hell up, you'll forever have my gratitude. Alright? Got it? Great." he snaps and the Britishness in his accent seeps into the water in one great vocal slap across the face. I feel the sting, but then I can't deny he's right. I hear him mutter something under his breath that sounds like 'bloody women', but I decide to ignore him. I continue to follow him into the dark depths of the tunnel, it moves through the rock like an eel's body, twisting and turning. All of a sudden I start to feel vibrations and I brace myself, preparing for the tunnel to collapse, burying me alive beneath its enormous weight. I hear Vex's voice travel gently toward me and I watch him turn, I can tell he's noticed my fear.

"Hush, pet. It's just the bass," he smiles wickedly, smirking at my fear, getting off on it.

What a shit head. I cuss internally, wondering where my anger is stemming from.

Normally I'd have left his smirking and his blunt demeanour in my dust as I swam away, but for some reason I can't help but enjoy our banter. Enjoy the challenge of trying to perhaps tame someone so aloof and dark.

Don't be ssstupid girl, you could never tame the dark. The voice moves forward from the recesses of my psyche once more, startling me. I slap it back.

"Shhh!" I exclaim, realising afterward that I must look insane. Vex doesn't seem to notice, or if he does he doesn't care enough to turn and ask me why I'm shushing invisible voices.

He propels himself forward with his long and suckered tentacles through the end of the tunnel ahead of me. I move past him and finally out into the open, out into the flashing lights.

The rave is terrifying, yet intoxicating and riddled with dark promise. The cave at the end of the tunnel is monstrous in size, from what I can see anyway. The lighting is strobe, intermittently flashing in brilliant short bursts of white, coming from eels that are suspended from giant and brutal looking fishhooks, writhing and sparking. Above them, hundreds of scarlet neon jellyfish pulsate, trapped in a heavy chained net, suspended from the ceiling, drenching the space in a bloody dim light.

The Psirens are huge in number, a mass of dark, mutated beings, clinging onto one another in desperate, lustful passion, allowing themselves to be engulfed in the remittent black.

I turn to exclaim my shock at the magnitude of the event to Vex, but realise anything short of screaming would be futile. The sound is so immense that the water I'm immersed in is blurred, vibrating with sound waves. The music is a primal rhythm with a pounding and potentially migraine inducing bass line. I source the sound quickly as I spot a group of Psirens, striking down on enormous metal drums with thick, alabaster whale bones.

I look closer, squinting until I can make out that the skin pulled over the broken submarine parts, making up the body of the drums, have scales. I shudder. Vex senses my awkwardness, my lack of belonging and grabs my arm, pulling me harshly into the thick gyrating layer of tails and tentacles. I look around, uncomfortable and being pushed against by other foreign bodies. Vex leans in, placing his lips against the shell of my ear.

"Relax, pet," his words, barely audible against the primal drumbeat, send a shiver through me as his fingers wrap around my waist. I don't stop him, if for no other reason than his muscular stockiness prevents me getting knocked around by other dancing Psirens. I do as he commands, ignoring the flashing images of black eyes and jagged, razor sharp smiles, smeared with the blood of their mates. I try to get lost to the music, finding a place of calm so I can let go. I throw my arms up above my head as the beat starts to increase in speed. I let the darkness take me and the sound and sensation wash over me.

This is exactly what I need, no responsibility, no royal duties, no Orion breathing down my neck, demanding more of me than I can be, or am ready to give.

In this moment, moving my body against Vex and letting the music take control is enough. I feel Vex's tentacles wrap themselves around my tailfin, I'd thought they would feel slimy and creepy, but instead the undersides feel like suckered, crushed velvet. I momentarily catch a glimpse of Vex's eyes, searching for mine as I've been busy gawking around at my surroundings. A chilling reality hits me as I realise the paleness of his lilac irises aren't icy blue and his blonde hair isn't tousled to perfection.

What the hell am I doing? I think for a second. This guy isn't Orion. In fact, he is so far off base from Orion he's a completely different species.

I take a second and still, watching him raving alongside the rest of his comrades and I wonder if maybe I've gone too far. It so isn't like me to be grinding in the darkness with a tentacled stranger.

But this feels good.

The voice shocks me, mainly because it's my own, and the words aren't a lie. Being here did feel good. In fact, it's the first time I've had this much fun in months. I feel good without Orion, even if I hate to admit it. It feels good being in charge of my own destiny, not worrying about what he would think. What I have always feared has happened, I had lost Orion and I am still breathing, still living. I don't feel awful, I feel powerful and excited. Excited at the prospect of being surrounded by the thing I have been most afraid of, and dancing among them, inconspicuous and untouchable. I can handle myself. I know that now.

Vex looks down at me before he closes his eyes and starts to shake his head, running his fingers through his hair and bringing his arms up so his abs become defined and his biceps bulge. The bass is about to drop and I feel his excitement as we wait for the music to change, moving together in a tangle of tentacle and fin. The rhythm drops and changes and Vex turns to a barracuda tailed Psiren beside him who passes him, I observe in two strobes of eel lightning, what appear to be chopsticks.

I watch him, in what feels like slow motion, take one of the chopsticks and stab himself in the forearm without hesitation or fear of pain. He slumps visibly, relaxing before he looks up and I notice that his pupils have dilated again.

He passes me the other stick and I take it in my palm, recognising it as soon as I hold it up to the strobing of the eels. Lionfish spines. What the hell? I'd seen them up close earlier on Caedes, but why would you want to stab yourself with them? By all accounts I know, Lionfish are deadly in the poison department.

I look down at the spine again and then notice something past it, beneath me. Below the crowd I'm dancing in, groups of Psirens are clustered around vents in the floor of the cave. They're sucking some kind of drug through pipes fashioned from diving equipment, that I assume has been pulled off some poor, doomed, deep sea diver. I look back to the spine in my hand, a drug?

Vex is watching me as the beat of the drums changes again, picking up. He smirks at my hesitation, making me angrier than I'd thought someone who wasn't Orion could make me feel. I look at him, narrowing my eyes, and then back to my palm before closing it. I bring my hand up in a sudden and brutal movement, before I strike down, ramming the tapered end into my skin. I feel the spine hit a vein and inhale deeply with the sharp pain as I think:

What the hell, right?

AZURE

"Get the hell off me, silent man!" I yell at Ghazi, his hand is gripping at my arms, which he has pulled behind my back, pushing my breasts forward.

"Azure that's enough," my brother's voice is cold, and I immediately know that he is the reason I'm currently bound like an animal.

At request of the Crowned Ruler. Perfect and easily predictable. I should have known my stupid brother was behind this.

"What the hell do you think you're doing?" I snap at him as my tailfin trails along the crystalline floor of the small council chamber.

"Well, I did ask Ghazi to ask you to come and see me. I'm assuming you weren't up for the idea?" he cocks a brow looking slightly amused.

"So, what? You just let your staff manhandle me? I'm not some bitch that'll come at beckon call!" I exclaim, feeling rage take over my motor function. I continue to struggle.

"Let her go, Ghazi," Orion mutters with a flick of his hand. He looks back to Saturnus, who I now notice is skulking in the corner, observing me with scrutinising emerald eyes.

"Get gone!" I bite at Ghazi, turning on him as soon as his vice grip slackens and then vanishes from my wrists and elbows. He doesn't cower, he just blinks a few times, looking unimpressed and turns to leave the room after slamming his fist over his heart and nodding to the stupid Crowned Ruler.

"Azure, I'd ask that you don't treat the Commander of the Knights of Atargatis like slime off a slug, but I know that won't happen. What I will ask you is where the hell you get off letting Callie swim off alone to the Psiren city, and not telling me about it." His face is stony, Saturnus moves out of the shadow towards us, an irritating smugness creeping across his expression.

I should have known this was coming, it becomes really hard to hide anything when your sister, the notorious, pink, sparkly suck-up, shares your mind's eye and can't keep her nose out of other people's business. Goddammit, Starlet!

"I didn't know you cared all that much about Callie's comings and goings. She said you told her to get out and not come back. I assumed that you say what you mean, being Crowned Ruler and all," I purr, twizzling a lock of my inky hair around one finger.

"Don't play stupid with me, Azure. You know full well how I feel about her. I proposed for Goddess' sake," he puffs out his chest, like some pathetic display of manliness. How the hell we are even related I'll never know.

"I think it's a good thing you sent her away, Orion. Something in that girl is broken. I felt darkness coming off of her like smoke."

"What the hell is that supposed to mean?" Orion looks taken aback and his dull, familial irises glower at me, demanding a response.

"I wouldn't tell her where the city was, so she went all Queen of darkness on my ass. Seriously. She tackled me... her eyes went like mine. You aren't telling me you haven't noticed the darkness in the girl you claim to care so much about? She's practically vibrating with it. It's just below the surface but even I can feel it." Orion looks to Saturnus but he shrugs.

"So you're saying what exactly? That Callie has been bitten by a Psiren? I'm pretty damn sure I'd have noticed that, Azure. She's barely been out of my sight since the Psiren attack when Titus died," Orion looks at me, his eyes searching for an even an inch of the lie that he thinks I might be spinning him. But why would I spin a lie, when the truth was so much more unthinkable?

"Titus..." I say the name aloud and my gut curdles like sour milk. "You don't think..." I muse the possibility for a moment, the cogs in my brain slick against each other beginning to whirr with inspired imaginings.

"What is it?" Saturnus has spoken this time, he is coming forward, suddenly interested in what I have to say.

"Well... Callie is the vessel right?" They both nod and I continue, my mind all the while going back to the depths of Callie's pupils, the darkness within, the darkness I had only once experienced with such gravity. "So she can absorb powers from us, and our powers are a blessing... light magic right?" I say again and Orion's eyes widen. God, I wish he'd stop gaping, he looks like a fish out of water. I mean, I know it's shocking but he's supposed to be the Crowned Ruler.

"So what if she absorbed Titus' powers... his darkness?" I drop the bomb and Saturnus remains expressionless. It makes me suspicious.

Orion on the other hand looks like he may throw up. No one knows how to undo you like family. I chuckle to myself internally.

"She... she... hurt me," Orion stutters and then looks up at me.

"Like say, Titus would be able to?" I ask him and he nods, shell-shocked. What an idiot. If you thought a magical beam of light energy with the power of thousands of bolts of lightning was enough to stop Titus, well then you were just stupid.

"Yeah. We were arguing and she hurt me. I don't think she knew what she was doing. It wasn't intentional," he looks so sure of this and I wonder why, I'd say he deserved some pain if he was trapping me like some kind of bird in a cage. "So what do we do?" He looks to me like a small child and I'm taken back, so far back that I can't believe I'm getting the memory, to when we were kids.

He was waving to me from father's fishing boat. I watch him, waving so enthusiastically he sways and loses his balance, tripping and then falling face first into the water. He comes up laughing with seaweed in his hair, careless and young. My heart constricts and I want to hurl. Being around family was making me soft. I need to get away.

"How the hell should I know?" I ask him, crossing my arms across my breasts.

"You saw her. Did she say anything?"

Oh so what, this is an interrogation now? Well next time I'm staying the hell away from little miss perky darkness, I can tell you that right now. I so don't need this hassle.

"She said she wanted to find her father. Said Solustus knew where he was. I don't know where she got that idea but she seemed pretty sure about it."

"Well I have to stop her. Can you take me to the city?"

"No," I mumble and he looks like he might slap me.

"You're telling me you're not going to tell me where the Queen of this city is? That's treason," he pulls rank and that makes me even angrier. What the hell is his problem? If he knew how to keep a woman happy this wouldn't be happening.

"Kill me if you want. It'd be better than hanging around this crap-heap anyway," I feel the truth of my words hit me. I am sick of this half-life. So many centuries and I've burned every meaningful connection I've ever had in the most spectacularly pyrotechnic way I can think of. What do I have left besides sarcasm and my anger? A whole lot of nothing.

I feel the air wave hit me before I see it as Orion expels me from the room. I am rushed with the newly born, manipulated current through the double doors, smashing my head on the back wall of the corridor outside the chamber.

Goddamn my sister and our so-called 'blessing'.

CALLIE

I am floating through a darkened milky way, ecstasy pulsing through me with the delicious thickness of blood and clotted sweetness of cream. Everything is sensational, sound that beats, making light flashes in certain places and dark holes in others.

I shake my limbs, feeling them, lighter than air, extended like an angel's wings. I wonder if I can fly away, through the green stars of phytoplankton that vibrate, shaking with the weight of their own existence. I feel crushed velvet enveloping me, wrapping itself around like twisted honeysuckle vines, climbing, exploring like I'm some kind of tropical forest, moist and hot. I turn around and there he is, head hung back in surrender to the dark, the thing that is making me wonder how anyone lives any other way.

How do they live never knowing this ecstatic abandon of the real, being given over to nothing but what is? The feeling of his flesh on mine, my hands running through his silver skull cap of hair and down the contours of his jagged cheekbones.

His arms wrap around me and he moves with blurred speed, though I can't tell if it's the Lionfish venom coursing through me or if he's suddenly developed superhuman speed. I find myself with my back to his chest as he grabs my hand and moves it up so it's draped around his neck. The beat of the drums is hypnotic and I close myself away, letting my eyes roll back into my head.

I feel Vex's breath hitting my skin, his exhale of water hot on my flesh. I tremble and I feel his breath hitch as he takes both of his rough palms and runs them down the front of my body, torturously slow, settling them on the top of my tailfin and moving my hips with his, swinging them in and out of his grasp, grinding my scaled buttocks into him over and over. There are no thoughts in my head, only feeling in my body. I hear his sentiment, whispered in my ear, moving through my mind like a snake in tall grass.

"You are so ripe."

I surrender again to the tsunami of sensory assault that is taking me, moment by moment, away from who I was and toward a place where nothing seems to matter but my own pleasure.

11
Strong
CALLIE

I stir hesitantly from a dreamless tranquillity I have not felt in a long time. I know mermaids can't sleep, so maybe I had found unconsciousness through other means. It's with this thought I remember how I had come to pass out, I remember the poison that ran through my veins, taking me away from myself. I open my eyes and my head is thudding like someone has been using it to break rocks all night.

"What the hell happened last night?" I exclaim loudly, too loudly. I regret making any noise at all instantly, bringing my palm up to cradle my throbbing temple. I notice the faint scars, already healed from my first Lionfish spine... and then my second, before I'd taken another in palm and thrust it into my spidery veins. I remember the night before in flashes, Vex's fingertips and tentacles trailing across my skin, the rabid electricity coursing through me as the drumbeat got louder and louder. I remember the high with relish and immediately crave it again.

"Morning, Love," the voice seeps through the water like sobering tonic and my stomach immediately falls as I notice the arm draped over my tailfin. I turn, realising I don't know where I am or how I got here. Or how Vex got here either.

"What the hell are you doing here? Get off me!" I squirm to get away from him before another shock hits me. My tailfin, no longer aquamarine, is now onyx like everything that surrounds me. The aquamarine lightning, forking across the scales, interrupting the darkness is now the only reminder of what was. I look down at my nails, black and hardened into claws. I recoil in horror. "You turned me! Oh my God!"

"No, I didn't!"

"Well then why do I look this?!"

"I don't bloody know, but I didn't bite you. Don't flatter yourself," he looks offended and I want to laugh, *He's offended?! Really?!*

"What are you doing here then?" I put my hands on my hip, head still throbbing, that however seems to be the least of my problems.

"You passed out so I brought you back with me. I didn't think you'd appreciate waking up and finding yourself being tortured by Caedes," he cocks an eyebrow and purses his lips as his eyes look over me hungrily. I bring my palms up to cover my breasts impatiently.

"I don't suppose you remember what happened last night then? If you're so sure you didn't bite me?" I attack him, feeling rage surging through me, causing the thudding in my head to get worse as I grit my teeth.

"We danced," he turns from his side to his back on the floor of the cave we're suspended in. The only light in the room are some kind of red bioluminescent worms that are packed into jars and stood on rock shelves that jut out of the barren, dark walls.

"That's it?"

"Well, it got a tad naughty, but we didn't kiss if that's what you're implying. I don't do that."

"What do you mean, you don't do that?"

"I don't do the kissing thing. Not my style."

"Right. So you didn't bite me? Did anyone else?"

"Nah Love, you were pretty pre-occupied with me, if I do say so myself. You're way more twisted than I would have thought. You should have heard the way you were begging me to…"

"Shut up!" I yell out remembering suddenly what it was I had been begging for.

"Ahhh… and so the Princess returns. Different packaging sure… but still a priss. You'd better get on finding your inner darkness Love, you so can't rock that look with your prudishness."

"I said shut up," I move over to a cracked mirror, lying on top of a rotting armoire in the corner of the room. It's fractured but I can still see

130

enough of my reflection to know that my appearance has totally changed. My scaled eye mask is still intact, though now it's black. My hair is black like coal and my eyes are black too, just like Solustus' and Titus'. I feel fear creeping in at my own appearance. I part my lips but my teeth are just the same as they've always been, not jagged or serrated. It doesn't make any sense. None of the other Psiren's have eye masks, and they all have jagged razor sharp teeth. So why don't I? If I really was a Psiren now why wasn't I showing all the traits?

"I look so…" I start and Vex cuts me off.

"Hot," he says the word and I turn to glower at him. "Hey don't get all bitchy on me now, Love, it's a bit late to pretend like you're not interested in this, isn't it?" He gestures towards his abs and I feel the urge to be sick clutch at my insides.

"God, you're such a pig," I snap at him.

"Yeah, I hear that a lot," he smiles at me, clearly not giving a crap about what I think.

"Must be true then," I shoot back. I move toward the exit of the cave, curious as to where I am. I get to the opening and can see that I'm in the rock wall that curves around the outside of the Cryptopolis. The white neon light from the clouds of jellyfish aren't that far above me as I am high up in the cliff. I notice as I look down from this angle that the light from above is casting shadows, exposing that there are many more caves hidden in the rock face, no doubt housing the rest of the Psiren army within.

"Better be going… training starts soon," I hear Vex call from within the cave. I feel him come up behind me. The way the water swirls is unnatural, due to his tentacles, "Later, Pet." He whispers, moving past me and brushing my shoulder blade with his thumb as he passes. I shudder and I can almost hear him smirk. He moves out into the water, descending slowly as his tentacles bloom out as he gets close to the ground. I settle on the ledge of the cave, lowering myself to watch them, secluded from view as darkness now cloaks me to invisibility with my black features. I watch as more Psiren's emerge out of their caves, slinking silently, red faced and irritable, clearly coming down from the high we'd all felt during the rave last night… or was it day? I couldn't tell without the sun.

"Cal?" A voice so familiar slaps me back into the moment and my head snaps around. In a cave entrance next to the one I'm sat in, a distorted but familiar face is peering at me from within the smoky shadows of the water.

"Daryl?" I gape, mouth hanging open in surprise... no... better word: shock.

"It's Darius now," he moves forward toward me, his body phasing at the waist into that of a great white shark.

"What the hell happened to you?" I look him up and down and he smiles at my shock, approval in the eyes which were once all-American baby blue.

"You could say I've evolved... you know, like those birds they taught us about, with that Darwin dude in biology." I gawk at him, still unsure how to react. The last time I'd seen Daryl... or Darius, or whoever the hell he is, he was trying to assault me in Chloe's beach house after I'd caught him with Mollie.

"You could say that. You shouldn't want to be a Psiren though Daryl. It's not exactly a step up," I cock my head and he snorts slightly, looking cockier than his human self, if that's at all possible.

"You can talk, you look just like us."

"But I'm not one of you. At least I don't think I am. I don't want to be anyway," I sigh and shake my head. He's staring at me and his brow is creased, dark pupils expanded outwards in the dim lighting, with blue lightning streaking through them.

"You look like one of us though. I mean, you were bitten right? They did the thing with the mixing of your blood?" He runs his hand through his hair, no longer the caramel brown it had once been, it's inky strands slip through his fingers, slick like they've been dipped in oil.

"No, I wasn't bitten."

"Could have fooled me the way you were letting that guy at your neck last night," he smirks and I scowl.

"Shut up. You're just jealous."

"Why would I be jealous of mister tentacles? Everyone knows I'm mother's favourite... and I'm not even one of hers. I don't even know why you like him. Is it the British accent?"

"Mother?"

"Yes, Alyssa, she made nearly all of the Psirens here. Well, the new ones anyway."

"Alyssa?" I repeat the name, something about it is familiar but I can't quite place it. Daryl blows bubbles out into the water in frustration.

"Yes. Alyssa. You know I remember you seeming a lot smarter when we were human."

"Shut up," I say the words, his rudeness is making my blood boil.

"So you never said, what is it exactly that attracts you to the British scumbag down there?" Daryl jerks his chin to Vex who is below us, still waiting for training to begin. He looks down his nose at him and I wonder where the hell he gets off looking down on anyone. He's just a child in a big man's suit.

"I'm not attracted to him. We were just having fun," I shrug and he smirks.

"I always said you were a tease, Pierce. Well I had better warn him what he's in for with you," he moves to begin his descent toward the courtyard in front of the Necrocazar, but I'm quicker and move with one slash of my charred tailfin, grabbing Daryl by the throat, reminding him of who he's dealing with.

"Excuse me? I didn't quite catch that?" I feel the electricity I had been able to muster recently prickling beneath my flesh, I taunt him with it, learning control of the ability in moments, sending his neurons firing like an execution squad, lethal and precise.

"Shit," I hear the guttural exclamation pass from his lips before I slam his head back into the rock face from which we've come.

"What did you say? About me being a tease? I'd say let's go all the way Daryl, really I would, but I don't think you can handle it," I let another pulse of electricity loose on his nervous system and he struggles against my grip, choking for breath as I cover his gills with my fingers, forcing them shut.

"Don't you like that? Maybe you shouldn't lust after women you can't handle!" I bite out the words, letting free one last pulse of electricity into his body, before slamming his skull into the wall.

I release his throat from my clawed grasp and watch him fall through the water to the ground of crushed bones and dead things, where he belongs. I can see that the eyes of the Psiren army from below are on me, including those of Solustus.

"You want to screw with me?! I invite any of you to try, I'm only too willing to teach all of you the same lesson. I'm not the kind of girl you fuck with. Not anymore." I yell the sentiment out to them, hearing the loudness of my voice reverberating back at me from the walls of the deep sea cave. I feel the power of my ability to cause pain flowing through me, making me untouchable. As I turn to move back into the darkness of the cave I hear Vex's British tone reach me.

"Well what do you know, there's hope for Little Miss Priss yet."

SOLUSTUS

The girl moves, turning around and retreating back into the cave from which she came. I can't quite get my mind around the concept of what I am seeing, she now not only acts with the power of my predecessor, but also looks like one of us, a poor imitation to be sure, but the darkness within her is evident and clearly ill-controlled.

The fodder turns toward me, their eyes are wide, unsure of what I expect from them. I wonder why they're such mindless, pathetic drones. I look over to the crumpled body of Darius, the boy I made to undo Miss Callie Pierce, limp among the bones of things too weak to survive among us. Well I suppose he is where he belongs. The fodder takes my looking to his defeated form as instruction to go and help him, but I give a warning look.

"No! He doesn't deserve our help. He was bested by a little girl, no more, no less. Let him rot," I snap and they nod. "Today I want you to pair up and fight one another until one of you is dead. Remember, it is not waste if you learn something and we can always make more of you. You are utterly and completely replaceable. So, fight well and you'll make it to training tomorrow. A gift in itself. The knowledge I'm imparting is the most valuable thing you will find down here," I issue the order and watch Vexus begin to move. "Not you Vexus. You're coming with me," I gesture for him to follow with a long bony finger, moving with all the speed I can muster back up into my throne room. I wish to observe the fighting from up high, so I can look down on them as they struggle to survive under my command. The boy lags behind me, making it to the throne room at the pace of a one legged tortoise. Pitiful.

"By all means, move at a glacial pace. I'm not getting any older, just impatient and irritated, that's not something you want," I seep sarcasm but Vexus remains impassive in his features. I look into his eyes and wonder what it would take for me to instil some fear into their hideous lilac depths. Probably not a lot, but this boy has been surprising me lately. Especially now that I know of his connection with the girl, something which my own prodigy has clearly failed to capture.

I move to the window to observe the fighting. "Come," I invite him to hover next to me, generous as always.

"Why did you want to see me?" Vexus asks, looking back over his shoulder, suspicious. I feel sort of proud, as though his paranoia is a sign that I'm succeeding in my teachings. He doesn't trust anyone, least of all me and that's exactly what makes him easily manipulated. Someone who can't trust is alone, and someone alone is weak. Everyone knows that.

"I wanted to congratulate you on your relationship with the girl, this proves most useful to me. I am pleased," at these words I expect him to look surprised but he doesn't, he just stares out the window.

"It was nothing. I just took her to a party. Gave her a little lionfish venom." I look over at him, *Lionfish venom?* Well that explains why half my army was turning up looking like they'd spent the night in a barroom brawl. It was because they had.

"Party?" I ask him with an eyebrow raised. I know the Psiren's in my city aren't on duty 24/7 but I didn't assume they actually had *lives*. It startles me, the idea of unity among their ranks. They aren't supposed to have minds of their own, connections with each other. They have two purposes and those are to kill and die… it is only a question of when and how.

"Yeah."

"I find it interesting that you're all off having a good old time and your fighting still isn't up to scratch," I mutter, running one of my sharp, clawed nails along my teeth.

"It's good for morale. Having something to look forward to, makes them work harder," Vexus makes the point and I wonder why he thinks he has the authority to tell me what's best for *my* army.

"You know what else makes people work hard, Vexus? The threat you're going to chop off parts of their lower extremities," I sneer and he looks at me with his eyebrow cocked.

"That is true, but you said you were pleased about me getting in good with Little Miss Priss and that's how I did it," he reminds me of his relationship with the girl and I remember the reason I asked him up here in the first place.

"With regard to the girl, I want you to help her. I need her for what I have planned and I need her trained up to fight, to control the power she has over darkness. Show her a good time, do whatever you need to, but I want her dark, Vex. I want her killing humans. I want her phasing. You know what I'm asking, don't you?" I look at him, serious in my expression.

"I get it, you want her dark, but I don't know why you don't do that yourself. You're the one with the power here and it's not like she's in love with me," Vex looks irritable and I wonder why, I'm bestowing a great honour on him in giving him this task.

"She tends to spit venom when I'm around. Darkness, it needs to be coaxed out of her. She needs to accept it as a part of who she is and embrace it. That requires a more... personal touch." Vex looks like he might burst out laughing at this statement, at the idea of my incapability to carry out the task. I consider briefly striking him across the face.

"Mate, if you think I have better luck in keeping her calm, you're wrong. She'd start an argument with a wall if it looked like it might question her authority. She's got more rage than you'd expect for someone so... perky," Vex laughs at the thought. I wonder momentarily if I'm seeing fondness for the girl or amusement at her futile expression of the darkness within. I decide it's the second, the first being too strange to contemplate or allow.

"Then find out what it is that's fuelling the rage. Use it. I need her dark. It's vital to our overthrowing of the mer. Do you understand?" I place my hand on his shoulder, sort of like a father, a real father, entrusting his son with a family secret.

"Yeah mate, I get it," he calls me by that hideous nickname again and I snarl.

"I'm not your mate," I remind him, feeling my rage crest as he waves away my remark like it were nothing but smoke. I want to pound him into the dust, I want to crack his bones and shred his organs but in this moment I bite my tongue, looking down over the Cryptopolis as I watch my fodder fighting each other. They've turned on each other so easily, so mindlessly under my command and it makes me realise that whilst Vex is infuriatingly blasé, at least he has a mind of his own, and that mind isn't stupid enough to disobey me. I need the majority of them stupid, this is true, but what harm can one extra pair of eyes do? After all, the second I want him dead he shall be so.

I feel him move across the throne room, but then something catches my attention. He's still in the doorway, turned, deviating from his path, staring with the intensity of the sun for which I was so named. I follow his line of sight and find where it lies. The black and violet, steel alloy trident. Titus' weapon, something he had taken from another mer warrior by force eons ago.

"What are you looking at boy? Get the hell out and do the job I assigned you!" I bark and he takes one last long look at the trident, intense and unwavering before he turns and reluctantly leaves the room.

I turn my back on the city, moving toward the giant mirrored surface at the back of the chamber and picking up the trident on my way there. I hold the weapon, thinking of its history. For something Titus was particularly fond of, he rarely used it and I can see why. The trident isn't particularly dangerous looking and I could name a hundred newer and more lethal weapons. Maybe it was sentimentalism, the fool, thinking it made him like Poseidon, father of our race. I throw the trident to one side, realising it as a useless display piece, one for looking strong but nothing more, not like Scarlette, who looked meagre but could slice a man in half without so much as a falter in her swing.

The trident clatters against the floor and slides into the shadows, next to the Scythe of Atargatis, which as it turns out, is becoming far more difficult to utilise than I could have ever anticipated.

12
Collide

CALLIE

Since my little outburst with Daryl, or whatever he calls himself now, the Psirens of the Cryptopolis are keeping their distance. Vex is now even giving me one on one training at the request of Solustus, which is leaving me exhausted but satisfied. I realise now there is a lot about my own senses I don't know or utilise effectively when it comes to awareness of what's around me. I feel powerful, more so than I had in the Occulta Mirum in spite of the crown they'd placed upon my head. It's not adoration or shallow envy that has led the other Psirens to bend to me, it is respect. It is the knowledge that I could take down any one of them, just like I had Daryl, with just a touch of my flesh to theirs. I'd always wanted to be liked, or so I thought, but fear is a tad more refreshing and works a lot quicker than the friendly alternative. It doesn't mean I am their equal, it means I am *better* than them. I don't hate it like I thought I would, it keeps me warm on the cold floor of Vex's cave during the chill nights where I lie on my back, blackened tailfin in the air, trying to forget Orion and letting my anger at his stupidity simmer silently beneath my skin. The feeling of superiority, that I am right in all of this, has become the more favourable option, especially when compared with listlessly desiring Orion every second we were apart.

I wonder now how I did it, allowing my life to revolve around a man.

It is something I swore I'd never do after watching my mother fall victim to Carl's venomous vice. But somehow I had fallen, just as she had, into the same trap.

I think back to Orion, his face, his lips, and his eyes… those eyes… *NO!*

I hear the voice inside my skull reverberating, like a battle cry, over and over, every time I think of him in any minute detail. I won't go back there. I was young and foolish, but I am different now. This place has changed me. Correction… is still changing me.

"Callie, focus," I hear Vex's Britishness and disdain seep through the water toward me. I can't see him, but I know he's somewhere out there in the shadow, ready to take me any which way he wants, leaving me bruised, sore and angry.

"I'm trying," I mutter, irritated at his lack of impress. We are floating in the crevasse, high above the jellyfish guarded entrance to the city which I had oh-so-gracefully navigated my first time finding the Cryptopolis. I look back on that now and cringe. The abyss is consuming both of us, but that's the point, I'm learning to fight without my eyes.

"Try harder. Focus. A Psiren is at his best when he's in the dark so you need to be too. Feel me." Vex has become like some sadistic version of sensei to my grasshopper these last few weeks. I snort at the comment 'feel me', thinking that's the last thing I'd rather do and yet I can't stop myself from admiring his body every chance I get. It sure as hell isn't love, I mean the man has the personality of a troll, but something inside me is lusting after something new and tempting.

I push this thought out of my head as I still for a moment, closing my eyes, allowing myself to hold steady in the water for a little while. I feel a tiny movement in the water to my left, *no… too small.* It's probably some kind of squid or fish. I concentrate on my breathing, sucking in cool stagnant water and breathing it out again through my gills. I feel him, for just a second, but he's there. I snap sideways, hand ready to strike him in his solar plexus but he catches my hand.

"Uh…uh…uh," he says it, a staccato of dirty promise as he licks his lips. "No spanking, Princess. You'll have to be quicker than that to get me over bended knee."

"Why are you so depraved?" I spit at him. He always knows how to make me disgusted, so why am I feeling disappointed that he is denying me touching privileges?

"I was made that way, Love," he saunters back into the shadows and out of view. I turn again and close my eyes, ready to try and focus on his scent, his movement… anything that can give me a hint as to where I need to turn to best him. I'm using the senses of a hunter, the senses of something primal that has long been disconnected from who I thought I was. I breathe in water, the taste metallic, and the scent of him wafts into my nasal cavity, trapped in the liquid that's flooding down the back of my throat and out through my gills again. I turn, seeking his scent, placing him correctly and hitting him smack damn in the middle of the throat. The impact of my strike sends him flying backwards into the shadow again. *Well,* I think to myself, *that'll teach him.*

It didn't.

Days pass and I start to harden, my body, my mind. My muscles become more defined and my tailfin moves with a preciseness I haven't ever felt before. My body has gained a sense of wholeness, each limb working with its connective in seamless time. My mind starts to work with a sensory awareness that has only come to me after hours spent with Vex in the darkness of the deep. Yet there's still something he wants from me that I can't quite reach. A speed and an intuition of a predator that I can't quite let go enough to gain. I hang in the crevasse once more, frustrated and irritable as Vex talks at me.

"So, for today's mind-blowing wisdom we're going to be setting you against me."

"We've done that already, so if you're going for mind-blowing…"

"I'm gonna get touchy feely, Love. We haven't done that yet and I can guarantee you, it will be mind-blowing," he smirks and I move backwards.

"What the hell is wrong with you… did you not see what I did to Daryl, did you not hear the big speech? What do I need a billboard that says 'Callie will kick your ass, back the hell off?'" I cross my arms, cocking my brow, a move inspired by him. He laughs.

"Not what I meant, Pet, but glad to know your mind is in the gutter, despite you saying otherwise," he purrs out the words and his tentacles undulate, spreading out and wrapping around me suggestively.

"You're going to attack me using your tentacles?" I look at him, surprised. He nods. I feel a shudder of fear move through me as I think of the unwilling pleasure at their velvet crush brushing up against my scales.

"You need to have the speed with two arms that I have with ten. Speed will be your greatest asset. Especially when it comes to Solustus," he looks me straight in the eyes and for a second I see the man behind the innuendos and sarcasm.

"Why do you care about Solustus beating me..." I look at him, suspicious.

"I don't, I don't care about him killing you either," he looks straight at me, nostrils flaring slightly, like I've caught him off guard.

"Oh... well that's good. Don't want to mistake your intent for compassion."

"Good," he is blunt. I feel his tentacles, which are still pushed against my tail, relax slightly.

"So you're going to teach me how to beat you? Aren't you worried I'll take you down?" I look at him seriously and he snorts.

"I'm not worried. Let's put it that way."

"Why not?!" I ask him, annoyed at his lack of respect for me in spite of all I have mastered.

"You wouldn't take me down, you're too busy being angry at everyone and everything to be a real threat," he licks his bottom lip and I falter in my strokes, letting myself fall slightly from his eye level, surprised.

"I'm not angry..." I start but he laughs, cutting me off.

"Don't lie on my behalf, Love. I've watched you trying to sleep at night, tossing and turning, exhaling like an asthmatic. I know anger when I see it and you, Pet, are angry," he points a stubby finger at me and I look at him.

"So?" I ask him and he laughs again.

"So? So, it's stopping you from really being lethal. You're too rage fuelled to see the woods through the trees. Real power, real violence comes from a logical calm that is seven steps ahead of its prey. Surely you've realised that by now. Solustus is always telling us that's what caused the guy before him to snuff it," he looks at me, serious for once, and unassuming. He is reaching deep into me, trying to pull out the truth of my rage. I recoil.

"Titus," I mutter the word, like it's a curse, magical and terrible all at once.

"Yeah. His rage, it blinded him. He wasn't observing what was around him closely enough." I think about the truth of what he's saying.

It was true; if Titus had been paying attention more closely he might have known Azure had been lying to him, playing him for the fool. I ponder this for a moment.

"I guess... I am pretty mad," I bite my bottom lip, self-conscious for the first time in ages.

"I'm all ears," Vex offers himself and I blink a few times, not sure I heard him right.

"You want to get personal now?" I expect him to joke but instead he does something that shocks me, he rubs the back of his neck with his hand. The gesture is one so familiar that I want to cry. It's what Orion used to do when he was vulnerable or guilty.

"I don't care. It washes off me like water off a duck's back." The phrase isn't one I've heard before and assume it's British.

"Okay. Well, I was Queen... back with the mer," I start and he cocks an eyebrow.

"So what, they didn't put enough sparkle on your tiara or something? Got into a spat with your favourite nursemaid, did we Love?" He rolls his eyes and I scrunch up my face.

"No! Are you going to let me tell the story? Or are you just going to make fun of me? Because that's not really how sharing works," I spit and his face immediately forces itself straight.

"Sorry. Please continue Your Highness," he says it, bowing, and I debate slapping him. Instead I choose to unload the weight that's been sitting on my heart, materialising as violence, ever since I fled the Occulta Mirum.

"Anyway, there was this guy. He and I... well, I thought we were made for each other. Things were great to start with, but then I died and things sort of got screwed up. Then he became the Crowned Ruler and proposed. But I didn't want to get married. I guess it was because he was too over protective and I felt trapped. Anyway, he screwed everything up. He was so controlling, he got paranoid and greedy with me. It was like, oh my god, am I not enough for you or something!? It was never enough. No matter how hard you try, or how much you change, some people are never goddamn happy! So now, I'm here." I breathe out, almost exhausted from my ramble and he looks at me, suddenly interested.

"You died?" He moves forward, like he may grab my hand, instead he folds his arms across his chest, wearing a suspicious stare.

"Yeah, I was kind of involved in this prophecy. Titus tried to sacrifice me and well, I died because of it. Only for a bit. Orion didn't deal with it well."

"So it's the guy, Onion, the one I saw you with at the coronation?" he runs a finger along his jawline, intrigued.

"Orion."

"Onion seems to fit, Love, he's making you cry for sure. I've heard you at night," he smirks and I roll my eyes.

"Yes. It's him! After I died, he wouldn't let me go anywhere on my own! He was too afraid I'd get hurt, like I'm some freaking china doll! It was pathetic! What's worse he had this whole *oh I'm so repressed and strong, I'll just fuck my woman to death*, routine going on. He takes everything out on me! It's not even my damn fault! It's just life!" I exclaim, imitating Orion's deep voice. I wonder what Vex will say next. I don't even like him, but I'm afraid his blunt honesty will be something I don't want to hear. "He's like a goddamn child for pities sakes."

"You didn't like that I take it?" He asks me and I shake my head.

"No, he was too controlling. It was like he loved me too much. He couldn't see what I really wanted anymore, and he actually really doesn't care, either." I admit.

"What do you want?" He looks at me seriously, bending his head slightly so he's looking down at me.

"I just... I don't know. That's what scares me. I had a life, I was a teenager, and then BAM! I'm a mermaid and a Queen in like the space of a few months. I lost myself. Completely. I think because falling in love with him came with also dying and turning into a mer... I think I sort of melded into what he wanted me to be. Which is the most awful, ridiculous thing that could have happened. So yeah, I don't know what I want, but I know what I

144

don't want. I don't want some man ruling my life, particularly not one that comes with the emotional capacity of a four-year-old! He's supposed to be like five hundred or something, he acts about twelve." I feel the confession free me, crossing my arms. I smile slightly to myself, the cruel things passing my lips are true and so I care little about whether they're fair. Vex's forehead is creased.

"That... wasn't exactly what I was expecting, Love."

"What were you expecting?" I ask him, boldness flowing through me. I look at him squarely, grateful that he is here for the first time since we met.

"I don't know. Something whiny," he waves a hand and I punch him on the arm.

"Hey!" I smile so he can tell I'm joking.

"Your smile..." He says, eyes narrowing and his lips spreading slightly.

"What?" I blush a little.

"It's just... you should do it more often. I'd say you aren't totally hideous."

It is the only compliment I feel he's ever given that he's actually meant. I'm not sure how to take it. I don't know what we have, it's not simple and it's not tender. It is raw, fragile, and borderline disdain. None the less, it is supporting me while I stumble around in the darkness of my own anonymity, and for now, I am grateful.

"Focus," his demand reaches me as his latest test looms.

Flashes of baited deep-sea creatures illuminate the space around me, a visual distraction. Finding calm amongst the chaos, the jumping of my own nerves, as Vex shoots in and out of the strobing light looking terrifying and threatening as his dark eyes reflect the whiteness of the light back at me. I close my eyes, breathing in and out, centring myself and concentrating on nothing but my own heartbeat. The calm has replaced the rage I was using to muster strength a few days ago.

I am now cool, calculating, untouchable.

I become the ultimate vision of myself, sensing Vex before he's even at an arms' length proximity, reaching out and slamming my palm into him.

Then, using a burst of electricity at the last second of impact, I send him falling backward. The light doesn't bother me anymore and neither does the dark. I am totally aligned with myself, with what needs to happen, with what I need to do and how I need to do it.

He moves again, stirring around in the shadow, and I manoeuvre instantaneously, pivoting on nothingness and catching one of his tentacles as it wraps around my wrist, using the limb against him as I tug its thick mass across my body, using his weight and length against him. I toss him sideways into the dark and here him hit rock.

"Well, I'd say my work here is done," I hear Vex sounding satisfied as I turn and see him rising up through the water, I'm glad to see he looks a little dishevelled.

"I. Kicked. Your. Ass." I declare, smug as hell and flushed at the power I feel running through me.

"I let you kick my ass," he folds his arms and twists his mouth into a smirk.

"Oh... don't give me that crap. I had you," I bob up and down in the water slightly, like a boxer rolling on and off the balls of my feet, waiting for the next strike and knowing it won't even get close to me.

"Had... me? Trust me Love, there was no having of anything. If you'd had me... you'd be a lot worse for wear," his smile is salacious and I act faux shocked, cocky and confident.

"So we're done?" I deflect away from the innate sexuality that thrums beneath every single word he utters.

"We're done. I thought I'd take you out. There's one more thing I haven't taught you yet," he smiles knowingly to himself, his flat forehead creasing at the thought.

"Why are you smiling?" I ask him feeling upbeat and ready for whatever he throws at me next.

"I'm smiling, Love, because for this next part, I get to see you naked," he gestures upward and we begin to swim away from the site we've been using to train and toward the exit of the crevasse.

"What do you mean? Naked?" I feel my skin tingling.

"I'm going to teach you to phase."

146

"Phase?"

"Yes, turning human again."

"Is it the full moon?" I pray momentarily that he says no.

"No, we don't need that," he looks at me, bored, like he expected my response, like I'm so predictable. We move past a six gill shark, skulking in shadow, moving silently and rise above it, my lungs feeling like balloons, deflating as they loosen at the decreased pressure.

"So you guys can just choose to have legs?" I feel joy stir in my stomach. I wonder momentarily if one could live a normal life as a Psiren. Choosing only to be in the sea when you wanted to be. I had loved being a mermaid, everything about it, except that feeling of being trapped at times, unable to re-join the human world.

It's weird what you miss when that is stripped away, like shoes, and walking in the rain.

"Yeah. It's a tad more complicated, Love. But basically," he doesn't give anything away, leaving me wanton for information. We move together, now equally matched in speed, despite the differences in our anatomy. Rising, we leave the darkness behind, and yet carry it with us, as we head toward the shore.

ORION

The sun is setting over the horizon. Another day gone and I feel her slip from me just a little. It's my own fault. I did this. I pushed her. I told her not to come back. Who knew she'd actually listen? That words could do as much damage as a fist or a sword... maybe worse. Who knew? The demons we had been so freed from had returned. I had sent the Knights out twice in the last few days to fight them back, to slaughter them, but I didn't go with them. I had lost my fight. They were breaking through the fault lines with no explanation as to why. I can't help but wonder if it's because the darkness is getting stronger.

I am in the throne room, my title the only thing left of me, and the only thing I hadn't wanted. The crown weighs heavy on my mind, my inability to think clearly without her is making me an inadequate ruler, crown or not. It isn't baubles that make a leader. It's action.

With that thought, I sit upright in the throne carved from the wood of olive trees, native to where I was born. I have been slumped in it for the last hour, watching the light fall over the city, over me, casting shadows. I'm not even sad anymore. Just angry. Angry with myself, angry at Azure, and everyone else for failing to help me get her back. Hell, I don't need them. I am the Crowned Ruler. If that isn't good enough for getting what I want, then what's the point in doing the damn job? I stick my head out into the vertical corridor.

"SATURNUS!" I bark, not the best etiquette, but I am far past patience. He appears from nowhere, alert and on edge. I wonder where he was lurking, maybe he's been watching me. Regardless, he's here and he's prompt so why should I complain.

"Assemble the Knights," I order him and he raises his eyebrows.

"All of them?" He asks, suspicious.

"Yes, all of them!" I snap and he crosses his arms.

"Are we under attack?"

"No."

"Then why on earth are we assembling the entire squad. It's sundown, Orion. They're exhausted, you know they've been pulling double duty with the demons' recurrence in our world."

"So? I'm the Crowned Ruler and I want them assembled," I remind him of his place as I turn into the throne room. He moves over me and blocks my path back to my throne.

"May I ask what you want them assembled for?" He folds his arms and floats, an immovable gold and scarlet statue of godly imminence. He doesn't scare me.

"I'm sending them to collect Callie. This has gone on long enough. God knows what they're doing to her down there Saturnus. I can't stand it," I reveal my intent and his emerald irises blaze angry.

"Are you serious? If you think we're assembling an army to fix your love life you are quite grossly mistaken, or delusional," he comes close to me, invading my personal space.

"I'm Crowned Ruler, I can do what I please. I need her here to help me rule. It's for the good of the Kingdom," I remind him of her place beside me.

"Then maybe you should have taken better care of your personal business, if you're so concerned about the Kingdom. I'm not having you, a reckless, selfish supplanter leave this city unprotected by sending our only militant force gallivanting after some girl because you couldn't tame her!" He spits the words in my face and I feel bile rise up in my throat.

"You can't tell me what to do, Saturnus. Now assemble the goddamn squad!" I shout at him, letting my anger loose.

"I don't answer to you. I answer to a force more sacred and more powerful than you can possibly comprehend, boy. Now sit down and go back to playing with your human women, or whatever it is you used to do before you got involved with that harlot you call a soulmate!" He shouts back and I've had enough, I feel rage climb within me like a wave, cresting and powering outward from my body in a burst of air that knocks Saturnus back, but only slightly.

"How dare you raise your hands to me!?" He comes at me, powering forward using his gaudy, jewel encrusted tailfin. I predict his assault and raise my fist, smacking him straight between the eyes with a large crack of my knuckles on his skull. He moves backward, disoriented from the blow.

"You forget yourself, Saturnus. I have more battle experience than anyone in this city. If you want to pick a fight, I suggest you choose a more meagre opponent," I sound calm but I'm not. I'm in internal tumult. He gets up off the floor and moves, quicker than I have ever seen him move before, so fast he's almost a blur and then he's behind me.

"No. You forgot yourself. You are nothing. You hear me. Nothing. I will have that throne, I'll have the crown off your head, even if I have to slit your throat and watch your blood run cold to do it." His words shock me.

What the hell is his problem? Does he really want the throne that badly? Hell, if he'd have asked I probably would have given it to him a couple of months ago. I'm not going to do that now. Is it that the power of the Goddess has gone to his head? Or that he knows I'm really not the right fit for this job? Maybe he knows what the Goddess wants, maybe that's not me.

Either way, something within him is snapping.

"Get out of my city," I choke out the words as his fingers close over my gills. I gasp, like a fish out of water. He laughs, whispering perversely in the shell of my ear. Delighting in my struggle against him.

"Stupid, stupid boy. You know what's funny? You overestimate your power. You may be Crowned Ruler, but I'm the one upholding the glimmer over this city. You can't get rid of me. Unless you want everyone slaughtered by sunrise that is. Or… maybe that is what you want? After all, why else would you be sending away our only defence?" His grip vanishes as quickly as it had clutched my throat and I sink to the floor. He's gone, moving out of the room in a flurry of bubbles.

I debate going after him, leaving him bloody, but I remember Callie's words to me. He's our link with Atargatis. Right now that's something I have to live with. He was right about one thing; we do need him.

I'm moving up off the stained glass of the throne room floor when Cole enters. He sees me looking breathless but doesn't ask why I look shaken. He knows when to pry; it's one of the things I like most about him.

"Sir, she's been seen off the coast, Sir… or at least we think it's her." Cole looks concerned.

"What do you mean you think it's her? She's not exactly subtle with that aqua tail!" I bark at him, irritated at the incompetence my men are showing.

"She doesn't look the same Sir. She's changed… her hair, her tail is different too. She's with a Psiren. I just got word," he says it, gasping almost with the speed at which he delivers the message.

"Right, let's go," I don't even think about anything else. Hearing Callie is out in the open ocean gives me a little relief, but she's with a Psiren, is he torturing her, leading her to her death? Am I too late?

"Sir, don't you want to let your right hand know we're leaving?" Cole asks me, looking troubled.

"No, Cole. I think Saturnus and I are perfectly clear on protocol for this kind of eventuality," I exit the room with Cole, toward the armoury to collect my weapons. Whatever Callie's business is with the Psiren, whether he be torturing her, killing her, or using her as bait, tonight will be his last night on earth.

13
Fun

CALLIE

The water at this depth isn't like I remember, it's lighter, fresher, and gives a clarity not unlike high definition as I zoom through it seamlessly. My time in the depths of the Cryptopolis has changed me, and it feels like I'm experiencing these coastal waters for the first time. They leave a fizzle of zest on my tongue and a refreshing tang in my nostrils. The low pressure means I move faster than I ever did before I journeyed to the deep, because my muscles are used to working so much harder at high pressures.

"Where are we?" I ask Vex as we reach a sloping incline of dust-like sand.

"Close to SDSU," he replies, the expression on his face is absentminded, something that somehow doesn't look right on him because he's usually so intense.

"How do you know?" I query him and he shrugs, mumbling in reply.

"One never forgets the place they breathed their last breath, Pet." I inhale sharply, I know he is right about that, despite the miles of ocean, the endless azure hue that seems to never end, I know I'll always be able to find my way back to that beach. The one where I succumbed to the kiss that killed me.

Then, I'm curious, I want to ask him how exactly it was he did die, but I don't have the courage, so instead I redirect the conversation, focusing on the task at hand.

My head breaks the surface of the cool shallow water and I blow liquid out of my nose, rejecting it as the dryness of the night air hits me.

"So how do I do this?" I look to him as his head moves above the surface slowly, seamlessly. He doesn't make any sound as he breaks the surface, not even a drop, he just slides like a ghost into the night.

"Well, seeing as how you're channelling whatever darkness is inside of you properly, it shouldn't be too much of a problem. It's all about visualisation. You just have to cleave yourself from the ocean, imagine yourself being independent from it."

"How do you know all this?" I ask him and he laughs.

"Mother taught me. She teaches all of us. She learned from Solustus I think." I shudder at the word 'mother'. I haven't even met this creature and yet I already can't stand the thought of her. She will always be a killer of innocents in my eyes, and that is wrong.

"Oh... okay... so I just picture myself being able to leave the ocean?" I cock my head in disbelief; surely it can't be that simple.

"What were you expecting? Sacrifice of an innocent virgin?" He chuckles to himself, a sound deep and hollow stemming from his throat.

"Have you seen the world we live in? You laugh, but I was sacrificed, remember?" I wonder if he realises the magnitude of what's going on around him, the world of Gods and Goddesses he's been brought into. He smirks and I roll my eyes, *no, of course he doesn't understand. He's a jackass.*

"Was there chanting? Did they sing Baa Baa black sheep?" He looks like he may laugh and so I slap him on the arm.

"Yes... it was very official. Officially shit scary."

"Well, as much as I'm sure it was terrifying, can we get on with it. I don't really plan on pruning up out here, that was supposed to be one of the perks of having to deal with tentacles, you know, not dying of old age."

"Fine," I snap and close my eyes. I focus, not needing to feel the rays of the moon on me, imagining my tailfin splitting in half and my scales vanishing. I feel a shiver run through me, not the normal tickling sensation, and when I look down at myself my modesty has vanished along with the black of my scales.

I move forward out of the water and Vex follows me, totally stark nude, droplets clinging onto him and trickling oh so slowly down the defined lines of his musculature.

"Try not to stare, Love. You'll make me blush." Then I do blush, unable to stop myself and his eyes roll over me, scorching. I scowl at him but despite myself can't stop staring at him either. He's shorter than Orion, around five foot eight, but he is tightly packed with sinew. He's stocky and pale, his hair gleaming white in the moonlight and his lilac irises spectral.

"I wasn't staring," I say, standing naked on the beach. I remind myself as I shiver, never to curse Georgia again as I wonder what I'm expected to do next. "What now?" I ask him urgently.

"Well, I was thinking we could not freeze to death for a start."

"You have clothes?" I ask him and he shakes his head.

"No, but I know where some bikers stash their stuff just up the beach, fancy breaking and entering?" I don't have much of a choice so say nothing as he breaks into a full out stride along the sand, totally unashamed of himself as I scurry after him, covering my boobs with one arm and my private parts with the other.

We reach our destination, a large wooden shed on the sand. It looks like it could be used to store jet-skis. There's a light on inside and the door is cracked ajar. Vex smiles and doesn't break his stride.

"Hey! What the hell are you doing! I'm not walking in on some biker's club like this!" I gesture down at my nudity. He looks down at me and then back at my face with a smirk.

"Calm your arse down. They're with us," he moves away, pulling my naked and completely not calm 'arse' into the lamplight of the oversized shed. Then he pushes me behind his body, covering me.

"Darius! Clothes, mate. Grab some chick stuff too."

"Please don't tell you me you brought her?!" I hear the exclamation and pop my head around Vex's shoulder.

"You bet your ass he did," I say, cheery just to piss him off. Daryl blushes in embarrassment, clearly still wounded from my take down, and a man next to him with dreadlocks throws a bundle of black clothing at Vex, who catches it and turns to me, shielding me from the rest of the room.

"Go change outside," he pushes me back through the door and into the chill night, I curse him under my breath. The San Diego weather never seemed cold to me before, but I stand, shivering and dripping wet on the sand, holding black garments to me. I hold them at arms-length, untangling them and looking at them with a cocked eyebrow.

"Oh you've got to be kidding..." I mutter getting dressed. Pulling on leather when you're dripping wet should never be attempted alone, I realise this as I fall on my ass, trying to pull up the black, skin tight leather pants that have been provided. There is no underwear, so I guess I'll be going commando. I pull the black corset around my chest, still sitting in the sand. It fits well despite being a little loose around the hips. I clip the silver buckles that line the front of the corset in place, pushing my breasts up upward. The attire reminds me of the night I snuck out to meet Orion, but I push this memory back as I flip my long black hair over one shoulder. I'm not that girl anymore. Not a chance.

"Got any shoes?" I walk into the bike shed, finally dry, and the boys are getting dressed behind large bikes. There are three of them, Daryl, Vex, and another Psiren I haven't yet met. He has dreadlocks and bloody red eyes. His dark skin glistens with sea water, forming in droplets over his abnormally large and faintly tattooed biceps.

"Over there, Love," Vex jerks his chin over to the pile of leathers and bike helmets that are hung along the wall. Boots are messily shoved against the wall, and to no surprise are all black.

"Aren't the bikers gonna be pissed we're stealing their stuff?" I ask.

"I don't think they'll need leathers where they are, Pet. No roads in hell." I shudder. I'm wearing a dead woman's clothes. That is wrong on so many levels. I pick up the smallest pair of boots in the pile, they're knee high, flat and made of soft leather, they had definitely belonged to a woman. I slip them on my bare feet, not thinking about the previous owner. I stare up from the floor as Vex pulls a black round neck t-shirt over his abs.

"The leather, it suits you," he compliments me and I catch Daryl glaring at me over Vex's shoulder, his buddy wolf whistles. I glare back at them and Vex turns around to stare at him.

"Bugger off, mate," he rolls his eyes and turns back to me. "Ignore him, and Tiberius," he gestures to the Psiren with dreadlocks and skin the colour of dark chocolate. "Ever ridden before?" He asks me and I shake my head, black hair surrounding my face in a shadowy mass that I'm not used to. "Great, you can ride with me." A glint passes behind the lilacs of his eyes and I recognise the mischief of his intent. My heartbeat quickens slightly in my chest as he walks me over to the largest black and silver bike.

It's shining in the light, a combination of masculine sheen, supple leather seats and an engine with the horsepower to outrun a pissed off leopard.

"Get on, Love," Vex purrs as he mounts the bike with a swing of one of his dark, leather clad legs. I get on the back, the leather of my pants pinching around the crotch.

I lean forward, placing my arms around his waist. I can almost feel a smile creeping onto his lips as his chest inflates slightly underneath my fingertips. Without a word he kicks the stand away and starts the engine. The roar of the machine makes desire pool in my stomach, dripping gradually downward like a slowly seductive waterfall.

Daryl and Tiberius get on two of the remaining bikes and do the same. Vex pulls his knee up and rests it next to mine as we lurch forward, my black hair trailing behind me like ink dipped ribbon as we race, engine purring beneath us, wheels spinning rabidly, into the darkness of the night.

The vibrations of the motorcycle rattle my frame as I cling onto Vex. We pull onto a road that leads to San Diego State University and weave past large white buildings and palm trees that are blowing lightly in the night air, their leaves like giant feathers. The campus is strewn with straggling students, walking home from the library after long evenings cramming for assignments or back from parties that they've left early, either too drunk or too bored to want to stay.

"Where are we going?" I yell over the roar of the bike. Vex's head turns, his profile outlined against the light of the streetlamps which is just a little too white.

"A party at a frat house," he says, revving the engine a little as we turn a corner. The street sign says 'Greek Row'.

"A frat party?" I raise my eyebrows and he nods. I feel excitement bloom in my chest, I'm finally going to get a look into the life I've left behind. I'm finally going to a college frat party with a hot guy. It's almost like the last few months never happened and ended up at SDSU for some reason or another.

As we pass the seemingly deserted houses that line the street, a vibration that's intermittent and familiar reaches through the tires of the bike, reverberating through the shiny metal work and up into my seat. It's a thumping bass line and it's coming from the house at the end of the street. All three bikes lurch forward once more before they pull up outside the house. People are spilling out onto the street. The lights are on inside and people are chanting 'chug, chug, chug!' in a primitive circle, not unlike cavemen, just inside the door. I dismount the bike and eyes turn to me, or should I say to us, as the others park their bikes. I hear someone yell.

"Hey! You can't park here man! You'll get a ticket." Vex shoots the stranger a stare not unlike one that would freeze the likes of hell. Pulling out a bottle of some kind of liquor and a plastic bag, he unscrews the lid off the bottle and takes a gulp, not giving a crap as always and sending the message that he won't be told what to do. I laugh as he walks forward, slinging his arm with the bottle in it over my shoulder.

"Ready to party, Love?" He winks at me as Daryl and Tiberius fall in behind us. We climb the stairs that lead to the porch and people part in front of us; boys are looking at me, my breasts, my ass, my face.

Is nothing sacred? I think to myself, wanting all too much to slap them, avert their eyes to some willing target.

"Yeah. So how did you get an invite to this thing?" I look at him and he snorts, taking another swig from the bottle.

"Who said we were invited?" He looks over at me. I throw back my head and laugh.

We walk through the crowds of dancing, smooching, and drunken students, finding a dark corner in the expansive living room in which to skulk. Tiberius and Daryl move to join the others, assimilating themselves in with the masses and starting up conversations with random women.

"Don't you want to go over and find yourself a hot young woman to prey on?" I look over at him as he perches on the arm of a barker lounger.

"Nah, Love, I've got the only woman I'll ever need right here." I open my mouth to protest against him making such an inappropriate comment about me and he brings the bottle up to his eye line and shoots me an amused stare. "Tequila."

"Why do men drink spirits? I mean, really? Do you think it makes you look cool?" I say, feeling irritated as he breathes salty musk over me.

"Oh, getting all high and mighty are we?" He snorts and takes another swig. "You think you're so much better than me, Pierce. But you didn't seem so high and mighty when you were fucked up on Lionfish venom."

"Is that what it feels like? Tequila?" I ask him, suddenly curious. I'd never been a drinker, but if drinking made you feel like I did that night at the rave, then maybe it is a tad more understandable.

"Not as much, but it's as good as humans can hope to get without the hard stuff, yeah. Don't tell me you've never had a drink?" He looks at me and I shake my head. His eyes widen. "Wait... you're not a virgin, right?" I slap his arm and snatch the bottle out of his fist, leaning back into the cheap corduroy hold of the armchair and throwing the liquid into my mouth. The salty burn of the tequila feels like sea water mixed with paint thinner, scoring its way down the back of my throat. I stick my tongue out and shake my head like a dog, closing my eyes and pinching my nose.

"Bleughh!" I exclaim and he laughs, pulling the plastic bag up from the floor where he'd perched it. "I don't feel any different," I say, allowing the burn of the liquid to dull.

"Keep drinking, Pet. I'll introduce you to Tequila's mistress, Ms Slammer," he pulls out a bag of limes, a knife, and a white box of salt from the bag as I sit back into the chair. He looms over me, leaning across the back of the chair, still perched on its arm next to me.

I watch as the humans buzz around the room, clinging to one another for dear life like insects. I see boys eyeing women and women eyeing Daryl and Tiberius. It was like the supernatural beings in the room were magnetic, pulling in and putting out sexual energy at the same time.

I look up at Vex as he starts to slice a lime and I wonder why nobody is looking at him. Maybe it's something you have to turn on, that attraction, and maybe, just maybe, he's content just sitting with me, drinking in the shadows. He may be invisible, but after a few moments it is clear to me that I am not. A young blonde boy, with baby blue eyes is staring at me, his eyes drawn to my darkness from across the room.

"You've got an admirer, Love. Why don't you go say hello?" He tips the head of the bottle in the boy's direction.

"Why should I?" I ask him and he smirks.

"Ahhh… but the real question, why wouldn't you? Take what you need, Love, but give nothing back. I'll be watching," he pushes me out of the chair and toward the crowd of people. A number of boys turn their heads to look at me, running their eyes over my form like hungry wolves. I breathe and flutter my eyelashes, unafraid… a lioness.

"Hey there…" A dark haired boy touches my arm. I pull away from him. *What the hell gives him touching rights?*

"Hi. What do you want?" I ask him pointedly, I see Vex out of the corner of my eye and he's smirking. *No.* I think. *Not what he wants. What do I want?* I ask myself the question and look up into the boy's dark eyes and square jaw. He's not unattractive exactly, just human.

"I…" He looks at me as I stare at him square on, losing his train of thought. I feel someone else tap me on the shoulder. I turn again, away from the dark haired boy and come face to face with the blonde boy who was standing across the room before, watching me with his baby blue eyes.

"Hi…" He murmurs slightly, I look up at him and he examines my face like it's a masterpiece of shadow and light.

"Do you guys want to dance?" I ask them, hearing the music change to a quicker beat.

"Both of us?" The dark haired boy asks with a raised eyebrow and a look of disappointment in his eyes.

"Take it or leave it," I say, sure of myself. Vex looks surprised from the corner, I smile, impressed with myself. Am I being slutty? Maybe. But at least I'm not pained with making a decision between the two boys in front of me. I don't want drama. I just want to feel wanted.

"Okay," the boy with dark hair nods and I turn to find the blonde nodding too. I smile. I can do this.

We dance together, the boys sandwiching me, using my body as a buffer between them. The blonde is at my back, with his hands on my hips, and the dark haired boy stands in front of me as I let my arms dangle around his neck. I can hear their blood, susurrations… pulsations and a throbbing fullness within their veins, like juicy stalks waiting to be ripped open and the nectar let run.

Vex watches us from the corner still and I can't work out if he's getting off on watching another man's hands running over me or whether he's debating killing both the boys for laying a single finger on my person. I watch him take another slug of tequila. It's odd. I'm loving the feel of strangers' arms around me, of their eyes brushing across my skin, painting an image of me onto their minds that will stay with them forever. However, I can't quite help but wish it was Vex who was adoring me. I wonder if it's because he isn't the adoring type. Is it because he's the one man who I could never love and who can never love in return? *Do I just want him because I can't have him? That must be it.*

I write off my fascination with him as being his taboo factor. The song finishes and the two boys look to me for further instruction.

"You can go now," I mutter and they both look disappointed again. "Shoo," I reiterate and I feel my eyes turn dark. They both flee at that, turning and moving back into the crowd. I return to Vex.

"How did that feel, Love?" He asks me handing me the tequila bottle.

"Good."

"Well, that was a successful lure if I ever did see one," he compliments me but I feel slightly horrified at the word 'lure'.

"I didn't lure anyone."

"Sure, because two boys just happened to want you at the same time. Look around, Love." I do as he suggests and turn, looking back over my shoulder. Male eyes are staring at me, transfixed on the back of my neck.

"That's just lusting, Vex, mermaids have that effect on humans," I explain to him and he laughs to himself.

"Sure it is, Love." I roll my eyes and raise the bottle to my lips.

"And you know… the thing about Onion, he asked me in front of everyone. AND THEN HE GETS MAD!" I lick another line of salt of my spit strewn wrist and throw back the shot. Vex leans in and feeds me a slice of lime, taking his thumb and running it to catch a drop of the zesty juice.

He licks his thumb. My head is swimming.

"Prick move. I'd kick his arse for you, baby. You know that right?"

"He's kind of good with the punching. Like this," I demonstrate with a few flailing jabs.

"I'd kick his ass, knock him into next Tuesday if it made you happy, baby."

"Stop calling me baby."

"Stop acting like one."

"I'm not!"

"I'd say you are, crying and waiting for some man to realise he's not good enough for you. Doesn't sound like something an independent woman would do, now does it?"

"And what would you know about independent women?" I take another shot of tequila into my mouth and his reply causes me to almost spit it out.

"Well, I have a Master's degree in British feminist literature."

"What?" I gurgle slightly, the last remnants of the alcohol still swilling around the back of my throat.

"I used to go here you know."

"You? Went to college??" I spit out before I can stop myself.

"Oh… I see how it is! Thought I was too dumb for college did you? I was here on a PhD studentship I'll have you know!" He looks self-satisfied. Smug.

"Okay, sorry professor Vex…" I hear how ridiculous my slurred insult sounds and burst out laughing all over again.

"My name wasn't Vex," his tone is suddenly dark again.

"What was it?" I ask him and he frowns.

"I don't tell my real name to drunk girls. I usually just shag them and then never call again," he smiles and I laugh.

"How very Mr Darcy of you," I think of the only literature reference I can remember with such a large amount of alcohol coursing through me, impressed I can remember anything I've read at all.

"Fuck Mr Darcy. That Ponce..." He smiles salaciously and holds out a piece of lime for me to suck on. I do and he rolls his eyes over my body which is spread out over the armchair now. I grab the sour fruit and throw it across the room; it lands in some guy's hood. I giggle and Vex does too. "You... are too naughty," he whispers and I laugh again. When did everything get so hilarious?

"And you... you're a bad...bad man," I slur my speech, bringing my feet up onto the seat and turning to face him.

"But at least you know I'm bad. I don't have a noble steed. Just a motorcycle," he reminds me and I nod, taking the box of salt and starting to make another pile on my wrist.

"I like your motorcycle," I say, not looking him in the eyes.

"I like you like this... the darkness. It suits you. You're like... some sort of dark Queen or something." I laugh. "No... no I'm serious. You are just... dangerous, Love. I mean... I misjudged you..." He takes another swig of tequila and passes me the bottle.

"Misjudged?" I say the word like a question but I can't remember what it means. I want to grasp the concept but it's not quite within my mental capacity to reach it. It sounds funny.

"The blonde you... before, you were so righteous I couldn't see it. But you've got power, Love. It's thrumming underneath your skin, I can feel it when you brush against me, when we dance, when we fight. He tried to tame you, but that's impossible, and that, Love, is why you ran. You're wild. Ain't no taming that and before you blame me, it's not something anyone did to you. It's who you are." He is inches away from my face but I don't recall when he got there. His lilac irises are burning into me. I snort and laugh, throwing my ladylike behaviour to the wind.

"You're so full of shit," I push him back and he looks disappointed, a cool mask of reserve sliding in quickly. I don't have it in me to care; the tequila is taking up too much room in my head.

"And you are battered, Love."

"What does that even mean? Battered. Such a guttural... manly word," I repeat the words, swinging my head from side to side to a silent song nobody can hear but me.

"Drunk, Love. I know, you don't have to tell me my British accent is an incredible turn on. Especially when I use words you don't understand."

"Do you put tequila in your tea in England then?" I ask him with mock seriousness, more giggles explode from my lips.

"Not all British people like tea you know. I notice you aren't an obese mess, sitting on a couch on her front lawn with a shot gun," he takes another swig from the bottle, which is starting to look rather empty. I want to cry.

"But you like tequila," I remind him and he smirks.

"Everyone likes tequila, Love. Even the Queen."

"So if you love tequila so much... why did you only bring one bottle?" I ask him and he gestures for me to lean in closer. I move forward and he puts his lips close to the shell of my ear, his breath hot.

"Who says I only brought one?" With that he is gone. I smirk to myself biting into a rogue bit of lime that has been left, wrapped up in the plastic bag. The zest is incredible and my mind is blurred, soaking in spirits that are apparently happier than my own.

Vex returns, another bottle and another plastic bag in hand.

"How many of those do you have in that bike seat?" I ask him looking surprised.

"Enough to get even me drunk... and to kill you."

"What's that supposed to mean?" I ask him and he smirks, sitting back once more on the arm of the chair. His head against the wall, he unscrews the bottle, handing it to me. I like its fullness; the glass is cooling to my touch.

"You are a lightweight, love. But that's to be expected, you're a twiglet," he brushes my arm with his fingers.

"Hey!" I slap his hand away, glugging more of the salty burn into my gullet.

"Don't get me wrong. I'd love a taste. Just say the word, Love."

"What is, 'The Word'?" I ask him, coming up close to him and feeling my skin heat.

"Hmmm... that's a good question. What do you want it to be?" He asks me, taking my bottle from me and screwing the lid back on. I ponder this for a moment before pulling on the only word I can think of.

"Tequila."

Vex laughs.

A few hours later and the house is starting to clear. The music has been pretty low key for the last thirty minutes, and Vex and I sit, tequila bottles strewn around us and empty with salt spilled out, looking not unlike cocaine. I look at them and pout, poor, empty bottles. Someone needs to fill them up. It's no fun being empty.

"You alright, Love?" Vex asks me again, he keeps asking me this and I keep nodding.

"It's so sad. They're so empty," I reply in a murmur and he laughs.

"I'm not giving you anymore, Pet. Not if I want you to remain conscious."

"Do you?" I ask him with a wry smile and he laughs.

"Yeah, you're not bad company for a priss."

"Why thank you, Vexy, you're not bad company for a per... perverted murderer," I pat him on the arm with a floppy hand and puff air out of my cheeks, a sudden and unfamiliar biological urge hitting me. I hadn't felt this way in a while. "I need to pee," I announce to him and he snorts.

"I'm not giving you permission, Love. Bathroom is through there," he points at the double glass doors that lead into the kitchen space of the house. I climb out of the chair, my legs betraying me completely. I stumble, feeling the room spinning and my vision becoming cloudy.

I move through the glass doors, pushing both of them open in a dramatic flair not unlike a movie star's entrance onto the red carpet. That's when I see it. Something terrifying.

"Callie?" The voice is all too familiar and is then echoed by somebody who I had never ever expected to see again, let alone when I looked like this.

"Hey, Mollie. Chloe," I nod to them and they gape, looking so stupidly human that I want to physically push their mouths closed.

Mollie is sat on some guy's lap and Chloe is standing in some extremely skimpy attire over by the sink with a beer in her hand.

"Oh that's right! You guys know each other! How could I forget!" The guy who's lap Mollie is sat on perks up at the drama and I realise I know him, too. Of course, it's Daryl. Right in the middle of an awkward sandwich, of my old life and new, is where he seems to belong somehow.

"What the hell happened to her?" Chloe asks Mollie and I turn to her.

"I'm right here. Why don't you ask me yourself?" I snap at Chloe and she recoils, I wonder if my eyes are completely blackened, do I look horrifying? Like some hideous monster? I retreat slightly, afraid of myself reflected in her flinching and stiff posture. "Sorry," I mumble and she rolls her eyes.

"Whatever. You're so weird." She takes a swig of her beer and I roll my eyes. Still classic Chloe.

I turn to Mollie, I want to say something, explain myself, but my brain is foggy from the drink and what could I possibly say. Really sorry I stopped being your friend because I ran off with a merman? Ummm... maybe not.

Daryl reaches around for a second and kisses the side of Mollie's neck, she giggles and as someone opens the back door a cold draft of air knocks my brain into overdrive and out of Tequila-Land, something within me clicks into place.

"Mollie can you come here please?" I ask her calmly, Daryl's lips slide back over razor sharp teeth and his pupils turn to black.

"Why?" She looks at me, her beetle black eyes so innocent. After everything I've done to her; disappearing, leaving a bruised and bloody Daryl on the beach house floor after he attacked me, and vanishing again with no trace. She is still as warm toward me as ever. I really did have a true friend in her. I love her for that, it's true, but not enough to want her to have immortal life.

"Please?" I feel my pulse heighten, blood thudding in my ears and Daryl catches my eye and smiles.

"Nah, I'm good here," she says.

Don't be stupid. Oh wait, she's human. I think.

I don't want to cause a scene so I turn on my heel and exit the room moving back into the living space where Vex is sat, lighting a cigarette.

"Can you come with me a sec?" I ask him and he raises his eyebrows.

"Bugger, I just lit up... can't it wait? I've been waiting to find a lighter for bloody weeks now, Love," he pleads with me, the alcohol still clearly making him fuzzy.

"Daryl is about to kill my friend," I say and his eyes narrow.

"So?" He says before inhaling and then blowing smoke into my face. I cough slightly.

"So, I'd really rather he didn't kill her."

"He's a Psiren, Love, it's what we do," he looks at me, something pitying behind his irises.

"Do you want me to kill Darius? I'm pretty sure that Solustus would be pissed," he shrugs but leans forward, stowing the lit cigarette behind his ear.

"Fine, I'll handle it," he gets up, kicking an empty tequila bottle against the wall so hard it smashes. The drink clearly hasn't lulled his violent side.

"Darius old friend!" He bursts through the glass doors, placing the cigarette in the side of his mouth.

"Yes, Vex? What is it? Out of lager?" He paraphrases the British word for beer, I know he's making fun of Vex.

"Nah, mate. I just wanted to say I think we should go, it'll be sunrise in a few hours and the calibre of women here... well, I mean look at 'em," he turns to Chloe, "Go put some clothes on, Love. You look like a street walker." He gestures to her and she storms out, looking embarrassed and frightened at his forwardness.

I look at Vex, his muscles straining against the thin cotton of his black shirt, which is speckled with salt. He takes another puff on his cigarette, moving to address Mollie.

"As for you, you don't want to get into it with this guy. I mean, look at Callie... that's what happens if you get involved with a guy who just wants to get you under him. Has he even taken you on a date?"

"No..." She mumbles fidgeting.

"Well then, what do you think he's here for? Cookies?" He raises his eyebrows and I want to roll on the floor laughing. Brutal honesty has never been so funny.

Mollie rises and moves away, one step, then another until she's out of Daryl's reach. I relax as I hear her footsteps following Chloe's out of the front door. I hear it slam and exhale heavily. Daryl doesn't move to go after

166

her, fully aware that if he tries anything me and Vex will have him on the floor with a smashed up face in seconds. I stand over him as he stays sat on the chair and he looks up at me.

"You're a real bitch you know that?" He spits at me. With those words Vex shifts, moving and slamming his fist into Daryl's nose. He is knocked back onto the floor, laying splayed out and bleeding on top of the chair which aided his fall.

"Hey. Nobody calls her a bitch but me."

Together, we walk from the almost totally empty house, Vex's arm slung around me, not because I'm his, but because it's comfortable. We clamber onto the bike in silence, unified in fury. I wrap my arms around Vex as we leave Daryl and Tiberius behind, making our way into the dark, alone.

The night hadn't been whatever I was expecting, and after everything was said and done I still haven't managed to go pee.

14
Free

CALLIE

For lack of a better place to go, Vex pulls the bike up to the edge of the sand, facing the beach from where we came. My stomach is churning and my head is clearing from the air of the night, which has been running through my hair on our journey here. We dismount in silence, shocked slightly at our unity in front of Daryl and Tiberius. Since when had Vex done anything that didn't directly benefit him?

"Why did you save my friend?" I ask him timidly. He sits down in the sand, lighting up another cigarette and taking a few puffs. I sit down next to him, stripping off my shoes, which are starting to pinch because they belonged to a dead woman. They aren't mine.

"Couldn't have you whining at me," he sighs out and I narrow my eyes. He seems irritable.

"Why do you think it is okay to kill people?" I ask him and he looks at me, surprised.

"Have you seen me kill anyone?"

"You're part of an army built specifically to kill the mer, what do you expect that means Vex? That you're going to send them cookies?" I snap, pulling on his metaphor from earlier.

"That's different," he looks out to sea, at the darkness of the horizon.

"Why is it different?"

"Because it's justified," he looks at me and blows smoke in my face.

"How? How is it justified?" I am desperately curious as to his answer. I hadn't ever considered the Psirens as people, with motivation behind their actions, I had always just assumed they were soulless killers.

"The mer, you don't deserve to live the way you do. All the luxuries and jewels, Love. I mean you cry diamonds for God's sake. It isn't right. Especially not while we're stuck in the darkness. Why should you get to be on top, because some Goddess says so? We belong in that city, we're stronger. The world would stand a better chance with us as protectors," he looks me directly in the eye, his lilac irises burn with passion for the cause he's been fed.

"Who told you this?" I ask him and he inhales more smoke.

"Mother," the single word I had been expecting passes between us. They have power, more than the mer know and it is because the Psiren children she had created believed they were the rightful occupants of the Occulta Mirum. I puff out air.

"Would you believe me if I told you that's not true?" I ask him and he shakes his head.

"After what you've told me about bloody Onion head I'm more sure it's true than ever." I nod. He's never going to believe he's been fed a load of lies.

"The mer aren't bad people. They dedicate their whole existence to saving this earth. If you think Solustus will have you do the same. He won't," I say absent minded, pushing my feet out against the sand.

"Of course you're going to say that, Love, you were one of them. I saw you at that coronation, it didn't look like you were defending much of anything, except the jobs of seamstresses everywhere," he laughs and I smile at him.

"You're not seeing the whole picture here, Vex. I've seen Orion and his father take down demons, defend humans. They're not bad people." I think back to the first time I'd ever seen a demon and Orion and Atlas moving in streams of bubbles and disabling the beast. They had been incredible.

"They kill Psirens. You aren't telling me people like that are good?"

"What if Psirens are the threat to humans?"

"We don't do anything to humans that's bloody awful, Pet. We hurt them, but only for a moment. Then they're free... for eternity." I think for a moment, observing the level of indoctrination in the mind of the Psiren sitting next to me for the first time.

"I'm sorry this happened to you," I make the statement unwillingly, the words falling out of my mouth like vomit.

"Don't be. When I died. It was bloody beautiful."

"It...was?" I ask him and he nods.

"She was there, in the middle of a crowd of people at a party on this beach. She was encased in scarlet silk, real clingy. I saw her and that was it. I couldn't have pulled away if I'd wanted to, and I didn't want to. She sang to me, she took me in her arms and it was like I belonged you know? She bit into me... and I was home." I hear his story. It doesn't sound awful. He offers me a puff on his cigarette and I shake my head.

"Sounds a lot nicer than when I died," I admit and he laughs.

"When you were in that ritual?"

"Well... both times I suppose. Being The vessel hasn't been easy," I remember my life slipping from me, the freedom I had felt after it was gone.

"The vessel, what's that, Love?"

"I can absorb the powers of other mer," I explain to him and he frowns slightly.

"You are powerful. I was right," he looks away from me again and continues to smoke. The silence envelops us for a few moments until a disturbance of the shimmering surface of the water breaks the dreamy pause.

It's small, barely a speck in the macrocosm of the surface's sparkle, but I know that it's the face of someone I haven't seen in a while. Someone whose face I've been trying to forget. I freeze, my blood coursing through me like an icy river, rushing at uncontrollable speed.

"What?" Vex senses my unease and follows my gaze, which is glued to the dark break in the moon's half reflection. I feel a breeze at my back. I know it's him calling to me. He doesn't need the air to summon me though. My adrenaline level spikes, icy blood at the mere thought of him is enough, and I hate him for it.

"It's him. He's here," I whisper, feeling my heart pound at the thought of another heavyweight fight. I swallow momentarily as Vex snorts.

"Onion head?" He throws his cigarette butt into the sand. I follow it's trail as it smoulders to black.

"Yeah," I turn back to the ocean and see that the speck of black is gone. I guess he's waiting for me underneath. I get to my feet reluctantly.

"What are you doing?" I look back at Vex as his eyebrow stands at its usual angle, cocked.

"I'm going in there."

"Why?"

"Because if I don't, he won't leave."

"Why? Why do you care?" Vex asks me and I stop in the middle of pulling off my leather pants.

"I..." I start but I can't answer the question. Why do I care? Orion turned his back on me because he couldn't force me into an expectation carved over hundreds of years. He's just the kind of man you can't change. He's too old, too set in his ways. I don't owe him anything. My black hair falls forward and I relish the shadow it casts on my face. I'm not the same girl I had been the last time he had seen me. I'm not his girl anymore.

But wouldn't it be nice to make sure he knew it.

The whisper is back, small and in the back of my subconscious. Not so foreign now, melded in with my own wants and desires, I listen to it.

"I've got something I need to say. I need to set the record straight. I need him to see I'm playing for the other side, let him see my power." Vex's face is surprised, more surprised than I've ever seen him in fact. I smile to myself slightly, I enjoy being the opposite of what he expects.

"Alright, Love, but I'm coming with. Don't want you getting kidnapped now do we?" He begins to get undressed alongside me, the wind whipping around our chilled bodies. I feel myself shake slightly at the thought of seeing Orion, but it's not nerves. It's determination, fuelled by my rage.

The warm water sloshes over my limbs as I descend, letting my tail return, scales running upward from my toes and binding my legs together in an onyx scaled seal. The aquamarine is long gone, no traces left, the darkness having leeched into my physical self, as well as my mind. I move into the dim navy of the water, seeing the icy blue of the eyes I can't get out of my head.

"Callie..." I hear my name from Orion, he sounds like someone has winded him, kicked him in the chest and taken his breath away, but behind that breathlessness anger stirs. I can tell this isn't going to be pleasant, and momentarily wonder if I should have bothered coming to speak with him at all.

"Yes," I snap out.

"You look.... Awful," he rubs the back of his neck as his form comes into view. My Psiren sight allows me to see through the dark of the water and my tail stirs. The water at this depth is nothing, easier to swim through than air.

"Gee thanks, so nice of you to say so." I feel the water at my back stir and I know Vex is moving in behind me.

"What is that... *thing* doing here. Did he hurt you?" Orion's chest is puffing out, trying to assert dominance, ownership over something he discarded.

"No. I want him here. He's my friend," I say the words and I feel Vex's eyes on my face as he moves in beside me. Orion's expression contorts, his statuesque beauty taking on a hardness that makes him look stunningly cruel.

"Your friend? It isn't your *friend,* Callie. It has tentacles. It's just a cold, dead *thing,*" he looks disgusted.

"Hey, mate! I'm right here you know." I hear Vex complain and I feel a smug smile crawl over my face.

"He's my friend, Orion," I repeat the statement and Orion's eyes bulge even further. I almost want him to keep acting like a jackass, it makes him easier to hate, it makes it easier to remind myself of why we can't, nor should, be together.

"Callie, listen to me," Orion comes forward through the water in one jerk movement, it stems in continuous undulation from the tip of his fin to his waist. I let myself hang in the darkness, looking into his face, into what lies behind the disgust at the darkness within me, the normal underlay of worry and fear is still there. "This isn't *you,* Callie. Titus, when you died, when he died, something happened. His soul latched on to you, or you absorbed it... or something," his words surprise me, not the apology nor the condemnation I had been prepared for. But an answer. An answer to the voice in my head.

I go to exclaim in reply but Vex pipes up as I inhale.

"Don't give her that, you just can't stand a woman who has more power than you. This is her decision. She chose to stop bending over for you. You just can't take it," he snarls the words and I wonder what is motivating his rage towards Orion.

"Pfft. What would you know about her?" Orion snorts.

"More than you, Nancy boy." Vex moves forward, his tentacles curling and recoiling.

"Look, stop!" I call out and both of the seething men turn to look at me. Orion looks somewhat ashamed and I square up to him. "You need to leave." I feel the sentiment roll out of my mouth, like a wave. It drenches Orion in the chill of my rejection and I watch him sigh.

"You're choosing him?" He looks at Vex and I shake my head.

"No. I'm choosing me." I look at him and he shuts both his palms into fists.

"You can't just end this, Callie. We're destined. We're supposed to be together," he spits out the sentiment and I feel Vex snigger behind me. I turn to him.

"Vex... can you just give us a minute. I'll be back with you in a second."

"Sure thing, Love. You just let me know if you need any.... assistance." I feel his eyes travel over my shoulder to Orion and he smirks. God I hate men. Why is everything some kind of penile measuring competition? I stare at him, letting him know I won't stand for anymore fighting. I need to deal with Orion in my own way. I need to let him know this is who I am now, and that he can't just come and find me when he feels like it and screw up my night. I move back to him, folding my arms.

"Look. You can't just do this."

"Do what?" Orion throws a faux innocent shrug at me.

"You can't just show up here. I'm not your concern anymore," I bite out the words and Orion's brow creases.

"You'll always be my concern, Callie... What I said... about you leaving and not coming back... I was angry. I didn't mean it," he puffs out air, blowing bubbles and looking uncomfortable.

"You think this is about that? Really?" I look at him exasperated. He seems so smart and yet he's totally obtuse as to what's going on.

"What's that supposed to mean?"

"It means I'm going to lay this out for you, one last time." I run my fingers through my stiff mermaid locks, frustrated at his determined single mindedness. "I've had a lot of time to think, so I'm going to tell you my thoughts. I don't want an argument. I don't want some bullshit show of masculine strength. I want you to listen. Then I'm going back to Vex. This isn't a window to get me to go anywhere with you. This isn't me bending to what you want. I just think I owe you an explanation. You don't seem to be able to see why I'm angry, or why I need to move on. So I'm just going to lay it out for you. No holding back or lying. Okay?" I exhale after my miniature rant and Orion looks like he's between exploding in anger or crying. I can't tell which anymore.

"Okay." The word comes from him, like a white flag, a show of defeat.

"Okay... Ever since we got together, a lot of stuff has happened. I get that it's not been easy for you either and I know that I lied to you about the prophecy. I know that. The reason I didn't tell you, is because you waited hundreds of years for me. That's a hundred years of moulding me into what you wanted me to be in your head. You wanted me to be like every other mermaid in the Occulta Mirum." Orion looks at me intensely and I almost melt into his eyes. Almost, but not quite. "But I'm not. I'm not a Princess or a Queen. I'm not a leader. I'm not a wife either. I'm just Callie. I don't do what I'm told. I know this world is dangerous, but I don't want to be sheltered. I have immortal life. So why shouldn't I live it? I feel like you had this amazing idea of who you wanted me to be, this perfect dream of your soulmate. But that's a dream, Orion. I can never be that girl. I am flawed and despite looking far from it, I am human. I have darkness in me, especially now if what you say about Titus is true," I take a breath and Orion's eyes are wide.

"I see," he whispers.

"The thing is, I do love you. If you'd have just given it some time. Waited for me to get comfortable and settled, let us work on the things that needed work, marriage wouldn't have been such a big step for me. But you couldn't wait. It was just your way of pushing me into this mould you'd created. That's not the way I want to be married, or loved," I say this and I think he finally understands. His eyes are glazed and his form is still, frozen under the power of my harsh words.

"And the boy?" He gestures to where Vex has retreated to.

"Vex is my friend. He doesn't expect anything of me and he trusts in me enough to know that I can look after myself. I'm happier when he's around right now," I say the last word and Orion looks like he might start becoming the source of Tiffany's next season collection. I want to comfort him. Apologise. I know I've done wrong too. This isn't all his fault.

Still a tiny and now recognisably Psiren voice is whispering in my head, *you've just got to be selfish, this isn't about him. It's about you. You deserve to be powerful, be unstoppable, it's what you were made for.*

I shake my head slightly, the black ribbons of my hair flowing outward in the shallow waters of the shoreline.

"I had better go, and please Orion. Don't come after me again. I'm a big girl. If I get into any trouble, I know it's my problem. I'll fix it," I breathe out and his eyes harden into two icy shards.

"I know. I get now that you don't need anyone," he looks at me with scorching condemnation. "I'm done waiting." He turns and disappears into the dark blue of the night's seething waters.

His last words sting me, I can't deny it. But instead of allowing them to swallow me and consume me, bring hardening tears to my eyes, I turn and head back to Vex.

ORION

It's over. I'd known she was unhappy, I'd known she was angry, but it is clear to me now that I am not good for her and that she is long gone to the darkness. Even if I was good for her, she doesn't want me anymore. But *him?* That monster; the brit with the bad hair and the tentacles? I shudder at the thought of his hands on her, moving across her skin, making her giggle and squeal, sweeping down trails mine had once traced. My heart convulses in a palpitation that feels like rain water hitting the surface of the ocean, or the lead pellets of a shotgun... right to where she used to reside. It's like a light has been extinguished. What have I done to deserve this?

True, maybe I had pushed her, tried to make her into something I'd dreamed of every night for years, but now... she won't even try to make it work. She had walked away, as usual. After everything that I'd done to try and make her happy, she still turned her back on me. Maybe it isn't that I'm not good for her. Maybe it's that she isn't good for me. The Crowned Ruler of the Occulta Mirum, running after a girl who doesn't want him. I think not.

I feel a shudder run through me. Have I really become this sick puppy? Getting kicked to the curb, not fighting back but whimpering and limping with one paw held up for sympathy? I used to be a great warrior... and now? My fist clenches as I begin my journey back to the Cole and the other Knights who are waiting for me, watching, just in case. Saturnus was right. Now is not the time for weakness and begging a woman to want me. Now is the time for action, for strength and for setting an example to the most important relationship in my life, that which I hold with my father's legacy, with the people that need me. Callie has made it perfectly clear that she doesn't need anyone. Titus' darkness had infected her that was for sure.

She had always been headstrong, longing for independence, but she'd never seemed power hungry before. The black hair and maps of dark magic that trace across her skin now, only prove to me the rivers of magic that run deep through her had been poisoned and that dark power is clearly more enthralling than I could ever be.

I sigh to myself, running my hand through my hair. I look down to the sand, sweeping along the ocean floor and miss my father so deeply I can barely breathe. I know one thing for sure, I am done fighting to keep her. I still want her. I will always want her. But I am suddenly overcome with the reminder that you can't make someone love you, just like you can't force someone who loves you to want to be with you. One thing is for sure though. I meant what I had said, and as I make my way back to my responsibilities, I know that I am finally, after all this time, done waiting.

CALLIE

I am free, finally. After everything I've been through, struggling and squirming to get free from Orion's possessive overprotectiveness. I am free. I am still in the darkness of the water, hanging there, limp and defeated. This is what I wanted. Isn't it?

Of course, dear. You are free now. Free to grow into the powerful killer you were born to be.

The voice echoes off each wall of my skull. *Wait... Killer?* My head snaps up and my eyes fall wide. Is that what this is? Was it Titus all along, making me into something dark, hard, and unfeeling? Is this all my fault? Had I just lost the only man who would ever make me feel so coveted... so loved? I look back over my shoulder as I begin to leave the ocean once more. I can't stand to be in it. I don't want to see its shimmer, its beauty. It makes me sick.

My head breaks the surface of the foam that has formed like a slime on top of the water and Vex is almost fully dressed, waiting for me, propped against the bike at the edge of the sand as he pulls his leather jacket over his muscular shoulders. I focus on cleaving myself from my curse, from the water, from Atargatis and I feel my scales shimmer out of existence once more. My feet pad across the sand in a light jog. My calves burn, an unpleasant side effect from the longevity of being in tailed form, and I feel the wind whip around my body, causing errant droplets of water to slither down my skin. Vex watches me, his eyes falling over my naked body and I instantly warm to him a little more. Orion isn't the only one who will ever love me. Vex wants me. He'd never admit it, but I know he does.

In that moment, as I watch him, pulling on my pants and wrapping the corset around me, an urge inside me surfaces, like a panther crawling into view through tall grass. I slick my wet hair back from my neck, running my fingers through it and throwing the long tresses over my left shoulder. I bend to put on my shoes, and look up through my black lashes to watch him, eyes rolling over me like wicked surf, salacious and wild.

I momentarily wonder what the hell I'm doing. He's a Psiren for Goddess' sake, but then I remember that he believes in me, more than anyone ever has. Certainly more than Orion ever would.

I stand, fully dressed and pace forward, running my hand through my hair again, nervous.

"So, Love, did you break the Nancy Boy's heart into hundreds of sparkly pieces? Did he cry? Ooh I bet he cried!" His lilac irises dance with enthusiasm, the kind he only feels for violence and pain.

"No, he didn't cry. He left. It's over. I'm free."

"Good riddance, Love. You don't need him. You're not a pet. You're a predator," his words sting me slightly, I don't know why.

"I'm not a killer, Vex," I whisper.

"Could have fooled me. This lone wolf act you've got going on isn't exactly the act of a saint, now is it?"

"I'm not a killer!" I yell in his face. His eyelids shut, hooding the light of his irises. He looks irritable.

"Why does it matter to you? You afraid the big bad wolf has been let out and you won't get it back into its cage? You have power, girl, whether you want it or not. Killing is just the next step up the ladder in using that power. Someone has more power than you, you want it, you take it."

"Oh and I suppose that's just life is it? No other choice, just going around killing people for what they have. God, you Psirens, you're so arrogant. You don't have the right to just decide whether people live or die, Vex!"

"Look, Love, you can act as innocent as you like, but it isn't life, it's evolution. You think you can escape those little voices in your head, the urges screaming around inside you for blood? You. Were. Built. To. Be. On. Top." His words penetrate me, a staccato of a statement which I don't know whether is true or false. He assaults my consciousness and leaves me bereft. I need to be held by strong arms and kissed by lips that could make me forget. I look up at him.

"Take me somewhere."

"Somewhere?" The air between us becomes charged as he bends his head, our noses are almost touching.

"Somewhere with….Tequila." I utter the word, cautious yet hungry.

"I think you've had enough of the hard stuff for now," he whispers, placing his thumbs in the tight pockets of his pants, as though he's bracing himself.

"The hard stuff is exactly what I'm looking for," I sweep my irises over him from bottom to top, letting his form fill my head, pushing out the images of Orion's broken expression. He smiles slightly.

"Oh… you want to go somewhere with *tequila…*" His eyes blaze.

"Yes, Vex. Take me. Now," I whisper the words and suddenly realise that I'm acting more forward than I ever have, even with Orion. It's like I'm on autopilot, not giving a damn and watching my body from the outside, performing the eloquent and seductive dance of a stranger, not me. I let the darkness take over. I feel my pupils dilate, turning black and empty, needing to be filled by someone's wanton grasp.

"Hop on." Vex turns to the bike, straddling it suggestively. I hop on the back, not bothering to look back at the ocean which had contained me, made me bend to Orion and rise to a place I had never belonged. I place my hands around Vex's waist and ride off with him into the night, accepting all the new parts of myself, like jagged puzzle pieces that grate, but are slowly falling into place. They complete an unexpected and fragmented image, hungry, wanton, dark, but also… free.

15
Smash

CALLIE

The fluorescent light of the seedy motel parking lot where Vex has parked burns my eyes. After so many weeks of being in the deep, and the months of only being a part of the surface world during the hours when the moon illuminates the sky, my retinas just can't take it. It sheds a stark and unpleasant light on the concrete covered space, showing discarded soda cans and cigarette butts that daunt me a little. Do I really want to do this?

It's what you want, so take it. Take him.

The hissing tones of the dark whisper to me, filling me with a primal confidence, a reliance on my senses rather than my ability to reason that is intoxicating. Vex dismounts the motorcycle and stands, his skin so pale it's practically translucent under the neon blatancy.

"I'm guessing we don't have a reservation," I mumble, suddenly nervous.

"Hey. Look at me." Vex pulls my chin up. "When you're a Psiren, you don't need invitations, or reservations. It's simple, Love." He walks over to the door of the room right at the end of the block. Pressing his ear to the wood for a few moments before continuing.

"See," he braces himself against the frame of the door. "Want," he steps back from the wooden barrier, preventing him from reaching the location he desires. "Take," he makes a grunt and forces himself against the door, pushing the weak lock past its breaking point. The door relinquishes, cracking open with a splintering sound and a jerk. The old me would be horrified about breaking and entering. The mer have everything together, they operate on a massive scale, always within the law and with a grandeur that never failed to impress.

The Psirens, unsurprisingly, don't have the same luxury, and so resort to petty crime and seedy motel rooms. I'm beginning to see why they so envy the mer. I wouldn't say no to a room at Lunar Sanctum right now.

He doesn't hold the door open for me, as would a gentleman, but lets it swing back in my face. I catch it with my palm, the peeling paint flaking away like dead skin onto the floor, before pushing it open and entering. The motel room is... well... what you'd expect for a motel room.

A simple metal bed frame is donned with black sheets, no doubt a giant mistake for an establishment that probably doesn't even wash their bed linen. The carpet is tortoiseshell, and the walls are a dirty looking green. There's an adjoining room with a double sink and a long mirror on the wall leading to the bathroom, two bedside tables and a desk with an old television to one side, it's aerial is twisted like a pretzel and I doubt it even works. The whole room sucks light into its corners and returns only shadow, no doubt a preference when one does whatever deeds are common for a motel in the middle of nowhere. This is the kind of place you come when you don't want to be seen or judged and where moral caution is thrown to the wind. There is no better place for what I want.

Vex throws his leather jacket onto the chair and then pulls his black t-shirt over his head. He doesn't have Orion's body, but it's still muscular. His black leather pants and belt remain where they are, thank goodness.

I'm doing this my way.

He walks over to me, passes me as I stand, a tall awkward reed in the middle of the room, shivering slightly. Pushing the door shut and propping a cheap metal chair under the handle, he turns.

"Don't want you escaping now do we..." He smiles salaciously, like he's been waiting for this ever since the day we met.

"I think you're forgetting that I asked for this," I remind him and he walks over to me, his boot tread lost in the distasteful carpet, grabbing me at the elbow and causing a vein to protrude across his left bicep.

"Yes... I just can't figure out why. I can't work out if it's because you're

trying to forget Nancy boy, or if you you're trying to forget what you are…"
He looks deeply into my eyes, his lilac irises too pale in the dim light, and his flawless stubble free jawline so smooth it could be ceramic.

"What I am?" I cock an eyebrow trying to seem uninterested.

"Dark. Untameable. Take your pick, Love. You had the perfect guy, and you couldn't let him love you. What do you think that says about you? You're dark inside… and you always will be," he spits out the word, his lip curling in disgust. I wrench my arms from his grasp and shove him in the chest. He stumbles backward, though his expression is unimpressed.

"Shut up!" I cry out taking a step toward him.

"Truth hurts, doesn't it, Pet?" He licks his bottom lip, abs flexing into six overly defined segments. He takes another step back, meeting the desk. I watch him and my mind races. I talk about Orion not listening, but maybe that's what I'm doing.

"Maybe," I relinquish slightly and he smiles.

"That's right, Love, you know it's true. You know you're rotten all the way through…" His words sting me, causing a torrent of raw emotion to come hurtling through me.

"You're no better!" I yell, angry once more.

"Oh I know, Love, and that's what terrifies you. It terrifies you that I, a cold, dead *thing,* might be the only one who can ever understand you. Not your soulmate, but *me*," he smiles slightly, but there's also some truth in what he's said, I can tell because his eyes are starting to remind me of the lilac flames, next to which Orion had made love to me for the last time.

"I hate you!" I scream at him, my blood rushing in my ears. The violence within me is rising, cresting, and readying itself to destroy everything in its path. The thing is though; I'm in human form. I have no power here.

Except… over him. I take a step forward and look into his eyes deeply. I run my fingers hard into the flesh of his arms, pushing him and causing his spine to bow against the edge of the desk. I clutch, digging my hard nails into his muscles. He exhales slightly, a tiny escape of the pleasure and pain that are melding into something confusing and forbidden.

"You can hate me," he cups my cheek, pushing my hair back and gripping the back of my skull like he might crush it.

"I can?" I look at him and he smiles.

"Yes. It's who we are." I feel a relief I hadn't known I had been looking for. He needs the violence, the pain, and now so do I. It's the only thing that makes everything real.

Orion had me in a fantasy, which could, and had, all come crashing down in a moment. Vex... he has me embracing the reality of life... death, violence, loss... it's all real with him. There isn't any hiding from the brutality of protecting humankind, of the job I've been tasked with. With Vex, clarity comes with staggering and uninterrupted momentum, knocking me down again and again until I have no choice but to stand through it. I pull Vex to me and he lets me have the control I need, I run my hand down the back of his neck, his skin is cold and he shudders as my nails graze him over and over.

"No kissing," he reminds me and I nod. I don't need it with him, it doesn't mean anything. I move my face into the crook of his neck where the smell of tequila and cigarettes diffuses and settles over me. I find myself brushing my fingertips down his back and then forward to the front of his pants. I rest my hand over his fly and look up at him.

"Yes, Love?" He asks me with a smirk. I can tell he's ecstatic in more ways than one.

"Will you show me..." I begin but feel nervous. He presses his crotch into the palm of my hand.

"What?" He pulls my hair, bringing my eyes up to meet his gaze.

"Teach me how to... be dominant," I ask him, gulping in air.

"Let me guess... You've never initiated before?" He looks at me with narrowing eyes and I shake my head. I wonder if at this he'll turn and run but instead he smiles, pushing his body flush against me.

"You know that darkness you feel... that darkness you're so afraid of?"

Oh... Yes. I nod.

"Just give in. Don't think. Just... do what feels right. Follow your natural instincts. No more talking," he puts a finger to his lips, silencing me. I close my eyes and feel my pupils dilate, the blackness overtaking everything. I shove him back into the wall and he grunts appreciatively, knocking the only piece of art in the room from the wall with a smash. The glass lies at my feet, shattered and jagged, but I ignore it. I feel my hands working the buckle on his jeans and I watch as his eyes widen in shock, and delight. I quickly remove and throw my jacket on top of his, holding his hips to the wall, eager, as his pants now lie around his ankles. I let my icy blue memories dissipate and get lost in the lilac ones staring at me with hungry anticipation, condemning myself to forget. I let the shadows consume me with a devouring, sharp, grating, and unquenchable desire for power.

The last thing I remember is licking my lips and dropping leisurely to my knees.

SOLUSTUS

He is late. I don't like answering to anyone, but particularly not someone who thinks my time unimportant. I have a Kingdom to run after all, it may not be as grand as what he's used to, but it makes my blood boil thinking that he's making me wait. Then again, he's the eldest, and that means he has a superiority complex rivalling that of Poseidon himself.

I float, innocuous before the looking glass; one half of a gift once passed from Atargatis, down to the people of the Occulta Mirum, and thanks to the thoughtlessness of Azure, now mine. It isn't really a looking glass at all, because it simply seizes the purpose of reflecting what you are back at you. Instead, it allows you to see how the other half lives, in part, showing you precisely what you are not. It had been used by Azure for months, allowing her to communicate in short, hurried bursts with Starlet. She had thought nobody knew, but I did. I let her carry out her torrid little affair with her sister, all in the name of getting Titus out of the way and gaining use of the mirror.

The looking glass is flawless, a miracle seeing how I have smashed it so many times, angry at my brother, at his obsession with beating the mer from the inside. In waiting for the opportune moment. I am patient, I always have been, but he seems obsessed with waiting for a single moment in particular, in fact, I'm not even sure if his cunning wit quite knows what it will look like, even when it does pass.

However, the looking glass is a gift from the Goddess and after each opportunely timed rendezvous with my older sibling, I feel the quite untamed urge to break it into a thousand pieces. I know the reason why I'm not taking control for myself. I know I need him, but it doesn't make me want to rip his throat out any less. I wonder if that makes me like our father, I mean, after all, he did shove a bottle into his eldest son's throat. Maybe it was because he wouldn't cease voicing his obsession over being the ultimate object of a higher being's affection. That's enough to make anyone turn violent, particularly someone with my pleasant disposition.

I exhale, tightening every muscle in my body simultaneously at seeing the looking glass turn foggy. He's finally decided to turn up. Well, aren't I special?

"Saturnus," I say the single word as his bloody tangle of hair and limpet green eyes come into view. He replies in a brisk and slightly bored tone.

"Hello, brother."

"I have news," Saturnus smiles, his teeth too white. The glimmer appearance he has going on never fails to make me smile. The epitome of a Goddess's love, and also a complete lie.

"I assumed," I cock an eyebrow and his smile drops into one twisted, one real. We set this meeting date every month and he always has some wisdom, some piece of knowledge that makes him superior to share.

"I think I have an answer to your communication problem with the Beast," he smiles and I feel my ears prick; I am, against my better judgement, intrigued.

"Yes?" I snap slightly and my brother smiles.

"The girl," his teeth are exposed again, too white and almost snarling with the glee of his latest discovery.

"What of her? She's merely a child," I snort, crossing my arms.

"You need not remind me. Need I remind you of to whom you speak?" At this sentiment, of his questioning of my power, of my diligence to our end goal, I find myself trying to supress a giggle of untamed hilarity.

Saturnus, my brother, would be nothing if it were not for me. It had been my teeth at his throat, my blood running in his veins that's made him what he is. I recall after I had thrown myself to the frothing, dog-like mouth of the ocean from the cliffs of the island on which I had grown, my first thought: family. I had sought out him and Caedes as soon as I was able, as soon as I could make sense of my new body. I had taken them into the arms of Poseidon, I had helped them ascend, evolve.

He may have forgotten that, but I never would.

I sigh slightly, itching my chin with a long, dirtied fingernail.

"So... the girl?" I prompt his frustrated expression and he once again becomes impassioned, loving the sound of his own voice just a little too much.

"She has the ability to absorb magic..."

"Yes... we already know this," I bite at him and he brings a fist up and moves to punch through the glass. His flesh makes a thud, impacting and causing spider-legged fractures to spread out from the epicentre of his palm. His eyes blaze yellow, his trueness seeping through the glimmer he works so hard to preserve. The fractures disappear in a moment, repairing themselves with threads of ancient, holy magic.

"If you don't shut up I'm going to terminate this conversation, Solustus. I won't stand for insolence. Least of all from you, little brother."

"Fine... fine... proceed."

"Thank you so much for your permission," he retorts, droll in both expression and tone. His gold tail sways from side to side, controlled in movement as my own. My hand brushes against Scarlette, his eyes follow my movement, clearly aware of the culling of violent tendencies. He says nothing.

"An old friend, seems to have found a way to cling onto life in this world," Saturnus smiles slightly and I feel my eyes widen.

"Titus?" I ask him, hopefulness only too evident in my voice.

"Who else? That bastard just won't die," Saturnus laughs slightly, finding himself hilarious at lack of a better audience.

"So you're saying that's why the girl... that's why she looks like one of us?" I ask him and he nods, smiling.

"The body of a mer, with the dark power of a Psiren. Lethal, I think you'd agree." His eyes sparkle with the untold possibilities of such a creature.

"Certainly. You think she can communicate with it?" I query, stroking my chin with long fingers.

"I'd say there's only one way to find out."

"She had the power to manipulate electricity for certain. I felt it when she…" I pause, not wanting to admit she had bested me in combat.

"No need for shame brother. The bitch has also used those powers on me. No one person so young should yield so much power," he admits, shaking his head angrily. His bloody hair moves silently.

"The Goddess… what is she playing at giving such power…" I ponder and Saturnus' expression turns grim. "You don't think…" I begin, wondering.

"That the Goddess has finally taken notice of what us mere servants are attempting? It's possible." He looks ecstatic at this thought. It wasn't hard to realise why Saturnus wanted the power of the Necrimad for himself, it was polar opposite to my reasons; chiefly killing mankind's hold over the land and making them serve the seas for once had always been my intent, I had been born to rise, to right the injustice against those of us trapped in servitude for eternity.

Saturnus on the other hand… wanted to be loved. Our father had torn him from the only woman who had ever loved him, and then that bitch Goddess had put him in second place to the Crowned Ruler. Besotted and hell-bent on making her and any other higher power see his true magnificence; it's become an obsession, and one that's only worsened with the Crowning of that fool, Atlas' son.

"So you want me to give her a little time in the vents. See what happens?"

"Yes, brother. We need answers. I want that seal unlocked, serving under *him*… that crowned fool, I'm about this close to ripping throat out," Saturnus looks grim. He's brave, at least I don't have to act. He's the Occulta Mirum's greatest kept secret, a Psiren, *the* Psiren right in their midst. He plays his role as though it were true. I certainly wouldn't have the patience.

"Speaking of the seal, have you noticed any changes?" I ask him this question in a quick, clipped tone, it's something I always ask and it repetitively sparks his rage.

"I've been sat on top of this damn thing ever since Regus erected the Alcazar Oceania around it over three hundred years ago. Trust me, Solustus, if there had been a change, I'd have already told you about it. Why don't you do yourself a favour and desist on asking every *single* time we have these meetings? Incompetence is not my forte," he narrows his eyes, so damn volatile, it's a wonder he *hasn't* killed Orion yet.

"Apologies, I was just being diligent," I bow my head, a sign of respect.

"Apology accepted. To be honest, I'm grateful nothing has shifted. The second the seal starts becoming active, my role in all this will become clear. I need the information from the Beast before we can move into the next phase." I nod at him, twisting my mouth slightly.

I relish the thought of the next phase, when we will shed the blood of the mer and take the city that is rightfully ours. After all, it is built upon the resting place of The Necrimad, Poseidon's most powerful child. Made from all the darkness he didn't think I could handle. I shudder, trying not to remember the day his angered expression had come to the forefront of my psyche, screaming at me to desist in the murder. He drained some of my power, giving me my mind, my consciousness back. I hate him for that. These thoughts move through my head at an accelerated speed, my intelligence surpassing that of a mere mortal.

"Where is the girl?" Saturnus asks, suddenly curious.

"Out with Vexus. He's helping her find her inner demons."

"I wonder if she'll ever be controllable. She is a loose cannon. The imbecile cannot rule, it's a joke. He's running after her like a schoolboy. It's a shame she doesn't realise just how much power she has," Saturnus muses, a sharp prick of anxiety seeds in my heart, the kind only the judgement of a brother can plant.

"Let's hope it stays that way," I mutter, wondering now if it is such a wise move to acquaint her with her inherited Psiren darkness after all.

"I have to go brother. There's another demon approaching the city limits and The Knights are asking for my assistance. I must leave," he looks over his shoulder, clearly distracted by something.

"Very well. I'll contact you again if the girl manages to yield answers," I nod at him, reassuring him of my future success. He vanishes as a grey mist falls over his end of the looking glass. I turn away from the mirror's reflective silver with a smile. I will have answers.

CALLIE

Pain, followed by pleasure, melding into a torrent of dark eyes, fingertips, and jagged, grazing teeth. A fight between two equally matched, hungry animals, clawing, biting, and scrapping for everything they can get. Vex is like a toy, a man-sized, sexually errant toy with the stamina of a prized black stallion. My fingertips spark electricity, coursing through the alabaster taught of his skin. He moans, hands behind his head...

"You are... wild," he pants, his compliment washing over me like warm water, this is the fifth time he's passed these words in a matter of hours. I feel the power of his appreciation flow through me, out of my fingertips and into his neurons, causing him to climb to the height of ecstasy against any remaining will of his own.

We had already destroyed the desk, wallpaper had been torn and scrunched in sweating, desperate palms, and the television had been smashed in the ferocious haze of seizing forbidden fruit. My pupils are fully dilated, light pouring in from the surrounding shadow and my lips throb, plumped and raw. I realise now that Titus *is* with me. I have his magic, his ability to manipulate electricity. I know now how he became so dark, because in watching Vex beneath my hands, it's easy to picture myself making him bend to my whim, causing him pain, making him submit. I don't love Vex, I just want him like a starving man wants meat, raw and succulent to taste. It's easier that way. Easier than it had been with Orion. So maybe the whole soulmate thing had been a load of bull.

Everything I had been afraid of, the darkness, the power, his touch, belongs to me now. He had given it to me along with the confidence to take control over another person, over my life, in a world where Gods and

Goddesses seem to have the only power over the drift and tug of life and its final destination. The power isn't like I had thought, it's better, a drug stronger than any venom coursing through me, making me invincible.

Maybe that makes me evil, maybe evil is just subjective; a word thought up by people who don't have power and need to justify being so weak. Regardless, the power was an immovable part of me now.

It's *mine.*

16

Bonds

AZURE

The back of my skull is still tender from where my brother thrust me backward into the wall outside the small council chambers. The look on his face, the anger there, pissed me off... and I can't for the life of me work out why.

I had been going over it in my mind for days... and I am done. I'm headed for the outskirts of the city, and this time I'm not coming back. I'm so tired of this crap, no wonder his soulmate had up and left him. He deserved it.

I bite my lip, feeling my heart palpitate slightly.

No. He didn't. A tiny whisper, a tiny slither of something resembling what had once been my moral compass, has somehow navigated the inky waters of my mind, surfacing unexpectedly.

Well, it doesn't matter. I'm still going. I think to myself, allowing a reprieve in the pattern I had sought for comfort all these years, *attack, recoil, retreat.*

I turn, reaching the outer limits of the bowl holding the city, looking back on it. The glimmer is all too familiar, the light seeping in from the surface too bright, but something about it holds my attention, not permitting me to look away. Her face wanders into my mind, like it always does at moments like this; *Starlet.* Her name a cursed prayer, carried on currents; those same currents that allowed my compass, long lost and broken, to surface once more.

The Kiss That Saved Me

I can see The Knights, floating as a unit on the city limits, Orion must have called them back after his return from seeing Callie again. I had heard rumours that demons were roaming these waters once more, but I figured, like I usually do in these types of life and death situations, that it's really none of my business.

I think back to Callie's face, the contortion, the twist in her soul that had allowed Titus to step in. I understand that more than anyone.

I frown slightly, rising and then sink to the sand, perching on the edge of the sandy slopes, surveying the city. The feeling I have toward Callie isn't one I expected and it makes me wonder, as I look down over the mer, over their pitiful attempts at beating back the dark, why I don't envy her, but rather find pity for her.

I think back to the night Titus had turned me, made me what I am. It's all so foggy, so grey and withered, like something rotting, that I can't quite remember whether I had given anything like consent. I remember him shooting me up with venom from a Lionfish, something he always had on hand from Caedes. I wonder now if consent from my drugged lips would even count under those circumstances... I mean, I probably would have said yes to anything.

It is perhaps the first time ever, that I have looked at what happened to me from my father's view. I was taken from him. I didn't swim away. It was something that happened *to* me, not something I had become by choice. All this time I always thought Titus had given me a gift, which is perhaps why Starlet thought that my leaving her was a choice. She had been in my head the whole time, seeing fragments of my degradation. That makes it all the worse.

I run my fingers along my arms, shivering at the gentle friction of my long nails across the white of my skin. It's true, I had loved Titus, but like with Callie, he had infected me. I hadn't asked to be bitten, he had just done it. No questions, no asking. Just an act that had changed the course of my fate.

I will never be the same. My lust for power, for darkness, is too great to ever leave me. I know that now. I wonder why I had returned here, why I hadn't just become nomadic, been free, not bound to any one place.

I find my eyes lingering on the tall, smooth glass spire of the Alcazar Oceania, my heart constricting. I let my defences drop, for just a moment, allowing myself to admit the truth. I had returned here, I had saved the mer in spite of myself, because the ties that bind me to her had never really fallen away. I have family here, family who desperately need a leader, someone strong to hold them together. My father is gone, that's true, but this is my home.

A thought that's not quite guilty, but curious occurs to me. I wonder now if Atlas would still be swimming around in his throne room, muttering to himself and looking over the Kingdom if it hadn't been for me. For my allegiance to a man whose heart was black as sin. I should have just killed Titus while his back was turned, or while he was passed out high. It would have been better for everyone. If nothing else, I know now that despite my being immortal, that does not mean I won't one day be sand, drifting along the sea floor.

The light from above sparkles, torturing me with the promise of atonement. It's all just too taboo, the idea of being… *good*. The word feels sticky, like my tongue is covered in syrup at the mere thought of uttering it. Could I even be better? Be different? Or am I too far gone?

I ask myself these questions, but I know that forgiving myself won't be the problem, I love myself. In spite of the fact I probably shouldn't. Self-loathing has never been a part of my character. I'm far too strong for that.

I know now, as I sit and ponder, the reason that I can't bring myself to leave and the reason I can't quite bear to stay.

I want to see forgiveness in *her* eyes, because if she can still love me like a sister after all this time, then maybe I'm not so bad after all.

I've been skulking in the doorway for hours. I don't know what possessed me to do such a thing or to even come back. I should definitely have vanished into the deep, never to return. But I didn't, and now I'm here.

I'm most definitely turning out to be a giant masochist. I suppose Titus' love of causing me pain has rubbed off and now I'm keeping up the habit, for old times' sake.

The Kiss That Saved Me

This is, as I now realise, an extremely bad idea and honestly all my fault. She has every right to be chronically pissed. I had broken almost every secret handshake and promise spoken in twin language that I possibly could have. I had shattered the oldest and most sacred bond in my life with neither spectacular grace, nor reason. I sigh, I am so bad at appearing humble. Centuries of feeling the power of the deep will do that to a person.

Especially one as narcissistic as I.

I don't want to do this, but something inside me won't let it drop. I'm afraid, for the first time in a long time, of her rejecting me. Of things never being repaired from how completely they had been decimated. I had risked it all for a relationship that was built on lies. I had allowed myself to be used for my power, and after watching Orion skulk around the Alcazar Oceania, I know that I can't let my soulmate get away so easily.

Things are screwed up, but nothing is too screwed up when it comes to family. Or so I'm hoping.

"I can hear you out there you know. You sigh when you're anxious." I hear Star's dullest tones move toward me and I smile.

"How do you know that?" I move around the doorway into her chambers, the room has pink crystalline flooring, so pink in fact it reminds me of vomiting as a child after eating too much salmon. I pull a face, before realising she can see me, something which after so much time in the shadow I'm not used to. I smile, trying to seem breezy.

Did I actually just say breezy? I guess I really am losing my edge.

"I know that because it's what I do when I'm anxious," she's sat at a vanity, near a stained glass window, the pattern on which is a wilting orchid. A metaphor of my life. It could have been so beautiful, but I lost my sunlight and died a magnificent death, plunging into rot and dirt instead.

"I'm sorry... I didn't mean to disturb..."

"I think you hanging in my doorway is the least of our worries with regard to privacy, wouldn't you? I mean you waltz through my head on a daily... no, make that hourly, basis." She's disdain filled. I move my charred scales left and right, swaying into the room. I sit down on the edge of her four-poster bed; the pink silk sheets look like liquid rose-petals. Beautiful and sweet, just like she once was. Before I destroyed her. "Make yourself at home, why don't you?" she snaps. I flinch, not having let words touch me in a long time, this is going to be harder than I thought.

"Look, I know I don't deserve your kindness. I don't want it even. I just want to apologise." Her head snaps around and a look of shock rests between her perfectly arched brows. She looks at me, at the colour returning to my scales, the blue of my eyes that match hers. I can feel the power of the dark fading. It's hard. But I know she can see it. She moves to open her lips, to retort in that bitchy way she uses as a defence.

"You... want to apologise?" she whispers, her eyes suddenly brimming. Whoa.

"Yes. I've been lost for a long time, I got poisoned by a snake. By Titus, but I shouldn't have let it happen that way. You're always going to be the most important person in my life. More important than any man," the words I speak cut me deeply. I remember now why I didn't want to do this. Vulnerability isn't really my style. Starlet places the conch comb down on her vanity, crosses her hands in her lap, and looks attentive, unable to resist the pull we feel to each other.

"You're doing this now?"

"Yes. Why? Is it a bad time? I can come back," I find myself totally disarmed. I didn't think my sense of timing would be the issue, I thought it had been that... you know, I had let her be captured and tortured...

"Our father died... he wanted nothing more than to see us together again Azure... and all you can do is this... it's too late," she lets a tear fall and crystallise, and I wonder if it's for what we've lost in each other, or what we've lost in our father.

"I'm sorry. I'm sorry about father. I am. I just... life is too short, even when you're immortal." She nods at me and I shift uncomfortably on top of her mattress. "I know things will never be like they once were. I don't want things to be the same, I want them to be better."

"How can things possibly be better, Azure? They're falling apart! Orion can't cope on his own, father's gone, Shaniqua left. Saturnus is becoming angrier by the second about not being Crowned Ruler. To top it all, now the girl who I thought could save us all is gallivanting off somewhere with a tentacled mess of a man, claiming she 'doesn't need anyone'. Things are about one step away from imploding!" She pants, slightly out of breath from her rage and then something terrifying happens. She begins to sob, uncontrollably and in an unstoppable torrent of emotion that has been mounting since the day I left. She breaks. I don't know what to do, but the only thing I can think of is to move from the mattress, dropping to the bend in my tailfin and reaching for her hands.

"Oh Star, please don't cry." The darkness within me is rising, condemning me for my pity out of habit. I remain strong, looking into the eyes of my sister, battling it back, for her.

"You left me..." She snots, Goddess, she isn't attractive when she cries.

"I know... Shhh," I coo her, and place my hand into her silky blonde locks, like time hasn't passed, wiping her tears away. I am the eldest, if only by minutes, and I had always taken care of her. I had died first too, and I wonder in this moment how I ever chose the dark over my twin. She used to be so innocent, the girl who had been trapped in a convent for her visions, who had never been with a man. A girl for whom there was only me. Time has hardened her, as it has me, but underneath she is still the girl who cried with me, who held my hand at my brother's funeral, who gave me a reason to keep going. I move up off the sand that is sweeping across the crystalline floor, moving my arms around her neck. She puts her arms into my dark hair and begins to weep diamonds down my spine.

"He's really gone... isn't he?" My sister gasps, unable to catch her breath. I feel the truth of her words hit me, and in an unexpected moment of weakness I feel the loss take the sustenance from my lungs for the first time. I had been kidding myself if I thought I could outswim the tsunami of my grief at this destruction of familial bonds. I know that now. Together, my sister and I sink to the floor, sobbing, and holding onto each other for dear life after all this time.

ORION

There isn't anything left to do but this. I need to get rid of all evidence she was ever here, ever filling the hole I had pushed her into, deforming her into something unrecognisable.

It's a tiny circle, a beautiful shackle that I can't let go of; I clench it in my palm, scared to set it free. I know I need to do this; I know I need to cleave myself.

I look out across the Occulta Mirum, the mer that move through the streets, The Knights on the outskirts, scouting weaker, lower level demons that have been slowly making a re-appearance. Something is coming, something powerful and it isn't good. I see Saturnus moving in the streets below. *Rat bastard.* He can have the stupid crown. I don't and have never wanted this.

Now, as I stare down at the streets, rather than seeing happy mer, chatting, unaware as to the encroaching danger that seems to be building every day, I see their lives in the palms of my hands. My decisions are the ones keeping them safe or killing them.

I had used Callie as a distraction and ruined my relationship in the process by putting too much onto her, because I can't handle it. I hate how she always flees from me. I need someone far stronger than that to help me rule. I hadn't listened when my father had wanted to teach me, I had always run too. I hadn't even wanted to stay in the Alcazar Oceania for fear of him trapping me under the responsibility. I wonder now how I could have been so stupid. Had I honestly thought he was going to live for eternity?

I suppose I couldn't imagine a world without my father in it. So the answer to that was yes. I move backward slightly and sit in the throne. The seat is too wide for me, far too wide. I don't fill it like I should. I think back to my father now, his silver hair, and gold eyes, the wisest of any man I had ever known. I should have listened to his advice, but there's no bringing him back now. He is dead and I am in a giant royal mess.

The crown sits on my head firmly, a burden I can't seem to get rid of. The ring still in my palm, I look down at it. I want to hate Callie for what she's put me through. I think of her, lying, splayed out with his hands crawling over her like parasites. *NO.* I mentally slap myself. I am not going there, and that's that.

I rise again from the throne, feeling my fin trail along the stained glass of the floor slightly, reluctant to take this next step. I release the ring, letting it float slightly in front of me before I push it away from me using the air in the surrounding water. I push it at such speed, never wanting to see it again. A silly human ritual. For a silly, too human girl. I watch it reach the panoramic glass window and shove it open with a larger blast of air, letting the ring and all my feelings wash out with the current. I stand and watch it zoom, exerting my will over this mini tide using the air within each water molecule to propel the memory of my love for her as far away as possible. The ring is a tiny, blue glimmer, like a star in the distance when I finally let the current drop. The ring is lost out there in the deep. Another piece of meaningless, worthless junk, sweeping across the ocean floor along with the ashes of a man whose place could never be filled. Let alone by me. The son who didn't listen.

I hear something move behind me and turn.

"Starlet, you can come out, I know you're there," I move, keeping my palm clenched. She comes out from behind the door of the throne room where I am suspended, motionless, unable to move forward. She isn't alone though, and much to my surprise, Azure follows her into the space of stained glass, stained with bad memories and bloodshed surrounding the throne.

"You're..." I start and they both give a slight smile, but Azure's eyes flash a warning.

"Together," Starlet finishes, turning to Azure. "She was worried about you... I mean, we both are. Orion... are you okay?" Starlet has softened, the presence of her soulmate, after all these years of absence, healing her broken heart. My spirits rise and then crash again, looking at their happy faces, a reminder of a kind of happiness I had only grasped for mere moments and will never share again. The kind you only get from finding the other half of yourself.

"She's gone. It's really over."

"No, it isn't." Starlet looks over her shoulder.

"You should have seen her Star, her hair, her eyes. That's not my girl. That's not my Callie. It's..."

"Darkness," Azure says with a soft simplicity, moving around Starlet's body, coming into full view. Her hair is still black, but her eyes are back to the familial ice blue.

"Yes..." It comes out, a breathless exhalation at the shock of looking directly into those ice blue eyes for the first time in years. Azure looks different, a slight improvement on how she appeared at the coronation. I can't help but smile. "You look different," I say, trying to be sweet.

"I got a rather large smack to the head. Put things in perspective for me," she quips and I rub the back of my neck nervously.

"Sorry about that," I apologise and she shrugs, moving toward me, head bowed.

"After everything I've done, I should be the one apologising. But I don't really relish the idea of getting all weepy," she breathes in deeply before continuing. "Instead, I'll say this... Callie and I, we may not be the same case, but we were infected by the same source. Titus. She can come back from this, Orion, she has to want it, but it's possible."

"How do you know that?" I ask her, imploring some magical solution.

"Because if it's not, then I'm screwed." Starlet snorts and Azure laughs, it's a beautiful sound, like a lost relic that's been missing for centuries, only to reappear, stunning you that you'd not noticed it was gone.

"Thank you."

"Don't thank me. It's not like I'm cured. I could turn back into super-bitch on the turn of a dime and if I do, please, just let me be. Tempting the beast only makes it worse," Azure is pleading with me and I nod.

"Okay. If you want a room..." I offer, gesturing to the surrounding structure. She shakes her head.

"It's best if I stay nomadic for now. I get smash happy when the darkness..."

"Say no more," I hold up a palm and she nods. Starlet grasps her hand and they share a look, like one they had shared when they were children, the night I left for war.

"Orion... we need a plan. This whole Psiren thing is getting out of hand," Starlet reminds me. It's something I'm constantly aware of, prickling my irritation levels. I quell them.

"Yeah... I know," I admit, not wanting to think on the amount of action I haven't taken.

"You know, Orion. Father always thought you could do this. He wouldn't have told me so if he didn't," Starlet puts her hand on my shoulder. She's being so kind and it's completely freaking me out.

"Azure... What did you do to Starlet? I think she's being... nice!" I give a pretend gasp and Azure covers her mouth to stop herself from laughing. I can tell their relationship is on new, very thin ice at her self-consciousness.

"Oh shut up! Hell, I always thought I'd make a good ruler. Give me that damn thing!" Starlet reaches for the crown and I swat her hand away.

"Oh, so you don't want any of the responsibility, but the pretty hat you'll take?" Azure cocks an eyebrow at me and Starlet laughs again. Moving back with one simple undulation of her magenta tailfin, she looks cool and collected once more.

"I suppose I don't have much of a choice with the responsibility. Everyone is looking to me for answers, and I'm just trying not to get everyone killed," I shrug and Starlet frowns slightly, a serious mood befalling the scene far too quickly.

"Orion, there are things here beyond your control, but there is also a lot *within* it," Azure pipes up slightly, her eyes sparkling. I wonder how much of the darkness within her is thinking about ripping the crown off my head for real.

"Meaning?" I ask her, crossing my arms attentively.

"Well... I was with the Psiren's for a long time. I know how they think. While you've been spending your time decorating ballrooms and throwing parties... you know what they've been doing?" She starts to swim lengths, a furious whirlwind of acute thought, coming to life. She's always been smart, been observant, it's a wonder I hadn't thought to put her to use before this. She looks at me... answering her own question. "Preparing for this war that you're all so determined isn't going to happen." She looks serious again.

"So you're saying we're not doing enough?"

"I'm saying you're comfortable... a predator with enough food and a warm bed can't evolve, Orion... it turns into a house cat." I realise she's right.

We do drills, we train, but there haven't been demons for over a century. The last time the Psirens had been in the city they had murdered so many... How strong would they be now that they've had an extra five months to train, recruit more?

"We've gotten lazy," I nod at Azure, her dark hair looks sleek as Starlet grabs her hand, calming the flurry of passion that had sparked her little speech. She's scared Azure is going to turn back to the dark, that she'll lose her again. I am free of that now. Thank goodness. "We need to start evolving again. Or this is going to turn into a bloodbath."

"Yes," they both nod in unison. A twin thing that has always been eerie.

"Will you help?" I ask them both and they look startled.

"You want our help?" Starlet asks me, looking proud.

"Of course."

"But we're only maidens…" She continues. "What will Saturnus think?" Her fear of him is evident. I wonder what he's said to her to make her so unsure of herself. Azure looks at her with a confused, but slightly angry expression.

"You're not *only* maidens, Star. Nor will you ever be. You're my sisters. The blood of the Crowned Ruler runs through you two and Azure has particular knowledge which will be incredibly useful." She looks at me with wide eyes and I realise that some decisions of a crowned ruler can be easy. It feels right, having all of Atlas' children helping to rule together. Suddenly I don't feel so alone. "Come on, we've got some family business to attend to," and with that decree, we get to work.

17
Shatter

CALLIE

I open my eyes, having banished my consciousness in the dark of the night before as Vex had fallen into a sex-induced slumber. I don't remember where I am for a moment, feeling slightly panicked, sore, and above all else: confused. I move, running my fingers through the black of the sheets. Nothing. Vex is gone.

I pull the sheets around myself. How long have I been out? Where the hell is he?

I turn, placing my feet down on the floor, the bare skin of my soles brushing against the cheap tortoiseshell pattern that sucks all light from the room. I stare over at the door in the gloom. The chair isn't propped under the handle anymore, and a stark, white, lethal light is creeping in through the crack underneath. I know the lock is busted and I instantly worry about the owner of the motel checking the room and finding me inside.

I creep over slowly, as if any movement will cause me to have a panic attack, placing the metal chair beneath the door handle again, barricading myself inside.

I collapse against the wall next to the door, the black sheets crumpling around my body as I pull them to myself like a cornered animal. My black hair falls around my shoulders in disarray as I feel the cold air prickle at my bare skin. I shudder, alone and vulnerable.

What the hell have I done?

My limbs stretch out in front of me, extending forward from the wall next to the doorway. I examine their tenderness. I'm black and blue with bruises and bite marks all down my legs, even on my feet. Why did I let him do those things to me? Why had I done those things to him?

It had felt good... I can't deny that, but it was too good, too good not to mean anything. The fact he'd left me here, vulnerable and naked, in a room with a broken lock and the sun at my back tells me exactly what it had meant to him.

I sigh, allowing the cold air to fill my lungs, shocking my system and letting my post-coital haze lift.

I had broken away from everything I had thought was causing the problems in my life, and yet I'm still not free, not really... who am I kidding? I'm more trapped now than I'd ever been. In a seedy motel room, caged by the light of the sun, by a man who I'd trusted with my body. I'm scared, no longer fooled with feelings of grandeur, of power; I am no more than a mouse in a mousetrap.

I get to my feet, feeling my joints creak in protest as I stand. Everything is sore on the outside, but my insides are numb.

I walk across the room, past the bed and stand in front of the double mirror, looking at myself hard. My eyes are bloodshot, really bloodshot. My skin is mapped with dark veins and my hair is black as soot, messy and knotted down my spine. My body is a paint by numbers of pleasures and pains that now haunt me... I had given in to the darkness, I had let Titus take control of me... I think. It couldn't have been me doing those things. That's not who I am. I know that now. I also know I'm alone. I have nobody, and that's just what I had wanted. How stupid can you get?

I had only ever been with Orion, and now I have given myself to someone who doesn't... who can't, respect me. I have given myself willingly and mere hours after I'd ended things with somebody who had meant so much.

I feel dirty, like my skin is crawling with the scent of perversion, it is invisible, but just like Vex's post-climax smoke it has crawled over me, leaving only memories behind.

Tears find their way into my reflection, the blacks of my eyes expanding as I watch the darkness move through me, following the regret that I am riding like a storm. I reach out to the glass, wrapped in the black sheet like some kind of gothic tragedy. The feel of the mirror on my palm is cool, hard. My reflection watches the outline of my hand as it traces over the image of my cheek, pale and spiked with black magic. I let a tear fall, the image of Orion's face slowly passing through my mind like a dream. It hadn't been like it was with him; it had been fuelled by careless abandon, of wanting to be free. It hadn't been right and I wonder if after this, anything would ever be again.

Oh stop whimpering. You loved it.

The voice of slithering, snake-like tongues comes to me just at the wrong moment and I snap.

"GET OUT OF MY HEAD YOU BASTARD!" I scream without restraint, slamming my fist into the mirror. It shatters. Blood trickles down my arm as pieces of the reflective glass fall into the sink below. The scarlet fluid runs down my wrist in lines. I try to mop it up but end up cutting my palm on a piece of shattered glass that's fallen behind the basin as I move to turn the tap. I gasp, *shit*, as more blood runs down the clean white skin of my previously uninjured limb.

I look up momentarily and the image that greets me is like something out of a horror film. My eyes and hair are a nightmare in onyx and my arms are stained and soaked with my own blood. The fractures of the glass edges crawl outward in jagged cracks, some pieces still remaining in the mirror's frame. The image of myself is broken, just like my insides.

I realise I don't want to be looking at the broken image anymore; its unfaltering reality is a display of how much of a mess I am.

Moving briskly from the mirror, I fall into the bathroom door, my arms held upward trying to stop the blood from trickling down my limbs. The door opens and I move inside, pulling back a cheap, semi-transparent and partially mouldy shower curtain that is falling off its rings. I turn the shower on, untie the sheet I'm wrapped in, and step into the bath, the showerhead looming over me. The water is scalding, but I let it burn, surprised at how good the pressure is considering how crappy the rest of the facilities are.

I watch the fluid run red, my blood mixing in with it and swirling down the drain in a torrent. I sit on the floor, huddled in the corner as I let the shower beat down on me, erasing the last twelve hours from my mind. I try to let everything clear in my head and with the achievement of this come to a startling realisation. I'm responsible for the decisions that I have made. Titus is with me that's for sure, but I had asked Vex to sleep with me, I had hopped on his bike with him, I had chosen to follow him to the rave the night we'd first met. Those were my choices. Nobody had forced me. Vex certainly hadn't. In fact, I doubt if he would have cared much for my company at all if I hadn't persistently hung around with him, drinking with him at the party and luring him into bed.

I could have gone with Daryl. But no. It was always him. And as with everything that has happened as of late, he was the wrong choice.

I have made bad decisions and there is nobody to pick me back up but me. In this moment I want so badly to feel my mother's arms holding me, making me the baby, taking care of me and fixing all my wrongs, but she isn't here. Orion isn't either and now I think about it, he's been cleaning up after me all this time. I had thought that he couldn't love for me who I am, but perhaps the problem was that I was too immature to love myself enough to make choices that were best for me. I place my head in my hands, my black hair beaten smooth and wet by the showerhead, my palm and wrist still stinging from the glass. I guess I hadn't really known what I was asking for when I had asked for independence. I had thought it meant doing whatever you wanted without anyone to stop you. I realise now that it's being wise enough to stop yourself, in having maturity enough to see the consequences of your choices before you make them.

That takes a kind of strength no magic can give you, only time.

SOLUSTUS

Something stirs behind me, prickling my acute senses. I turn, as though pivoting on a knife's edge, irritated at the intrusion. The throne room isn't somewhere you just decide to visit. I really need to get some guards up here. After all, I am ruler.

"Solustus," Vex is inching around the doorway, a look on his face familiar to me only in one respect. I smile to myself slightly, amused.

"Yes?" I move back from the mirror where I've been hovering, going over the conversation with my brother, intrigued as to the girl's new role in events. Who would have thought someone so pure looking would have the devil in her, so to speak? Who would have thought she'd be the one communicating with the Necrimad?

I let myself drop, stretching out in the water as I fall, draping myself sideways across the throne of bones. Vex hovers above the floor a few feet, his tentacles pluming outward, curling and recoiling as they propel him through the bloody dim light.

"I've just left the girl, but I have to admit, she's not as powerful as you indicated, Solustus. I find myself... disappointed." I almost snort at this statement. What does he think I am, stupid? It amuses me that he thinks he's less than completely transparent.

"Oh I see... what a shame," I faux pout, playing it up for the smitten man in front of me. What the hell had that girl done to him?

"So that's what you came to tell me?" I ask him, stroking a long fingernail along my scales, it makes my internals whir with satisfaction.

"Yes..."

"Very well, there's no reason to keep the girl here if you don't see any usable power in her. Tell her to come to me. Tell her... it's about Gideon. She'll know what I mean," I find myself playing this casual character rather skilfully. Vex's face falls and I almost want to exhale, hysterical at the mere thought that he could outwit someone as old as I. Stupid boy. Surely, someone with the dark magic of Poseidon running through their veins doesn't think the first of his kind wouldn't see right through him.

"Vex..." I begin, wanting to give him some indicator that I know his game, rattle him.

"Yes?" He looks back over his shoulder as he turns to leave.

"Remember... Psirens can't love. It's not who we are." With that, his eyes narrow and an angry flash passes beneath the darks of his lilac irises.

"I know that," he snaps, leaving with increased speed. I smile to myself, thinking of the one person who I know had learned the truth of love the hard way…

The door creeps open, a draft from the sea spilling into the stagnant air. I watch under the crack… relieved that Saturnus is finally home. Caedes is asleep behind me, his hair ratted and his body bruised. He could be dead for all I know. Father's beatings were taking their toll and he has found a deep unconsciousness that I pray will, at some point tonight, be mine.

"Father… We need to talk." What's this I wonder? A stand… has Saturnus come to take us away from all this? To somewhere better.

"What is it boy? Have you got my money? I'm out of spirit," my father is drunk, as usual. Saturnus stammers.

"No… I'm leaving… I'm marrying Delphine tomorrow. We're leaving," he almost vomits the words, like he's been waiting to spew them for months. My heart drops, how can he leave us? How can he leave us with him?

"Listen here, boy… You're responsible for this family. Your brothers need food in their bellies and I need spirits in my tankard. You're not going anywhere," he barks it, not as angry as he would be if he were sober.

"No, I've had enough. You treat us like dirt. I'm leaving father. There's nothing you can do."

"Oh really?" I see him get to his feet, swaying slightly, massive in every attribute. From underneath the door I can see Saturnus' feet lift off the floor. I know my father has him by the throat.

"You're going to get married? Leave us? Why would some bitch ever want to marry you? You're worthless… Everyone knows it. Your mother knew it, too." My father is vile when he's angry, worse when you mix in alcohol.

I wince as I hear choking coming from my brother. I want to cry out from behind the locked door, say something, but nothing can stop my father. I hear something smash, glass I think, and then see the evidence as several green fragments tinkle to the floor.

"Father… please…" I hear Saturnus choke out and I want to cry out, but I'm too scared to make a sound, fearing I may make things worse and make myself a target in the process.

"You want out? Is that what you want?" My father spits the words. I can

hear his hurried breathing from lack of physical exertion and drink.

"Please..." Saturnus begs.

"Fine... I'll give you an out!" I hear a muffled blow, a gasp, and then I see Saturnus' body fall to the floor. His head lolls sideways, his open, terrified, and blood stained face peering under the door.

I want to scream, but can't find the breath. He's gasping out for breath that will never come as his carotid lays weeping scarlet from the bottle my father has shoved in his throat.

I lay there, staring out into the light at the dying face of my brother. His blood reaches under the crack, filtering in among the cobblestone, as my father sits back down and begins to whistle a merry tune, the murdered body of his eldest son at his feet.

The throne holds me as I find myself feeling something I hadn't ever felt when recalling this memory. Superiority. I would never have fallen for something as fleeting and weak as a woman, let alone have found myself in a state such as love. Love has no place in the heart of a King.

CALLIE

The sound of my feet pounding against the sidewalk echoes in my ears long after my legs have returned to their natural form. I've made the long and embarrassing journey back to the shore from the motel room at a sprint, fleeing the night that has passed, longing to feel the salt water once more claim me as its own. My black tailfin no longer glitters under the moonlight as I break the surface of the water, rather taking light in and holding it hostage. I arch out of the water, enjoying the low pressure and the freedom of the night's rough waters. Returning to its depths with a crashing mass, I remember the last time I had rode the waves like this. The night I had fled from Orion's proposal. I try not to think on it too hard, making the journey back to Cryptopolis about me. I have been with the Psirens too long and my intention is now to get in, find out about my father's location, and get out.

No more games and certainly no more boys. I think I've had enough of the opposite sex for a lifetime.

I approach the chasm that leads down into the darkness and propel myself deeper and deeper into the shadow. This time however, the darkness doesn't swallow me whole. It doesn't need to.

I've only just made my entrance into the city via the neon cloud of jellyfish that no longer terrify me, when I hear my name called.

"Callie!" I hear his voice, curling out toward me like the tentacles that now attach to his waist in a flurry of black scales. I feel my heart stop momentarily. I don't want to see him.

"Aren't you surprised to see me here?" I sigh out, narrowing my eyes as his angular face comes into view, spiking adrenaline induced flashes of the night before. His tongue stroking across my... *oh God no, please stop with the memories...* I want to erase those images so badly, but in an insane kind of way, I can't help but find them titillating. What the hell is wrong with me?

"Whatever do you mean, Love?" he purrs.

"Well, you left me in a hotel room, naked, with a broken door, trapped by the sun. I'm assuming you were trying to kill me... or at least get me arrested for breaking and entering," I do my best pissed off face. I expect venom in return but instead he just strokes the back of his neck with one hand. I've seen that move a hundred times, from Orion when he was guilty. So what the hell is it doing here... on this man?

"I didn't think..." he mutters looking worried. He licks his bottom lip and I roll my eyes.

"Yeah clearly not," I bite out, folding my arms, letting myself hang above the hustle and bustle of the Psiren soldiers below.

"About last night..." he starts, but I cut him off.

"I know, I asked for it. It's not your fault," I admit, straightening my spine in the water. The movements of my tailfin are reserved, precise. I don't want him thinking last night meant anything.

"My fault?" He looks at me, his lilac irises foggy. Is he confused or something?

"It was my mistake. Don't worry about it," I clarify and he opens his mouth to speak.

"Oh… Okay. Fine… I mean, whatever, Love," he looks confused and I wonder what he's expecting, does he want a declaration of love? I know love… and that wasn't love… it was perverse pleasure… nothing more, nothing less. I turn to leave, feeling agitated at his forwardness. "Callie?" I hear him call my name again, a crestfallen beast.

"What?!" I pivot, finding myself facing him instantaneously with the quickness of my own momentum.

"Solustus wants to see you. It's about Gideon," his eyes are glazed over, like he's in a trance or something. I nod and swim away once more, enjoying the feeling of moving away from him, away from what had happened. I am leaving it in the past and that's that.

I move toward the central building of the Cryptopolis, taking in the palace, if you could call it that, and its towering vent made structure. I wonder who had made it, or if they'd just found an old vent and moved in. That seems more likely knowing the nature of the Psirens.

I look around, watching them in a pit below, toiling over anvils, practicing their manoeuvres and I wonder if the mer really are right about them. I know they have darkness in them, but maybe if they were given the right opportunity they could be given purpose. The mer don't understand what it's like to have darkness inside you, when you yourself hadn't asked for it. It's easy to let it control you; it's easy to let things get out of control.

I enter the dark archway of rock, practically ashen, only a little underwater lichen hold it together. Once inside I navigate the corridors and hold my breath, heart beating fast. I can't wait to get out of here and find my father. Who knows, maybe the open ocean will quell some of this turmoil that won't seem to rest within my chest.

I move upward through a hole in the ceiling, which has collapsed, and into the next layer of burnt tunnel which leads to the throne room. As I enter the bloody red water of the throne room, I feel a dirty, pale, and cold hand cover my mouth and another pull my black hair. It yanks my head back, hurting my neck. I stiffen, feeling suckered tentacles wrap around my wrists. What the hell is Vex playing at? I see Solustus coming from around the back of the throne, where he was previously eclipsed from view.

"Come on, Alyssa. This one is going on a little trip."

18
Mother

CALLIE

They begin to slide the giant boulder in place, sealing my fate, locking me in with the vents inside. What the hell is going on? Why have they brought me here?

I am sure now that I've been played for a fool. Not surprising really when you think about it. You don't make a deal with the devil if you want to get out unscathed.

I get up, flexing my tail in one powerful motion, propelling myself toward the still moving rock as the last speck of light vanishes from the basement level cavern. I hit the rock hard with my fist but it doesn't budge. I hear murmuring from outside as I push my ear to the stone.

"Let me out!!!" I scream, the walls closing in on me, leaving an echo of my claustrophobic plea resonating between the walls of my skull. I pound on the boulder once more, trying to shift it. Nothing. Not even a smidgeon of give.

I wonder what I'm doing down here. Is this just a containment cell, are they keeping me for something worse? Torture perhaps? I cringe, wondering how well I'd hold up. Goose pimples rise in a wave across my flesh, travelling up my arms and down my spine as my senses heighten and my eyes adjust to the dark.

I turn away from the boulder, knowing there is no way I can shift it without some serious mystical help. I face the cavern, which is filled with old vents that don't seem active any longer, exhaling heavily.

I'm trapped. Or at least, it seems. I swim through the dark water, feeling my way along the wall, looking for weaknesses.

That's when it happens.

A shudder in the earth causes the cavern to shake and the water to vibrate in simultaneous motion. I find myself looking at the stalactite encrusted ceiling, fearing a cave in at the jerking, rumbling, grinding of crust beneath. I cling to the wall edge, my heart pounding.

That's when I notice that something has escaped the vent. Like squid ink, a black plume of something has been released from each vent of the deep earth.

I inch forward slowly, fearing what it may be. As I get within touching distance, the black cloud takes on a life of its own, collecting in a dense stream and climbing up into my nostrils.

I blink a few times, my head feeling like someone's shoved a balloon inside and is slowly inflating it. I clutch my temples, feeling my eyes burn with the pain. I lose the will to keep myself suspended in the water surrounding me as the smell of burning takes over and I fall to the cavern floor.

A shifting, burning, bloody mass is stirring in the dark. All shadow and night. I feel it infecting me with its ancient tongue. The taste of ash fills my mouth, the scent of death in my nostrils; it calls to me. Whispering words in shadow, forming ancient symbols on the back of my eyelids. The earth shifts, deep down in its molten core.

Something is coming for me. Something is ascending. Now.

I know it, but at the same time I cannot know it, do not want to know it. For it is what will kill us all.

I have been in this place before, but only in my dreams and only once. On the ocean floor, the night I had fled the city. When Titus had first taken grip of my senses.

"Girlllll," it roars, deafening me. No longer a whisper but a shout.

"Why are you doing this?!" I scream at the beast, as it emerges through black clouds of smoke.

I do not question how there is black smoke underwater, for I know this isn't a vision of the world I've just come from. This is a window into a prison cell. A kaleidoscopic, blood stained pane into something old and forgotten.

"Need... blood," the monster snarls, wanton and hungry.

"I don't understand!" I wail, clutching my hands to my head.

"Need, blood, need pure... blood."

"Please, let me be!" I scream again, covering my ears, trying to keep out the blood curdling essence of fear. It clutches at me, causing my senses to run away in an evasive riot.

"Girrrrlll...listen!" The beast roars again and even though my ears are covered, the voice echoes inside my skull. There is no escape.

"Okay... Okay..." I beg, breathing deep and feeling myself wretch at the scent of rot and decay surrounding the Necrimad. It's dark so I can't make out any detail, just a great black mass, full of unrest, with two luminescent yellow eyes, like those of a cat.

"Need blood... Pure blood..." The beast repeats its request. My heart is in my mouth, pounding, racing, terrified.

"Blood? But why?" I ask it, suddenly finding my curiosity.

"To rise..." The two words are clear as crystal.

I know now what all this has been about. Solustus wants to raise the Necrimad using my scythe, to finish what Titus started. But how?

"Pure..." I utter the word like I've never heard it before, trying to clear my mind and ignoring the fact I'm in a trance like state, away from my body, the world I know. The only way is to listen and listen well. "What do you mean pure?" I ask the question and the Necrimad stirs, seemingly affronted by my forwardness.

"Untouched..." it says the word and I feel myself repulsed... does it mean what I think it means?

"I don't understand," I reply. The fog rolls forward and a blast of scalding hot air blows me backward, taking my breath from me. The beast banishes me back to my body with only one sentence in reply.

"You are not supposed to, dark one."

AZURE

I'm meditating, trying to beat back the darkness within after losing my temper with Orion. My brother sure does know how to make some stupid decisions for someone entrusted with a whole Kingdom, I know I wouldn't like that kind of responsibility in my hands, but even if I had it, I wouldn't be making the mess of it he is. It's almost like Callie took the last of his common sense with her.

As I sit on the sand, tail tucked beneath me, I shut my eyes, the Occulta Mirum becoming lost, insignificant, behind the black of my eyelids. It is time to focus. Time to find my centre.

I think back to where this had all started, being brave enough perhaps for the first time to think about the past. The visions hadn't always been a part of me. They'd crept in for both me and Starlet after the death of our father. We'd always had a sort of foresight, but nothing compared with the clarity brought on by the visions from the Goddess. I was marked, always destined for this life, even when I was a human.

Starlet and I were terrified when the visions first started, nothing made sense and nothing would make sense again until our human lives ended. It was torture. Seeing things, things you didn't understand, that terrified you. Images of your father, your brother, as strange new creatures beyond anything your tiny, sheltered mind could imagine, took their toll.

I think back to Arabella, something I don't allow myself to do very often, letting myself be lost to the only memory I have of her.

"Push!! Push!!" The dark sweaty forehead of the midwife pops up from in-between my trembling, blood stained legs. Why the hell is she sweating? Aren't I the one doing the hard work? My white woven undergarment is stuck to me, damp and cold against my bulging, hard, lump of a stomach. The pain is too much. I can't do it anymore. Everything is just too excruciating and I am exhausted, it has been days since the pains started and my baby is still

nowhere to be found. Maybe she'll never be here.

The weather outside is stormy, the roof of the medicine woman's hut shaking with the force of the coastal wind. I prop myself up on my elbows.

"I can't...." I sob, screaming as another contraction hits. I feel myself weaken under its hold, crushing the life out of me.

"You don't have a choice. Do you want your baby to die?" The medicine woman looks up at me with dark eyes, no sympathy, just a cold, hard dose of reality.

I feel tears running down my cheeks. Is it supposed to hurt this much? Take this long? I think back to the vision, to the image of me covered in blood and dying at the birth of my own child. It terrified me, scared me enough into telling Ethan, but he had simply shaken his head and walked away, saying that he didn't care for women's troubles. I want so much to hear my mother's voice now. Telling me it will be okay, that it would be over soon, but she is dead, lost to me forever. I feel the next contraction coming and suddenly I don't have time to wish for anything. The pain is too immense. I scream out, bearing down and pushing with every fibre of my being, praying that my last ounce of strength is enough to birth the baby I have come to love so much and yet have never met. I lay back, feeling a rush of wet and a scream of innocence so pure my heart swells, ready to burst with the need to hold my child. My baby is here.

A rush of cold enters the room, the burlap fabric that hangs over the doorway being brushed aside by my husband, coming forward to see his bounty. I lay there, my heartbeat weakening.

"The child... is it?" I hear him ask the medicine woman.

"A girl..." the woman replies. I have never met her before; I don't even know her name. Ethan had brought me here when the pains hadn't yielded a baby after two days, not sure of what to do with me as I sat, begging with him, telling him that I knew I was to die.

"Arabella," I whisper, sitting up and moving, using the last of my energy to try and catch a glimpse of my daughter. I had known all along that she would be a little girl, the images in my head had told me that much. I had kept that knowledge to myself. I had attempted to tell Ethan about my visions once I had found out I was pregnant; I had all but given up trying to

convince him. He takes my baby into his arms holding her, but there is no smile on his face. Only anxiety.

"Give her to me," I demand, reaching out, the emptiness in my arms like a void.

The medicine woman moves forward, looking at me with a concerned expression.

"There's a lot of blood here. I'm not sure..."

"What... what's wrong?" I ask her, no longer feeling any pain, only weakness. The urge to hold my daughter is fighting any physical discomfort.

"You're bleeding... I don't know how much I can do."

"Fix her up. I'm leaving," my husband utters. Arabella grabs onto his finger but he pulls away. My heart breaks and panic clutches at me.

"Give. Me. My. Daughter." I want to scream at him, how dare he keep her from me?! She is mine!

"I'm not giving this poor innocent baby to someone with the devil in her! Are you mad? She's better off with no mother than one who's possessed." My husband's strong, dark features are terrifying in the dim candlelight of the room. My Arabella lets out a cry and I physically ache.

"What? What are you talking about?"

"You've been seeing things, Azure... evil things. I've been waiting for the baby, but now... I have to take...Arabella," he utters the name for the first time. I can't tell if he's disgusted or guilty from the expression on his face.

"Please... please don't take her... I need her Ethan... please," I beg, beginning to see what's been happening right in front of me. He had believed my visions, but he had waited until his child was out of me to do anything about it.

"I'm sorry," he utters, moving to leave the room.

"Please... please! I'll do anything... at least let me see her," I plead, my eyes streaming and heart hammering. I can feel myself weakening. How can he do this to me? He sighs and tilts the baby wrapped in burlap toward me. Her huge, icy blue eyes stare at me, runny from the shock of entering the world. I love her so much and I've never seen her face before this... how can that be? Ethan pulls away and I scream as he takes her out into the rain, into

the cold...

*"NO! ETHAN YOU CAN'T DO THIS! I NEED HER! SHE'S MY BABY!
PLEASE... I'LL DO ANYTHING!!!" I scream until I'm hoarse. The medicine
woman covers me over with a blanket. I cry until I have no energy left,
weeping over the loss of my daughter. Slowly, under the stormy night sky...
my blood trickles off the edge of the table I'm laid on and onto the floor, I
bleed, letting out a final, slow and heartbroken breath, with my only thought
before death being of the ingrained image of my beautiful Arabella.*

I return from the memory, a single tear falling down one check. She would
never have known who I was, who her own mother was. I had failed her in
the most important way. I only had to be there, but I never was. Ethan had
taken that chance from me. I wonder about my Arabella, what she had
become. I'd like to think she went on to be happy, but in the world I had
grown up in, where having visions left you bleeding to death or in a convent,
I wonder how likely that really is. For a moment I let myself fantasise,
wonder how it would have felt if I'd ever held her in my arms. Had her tiny
eyes looking up at me, her little fingers clutching mine.

I ache, intensely, deeply, letting my head fill with the image of her. The
fog rolls in, pushing the image away, instead putting something else in its
place... something bad. My eyes snap open. The time for meditation is over.
I need to get to Orion and fast. The time for evolution is upon us.

CALLIE

I come back from my trance like state, finding my body not where I had left
it. I open my eyes, meeting with those of the two people who had put me in
the vents to start with. Alyssa and Solustus.

"Did you get that?" Alyssa turns to Solustus and he smiles slightly. My
body is lying sideways and I'm trapped in what appears to be a naturally
formed prison cell, with stalactites and stalagmites instead of bars.

Shit, I think to myself.

My head is thudding. Solustus speaks, his eyes gleaming with deadly promise.

"Yes. Blood of someone pure. I got it. Now, I must go ready the army. We will take the city at dusk." That gets my attention as I find myself upright and acutely tense in mere moments. Alyssa looks at me and laughs before turning to leave with Solustus.

"What do you think you're doing?" Solustus asks her, her tentacles a bloody rust.

"Going to help you prepare my children for war? Where else?" She sounds annoyed at Solustus' lack of ability to see her intent. She has her back to me and all I can see of her is a cascade of black hair longer than any I've ever seen.

"I need you to stay and watch her. I don't trust her. Besides, you two have a friend in common..." he dismisses her with a wave of the hand, darting out of the corridor where my cell is situated. I can tell Alyssa is pissed.

"Great, so now I have to babysit the brat!" I hear her protest.

"Hey! I'm right here!" I cross my arms. Pouting. After everything, I'm feeling cocky now that rock separates us.

"Oh, I'm well aware of your existence," she snarls.

"So what? You've heard of me then?" I cock an eyebrow, wanting to make out like I'm not afraid. Maybe she's heard about me kicking Daryl's ass, if that's the case then I had better live up to my reputation.

"Heard of you? You ruined my life!" She bites out, wrapping two tentacles around the rocky teeth that make up the bars of my cell. Suddenly something clicks about the name as her face comes toward me, too close for comfort.

"Alyssa... wait you're..."

"Your father's soulmate! Yes, that's me. The one he left for your harlot of a mother."

"But I thought you were dead?" I cock my head, confused as to her existence. Saturnus had said she'd killed herself.

"No, it'll take more than a broken heart and being outcast from the Occulta Mirum by Saturnus to kill me off, dear. As you can see, I've made quite the comeback," she gestures to her surroundings, laughing.

"What happened to you?" I ask, furrowing my brow.

How can this be? How is it that nobody knew she was alive?

"I found my true calling. Much more than anything I could have hoped for up north with your stupid father. You won't find me sticking with some sap, mooning over his wife and baby daughter, freezing my tailfin off up there."

"North?" I snag onto the word, finding my eyes widen. She smirks.

"So... I found my children. Young men who would love me forever, who want me, but can't have me. You see, child, as soon as you give someone your heart, they no longer want you. That's why your father went for your stupid mother. She was nothing but a taboo. How could she ever mean as much as hundreds of years together?" Alyssa is angry, but beneath her pale, rust coloured façade of clutching, suckered tentacles and eyes that lead to an abyss, I can tell she's still devastated.

"So you're responsible for all your... children," I gulp as I utter the last word, feeling physically nauseous.

I hover, suspended in the tiny volume of water that my prison cell allows.

"Yes. After I saw how your father..." she begins but cuts off... "Why am I telling you any of this? I don't need to be stuck here. Those are my children out there! Screw this!" She waves a hand, her tentacles sliding back from the rock formations holding me captive. "So long, little girl." I hear her mumble. What an odd woman, she's entirely desperate. It's like she needs to be loved, wanted, so badly that she'd tell her worst enemy a story just to have someone to listen to her. She has a cruel face and I wonder how Vex or any of her other prey had thought her beautiful. I feel pity for her, but then remind myself that she's frenzied enough to murder young men to be loved. She is dangerous to say the least and she has a personal vendetta against me. Great.

I think back to where she's going, to help Solustus put together the army that's going to take apart the city I am supposed to be ruling over. I feel guilt wash over me slightly, sure, now more than ever, after my encounter with the Necrimad that the Psirens are on the wrong side.

If there had been any doubt in my mind, it's long gone.

I am trapped by the earth with nowhere to go while the people who had taken me in as family are left to be slaughtered. They are strong, but they're also outnumbered. I wonder about Orion momentarily and my heart constricts. No matter my romantic feelings toward him, I can't stand the thought of him turning to sand. In fact, it makes me feel very violent. Orion had always said I run away from everything, when things get tough. It's true, I had fled from the masked ball when I had discovered I was the vessel, I had fled from the site where the demon rose out of the earth the first time I had seen Orion fight. Now I think about it, the only time I hadn't run was when Titus had bound me to the scythe and sacrificed me... but then death in itself was just another form of escape... wasn't it?

When I'd sat with Atargatis in my car she'd given me the option to become a Goddess. I'd turned her down, saying I didn't want the power she had to offer, but perhaps it wasn't the power I had been afraid of, perhaps it was the responsibility that came with it.

I was scared of responsibility. I was scared of being Queen and I was certainly scared of being somebody's wife, especially Orion's, someone who had such high expectations and had set the bar infinitely higher than I could ever hope to repay with his own perfect ways. I have been looking for an easy alternative to being a mer, being a warrior and a leader, but the only alternative has damaged my trust in my ability to make even the simplest decision.

When I had been a child I had thought being a grown up meant you had all the answers, it's only now that I realise you can only make the best decisions you can with the information, time, and resources you have. I also realise that I'm not brave enough to deal with the consequences that come from making mistakes, but not docile enough to take instruction or advice from the one person who had my best interest at heart. I had pushed Orion away because I was scared I wasn't good enough. Vex was right when he had said I couldn't let him love me, because I couldn't. How could I when I didn't even know how to love and trust myself?

I have made a mess of things and one fact, more than any other has become increasingly evident:

I am a coward.

I allow myself to sink to the floor of the cell; the dirt beneath me is mixed in with sand and the bones of dead animals. I let myself lie there, in the dark of the ashen, burned corridor inside the giant vent palace, gathering my courage and trying to quell the voices in the back of my mind that are telling me I can't save the city. That it's already too late.

I rise slightly after a few minutes, ready to try dismantling the natural formations that are barring in me in. I know ramming them isn't the most sensible idea, and that I'll probably somehow impale myself and die, but this is no time for caution and fear, I have to try. I'm about to begin gathering as much momentum as I can toward the rock teeth, hoping to break clean through, when I see something behind the corner. A tentacle, and a familiar one at that.

"Vex is that you?" I call out.

"Oh bloody hell. Shut up! This is a rescue mission not a bloody news bulletin."

"Rescue?" I cock my eyebrow as he turns the corner. He's in a chest piece made of black rock, like a crust, with a helmet of a similar material on his head. All kitted out to go and slaughter everyone I love.

"Yes, you need it, don't you? Or would you rather stay in the nice cell?" He comes forward, hurrying along the long corridor.

"How are you going to get me out? Did you bring, like, a chainsaw?" I ask him and he shakes his head.

"No... I brought some extra hands though," he smirks and wraps his two thickest tentacles around a central stalactite.

"You're going to pull it out? That's your big plan?!"

"Hey, I abandoned my army and came back for you. Don't make me regret it. I didn't exactly have time to think out a detailed plan." He looks up at me, his head bent from concentrating on forming the best possible grip around the rock.

"You're right. Sorry," I apologise, trying not to laugh.

"Don't mention it... like seriously don't. I don't want my irrational desire to not see you killed discovered. It makes me look like a bloody nancy, alright?" He mutters and I laugh slightly.

222

Not quite prince charming, but he'll do.

"Your secret is safe with me," I promise.

"Okay, get back..." he orders, bracing himself with his other tentacles against the floor. He heaves, his face turning red and after a few moments, the rock comes away, disturbing sand in small plumes that disperse in its wake. A normal person could never have mustered the grip to remove it. It seems tentacles have perks. Who knew?

"How did they even get me in here?" I ask him as he places his tentacles around the next tooth along.

"Regus. He has powers to manipulate earth. He must've done it."

"But then how do they get prisoners out? Does he have to release them?" I ask him, his eyes turning dark as he prepares to brace himself against the burnt floor once more. Summoning the darkness to gain maximum strength he replies.

"Most prisoners don't get out, Love." I wonder now if the bones at the bottom of my fin are animal. Maybe they're just people who rotted away in here. I shudder. I'm thinking on this awful thought when I hear a crack as the calcium of the stalagmite falls away. One more and I'm free.

"Save the best til' last," Vex mutters.

He's right; the last stalagmite is huge, thick at the base and looks completely solid. However, if he can't break it, it'll all have been for nothing, as I can't fit through the gap he's created without its removal.

"What if I try slamming into it from this side?"

"That might do it." He wraps his black tentacles around the stalagmite at the middle point, this time using his two thickest and one slightly smaller tentacle. I take two strokes backward so my back presses against the end of the cell.

"On three," I say and he nods, his mouth a thin line of focus.

"One..." I feel my tailfin twitching, the musculature ready to power me forward.

"Two..." Vex follows on, shifting his grip slightly.

"Three!" He pulls back with a grunt and the stalagmite falls away before I even get to it, my momentum carries on, unable to stop in time.

I sail through the now open gap, smashing into Vex's chest and causing us both to fall to the floor. I'm lying on top of him, panting, blood coursing through me, heating my face and chest, which are now pressed into him.

The sand clears and our eyes meet, black to black.

Then something I don't expect happens. Vex is putting his hand on my cheek and then he's kissing me. Holding me to him in a rush of passion that has come from nowhere. His lips push against mine and a heat grows as I feel the energy drain from me. I start to get into it, kissing him back until I feel something heat, really heat between us.

The heat I can't quite describe, but one minute I'm smooching the tentacles off him and the next I'm being thrown at the wall, hurtling away from him like we're two magnets of the same polarity. Vex is thrown to the end of the corridor opposite me, the force of the kiss sending him flying through the water too. He looks confused.

"See…" he pants, "This is why I said no kissing."

19
Converge

ORION

Starlet's eyes cloud over, turning a brilliant bone white. She's having a vision and as her mouth contorts in horror, I know it can't be good.

"Starlet! What do you see?" I thrum my musculature backward, propelling the water away from me and moving toward her. I place my hands on her shoulders gently, shaking her ever so slightly.

"They're coming... the city... the city is tumbling... cracking. Glass, everywhere," she's mumbling but I get the general notion of what she's saying.

"When? When are they coming? How much time do we have left?" I shake her again, harder this time. Her eyes clear, turning that familial glacial blue, and I watch her lips form the word I most dread in a single, terrible exhalation.

"Now," she looks like she might lose her tread in the water, tumble backwards.

"We need to summon The Knights of Atargatis! Someone get me Cole, Ghazi... Everyone! Someone find Saturnus!!!" I'm babbling, freaking out, as Callie would say. They're coming. A swarm of darkness larger than anything we can hold back. We're out of time. Luckily for us, I suddenly remember, we don't have to hold them back at all.

"Where the hell is Saturnus!!!" I bark. Nobody is here... I'm suspended in the throne room barking orders and there's nobody to hear them. I have asked the guards to back off, leaving me with my misery.

How stupid am I? I'm wasting valuable time.

225

Panic stricken, I speed through the water shoving the double doors of the throne room forward with a blast of air exuding from my outstretched palms.

"Starlet! Come on!" I bark behind me.

I hear her gasp slightly, as though I'd broken a sort of daydream with my abruptness, but I don't have time to check if she's okay, I have to make sure everyone else will be first. I move into the column that runs through the centre of the palace, plunging as fast as my tail will allow, pushing through the water with a wilfulness I haven't found for a long time.

Cole is floating, diligent, at the double doors as usual, he sees me and his mouth forms a grim line.

"Cole! The Psiren's, they're coming! We need to get everyone ready. Summon the Knights. Ready the weapons!" I bark at him. He nods, looking concerned. He has every right to be. I know we have the glimmer protecting us, but I'm not taking any risks. Not after last time.

"Sir, yes sir. I'll get Ghazi."

"Good. I'm going to find Saturnus. Do you know where he is?" I speak quickly, unable to find patience, my heart beating heavily within my chest. I'm a fine example of a ruler. I should be calm, but after the centuries I've lived through, the wars I've fought, when it comes to laying the responsibility of it all on my shoulders I feel like I'm ready to crumble.

"I think he's in his study. He said he didn't want to be disturbed," Cole muses.

"Well, I don't think he'll mind on this occasion," I mutter.

Starlet catches up to me, touching my back gently. "Come on, we've got to find Saturnus," I remind her.

"What about Azure?" she asks me, the concern for her soulmate evident on her face. I wonder why I haven't thought about Callie. Maybe she'll be a part of the army, so far gone as to attack a city she had once loved. Maybe she hadn't entered my mind because I'm finally grasping that nothing could ever be as important as my role as Crowned Ruler, or maybe I am just too afraid of the consequences of her attacking my city.

"She'll be okay. Azure can take care of herself. Come, we need to find Saturnus," I repeat myself, Saturnus' name a prayer, a magic solution, on my lips.

I know we've had our differences, but maybe this was what we need to come together. He had been right when he said we needed him and I had never felt more thankful for his protective walls around his city than today.

I grab Starlet's hand and pull her out of the now open doors of the Alcazar Oceania.

As we glide among the coral stalks of the palace gardens I scan our surroundings, paranoid of every single speck and sliver of shadow.

After a few moments of looking around, desperately hoping to see nothing, I breathe a sigh of relief. No sign of the Psirens yet, but it's high noon on the surface world. Perfect for mer slaughter, you need only expose them to the sunlight above for half a minute and they'll turn to sand.

I frown, hating that glowing ball of light. We need to stick low to the ground today; I'm not taking any chances.

"Orion! Stop!" I feel Starlet grab at my wrist, but I jerk it away. She isn't having any of it. "ORION!" She yells. I stop, turning on her, irritated.

"What?" I bark.

"Calm down," she reminds me.

"How does that help anything?" I demand, as she narrows her eyes, crossing her arms and smiling, like she has some big secret.

"You're forgetting, brother, that you've done this before, so have I. Maybe not with an army this size, maybe not with the Psirens, but we've done this before. We're still standing. So breathe. You fluttering around like a pissed off butterfly isn't going to help anyone. You need to be thinking clearly."

"I'm wounded that you equate this with fluttering," I say, my expression deadly serious. She cocks her head to one side, her white blonde hair falling over one shoulder and her magenta facial scales shimmering wildly in the light of the high sun. "Okay. I'm breathing," I respond, annoyed at how right she can be. Out of everyone in our family, I'd never peg her for the smartest, but if there's one thing Starlet is, it is reason in a sea of chaos, calm in a crisis.

"How do you do that?" I go limp slightly as I ask her this one, very important question.

"Do what?" She asks me, taking my hand in hers and squeezing it.

"Stay calm and rational when everything is falling apart?"

"I watch," she says the sentiment simply as I feel the blood pulsing around me begin to slow. I'm looking deeply into my sister's eyes, being lulled into what I know, letting her ground me.

"What do you mean, you mean like how you see with visions?"

"No. That's seeing. I watch." I frown slightly and she inhales, smiling.

"Dad, he used to know what to do in a crisis. I watched him for so long, it's what happens when you aren't allowed to fight, you observe. You learn," she admits, looking like she might cry.

"He'd be proud of you Star... At least he raised a ruler in one of us." I lean forward and kiss her cheek. She blushes slightly.

"Thank you," she whispers.

"For what?"

"Being the man I know you are," she winks at me and smiles, the biggest smile I've seen pass her lips for years. She reaches up and puts her arms around me, an uncertain gesture but one that hasn't lost its nostalgia, even though it's been years since we last embraced. "Come on. Let's go, before we both turn into blubbering idiots," she laughs, wiping underneath her eye, embarrassed.

"It's going to be bad, isn't it?" I whisper to her, as we begin to move out of the coral gardens, close and synchronised in our strokes.

"What makes you say that?" She tilts her head. I look out onto the horizon, watching as a black mass begins to rise into the aquamarine hue of the midday ocean.

"Because," I say, looking deeply into her eyes, "something about that embrace you just gave me felt like a goodbye." Her eyes widen slightly and her lips sag, unable to form words to express what's running through her mind.

I wait, but she doesn't answer. She doesn't need to.

I just hope she's wrong.

228

CALLIE

We sit, opposite each other, aching as the sand from whatever blasted us apart settles. I look down at myself.

I have changed.

My tailfin is aquamarine again, my hair falls in blonde around my shoulders. I stare into the now murky water, head throbbing. Vex is slumped against the opposite wall, holding up his arm to the light.

He's examining the white flesh of his limb, which is now mapped with dark veins of black magic. I examine my own skin, nothing but pale white flesh and aquamarine scales, shimmering madly.

I look between my own form and Vex... his eyes have turned dark... almost like he's taken on my own darkness along with his own. Wait a minute...

"You... you took my darkness!" I exclaim, not sure whether to be relieved or angry.

"Wait... what?" Vex rises slightly, looking at me from across the length of the corridor. He looks just as confused as I am and his voice sounds husky, like he needs to cough. I move back from him slightly, scared as to what such an influx of power will do.

"How did you do that?" I ask him, my eyebrows raised. He shrugs, shoulder rising with an angry suddenness.

"How the bloody hell should I know! You're the one with the bloody 'kiss me, kiss me' eyes!" He flutters his stumpy fingers around his eyes, batting his eyelids.

It would be comical if he weren't so terrifying. His face is covered in black veins and his eyes are completely black too, rage filled. He looks like Titus from here, just with tentacles.

It's with this recognition that I remember staring at my reflection in the shattered mirror of the hotel room. I know that's exactly what I had looked like.

"You kissed me!" I exclaim, disgusted at his insinuation that I had been the one to initiate.

"Don't give me that bollocks!" He sweeps a hand around himself, as though he's pushing my retaliation away.

"What bollocks? There's no bollocks here! You came back to rescue me, remember? You're the one who started all this! You should have just let me rot!"

"Well...maybe I should have! Don't worry, Love, I'll be letting you next time! You're a bloody lousy kisser anyway!" His argument is weakening as the hysterical nature of what's going on seems to infect his thought process. I'm slowly lulling him back from the edge with banter. I continue.

"Me?! At least I don't taste like an ash tray!" I spit, pretending to expel his taste from my mouth.

"Better than the taste of Nancy boy..." he quips. This comment suddenly reminds me of why I was trying to escape in the first place.

"Orion! The city! We have to go, stop them from leaving!"

"Bit late for that, Love. They're gone," Vex looks at me, his eyes slowly returning to their usual lilac. His skin is still mapped with veins, but he is beginning to look more like himself again.

"What do you mean?" I ask him, immediately rising off the floor and straightening my spine, tense.

"I mean they're on their way, Love. The revolution has already begun."

ORION

"Saturnus!!" I am hammering on the door with my fist, Starlet at my back. The door doesn't open. "Back up," I order Starlet. She does with one quick movement of her tailfin as I expel a blast of air from my palms, knocking the door back, swinging on its hinges.

I enter quickly, looking up at the high tower where Saturnus keeps his extensive collection of books stacked tightly into the curving shelves of the cylindrical tallness of the study. He's there.

"May I beg an explanation of this rudeness?" He barks, sinking through the water, unmoving, as though he's a God. His golden scales are shimmering, the jewels encrusted into the scales sparkling with blinding intensity.

"The Psiren army is coming!" I exclaim and his eyebrows rise slightly, not missing a beat.

"Ahhh," he doesn't look worried, merely stern.

"Aren't you concerned?" I ask him, slightly confused as to why he's not panicking.

"Not at all. We have all we need here to beat them back. Let's just stay calm and prepare. I still hold the power to protect this city. Worry not, Orion. All will be well," he places a hand on my shoulder.

"What should we do?" I ask him, desperately needing his guidance.

"You're asking me? You're crowned ruler," he smirks and I feel irritated. This isn't the time for grudges.

"Yes, but you've guided the crown for longer than anyone," I remind him. He smiles, his pale skin radiant against the bloody mess of his mane of hair.

"Very well. If you wish me to guide you I will," he nods and I smile.

"Thank you," I exhale slightly, feeling relief wash over me.

"Starlet is with you?" He queries.

I nod as she moves around the doorway.

"Very well. Starlet, I'm going to lock you in my office. You shouldn't be out in the city." Starlet looks at me with alarm on her features. I place a hand on her shoulder, bending my head.

"Don't worry, I'll come back for you as soon as I can. We need to trust Saturnus. It'll be alright now, you'll see," I comfort her but she still looks unimpressed. "I can't risk anything happening to you. I won't lose any more family to these creatures." She pulls a face but heads over to the red velvet sofa, picking up one of Saturnus' books and flipping through it, looking bored. Something catches her eye in the corner and I watch her gaze fall to a mirror in the corner of the study. She frowns slightly, her eyebrows knitting together.

"Is that my mirror, Saturnus?" She asks him and he nods.

"Yes… I recall you asking me to move it out of your room for you. A safety measure, remember?" Saturnus looks at her and her eyes search his face. He pulls a leather satchel from a nearby table, throwing it across his body so it hangs at a diagonal.

"Yes, but why is it here?" She asks him and he shrugs.

"Why, because I can't find anywhere to store it of course," he laughs slightly. She nods slowly, like she's unsure of something, but sits back into the hold of the chair, returning to the book she was previously reading.

"Come, Orion. We have work to do," Saturnus commands. He moves from the room and I follow him out. Looking back over my shoulder at Starlet.

"I'll be back before you know it," I wink at her and she raises her eyebrows, her expression deadly serious.

"See you later then," she replies. I nod and close the door behind me. Saturnus removes a cord from around his neck with the key to his study. Placing it in the lock, he gives it a quick twist before returning it safely around his neck.

"Better safe than sorry eh?" He smiles and I nod. Unamused.

"Let's go," I urge him on.

We sink through the tower and immediately, with Starlet's safety ensured thanks to the quick thinking of Saturnus, my thoughts move onto battle strategy.

"So, I need to position the Knight's around the city, I was thinking a strong hold at the place where the Psiren's entered last time, what do you think?"

"I think you don't want to risk it, set them in a ring around the city," Saturnus sounds so sure. He must know something I don't. I knew I was going to screw this Crowned Ruler thing up.

"But then the line will only be one man thick. The border around the city is large," I remind him, but he shakes his head.

"I'm telling you, Orion, you're better spreading them out and having better coverage. There's no way they can take out the entire glimmer. If they do manage to get through, say they've found a spell, or an object that can damage my magic, then it'll be concentrated in one spot. What we don't know is which spot. We need to cover every possible side."

"Very well. If that's what you think is best," I relinquish, still unsure, but knowing my judgement has done nothing but falter since I've been crowned. I can't risk screwing this up.

"It is. I wouldn't be telling you this if I thought otherwise now, would I?" He asks me the question as we move out into the street, the bottles embedded in the paths are glistening. I assume it rhetorical and keep my silence.

Cole and Ghazi approach from the centre square in front of the Alcazar and I turn to face them immediately.

"You're to spread the Knights of Atargatis, shoulder to shoulder in a ring around the city," I order them. Cole looks at me, confused.

"But sir, we don't have enough Knights to put shoulder to shoulder without the ring only being a single layer thick," he questions me.

"I am well aware, Cole. Isn't it slightly above your position to be questioning my decisions?" I ask him, feeling the venom leave me unexpectedly. I have never spoken down to him before.

I immediately feel bad. His expression hardens and Ghazi looks shocked.

"Sir, yes sir." His eyes are glazed over, I can tell I've hurt him, but I don't have time to make amends now.

"Do it," I command, stern, and they both turn from me without a words parting.

"Good. Nice to see you finally taking your role seriously," Saturnus nods, placing a cold hand on my shoulder and squeezing hard.

"What now?" I ask him and he smiles, like my asking him for advice is how things should be. Like it's right.

"Now, we rise above the city and watch. You want the best vantage point possible," he reminds me and I nod. Something inside of my falters suddenly, I narrow my eyes and turn to him.

"Don't I need a weapon?" I ask him, feeling fear clutch at my heart.

"You are enough of a weapon already Orion. You have your ability over air, a gift from our Goddess. That's better than any spear." I smile a little, his confidence in my abilities making me feel sure of myself.

"I'd still feel better with a spear or sword. I'll head to the armoury."

"You're out of time!" Saturnus says, looking out to the horizon and pointing. His eyes wide.

The sun is high overhead still, and now I can see the Psiren army for what it is: huge. They've grown.

Saturnus and I rise high above the city, watching the Knights assemble around its borders, diligent to my command and unthinking in their loyalty.

"Quite a sight to see, isn't it?" Saturnus asks me, his bloody tangle of red hair wavering around his head. His gold scales and jewel encrusted flesh glistens under the midday sun.

"Of course," I mutter, uninterested in platitudes.

The streets below are packed, the people of my city having noticed the encroaching dark cloud, like smoke, I can only hope it's easier to capture and destroy. The mermaids below are stirring, I watch them from this great height like insects, scurrying and forming tiny clusters, no doubt gossiping and spreading fear amongst themselves.

"You need not worry, Orion. All will be well," Saturnus comforts me and I turn to him.

"Thank you. I'm not doing a great job at this leader thing. I know that. You would have been the better choice," I admit this, trying to show my true feelings about the position, hoping he will understand that this isn't a responsibility I ever wanted and that I in no way feel superior to him or anyone else.

"Oh I know," he smiles, his mouth spreading into a joyous chasm. My heart begins to drop slightly at the look in his eyes.

I ignore it, turning away from him as a slight sickness churns in my stomach. Is it just nerves? Probably. I dismiss it and turn, facing my fear and watching the black mass of Psirens fall upon us.

They reach the outskirts of the city limits and the effect is staggering. They dwarf our army entirely, especially now that the army is spread, shoulder-to-shoulder in a single band around the city limits. They look like a piece of string, flimsy and weak compared to the fist of an army they face. I swallow hard, blood pounding around my body.

"So what now?" I rotate in the water. The armies are facing one another, floating and waiting, innocuous.

"Now... I think it's time that I impart a lesson that your father learned the hard way. He would have wanted me to impart it and seeing as I might not get another chance, it should be now," he looks deeply into my eyes, his voice lulling me into a familiar security.

"What is it?" I whisper, slightly awe stricken at the lushness of his green eyes.

"Come closer…" he gestures for me to move toward him, the heat of his breath touching my face as I slip through the water. He moves in too, sliding his mouth in beside my ear.

"Trust…no one," he whispers the words and I feel myself frown, confused. Something is thrust into my flesh and with a sharp convulsion I scream out. I look down; he's stabbed me in the gut with a dagger.

I watch as he shifts, magic falling from him like a curtain, unveiling the performance of a lifetime. His body is deathly white, his eyes black, with yellow feline pupils. His hair changes from bloody red to black as night and his tail morphs from one of a Goddess' love to that with characteristics of a white dragon king crown betta. The body of his tail is white, pale and leeched of all colour but its edges fray and morph outward in crisscrossing blades of onyx flesh.

This is all I manage to take in before a sick smile spreads across his lips and he pushes me away from his true form, wrenching the dagger from my insides as I gasp in surprise. I fall backwards through the water steadily and in slow motion as I reach out to grab at Saturnus. My body is in shock, damaged and unable to respond as I crash downward. The glimmer surrounding the city falls as Saturnus commands it, ripping our only chance of survival away as though it were no more than tissue paper.

The last thing I remember before the unconsciousness takes me are falling, flaming stars and a swarm descending on everything I love.

20

Decimate

SOLUSTUS

The glimmer falls and there it is: the promised land, all gleam and shine in the sunlight which burns my eyes. The Occulta Mirum, the Kingdom I had longed to possess as my own for so long, to watch the mer kneel before me as I slit their throats. I smile to myself seeing my brother, a speck at the height of the city, a figure falling from him, leaving a trail of scarlet behind it in intermittent plumes.

"Fire!" I bellow. My arrow masters pull back their bows, constructed from whale ribs, and ignite their arrows. It was an ingenious creation, sparked by the discovery of a flare, still burning in spite of being at the bottom of the ocean. Magnesium, that was the key: a chemical that burns so hot that it makes its own stream of oxygen from the surrounding water, keeping it lit. Saturnus had been impressed and I watch as the arrows, flaming, fall upon the city.

A satisfying panic rings out as the people below scatter.

I move forward, pointing with my long fingers, signalling for the army to descend. They move, a black mass of intense power, each beast armed with some kind of weapon, many with little more than boards of rotting wood with fish hooks stuck through, but each as lethal as the next. I am glad in this moment that I have trained them personally and I watch as they move, meeting to clash with the flimsy band of warriors that the mer call an army. My next command isn't necessary, but I feel I need to exert my dominance and keep some semblance of control over the mass of soulless killers I have harboured. It is simple.

"Decimate."

I swim like a dart, lithe and with quick momentum, through the water with such accuracy and pointed speed that one might not discern me unless they really try. I am a blur, high on the bloodshed occurring beneath me. Scarlette at my hip and the scythe strapped flat against the length of my spine.

"Brother!" I bellow, my mouth wide in a smile, Saturnus has shed his costume of light and is back to what I made him. His tail had always made me feel like I was on a knife's edge, proud in one aspect, that I had created something so wicked looking, and jealous in another that my own appearance did not exude such power.

"Solustus. My how they have grown," Saturnus smiles, his jagged teeth showing gaps that would make anyone shudder.

"Indeed. Alyssa has been busy."

"I can see that. I swear outlawing her was the best thing I ever did. I knew she had greatness in her, even if I did have to pull it out of her." He looks smug, of course he feels this is his victory, pulling strings, manipulating from afar.

"They will dismantle this army in moments," I watch as my creatures set about the Knights with relish. The mer bend and buckle beneath the weight of so many vicious, clawing bodies seeking out flesh to tear from bone.

Saturnus smiles as the line breaks, heads falling from bodies, and the Psirens pour forth, moving out into the streets.

"Welcome home," Saturnus turns to me smiling. Victory looks good on him. He clasps my hand in his palm and pulls me in, patting me on the back. I close my eyes a moment, savouring his approval.

"I brought Regus," I enlighten him, knowing we need him for the next part of our plan.

"Good, we need him to shift the decoration from around the seal. I've captured the seer based off the information you retrieved from the Necrimad, she's in my office. However, there's still one mer in particular we need."

"Who would that be?" I request, keeping my eyes on the army as my soldiers move into the streets like a plague, grabbing brightly coloured maidens and taking them apart.

"The metal master, Oscar," Saturnus says the name with disdain, like it's toxic.

"What need do we have of him?" I enquire as the sounds of screams start to reach me.

"You can't tell me you think we're going to raise a pure blooded demon and let it run free. We'll be needing containment," Saturnus cocks a black eyebrow as if I'm stupid. It is true that I hadn't thought of it like that.

I say nothing, allowing my palm to stroke the edge of my rapier's handle.

"Where's the boy?" I ask Saturnus, dying to change the subject. Saturnus' smile widens as he points downward. I look down and far below is the Crowned Ruler, splayed out and broken on the ground, I can see that his eyes are open, unblinking and I wonder if he's alive.

"Dead?" I enquire.

"Why should I care? He's nothing special," Saturnus dismisses my comment with the wave of a hand.

"Come, and get Regus. There is work to be done."

We float, impatient before the giant sea glass shard. To so many mer it is a symbol of hope, and yet all along it has been window dressing on the real power, the real reason this city was erected. It stands over the seal of Poseidon, where he trapped my power and stripped me down to what I am.

"Can you do it?" Saturnus turns to Regus. His tail, that of a hammer-head shark, barely moves and his heavily muscled torso is tense with concentration. His bald head moves up and down, never one for words; he could be a mute.

"You might want to get back," is his only sentiment. His bulging muscles disgust me as the thought of so much excess of flesh on his bones makes him slow and cumbersome.

Saturnus flexes his tailfin, giving Regus a wide berth, and I move minutely but gain a large distance. I smile at my speed, one of the only things I have over my brother.

We stare at the palace for a few moments, nothing happening until a sudden and mighty rumble erupts from the earth below. Regus raises his palms, his muscles tense to the point where veins burst from their surface.

Saturnus and I watch as the palace begins to shatter, unable to bear the violent cracking of its foundations beneath. Regus brings his palms down in one fail swoop and I watch as a trail of black follows them, the darkness of his magic showing itself. With this gesture the palace shatters from the base upward with a sharp, mind-numbing crack. The glass falls like jagged crystal rain and sand flies up from the sea floor.

I turn away from the destruction, bored, staring at the war going on at my back. My Psirens are owning the mer, showing them where they belong. I watch as they rise, taking members of the Knights with them, taking them for a bath of sunlight and leaving them as nothing but sand. Others go for a more abrupt approach, simply ripping heads from bodies in mushroom clouds of scarlet hue. I turn back to the giant pile of glass.

"Removing that debris is going to take a while," I run my fingers through my hair, flexing my spine and puffing out my chest. Saturnus raises both his eyebrows and his eyes sparkle, white from the depths of yellow and black. He looks practically feline.

"We have nothing but time. Our enemies are sand, brother." He turns to the mass annihilation occurring on the streets below us; sand swilling in with the blood that is spilling out into the water by the gallon, he purrs, "Nothing can stop me now."

AZURE

The streets of the Occulta Mirum are in chaos and all I can do is be still, surrounded by the din and incapable of taking in what's going on around me. It's like everything is in slow motion, a merman with a violet tailfin and blonde hair has his body removed at the neck, falling and then disappearing in a plume of blood and sand that swirls together in a sickly sweet and gritty concoction. It falls around me as I inhale it, feeling the bloody water coat the back of my throat as it's taken inside by my gills. I had been out of the darkness too long, away from this violent world, sleeping in soft beds and surrounded by those who pity, those who care. That's not what I need right now. I realise this as I watch a maiden with blonde hair being taken and shoved into the wall of a cylindrical tower to my right. I need the darkness; I need the power. Everything that I had known is tumbling around me. They've done it, they've really gone and taken the city. They are slaughtering everyone. I had seen it in my vision, but in person, with the screaming and the smell of burnt flesh in the water from the impossible fire, it is different.

Something comes out of nowhere, smashing into the side of my skull, my head takes the impact but I manage to maintain my upright position in the water. A Psiren, a male with the tail of a great white shark is grinning, looking pleased with himself as he pulls back on his slingshot again.

"Oh you're going to wish you'd aimed that at someone else you little..." I mutter to myself as I start to feel darkness bubbling up from the deep void within me.

I move, like a killer, like Titus had shown me. It's only a twitch, but as I fall through the street at high speed, the boy who hit me in the head with a luckily aimed rock gets tackled, the air blown from his lungs as I set about dismantling him. The smile vanishes from his face as my jaw opens wide, bending down to bite out his trachea, ripping it from his form. As I rise to plunge and take his life, the blue of his eyes becomes non-existent and his pupils dilate, not with darkness, but with fear. I stop.

"Get out of here," I move from his body and he looks confused. "GO!" I scream, wondering what I must look like to him, a monster. I was the thing monsters feared apparently.

I don't know what makes me stop myself from killing him, but I realise in this moment that killing him isn't going to save anyone I love. I turn my back on his shocked expression as he rights himself, moving back into the mass of bodies, locked in immortal struggle.

My thoughts go to my priorities, trying to see clearly through the anger that mists my thought process.

Starlet.

I remind myself of my soulmate, quickly picturing her face and then realising I need to find somewhere quiet, only for a few moments, if I'm to locate her.

I move across the street, where I dodge a few Psirens who are fighting with Ghazi and Cole. It amazes me as I move quickly past them that they're not dead, but instead beating back an enemy that is overtaking them at a ratio of six to one. They are incredible fighters and as I turn from them I hear metal armour clang against weapons and the cries and grunts of exertion from fending off the enemy. I hope silently that they make it, we'll need them for after, if there is an after.

I take cover in the shadows of a cylindrical surface scraper and try to drown out the sounds of the killing and fighting going on around me. The water remains tinted slightly red and the noise is overwhelming and barbaric. I breathe, ignoring the metallic taste in the back of my throat.

Please, Goddess, if you're out there, let me see into her.

I make this silent prayer before the fog rolls in as I will it.

I'm in Starlet's mind, looking through her eyes. She's in Saturnus' study and she's reading a book. I wonder what the hell she's playing at, reading during the biggest war I can remember, but then I notice something. She's underlined words in a red ink that could be blood for all I know. I trace them through her sight, scanning the page. The message from her is clear.

Do Not Save Me. Run. Save Them.

I'll give her some credit, she's done well getting the correct words on the same page to send the message, but I'm not leaving her behind, no way in hell. I know where she is and I'm getting her the hell out of here, we're family.

I open my eyes, coming back into my body and suddenly realise that the building I'm leaning against is shaking, as is everything else around me.

An earthquake? Now? This can't be a coincidence.

I peer out into the street, but instead of focusing on what's going on around me in the immediate vicinity, I look up. I don't know what makes me look up, but once I do I know why I have.

Three figures. Solustus, a black tailed Psiren, and what appears to be Regus are standing near the Alcazar Oceania.

Shit. I cuss internally.

It was Regus. His power over earth is incredibly powerful, not that Titus would have ever used it, because that would have implied Regus had power he didn't. Another Psiren however, take Solustus, wouldn't hesitate to use his abilities to get what he wanted.

I flex my tailfin propelling myself forward, moving toward the central square where Saturnus' office resides, ducking in and out of the fighting, clenching my fists to hold back the darkness which is telling me, over and over, in constant dull rhythm, to take each one of these Psirens and rip their throats out.

I weave between them, trying not to get clobbered. You'd think I'd be feeling my heart race, or be unable to order my thoughts, but suddenly I'm finding clarity among the chaos. I wonder if it's because I've known this was coming all along, or because I'm so used to death and pain and the fall of everything beautiful in my life that I've lost the ability to really care.

I study the fights going on around me, scrutinising the details someone panicked would miss, trying to avoid any errors while whipping through the water at a speed rivalling even the fastest marine life. They're attacking more maidens now. I look back over one shoulder and realise that's because there are hardly any Knights left.

I refuse to dwell on the implications of this, moving ever forward, until I come to a roadblock, and a psychotic one at that. Caedes is hovering in the street looking straight at me. Every muscle in my body tenses and I feel the sinew in my tail readying to manoeuvre. I don't want to get into a fight with Caedes, but knowing him, he's not going to give me much other choice.

It's minute, a movement so small it's barely perceptible to the most inhuman of eyes, even mine. Nonetheless I notice Caedes recoil the spines which protrude from his tail, that of a lionfish, ever so slightly. I know he's got me in his sights and I know I'm going to have to fight him, so I just manage to breathe in before I see him smile. All of a sudden, he's on top of me. It's a silent struggle as his hands close in around my throat, his eyes manic with a lack of logical reasoning. I had seen darkness in the eyes of Titus, but there is something eerie about looking into Caedes eyes, like he's in a trance or a dream from which he can never awake.

As this occurs to me my thoughts start to evaporate, like the lack of oxygen is smothering my ability to think. My gills are trying to open, but Caedes' grasp is too tight. I reach out, flailing with my arms until I feel something solid knock the back of my hand. I grab it, pulling it up and slamming it into my attacker's skull. Caedes falls back, disoriented as I gasp for air, pulling water into my lungs as they open and close in frantic rhythm. I know the only way I can beat him in a fight is to become just as twisted as he is. I wonder momentarily if it's worth risking my own sanity to kill him.

No. I think to myself as I put a slender hand up to my gills. My blue fingernails gently move across the skin, which feels tender, and I'm angry. I look at my other hand, realising I'm holding a helmet full of sand. It belonged to one of the Knight's by the looks of the design and I wonder if the sand pouring out of it is all that remains of the soldier it once belonged to. I watch as Caedes rights himself with one flick of his tail, his spines flared out, his red hair dishevelled, and his black eyes spinning in their sockets.

"Ow," he spits blood into the water and it dissipates before our eyes. He begins to move, circling me. I compensate, circling him too, two lions waiting for a weakness in the other. I'm clutching the helmet in one hand as epic battles continue around us, dances of death and struggles for survival raging on in an unending clamour. I drown out the noise, the cries of pain and the grunts of victory, focusing on the problem in front of me.

I feel the tension in the water rise momentarily; something is going to happen. He might kill me. It might finally be over.

Something does happen, but it's not what I expect as a mighty cracking sound explodes through the air. I try not to let it distract me, as I don't want to give any inkling of lapsing focus. Suddenly, as though fate has stepped in, Caedes falls to the floor unconscious. I gape, confused, looking around for an explanation. The back of his head is bloodied from a rock, the red fluid rising into the water like a twisting serpent.

In the distance I see the shooter; it's the boy I saved, smiling at his improved accuracy. He nods at me and then turns, going back to shooting the people I'm defending with one flick of his muscular shark tail. I don't have time to react because in what seems like only a moment, a shuddering is making the water around me vibrate visibly.

I turn and see a gargantuan cloud of sand and shards of glass hurtling towards me. The Alcazar is falling, a hundred tonnes of glass, stone, and debris collapsing in on itself and falling to the ground. I hear the sound around me seize as others finally notice what's happening. I pause before turning and swimming, getting out of the main street, taking cover against one of the other buildings.

I look up as the cloud reaches us. The sand and displacement of the water feels like an immense wind, stinging my eyes and prickling my skin. I turn, trying to get out of its path, entering the building I'm leaning against to try and escape. Inside the doorway things are slightly calmer as the debris from the castle washes over the building. The rumbling eventually stops as I wait it out, suddenly realising where it is I've ended up. The armoury.

I look around, the walls are practically barren but there are a few pieces of armour that haven't been taken. I frown. They look like Orion's. I know I've seen him wearing something similar before. This thought suggests an interesting concept to me. Where are he and Saturnus? The Crowned Ruler and his Right Hand are two of the main people you'd expect to find either fighting or in the Alcazar, but now that is gone. I wonder if they are both trapped inside... or worse. My heart constricts a moment for my brother, who has been trying so hard to keep the city safe mere hours ago. I place the helmet on over my black locks and take some chainmail to wrap around my tailfin while trying to find a chest plate that fits, but nothing works over the top of my breasts. I growl at the lack of attire for women. Starlet was right; this city has major issues. I wish I had my pearl strung whip, but I had gotten rid of it after the last Psiren invasion... or rather Orion had confiscated it, not trusting me with weaponry. I sigh before pulling a broadsword down from the rack feeling the weight of heavy steel in my palms.

Yes, this will do nicely.

Out in the streets once more the fighting is still going on, but the numbers of mer are drastically reduced. Psirens are everywhere, some looking bored and others seem to be looking for something. I don't know what it is, but I don't want to be noticeable so I focus on the thought of Arabella, feeling my pupils dilate so they're black. My tailfin has been reverting to its old electric blue lately, but I'm hoping the chainmail makes it look duller somehow.

I move forward toward where the Alcazar Oceania had stood only a short time ago, the streets scattered with broken sea-glass and the remnants of stained glass windows. I see wood too and I can't help but cringe slightly because I know where it's from. The thrones made from the olive trees native to where I was born. I hear a sudden inhale, something broken and strained as I move through the streets. I jump slightly.

"Az..." I swear it's a call out to me, but as I turn around, nobody is paying me any attention. I look down, piles of sand and glass everywhere.

Suddenly one of them shifts. There's someone under there. I look behind me again, making sure I'm going unnoticed before I allow myself to fall to the floor. I set about moving sand from the pile, clawing it so it's behind me, taking care to keep brushing my palm back against the handle of my weapon, ready to grasp if it I have to. As the sand moves away, I realise that what it's covering isn't just anyone. It's Orion.

"Orion," I exhale. "Not an ideal place for a nap." I snap, trying to seem mad at him. I can't have him thinking I've gone totally soft.

I work about moving more sand, but in the end I figure it's faster to pull him out instead. I rest my tailfin flat against the path; it was once lined with glass bottles but is now spiked with their shattered remnants. I feel my scales ripping slightly from my tail as I strain against the jagged glass, but it has to be done. I wince, trying not to cry out. Eventually, after much heaving and grunting, I've managed to prop him up against the walls surrounding the alley and away from the main street, that's when I notice he's injured.

"What happened?" I ask, moving to touch the stab wound, it's red and angry in his gut. He winces.

"Saturnus. He..." he winces again, pulling himself so he's sitting upright properly.

"Saturnus? You mean Solustus..." I begin; the Crowned Ruler is delusional...

Greeeeat, I snipe internally.

"No! Saturnus. He's evil, Azure. He can glimmer himself. He dropped the city's defences. He was a Psiren all along," he is gasping a little. I wonder what internal damage the knife has done. Fortunately for him he has accelerated healing, but it still probably stings like a bitch.

"Saturnus?" I say his name once more. I think back to every time I'd had a dodgy feeling about him. My gut clearly knew more than my brain did. I knew something was off there.

"Okay... I need to get Star. Then we need to get out of here. Can you move?" I ask him and he nods, wincing.

"Yes, I'll be okay, I can feel the wound healing already," he goes to rise.

"Rest a moment. Then you need to find anyone who's still alive and get them out. This is a bloodbath. There's nothing left for us here."

"Go... Go where?" He looks up at me, his icy blue eyes full of fear.

"Anywhere you can think of that's safe. We need somewhere to regroup."

"How will you find us?"

"I'll manage," I promise him. He rises again, putting on his tough face and pressing his mouth into a firm line.

"Okay. Be careful," he warns me and I cock a brow.

"Says the man who got himself stabbed. Yeah, whatever," I turn from him, shrugging. I don't do big emotional goodbyes after all.

I make it to the outskirts of the building where Saturnus' office resides. Swimming as quickly as I can muster, darting in and out of the shadows while I try to stay out of sight. I am good at this, the high pressure, blood pounding, heart racing type situations are what every day had been like as a Psiren and so I relish my time invisible. I look up at the tower now that I'm here, the noise of a nearby Psiren smashing something makes me jump momentarily.

Okay, so maybe I'm not totally fearless, I remind myself.

I could go in through the door, but that would be too easy and odds are it's locked. Slowly, I rise up against the cylindrical turret, ascending to just outside the window.

"Psst," I hiss over the top of the window, not looking first.

That was a stupid idea. I chastise myself.

I place my hand on the ledge and suddenly something is gripping onto it, something pale and with dirty fingernails.

"Can I help you, dear?" Solustus' tone reaches me, my heart stopping cold in my chest.

"I want my sister. That's all," I bite out, yanking my hand away. I ascend further upward, moving back so I can glimpse into the window properly.

"Oh, is that all?" Solustus has his pointed chin resting in his long bony fingers like a wistful teenager.

"Yes," I glance behind his head as I reply and see a flash of icy blue. Starlet's eyes catch the light and instantly I know the terror she feels. She's bound and gagged.

"I think not," Solustus smiles at me, his pointed features cutting me with their cruel response. I know he can't get to me through the window, it's too narrow, but I don't like conversing with him none the less.

"Why? You don't need her for anything! Let her go!" I retort and he laughs.

"Quite contrary, my dear, but if you want to fight me and my brother and the five guards I have posted outside the door, be my guest, but I have the distinct feeling that would only lead to your death." He cocks an eyebrow, challenging me with a smile.

I think for a moment, my finger touching the handle of my sword. His eyes trace over me. "You? Think you can beat me with a sword? Dream on girl," he laughs and draws the curtains, sick of the discussion. I debate stabbing him through it, but I worry he'd situate Star on the other side of the lush red velvet as punishment for my defiance. He's wicked that way. I could take the door approach, but I don't have enough strength to take on five guards, Solustus, and Caedes. I could barely handle Caedes on his own.

Instead I hang, placid and useless in the water, I need to launch a rescue mission for Star, but I can't do that alone. I need mer with offensive magic. I cuss internally, what the hell use is being good if it means you have no power or control? I wouldn't be in this situation if I'd stayed with the Psirens. I could save her.

Yes. But she wouldn't want you to. I remind myself that with the darkness Starlet and I would never be Starlet and I, because she wouldn't want to be a sister to someone so despicable.

I look down on the rubble of the Alcazar Oceania, where Psirens are scavenging treasures from the ruins, moving rubble and picking off the last few mer who remain. I wonder how successful Orion has been in finding survivors.

I look back to the red curtain and hear screams from within. Turning away a single tear falls from my eye, devastated that I can't save her. I had only just gotten her back. I should have heeded the warnings, the visions sent to me, but instead I had wallowed in my own darkness. I think of Starlet's face, terrified and sparkling with tears, and my breath catches in my throat. I know we are supposed to be together.

It seems however that destiny, the bitch, has other ideas.

21
Sanctuary

CALLIE

Vex and I propel through the water, leaving the Cryptopolis long behind us, not talking and reaching a speed bordering on urgency. Things are awkward after our kiss. I don't want to give him the wrong impression, he's hot and all, but now my form has returned to its old self, I can't help but feel momentarily repulsed by him. His silver hair is greasy, his skin too pale, and his eyes too intense. He's striking, but he's not beautiful like Orion, or like any of the other mermen who were created by Atargatis. The lilac in his eyes is too pale, so much so that I feel shivers run over my skin whenever he glances my way. It's creep inducing.

"Can you stop looking at me, it's freaking me out," I ask him, snapping slightly. An anxious knot has formed deep inside me and he's only making it worse.

"I liked it better when you were dark. Come here…" he moves to grab me, to kiss me again, but I punch him in the nose with a sudden, and unplanned, jerk of my arm. He swears. "Shit!!! What the hell did you do that for?" He backs away from me and I continue swimming forward, ignoring him as blood seeps out from his nostrils into the water.

"Don't touch me," I mutter, all business as I race through the waves.

"Alright, Love! No need for bloody violence now was there?!" He exclaims, his eyelids fluttering as he pinches his nose. It's probably broken, but I'm too worried to feel bad.

"Do you realise what's happening here? If the Psirens succeed they could kill thousands. I don't have time for your crap, Vex!" I shout at him,

249

not in the mood for banter.

"Alright miss bossy britches. Keep your bloody hair on," he exclaims, making rage rise up in my throat. I don't take the bait for another argument though and he doesn't try to interrupt my rhythm against the water again. The silence resumes.

After a little while we begin to get close to the Occulta Mirum. I make way to see its towering green, sea-glass spires coming into view over the sea floor horizon. I'm fully aware that Vex won't be able to see them because of the glimmer, but I'm also expecting to see masses of Psirens on the outskirts of the city trying to breach its defences and that he will be able to see. I'm keeping my eyes peeled for the stone edifice, marking the city's entrance too, but instead I see nothing. As we move closer the Occulta Mirum comes into view, but its towering palace is gone.

"Oh my God..." The palace is a pile of shattered crystalline pieces and even from this distance the area where it was once erected is now crawling with Psirens. My heart drops and a single name screams out within me.

Orion.

I drop to the ground, losing all momentum, sounds lost to me. The city, the city I had loved, that I was supposed to be protecting was a pile of rubble. What had I done? What had happened here? How had the Psirens won so easily? We couldn't have been more than a few hours behind them, so why was the place in ruins with Psirens crawling everywhere in a swarm of dark black fins and tentacles. I sit in the sand, silent, letting the weight of what has happened sink in as I look down upon the rubble. Suddenly, my senses return to me. This is when I realise that Vex is talking.

"This is what we've been fighting for? Looks like a crap-heap to me," Vex shrugs and I turn to him, finding the strength to rise in the water.

"You can see it?" I ask, desperate, and he nods. He furrows his brow at me like I'm insane. "Don't look at me like that. We're too late. It's all my fault," I say the words, a cold torrent of realisation drenching me with guilt.

"The Psirens... you mean we won?" He looks hopeful, a spark igniting in the back of his too pale irises.

"No! You can't want this. The whole human world is now defenceless."

"So?" He shrugs again and my eyes widen.

"So..." I place my hands on his shoulders, feeling the need to shake him gripping me. "Everyone you ever loved in life, they will die. Screaming, bleeding, they will die... because of this. There has to be someone, someone who meant at least a little to you. Well... with the Psirens in charge the demons will come... and there will be no more sanctuary. Only death." I sound like an oracle, but in this moment I need him to understand. I watch a memory flash across the back of his eyes.

"Okay, what do I do?" He looks at me, his expression deadpan.

"I know what you can do." I hear the familiar tone and I turn, whipping my head around so my hair falls around my shoulders, long and blonde.

"Azure," I utter her name. She looks different. Her eyes are icy blue and her tailfin is coated in chainmail. There's a helmet on her head.

"So nice of you to finally show up. You missed the show," she bites at me and I feel her insult sting. She's right; I should have been here.

"I'm..." I begin to apologise but she holds a hand up. I blurt, abandoning my remorse and addressing the more pressing question at the top of my priorities. "Orion! Did he get out? Is he..."

"He got out, he was a mess though. Stabbed in the gut." My heart plummets and I feel my breathing quicken. Azure continues, un-phased. "Vex..." She turns to him and I watch his attention focus in on her, his eyes dilate, I've seen that happen when they fell on me, too. He's clearly attracted to her. As his body straightens and his chest bulges forward, I wonder if I should feel jealous that he's having this reaction, but my insides are desolate.

"Yes?"

"I need a man on the inside. It's not an easy job, trust me, and you might betray us, but right now, you're all I've got." I look at him and then back at her, surprised.

"You want *him* to work for us?" I say it, sounding as incredulous as I feel toward the idea. It's insane.

"Hey! What's that supposed to mean?" He looks at me offended.

"It means that you're not exactly the most reliable man I've ever met, you abandoned me remember?" I snipe back.

Azure looks between us and cocks an eyebrow, clearly amused.

"As I said, he's the best I've got. I need someone in there. My sister is inside, Vex, and I need her protected. You up for it?" She brushes some of the sand up off the ground with her tailfin, moving toward us.

"Starlet?" I whisper, horrified. Another one of Orion's family members is in danger because of me. I think back to the times I had felt jealous of her connection with her brother, with my soulmate, but it all seemed ridiculous and petty now.

"Yes. Solustus…"

"I'll do it," Vex cuts her off.

"Are you sure? If you promise to do this for me, I'm holding you to it. If you betray me or she dies, I'll kill you," Azure looks him straight in the face and gives a small smile as he chortles slightly. She comes up close to him with her sword, pressing it to his throat. "Do you know what takoyaki is?" She asks Vex and he shakes his head, gulping. His Adam's apple bobs against the edge of the blade and his tentacles still.

"It's what the Japanese call octopus that they grill and serve up on a platter. Now… listen up and listen good. I don't care how bad you think you are. I can guarantee you if you've done it, I've done it fifty times worse. Think you've been through a lot? Well, I've been on this earth a hundred times longer than what you consider your mighty lifespan, so just think about that… unless you want to end up an entrée," she threatens and I can tell Vex is on edge, but I think he's also turned on. Azure drops the blade and gives a casual smile, fluttering her eyelashes. "Great! Thanks!" She's acting so carefree, I've never seen her like this.

"Okay, so Callie are you coming with me?" Azure turns to me and I nod, twisting to face Vex. His sallow skin and sunken eyes are watching.

"This is where I say goodbye. Thanks for…" I don't quite know what to thank him for. Has he really made me into a better person? Or was my time away from the mer just a sabbatical from sense and reason? My internal voice whispers *he took away the darkness,* but I shake my head, dissolving the thought. I still don't understand what happened, why the darkness within me vanished, especially not when he was the epitome of darkness and I was kissing him.

"The tequila," he finishes my sentence with a wicked grin and my mouth pops open in shock.

My mind flashes back to my lips gliding across his skin. His hands in my hair, pulling my head back. His finger's clawing into my ass... us smashing in the television, breaking the desk. His expression feral and unyielding and his eyes alight with an eerie lilac glow. His eyes bare into me from memory, scorching themselves into the forefront of my thoughts. No! I snap internally, feeling my heart begin to pound.

I realise my mouth is still hanging open and I quickly return my expression to one that's uncaring. I don't have time for his innuendos.

"Sure. Whatever," I bite out and he recoils, looking hurt.

"You know you can be a real bitch?" He looks me square in the face. He wants me to retort, to return to our normal argumentative banter, but instead I turn, sighing.

"I know," I mutter as Azure and I turn away from him. Azure looks me in the face, curious, before something passes across her features, an idea or a memory, I can't tell which.

"Vex, wait!!" She calls out, turning. Vex spins, his tentacles flaring out with his momentum. She moves over to him quickly and they talk for a few moments, I can't hear the conversation but Vex bursts out laughing at something she says to him.

Behind them the Occulta Mirum lies in ruin. Some of the surface scrapers have fallen and the Alcazar is a pile of rubble. I want to sob for the loss of something so beautiful.

Azure returns to me, her tailfin undulating beneath her. Her brow is furrowed slightly and she's studying me with a curiosity seldom seen crossing her features because she rarely cares enough for this level of intrigue.

"I don't know what you got into with him, but whatever it is, you can be sure Orion won't let him live for long once he finds out," her eyes fall across my body.

She's judging me? Really? I take a deep breath swallowing down my instinct to sulk.

"I know. I don't know what I was doing with him really. It was just...

there was no expectation."

"You don't need to explain to me, Callie. I was with Titus, remember? I'm not exactly the Queen of great decisions," she pulls her helmet from her head, shaking out her hair. "We should move on, away from here. I don't want to know what it'll be like in these waters once the Psirens get bored of smashing up the city." She frowns, but her eyes are glassy and as we pass over a small section of coral reef, crawling with crabs, I notice how much she really has changed. She's no longer twitchy and the veins that once mapped her skin intermittently are gone. Other than that she seems to have found a kind of control over her rage. The Azure I had known before would have tackled Vex to the ground without a second thought. This time she'd only threatened violence. It isn't a completely new Azure, but Rome wasn't built in a day. It makes me think about my own actions and I realise I owe her an apology.

"Hey, I'm sorry about before. When I, you know, attacked you," I lack the ability to feel bashful like I once had, but I can't help but notice my cheeks warming slightly.

"I killed you. I'd say we're even," she isn't looking directly at me, always uncomfortable around public displays of emotion. I nod in response, not wanting to make an issue out of it just to make myself feel better. We move together, silently, but it isn't as awkward as I thought with her, in a way we're more similar now than I'd have ever thought possible. She's seen the darkness too, but she hasn't been so lucky in getting rid of it. It's a part of her now and I don't envy her. Always keeping her emotions, her rage in check. Not listening to the voices in her head telling her to kill, to destroy everything she touches. I look at her differently now and I know she's stronger than anyone gives her credit for.

"So where are we going?" I ask aloud, not filtering my thoughts as I watch a lowering sun throw silver lines across the ocean floor.

"I told Orion to go somewhere safe. He wanted to set a place but I was too distracted by the news about Saturnus and I told him I'd manage," she shakes her head, clearly regretting her decision. She increases her speed as she rises toward the surface. I follow her.

"What do you mean the news about Saturnus?" I ask her and she looks at me. Her expression is impassive, which for Azure is a restrained translation of grimness.

"He's evil, Callie. We don't know how long it's been going on for, but he dropped the glimmer and left the city defenceless. He turned it from a fair fight into a blood bath. According to Orion, he can glimmer his own image, like a chameleon. Lucky bastard." I can't tell if she's scared or jealous, but her pale skin glows slightly as we near the surface, the sunlight making her ghostly.

I pause a second as I feel the water run across my skin, the light pressure from the lack of depth exhilarating me. No matter how bad things get, I can't deny that slipping through the ocean's liquid bounty brings nothing but pleasure, despite the desperately melancholy knot tied deep within my gut. I try to wrap my mind around the information that's just been imparted. Something inside my brain clicks into place and my synapses fire in a quick assault.

"Yes!" I suddenly burst and Azure falters in her stroke.

"What the hell?" She exclaims, demanding I answer for my outburst.

"It all makes sense now! I touched him… and he freaked out, the first time in his office right before Titus tried to kill me, he practically tackled me to the floor. Orion was furious. I knew it was about more than me seeing that stupid prophecy! He was worried I would steal his glimmer! It happened again right before the coronation… Why didn't I see it before? I kept seeing this… weird alternate version of him in my head." I'm pleased with my own ability to see what before was a mystery.

"Thanks for letting us in on that little titbit," Azure's tone is droll and her expression is unimpressed.

"So you share every vision you have?" I ask her, she frowns slightly.

"No." Her reply is a mumble.

"I didn't think so," I retort, feeling numb.

I don't want to feel bad about the past anymore, it isn't like I can change it now. I feel myself let go, and a weight lift off my shoulders. I can only move forward. After all, I've come so far from the girl who awoke a mermaid, so confused and weak... I think about Orion, about that first afternoon were I opened my eyes and went crashing to the floor of the marble chapel. I remember how he held me, how he told me to breathe. How he became something for me to cling to among waves of disbelief that continued to crash down over me despite my lack of readiness to believe in Atargatis, in her magic. He had been my rock on that day and for many that followed, I couldn't deny that, even if I didn't like him very much. Suddenly something within me clicks again, sparking more inspiration.

I speak my mind, unable to help myself as a knot tightens in my stomach again. I don't know if I'm ready to see him yet.

"I know where Orion would go for sanctuary."

ORION

The white marble walls rise high around us, like a physical manifestation of Atargatis, the Goddess I so sorely need to protect my people and I. I have failed, I have let everything my father worked for collapse and shatter. His legacy is gone.

"Orion!" I hear someone's voice calling me, parting the tides of grief that seem to be rolling in with unstoppable force.

"Yes, sorry..." I say mumbling. It's Sophia, I found her with the rest of the mermaids, cowering in Oscar's study surrounded by his personal supply of weapons. I was only looking for a sword or spear, and yet I found a mass of maidens, huddled and shedding diamonds, terrified.

"It's okay. You lost just as much as we did, if not more... but the other maidens, well... they're scared. They want to know what you're going to do," she looks at me, her brown eyes so filled with sorrow. She is now alone, having lost her mate. He is dead, or worse: being tortured for information. She is not alone, the maidens here have lost much and many are now alone. Just like me.

"What I'm going to do?" I look at her incredulously. Doesn't she see that I'm the last person who should be left in charge? A familiar voice travels towards me, angry.

"Yes, you're the Crowned Ruler, remember?" I turn and come face to face with Cole; his eyebrows are knitted together.

"I..." I start but I can't quite bring myself to make a single syllable. I screwed up. I listened to Saturnus; I trusted the wrong man and I spread my men too thin. Now they're dead.

"Well?" Cole jumps on me, no mercy. He's pissed.

"I'm sorry I..." I can't speak again. My voice seems to have disappeared along with my confidence.

"Don't be sorry! Be what we goddamn voted for! You think you're not up to the job? I get it. But people are dying!!" He's yelling, clearly distraught.

"Don't you think I know that?" I look at him, feeling deflated and his eyes narrow with frustration.

"Then do something!" He snaps, hovering angrily above the sand swept white marble floor.

"Every choice I make ends badly. I don't know what to do... This isn't simple. I trusted the wrong person, Saturnus... he betrayed us all." I look deeply into Cole's eyes as they widen. I also notice a silence fall and I know that the mermaids are listening in.

"Saturnus... but he's the Goddess' soulmate... he's our connection to her. How..." I can tell he's totally stunned.

"I know," I turn to the rest of the mermaids, watching their hunched forms perk slightly as my eyes fall onto them. "Saturnus was a liar. He dropped the defensive glimmer of the city. We didn't stand a chance. His alliance is with the Psirens now." They gasp, slightly melodramatic. I can see that they aren't cut out for this.

"What are we going to do now?" Alannah looks at me with her mint green eyes and scales glimmering intensely. I don't have an answer. Her tailfin is stone still and I feel the eyes of all her companions bear into me, needing something I can't give them. I turn as a voice comes from the opposite end of the chapel, a voice that ices my blood, yet sets my skin on fire. She speaks.

"Now, we fight."

CALLIE

My words ring out through the water and ricochet from the white marble walls like bullets. Heads turn and eyes fall upon me as the impact of my words takes hold. Orion's face is harrowing to witness as his icy blue irises clamp onto me. I feel myself drawn to him suddenly, an acknowledgement of what I have lost. I cannot help but want to hold him, for I realise now he has lost far more.

"Callie." The word doesn't come from where I expect, but my name is instead called out in exclamation by Sophia. I feel Azure at my back, pushing me forward into the room. "Where have you been?" Sophia asks, raising her eyebrows.

"I was…" I begin, but Orion cuts me off.

"She was with the Psirens." I hear a number of gasps from the mermaid crowd. I notice Alannah, Skye, Marina, Rose and a few other maidens who had become a part of my friendship group quickly, as well as one or two Knights who are injured, lying against the wall with their fins outstretched and covered in blood stained chainmail. Fahima is with them, her tangerine scales starkly contrasting to her dark skin, her eyes travel and I wonder what she's looking at. As I move further forward through the smashed in stained glass window I notice the object of her adoration, Ghazi, who is floating diligently next to Cole. They are both watching me like I'm dangerous.

"You… why would you go to them, Callie?" Sophia is looking at me with wide, bloodshot, brown eyes. She's clearly been crying. I look around but I can't see Oscar anywhere.

"I needed to find out where my father is," I explain it to her in the simplest way I can think of. Orion rolls his eyes behind her and Rose speaks up from over his shoulder, her dusky pink tailfin swaying from side to side in that ethereal way that all the mermaids seem to adopt.

"That's all well and good, but you are supposed to be our Queen. How could you leave us? Shaniqua never would have done something like that." I look at her, narrowing my eyes, feeling like I've been slapped. I want to yell and make a fuss, have someone defend my honour, but I've blown that bridge with Orion to smithereens and I guess it's time I square up to the consequences.

"I know. I'm sorry. It was selfish of me." I look down at the split in my tailfin, to the sparkling sinew and shimmering flesh, feeling guilt wash over me. I look up again and Orion looks surprised.

"So..." he coughs, clearing his throat, trying to bring some authority to his tone. He might be able to act to the others, but I know inside he's broken. "Will you be gracing us with your company? Or is this just another stop on your travels?"

Damn. That stung. Okay, damage control. I take a deep breath, exhaling bubbles.

"No. I'm here to stay. I know I've made a mess of things, but I'm not fleeing any more. I have to be the Queen *all* of you deserve and that means never abandoning any of you," I inhale sharply as my next words cross my mind. I don't want them to be misconstrued, but I really do feel I need to vow them to my people, "'til death do us part."

Orion doesn't react; instead he crosses his arms and furrows his broad brow.

"Did you know?" He looks at me suspiciously.

"Know what?" I ask as the mermaids lean in, they can sense he's raging for an argument, but after everything I've been through I realise that arguing with him is something I can handle.

"That Saturnus was working with the Psirens. I mean, I find it rather convenient that you just turn up looking the picture of virtue. The last time I saw you... you were like one of them. How do I know Saturnus isn't using you to play me?" He presses his lips into one, unforgiving line. The mermaids behind him narrow their eyes also.

"Really? You really think Saturnus would use me to get to you?" I feel offended. I feel the sinew and muscle in my lower abdomen twitch, willing me to flee. Instead, I ignore it, staying through the unpleasantness.

"He already has," he gripes.

"What... when?" I demand of him. Suddenly, as I refuse to crumble under his scrutiny, something shifts behind his irises and he looks uncomfortable. He rubs the back of his neck and I notice a large gash in his abdomen that has started to heal. He doesn't answer my question. "Well?" I demand, irritated.

"Maybe we should talk about this in private..." he replies hesitantly.

"Uh... no. You wanted to do this here. Let's do it here. When has Saturnus ever used me against you?" I look behind him, at the transfixed stares of the women.

"When he told me to propose!" He bursts, like it's been welling up inside him since the day I left him. He throws his hands up, dislodging water and frightening a silver fish that's swimming past him, minding its own business. The movement stirs his tousles and his eyes look lost.

"What?!?" I exclaim and Sophia's eyes almost pop out of their sockets.

"Saturnus... he said he'd overheard you saying that you wanted to get married..." he mutters under his breath.

"So what? You couldn't have just asked me?" I look at him, confused and hurt that we'd been so easily manipulated.

"I did ask you! I proposed!" He looks at me like I'm stupid, incredulous. His voice is shaking and I wonder if he might cry.

"Yes, in front of everyone! That doesn't exactly give me any say, does it? Saturnus knew I would say no! That's why he got you to buy that ring, so I'd get scared and run. He wanted to break us apart, because he wanted you distracted," I feel my chest rise and fall as my heart races.

"Yes and he got exactly what he wanted, didn't he? If you really loved me he wouldn't have been able to make you run so easily!" I'm taken aback by his logic and I realise that if I retort this will escalate to a full on screaming match. That's no good for anyone right now, especially not him. He's lost his home, his men, his sister, and all closeness to Atlas' memory. That is enough.

"You're right. I'm sorry," I reply. He moves slightly backwards in the water unintentionally and his eyes lose their fire. Instead they become reserved and guarded.

The mermaids stir behind him, sensing the storm has passed.

"Okay you two. Break it up," Azure comes past me, having been sat on the step of the altar, spectating and probably amused.

"Sorry," I mumble again.

"I couldn't get Star out," Azure says to Orion. His face contorts but then a mask of unfeeling calm comes into place. It's not unlike that which I have watched Saturnus implement.

Ghazi moves forward, turning to Cole and makes several hand symbols in quick motion; sign language which I can't understand. Cole translates quickly to Orion.

"Ghazi wants to know why they need Starlet? I mean, why not just kill her. Is it her visions?" Ghazi's eyes greet me with a certain warmth. I smile back at him, glad that not everyone here totally hates me.

"I might be able to answer that," I interject as Orion moves to speak, his eyebrows rising.

"Do tell."

"I think it's something to do with them raising the Necrimad."

"They're still singing that same old tune?" Azure laughs, as I turn to her with a surprised look.

"Yes, why?" I enquire. The other mermaids are rising, moving to join in the conversation. Ghazi eyes them with a frown

"I didn't think Solustus was that stupid," she crosses her arms. I raise my eyebrows, a silent question and she exhales heavily.

"Okay. So Solustus isn't a good guy, but he's not destructive like Titus was. A beast the size of the Necrimad will kill everyone, him included."

"So why did Titus want to bring it forward?" Orion sounds smug behind me.

"Titus had a lot of darkness, so much so he couldn't see clearly, he was purely and instinctually power hungry. He didn't think about the consequences, whereas Solustus will, he's logical, drastically so," she shrugs, like the words she's speaking mean nothing to her even though I can't deny that they send chills through me.

"Okay. So seeing as we can assume Saturnus and Solustus are aligned toward the same goal... why do they need Starlet?" Orion demands the answer of me, cocking his chin with a cocky exuberance. He's using it to cover his pain, but it's pissing me off.

"Solustus stuck me in the vents with these like... fumes or something.

Said I could speak to the Necrimad because of Titus."

"What do you mean?" Sophia looks over at me and I sigh, I guess lying would be nothing but painful. I shift in the water, calming myself.

"As the vessel I can absorb magical power, so when Titus died a part of him stayed within me. His darkness. It's gone now... but I don't know how." Sophia and the other mermaids back away. Azure barks, making everyone jump.

"Hey, she's clean. I'd be able to tell," she nods at me, giving me permission to continue speaking. I know she wants to hear what I have to say, because it's about Star. Regardless, I'm grateful for her support.

"Well, I spoke to it. It said something about needing pure blood," I say and Azure groans.

"Oh for shits sake that's so cliché. Blood of a virgin? Seriously? What on earth kind of ritual requires that?" She barks. I feel a slight sense of shock. Starlet was a virgin? She seemed so... not the type. I shake my head, my long blonde hair tickling the base of my spine where flesh turns to scale.

"An old one," Marina comes through the crowd of women who are in a horseshoe formation behind Orion. She looks awful, her breast is slashed and she has a black eye, it's healing already, but her wounds still shock me. It's the first time I've ever seen her without her hair pristinely kept.

"They have my scythe, too," I drop this bombshell.

"How?" Cole demands and I shrug.

"I don't know. Solustus must have had it all this time, but it's useless, it served its purpose," I remind Cole of this fact but he doesn't look so sure I'm right.

"We have to go and get Star," Azure says fiercely. "I have someone looking out for her but we can't leave her there." As her words reach Orion I watch him debate this momentarily.

"We can't, Azure," he shakes his head, looking grim.

"She's your sister, Orion!" I remind him, shocked at his lack of compliance on the matter of family, which he usually held so dear.

"Her life is not worth the extinction of our race. We need to get far away from this place. We need to regroup and heal." He looks at me, his gaze softening, as if his façade of coldness is cracking under the weight of his decision.

Azure is about to retort when we hear something suddenly stir from outside the silent walls of the white marble chapel.

We freeze, instantly forgetting the passionate tongues of the argument that clash together like swords. My blood begins to pound in my ears but I remind myself of Vex's voice, telling me to focus and I hone my senses. After a few moments I hear the stirring again and I move high above the height of the group and swim towards one of the windows.

"Callie! What are you doing?" Sophia hisses at me, looking distraught. I expect Orion to give me grief about endangering myself again but he says nothing, letting me go as I please. I smile to myself slightly at that; relieved he isn't going to argue with me on every little thing.

As I reach the window, I place my hands on the ledge and stare out at the vast expanse of sand and empty ocean before me.

I see something, a blessing, and it makes me smile. I fly from the window, my heart rising in my chest. He is here, against all the odds.

I lower myself to eyelevel with him, smiling with a crazy enthusiasm.

"Hello, Philippe," I sigh, feeling myself relax. I pat his neck, stroking and kissing him. I had never been a true lover of horses, but in this moment I adore every inch of him. He is safe and he is here, a symbol of all we have lost, but also a sign that Orion is right.

The others follow after me, helping the Equinox into the chapel, his hooves clopping and clipping against the marble, sand dusted, floors and his gills blowing bubble filled snorts into the darkening water of dusk.

I do not know how he found us, whether he had felt the calling of our sorrow, or that of the Goddess, telling him we were in need. The message of his aid however is clear.

We are on the move.

22
North

SOLUSTUS

A knock at the door stirs me from contemplation, from staring upon the face of my brother. I have not been in close proximity with him since the night Titus was taken from this earth... I remember it well.

"Saturnus!" I hiss, desperate to make sure he is still abreast with the plan. I am hidden from sight by the shadow of a doorway.

"Brother. Quiet." He stirs slightly from the sand where he is pretending to lay unconscious.

"Sorry. Everything is in place? She will yield to us?" I look into his too green eyes as I hear the army fighting above us and my heart races with the effect of adrenaline. I can be gone but a moment, making sure that nobody notices I am absent among the fighting.

"Yes. The girl will not fight the prophecy I have fed to her. She believes she is dying to save them all. We just have to hope Titus will keep a close enough proximity to be in the path of the lunar energy we so seek," he looks up at me, irritated, as though he can't work out why I'm still suspended in front of him. I look over my shoulder, I need to get back to it, to dart back in as if I had never left. I turn my back on my brother and return to the ritual site, seamless in my invisibility.

"What?" Saturnus barks, noticing me staring. The water is still slightly cloudy with the dissolution of sand and glass shards mingled in with the metallic sting of blood. The ruddy taste clings to the inside of my throat, an old friend.

"Nothing..." I mutter, slightly averting my eyes. They travel into the room, settling on the sickly pink tail of the mermaid, Azure's sister. Her eyes narrow as she catches my gaze.

"What are you looking at, bitch?" I find my body erect and her eyes widen, she tries to say something but the gag across her mouth, shoved between her lips and pressing down her tongue, prevents sound. My tail twitches, willing me to move, to spill her blood. I feel Saturnus shift, pushing his palm to my chest.

"Brother. Not yet. She must die, but in the right way," he reminds me that we need to kill her over the seal. I turn, disgusted by the sight of her sparkling demeanour, and move to the window. We are silent in these moments, savouring our victory. I look out over the city, the city I have waited several lifetimes to grasp, only to crush and let fall like sand. A harsh knock at the door disturbs me and Saturnus is there within the time it takes me to blink, opening it and revealing Vex, he is smiling and his pupils are diluted black, his lip is bloody as he sweeps it with his tongue.

"Who is this?" Saturnus turns to me and I beckon the boy forward. He moves into the room, pulling his cargo with him. A mer.

"Vexus. One of my more useful minions," I explain as Vex bows his head in respect to Saturnus. I wonder if he can feel the darkness radiating off him, he had never bowed that way to me. My eyes narrow.

Vexus pushes his captive to the floor, next to Starlet.

"I believe you're looking for this?" He snarls, his lip upturning in disgust of the merman's glimmering scales, rebounding light at all angles. I share his disdain for the creatures so clearly in favour with the Goddess, more beautiful than we could ever be, even in the best light. Not that I want to be beautiful, I like my dull ruggedness just fine. I raise my eyebrows again as Saturnus smiles.

"Yes, indeed I am boy. It's nice to see Solustus is valuing brains and not just brawn I must say..." His impressive tail sweeps out from him as he closes the door and rounds Vex's wide circumference, its spiked flesh flaring slightly with each of his motions. I lean back against the windowsill, contemplating my memories.

"I do not recall seeing you at the fight Vexus…" I begin and Saturnus cuts me off.

"Now Solustus, surely you cannot hope to remember the whereabouts of every one of your recruits. You are but one man after all…" Saturnus looks back over his shoulder at me, his yellow cat eyes are terrifying and his pupils are but fissures into nightmare.

"I was there. Saw the whole bloody thing, didn't I? It was nice of you to warn all of us *minions* that you were going to upend the ocean's sand into the open water though. I'll be getting it out of my hair for weeks, bloody stuff," he rubs his hand through his locks vainly and Saturnus smiles, almost too sweetly. I know he's fuming, volcanic.

"What makes you think I need to tell a bottom feeder like you my plans?" I move quickly, sensing confrontation and wanting immediately to be in on the action. It's the moment I've waited for, holding the Occulta Mirum in my palms, and I don't want to miss a single second. Vex's eyes widen.

"Mate, I didn't mean it like that…" It's the first time I've heard him on the retreat, and once again it's not from me. What is it about Saturnus that chills him? I've made threats, I've spoken harshly and downward to him before, and yet I cannot quell his rebellion. Saturnus does nothing at all and has the boy's tentacles twitching. I clench my hands into fists until my long fingernails carve my palms.

"I don't care how you meant it," Saturnus snarls.

"You're right. It was rude of me… sir," Vexus bows his head again and moments pass as the mer begins to stir beneath us. Saturnus relaxes, moving his fluke fluidly once more. I feel like rolling my eyes but abstain.

"Well, you have brought me my metal master. So I suppose I can forgive you this once," Saturnus turns away beside me and Vex relaxes. It's as though my brother can sense his muscles unfurl, because in one swift slash of his burnt, black fin he comes reeling around sideways and strikes Vex along one of his high cheekbones, sending him crashing against the wall and sinking to the floor. A break in the skin is visible and weeping blood from where Saturnus' fingernail has punished his insubordinate tongue.

"I'll tell you something right now, boy, true rulers don't forgive. Forgiveness is weakness, and I've played the weak one for far too long," Saturnus towers above Vex and I watch the boy stutter, quite unsure of how to react. I smile to myself, daydreaming of how many others will have this look upon their faces, gazing up instead at me. Vexus rises through the water, his eyes masked over with cold reserve. It makes me sort of proud because I can tell he has mastered the skill of acting far more invulnerable than he truly is. I have taught him well.

"Feel free to step in and discipline at any time Solustus…" Saturnus turns to me and glares, his black hair and pale skin looking strange, it has been so long since his true form was this much of a permanence. "Not boring you, am I?" He raises one eyebrow and I shake my head.

"No. Not at all," I speak in a clipped tone. How can it be that I find myself still in second place? I have waited centuries to supplant Titus and yet here I am once more, taking orders.

"Good," his tone is cold but I can hear a smile spreading across his expression as he turns, moving away from Vex and hovering over Starlet once more. He stares down at Oscar who is moving slowly away from him, eyes wide.

"You…" the merman stupidly opens his mouth and his courage surprises me.

"Yes… you can skip the dramatics, Oscar. Everyone here is fully aware of how corrupt and terrible I truly am…" Saturnus almost sounds bored as he twists in savage momentum once more. "Where do you think you're going?" He barks to Vex, speeding toward him without warning and slamming him into the wall. I yawn, torture and lording power really is more fun when I'm doing it.

"I thought…." He chokes as Saturnus' black fingernails close around his throat.

"What's that? You had a thought? Well, quell that urge boy. You're staying here. You've earned yourself the position of personal guard dog. I want you where I can make sure you've got the message about who's on top. Hmm… I might even get you a collar and leash. Who knows," Saturnus releases him and clicks his fingers.

"Come, Solustus. We have much to co-ordinate," he doesn't even look at me and I feel my gut begin to churn with agitation. When did he become so demanding? I had thought we were in this together as brothers, but he's expecting me to follow in his wake. A typical big brother. My finger brushes the handle of Scarlette and my eyes wander to the scythe, which is propped against the edge of the two-way mirror that we had used to communicate.

I follow him out of the room, shutting Vexus in with the two prisoners and bypassing Caedes and Regus who stand guard at the door.

"You know I don't respond well to finger clicking. I'm not your sidekick," I grumble and Saturnus turns on me.

"Excuse me, brother?" He looks hurt, or what would be hurt if he had normal eyes. The feline quality to his irises creates a disturbing parallel.

"I said I'm not your sidekick. We're supposed to be in this together."

"You can step up anytime, brother," Saturnus turns and moves away from me, leaving me in a flurry of bubbles as his words reach me. I don't know what to make of them, I only know I can't let him take everything I've worked for from me.

I catch up to him in a single push through the water and say nothing, unsure how to reply. We reach the site of shattered sea glass in mere moments.

"I'd expected your army to have assembled by now. What kind of loyalty is that?" Saturnus questions as we rise to a great height. I look over the city and find that the Psirens are scattered, kicking up rubble and smashing things with gleeful abandon. I find myself embarrassed.

"They're ensuring the rest of the mer are dead," I assure him, knowing full well that the last of the mer are long gone.

"Whatever you say. Their numbers are low. So low in fact that I believe as soon as the Necrimad is released from the seal that we won't have a problem with the final part of the ritual," Saturnus smiles to himself.

"Whatever do you mean?" I ask him and his brow creases.

"Didn't you listen when we had those long early meetings, brother? Don't you remember?" He seems more hurt than irritated which is an odd reaction from him. If I'm honest I wasn't really listening to his infernal religious ramblings.

"It was so long ago…." Lies spill from my dry, cracked lips, seeping between my jagged teeth. Saturnus looks down at me as he rises slightly in the water. "If you would jog my memory. It has been a long day." I fold my arms and look up to the setting sun; it's light is blinding.

"Very well, but listen up Solustus, I will not be repeating this again," he looks agitated but I can't quite believe it, he loves reciting ritual and scripture, he thinks it makes him closer to being one with the Gods.

"I'm listening," I reply sharply.

"Well, we have two more phases of the ritual to complete. Phase one was, as you know, the siphoning of lunar energy into earthly matter."

"The scythe," I remember how hard it had been to manoeuvre the scythe and its bearer into the right place at the right time without revealing our true intent and I shudder.

"Yes. Well, phase two involves releasing that energy via the sacrifice of the seer. She is pure, I am sure of it. Her blood will release the beast under the next full moon," Saturnus is smiling, pleased with himself.

"But we'll still need to release the Necrimad's powers from its flesh," it all comes rushing back to me.

"Yes. That itself unbelievably, is the tricky part. In order to release the raw power of the Necrimad, there's a tad more we need to prepare for," Saturnus reminds me, I try to recall but I forget the specifics.

"Okay, more rituals… seems simple enough to me," I remind him and he snaps.

"Don't you think I know that? Of course it would be simple if it were merely a phase of the moon or a naïve blonde we had to manipulate alone, but there are more factors at play here. Poseidon put a damn lock on this beast for a reason. There are so many conditions to its release because there is only one instance he could think of in which anyone would want to release it."

"Which is?" I ask, finding myself strangely enraptured.

"That the world needs to be purified. Cleansed and wiped clean. Poseidon hates mortals don't forget. It wasn't difficult for him to foresee a day when they'd all need to be eradicated," he speaks with such superiority, as though he has a direct line to Poseidon's inner thoughts and I'm tempted to remind him that the one of us who has been closest to him is me. Unfortunately, I can't deny that he's right.

"So what does the last ritual entail?" I ask him, shaking my head slightly. I'm becoming tired of all this chatter and crave the silence of the dark.

"There are scales of good and evil, as long as the mer exist they will tilt those scales to keep them in balance with the evil of this world."

"But why?"

"When they're made they're infused with the magic of Atargatis. It's what keeps them immortal, that Goddess' magic on this plane of existence is what keeps the scales balanced in favour of good. Once enough of their blood is spilled and her magic released into the aether, the scales will tip and the ritual can be performed," Saturnus' forehead is creased as we look out over the city and faint smashing sounds reach us from the brutal beasts of my army.

"Brother, that sounds impossible."

"Not impossible, easy. There aren't enough mer left to do any real damage. They'll make a foolish final stand at some point, what with their romantic notions that hope and love will conquer all. When they do, we'll be ready and waiting. We don't need to kill off all of them, just enough to tip the scales. The Psirens' increasing numbers have made the task easier. We are many." I nod my head, hearing what he is saying. I find myself being able to recall our prior conversations now. I had known all this information subconsciously, but I had been too romanticised by the notion of finally being able to raise an army of the undead, those who had been claimed by the sea.

CALLIE

My head is pounding. The sun is hanging low on the horizon about to pass through the division between worlds. I haven't moved an inch in quite a while. Orion is opposite me, Azure at my side and everyone else who has decided they want a say in what is debatably becoming a giant shouting match are encircling us.

"We've already been over this Azure! I'm not going back there!" Orion throws up his hands again; agitated at the fact he's having to repeat himself for what seems to me like the millionth time.

"She's FAMILY!" Azure yells, getting up in Orion's face again. I raise a hand and rub my forehead, trying to release the tension that's building there from trying to refrain from laughing. You'd think being a centuries old civilisation of people chosen to save the world they'd be more organised.

"Yes, okay. We get that you want to save Starlet!" I burst, suddenly feeling that I've had enough. Orion turns to me, his eyes blazing fury.

"What gives you the right to an opinion?" He is acting snarky, but I know it's because I've hurt him. I take it and breathe deep.

"I just think that maybe yelling the same thing at each other over and over might not be the best way to resolve things. But hell, what do I know?" I cock an eyebrow at him, trying to come off cool and collected like Vex. In reality I hate the fact that I'm going up against him in front of everyone. I don't want to make him look incompetent, I've already done that enough.

"Well, if you're such an expert what do *you* think we should do then?" Orion thinks he's backing me into a corner, trying to make me look equally as incompetent. Rather than stumbling I pause for a moment, ready to prove myself to the rest of the mer.

"Well, I think this is a decision both of you are too close to the picture to make. We have military experts here, don't we? Why don't we ask them? Nobody can claim to know more about the capabilities of the Psiren army than the leaders of The Knights of Atargatis. Ghazi, Cole, what do you think?" I smile to myself, pleased with my answer. Orion purses his lips as silent fury consumes him, but then something else unrecognisable passes beneath his irises and his tail visibly relaxes. I turn in the water, my hair moving around me and lock eyes on the two men who I know will make the decision that neither Azure nor Orion should be charged with.

"Thank you, Callie," Cole says, turning to Ghazi who nods, signs a reply, and then shakes his head viciously from side to side, his black locks feathering outward in the water.

271

"Ghazi and I agree. It wouldn't be wise to host a rescue. We were lucky to get out of the city alive the first time. Going back in is a suicide mission."

"There you have it. Decision made. We're going to move away from this place," I nod and smile at the both of them, they bow their heads and despite everything they have lost I am glad that I have managed to maybe earn a little respect back from them.

"Go where?" Rose pipes up from the circle of mermaids, she looks concerned.

"Our home has been destroyed, remember? Where on earth could we possibly go?" Alannah joins in too. Sophia looks at me from behind Alannah's shoulder, her eyes searching mine for a speck of comfort. I cannot forget that Oscar didn't make it out of the city. He's probably dead, or worse. She needs anything I can give her right now and as her brown eyes, that remind me so much of a very special little girl, sparkle with unshed tears, I know I have to give them some kind of reprieve.

"Look, I know the city is gone, but that's not our home. Not really. I mean we're mer. The Occulta Mirum was just a lot of pretty buildings, but nothing is as beautiful as our actual home and that's the ocean. Nothing can take that from us, except death, and as far as I can tell everyone here is still breathing." It's probably the lamest cliché I could have spouted, but something within the maidens unconsciously lifts as their eyes fixate on my face. Or most of them, anyway.

"That's all very nice, but it doesn't solve the problem of where we're actually going to go," Rose's irritating tones cause me to roll my eyes slightly.

"Right you are. What I'm trying to say is that we're not bound to somewhere that has buildings, walls or even a roof. We can go anywhere we want. However, if you want walls and a roof, if that's what makes you feel safe, there was this place I read about... From the silent times?" I look around at them and their eyes widen as they all remember.

"The what? I have no idea what you're talking about!" Rose bursts again and this time Sophia speaks up before I can defend myself.

"That's because you're too young. However, if you'd have done your reading and worried about filling your head instead of the hair covering it, you'd know that Callie is referring to the Ice city. The mer used it to stay away from prying human eyes." She turns to me and her eyes are still red, but this time they're rage filled. She puts on a polite smile, totally not hiding how pissed she is. "I think it's a great idea. It's low key and it's protected. We all know that demon activity has been on the rise."

"It has?" Rose speaks again, unable to grasp the concept of shutting the hell up.

"Yes, Rose, where do you think Jason has been going, the pub?" Sophia says this, gritting her teeth and not even bothering to turn. Rose falls silent again and I really want to laugh, then I catch a look on her face and I avert my eyes. I wonder if Jason made it out alive. I turn to Orion, knowing that I need to respect his authority here.

"What do you think?" I ask him, trying to appear sweet.

"Does it really matter what I think?" He shrugs and then rises, moving quickly out of the chapel and into the blue beyond.

"Is he coming back?" Alannah asks me looking worried. I shrug.

"Well, don't you think you should follow him? He is *your* soulmate," she makes a little shooing motion with her hands, all the while moving her mint green and pastel pink scales from side to side in hypnotic time. I sigh, exhaling a large cloud of bubbles and turn to Azure.

"I'll be right back," I launch upward, tensing all my tail muscles together, zooming off after Orion. He's not hard to find, he's only a little way from the chapel, bathing in the dimming light from the sunset above, practicing some kind of martial art routine or drill.

"Hey…" I say awkwardly, wanting to get this over with as quickly as possible. There are still decisions to be made.

"If you've come to apologise, I'm not interested," he doesn't look at me.

"I'm not apologising. Why should I?" I ask him, he's got a real bug up his butt.

"You come back here, after everything that's happened, and you want to play hero. That's pretty shitty in my books."

"I'm not trying to 'play' anything, Orion. I just want everyone to be safe. I don't want anyone else to die," I speak honestly, realising that every single time I've watered down my feelings, twisted the truth, or not spoken up I've

273

been lying to myself and pushing him away. He scares me as I watch him strike out with his fist, but it's not the physical damage I know he can inflict which disturbs me. As always it's the emotional scars he can leave without even laying a hand on me.

"Could have fooled me…" he starts but I interrupt him.

"I get it. I get that you're pissed at me. I let you down and I ran. But I'm not going to do that again," I go to move toward him but he flashes me a warning with his eyes.

"I don't believe you," he strikes out with his other palm, impacting nothingness. I wonder if he's picturing me.

"You don't have to believe me. There are bigger issues than you and me here. I'm not saying that I want you and I to be besties, I know that's too much to ask. I just want us to work together. For those people in there. I've let them down too. I need to be there for them now. So do you." He stops punching out, stilling, his shoulders slumping.

"I don't think I can." All malice has left his voice and all that resides in the space between us is water and despair.

"Of course you can," I laugh slightly, snorting. The Orion I knew wasn't this full of self-doubt. What has happened to him?

"I'm the reason the city burned. I was too busy being caught up in losing you and I missed what was right in front of me," he blames himself for everything.

"You didn't miss anything. I was around Saturnus just as much as you and I didn't suspect anything either." I move over to him, positioning myself and placing my palms on his shoulders. He doesn't pull away.

"Let's go back inside. It's no use worrying about what's already happened. We have to move forward." He nods, not fighting me. I turn and pull his hand behind me; this small touch sends a familiar jolt of sensation up my arm. I look back to him and his face has turned glacial again. The sea is still around us and I wait as he draws breath, wondering what he'll say.

"I'll follow you… but I don't trust you." I'm surprised to feel the wind knocked out of me at such a simple expression. It's perhaps the first time I've realised that for all my complaining and whining about being vulnerable and not wanting to get hurt, I can hurt too. I close my eyes slowly, looking away from him. My heart breaks.

Back inside the chapel all talk has turned to the journey north. Apparently my suggestion of a destination is the only one anyone has been able to come up with.

"We need weapons. Supplies. We have nothing," Cole says aloud as I re-join the conversation.

"What would we need weapons for?" Skye looks worried.

"What do you think, Princess?" Azure chimes in and her deadpan facial expression is so intense I'm impressed it's not melting off her skull.

"Surely you don't expect us to fight? We're mer*maids*," she puts emphasis on the last part of the word and I laugh.

"We can't be picky about who picks up a sword anymore Skye, the army we had are gone. You'll need to learn to fight, all of you," I turn around to them. A mermaid who I have not noticed before says something; it's barely a whisper. Her powder blue tail, pale skin, and white hair are dim now in the dying light, and her giant baby blues make her look like an angel.

"What's your name?" I lower my height slightly, bending my tailfin under me and she looks terrified.

"Emma," she whispers.

"What was it you said before, I didn't quite catch it." The conversation resumes around me as people lose interest in what I'm doing.

"We're not all like you... I don't think I could fight." I turn from her, rising slightly in the water.

"Listen, all of you. If I can fight, so can you. Atargatis made us all who we are, she wouldn't give us anything we couldn't handle," I look down at Emma, her kind sweet face is looking up at me like I'm Atargatis herself.

"Yeah that's great, Callie, but if you were listening rather than indulging what's-her-face down there you might have noticed that we don't have any weapons!" Rose scolds me and Orion looks like he might legitimately punch her in the face. The sand stirs around us and I have a brainwave.

"Hang on! I know where we can get some weapons... but..."

The group looks up at me once more and I trace each one of their faces.

Do I really want to put them in danger again? I don't know if the maidens can handle it. I look down at Emma; she isn't exactly a warrior. She looks more like a scared teenager. Then I remember, I *was* a scared teenager. If I can do it, so can they.

"But what?" Sophia asks me as the final light of the day vanishes below the horizon.

"It'll be risky," I reply.

23
Risk

CALLIE

A few hours and a lot of yelling later the remaining mer and I hang, suspended above the crevasse to abyss which holds the Cryptopolis and Necrocazar in its belly. Rose doesn't look impressed.

"Are we really doing this?" She looks down, her eyes sparkling in the dim moonlight, shimmering from the surface refraction.

"Yes! We are actually doing this. We've argued enough! We're here, so let's shut up and get on with it!" Sophia bursts, yelling and Cole gives her a small smile. Orion floats next to me, still. His brow has remained in the same furrowed position since I shut him down. He had objected to the idea of raiding the Psirens home turf for left over weapons, just like he was objecting to any ideas that were potentially risky in any way shape or form. He had lost his nerve, and the lack of courage doesn't suit him as a leader, or a warrior.

"Okay, come on..." I coax the rest of the group, those watching the banter with bored stares. They've had enough of debating, of feeling the anxiety build within them at the thought of going down into the dark. So have I.

I turn to Orion, who looks away, refusing to catch my eye, but Azure gives me a kind of impressed half smile as I hold her gaze for a second. She's been fairly quiet. She didn't, however, object to the idea of raiding the Psiren city and in a way I wonder if it's because she's craving blood.

I revolve in the water, diving at high speed as I anticipate the increase in pressure and I see Azure and Orion as they overtake me, plunging ever downward into the dark. I can see the shimmering of Orion's scales, however dull, radiating royal blue beneath me, but I can't see Azure, her tail has lost its shimmer after everything she's been through. I look up at my own, it still sheens, like that of the rest of the mer, demonstrating once more that my dance with darkness had been temporary. Still, the repercussions from my time with the Psirens isn't and though I might now swim among Atargatis' own once more, my time with those made by Poseidon has left more of an impact on me than is visible from the outside.

As I descend deeper into the darkness, I get the eerie feeling of other eyes watching me, eyes I cannot see, and I miss the enhanced vision that Titus' magic had allowed. I feel a hand gripping onto mine, warm and unexpected. I look back, expecting to see Orion, but instead am met with the scared, large blue eyes of Emma. She is so out of place here, and I hope my decision doesn't put her in harm's way. She seems too delicate.

I stop, falling though the darkness, letting gravity pull me down and wonder momentarily if that's how Orion feels when he looks at me. I let go of Emma's vice like grip, knowing she needs to learn to face her fear.

We near the bottom of the canyon, bathing in the eerie white of jellyfish that crowd the entrance to the city.

"What now?" Sophia whispers to me, her eyes as large as dinner plates. I can see from here that her flesh is goosed all over.

"Now, we sink," I say, but everyone is already moving. Azure is already neck deep in the jellyfish cluster, entering the city from above.

"That was messed up." I can hear Skye muttering as she pats her hair down with one hand.

"This place is named Cryptopolis... what did you expect?" Cole asks with a cocked brow.

"I knew I should have stayed behind with Philippe," she blows bubbles in a half-irritated sigh.

"It's better if we stick together. Besides, Philippe can take care of himself," Orion remarks and she suddenly looks embarrassed.

"Whoa," I hear the word fall from Rose's lips and I know she's looking down. I follow her lead, looking down on the Necrocazar, the blackened walls, the crushed bones and the eels sparking light into the central square from jars hung on old ship masts.

"Azure... did you know it was this... big?" Orion asks his sister and she looks amused, licking her bottom lip and crossing her arms. "Of course you did," Orion answers his own question.

Come on, we don't want to be stood out here, anyone could be lurking, Fahima's voice echoes in my head as her hand grips onto my elbow and I know she's repeating a concern of Ghazi's.

"We need to move. We can't just sit here ogling." I remember the first time I had seen the city, the need I had felt to stare. It was unbelievable, but to me everything is, including the fact I'm half fish and maintain perfect hair underwater. The fact these mer, who are hundreds of years older than me, are struck with disbelief too tells me I was not wrong in my first reaction to this place. I have lived here and yet it still sends a chill over me. "Azure can you take everyone to look for weapons? I have something I need to retrieve," I look at Azure; her pale flesh is practically glowing down here. I can tell she's adapted for this kind of world. Her pupils are dilated black and I know that she's using her enhanced Psiren vision to see details I'm no longer privy to.

"Why do I have to babysit?" She grumbles, her tailfin hypnotic in its motion.

"Because you know this place the best. You're the expert here." Her eyes light up at this and she takes a large breath, shifting slightly in her posture and puffing out her chest.

"Oh... okay, come on you lot. Follow me," she leads them down until they're beneath me and tiny in retrospect.

"What are you going to do?" Orion hasn't descended with the rest of them. I can't work out if he's suspicious or concerned.

"I'm going to see if Solustus left the scythe here. It was in the throne room of the Necrocazar last time I saw it," I explain. His tail twitches slightly and I see his abs tense.

"They have a throne room? Like seriously? Wow. They're more deluded than I thought," Orion chortles. I don't know why but his response irks me, he's so sure of himself and I'm surprised to find myself thinking he's a little ignorant.

"Yeah well, Solustus certainly is." I think, trying to avoid saying something that will start an argument. I have work to do.

"They all are, Callie," he retorts and I roll my eyes. Nope, okay... argument it is.

"They're children, Orion. Most of them aren't much older than me, some are younger. I know they've done wrong, but I can't help but feel like they've been manipulated by Solustus and Alyssa. It's scary waking up and being half the person you once were. I'd have clung to anything that helped me make sense of what had happened," I explain and his eyes narrow.

"You really think those things are just misunderstood?" He looks at me. I decide to turn the tables on him.

"Maybe... I can't forget the fact that could have been me. If I hadn't of died in your arms. If Azure had gotten to me before you... If I'd have become a Psiren and hadn't had you to take care of me. I could have been one of Solustus' army." His eyes widen and he says nothing. I swim past him, descending into the streets of the dark city. As I fall through the water, I can't help but despise Orion a little for his ignorance. He's so obtuse to how the real world operates for someone so old. He sees things black and white, and I am very much a modern dove grey. I contemplate this as I move over vertebrae and teeth silently, wondering now if it's the fact he can't quite place me, can't guess what I'm thinking or understand my motivation that is what makes us incompatible. He wants me to be safe. Predictable. But I am not. The last of my predictability was washed away with my curls and tolerance for the sun.

I enter the throne room, empty now except for the throne and a mirror.

I look into it, suddenly wondering why I hadn't taken greater interest in it before. I have always seen it as belonging to the room, an expression of Solustus' narcissistic personality, but it seems like an odd object to have now I think about it. The rest of the throne room is so primitive. The throne made of bone, the animals used for day-glow. Bones coat the floor and it suddenly seems that this highly polished, ornate, pristine surface is completely out of place.

I swim over to it, rising over the pointed bones which form the high arc of the throne and place my palm on its cool surface. It's then that I notice, not the scythe, but the trident in a worthy second place propped behind the throne, reflected in the mirror, hidden from the view of anyone in front of the bone construct. It hadn't been what I'd wanted to find, and as I do a quick sweep I know in my gut the scythe is gone, but it's better than nothing. I move to take it in my palm.

I feel the flesh on the back of my neck tingle, a primal warning that I'm not alone.

"Alyssa," I speak the name, knowing instinctually that hers are the eyes resting on my back.

"Did you know, Callie, I didn't think you could ruin anything more for me than you already have. But I guess I was wrong! Because of you I missed my revenge on the race that betrayed me, my whim, performed by my children."

"I didn't keep you here," I remind her, wondering why she hadn't left and joined Solustus long before now.

"I've been looking for you though, haven't I? Solustus wanted you detained. Imagine how disappointed I was to return to your empty cell," she sneers. I wonder still why she's here.

"You're scared of him…" I articulate the epiphany as it hits me.

"No, stupid girl. I worship him and he worships me. That's something you couldn't hope to understand," she spits at me, her tentacles bringing her to my face in one rapid pulsation. She's inches from my nose, her dark eyes bearing into me.

"I don't want to," I retort, smiling slightly. She doesn't scare me. I've had practice dealing with tentacles and I've never been so glad for Vex's hard learned lessons. I've looked into eyes darker than hers. My own.

"You should. You should want to know the reason I'm going to slaughter you. You're useless to him now, and so he'll revere me once I give him the news that I've killed you," her eyes are wide like her pupils, dilated and crazed. She really believes Solustus will bow down to her superiority once she's killed me? How deluded can you get?

She doesn't go onto lament her wickedness, thank God, I've had enough of that from Titus for a lifetime. Instead she wraps her tentacles around my wrists, binding them back as her suckered grasp extends and winds around my body. I still, clearing my mind and not allowing panic to set in. I've seen the move a hundred times, from Vex, and so don't hesitate to swim upward, and revolve my body around backward in an arc, twisting her tentacles around and slapping her in the face with the end of my tailfin. She gasps, her head snapping backwards with a gross crack of her neck. She releases me, but another tentacle grabs onto the base of my tail and she pulls me through the water, smashing my head into the floor, my eyes roll backward and as they do I catch two people out of the corner of my eye. It's Orion, looking like he wants to lurch forward. Cole has his palm on Orion's chest and then I faintly hear the words pass his lips, "No, this is her fight." Before I can respond to either of their presence, Alyssa is dragging me across the floor.

I slither free, using muscles that feel like they're being crushed by her grasp and push myself upward with both palms. I whirl around backward, swinging with my fist, it hits her face with an echoing crack and I smell blood as her nose begins to weep scarlet. She's disoriented, unable to think straight, as I know the pain is now reaching her temple. I use the time she's distracted and move behind the throne where the trident is propped. It's not really my style but I don't have another weapon within reach. I skim the edge of the room, heart thudding, gills opening and closing in accelerated rhythm. The blood is pounding in my ears and I almost forget to check the location of Alyssa when a near miss from an outstretched extremity reminds me to face her. I spin, nearing the doorway where Orion is watching, itching to jump in and save me. He backs away as I slow my momentum, not bothering to look at him, and turn to face Alyssa.

She's pissed. Her nose is a bloody mess and I'm kind of amazed that my small fist did so much damage. I guess I really have gotten stronger. Her tentacles are erected, all of them, twitching like angry snakes with the rage that I can see is trembling beneath her flushed composure. I remember something Vex had said… *dammit what was it?* My time is out, so I fall back onto one of his earlier lessons, going on my instincts. I rush at her, aiming the trident's pointy end for her face. She raises a tentacle to block me and at the last minute I power upwards, a move Vex had told me he's once used to outwit Solustus. I flip, rotating my tailfin over my head, like some kind of gymnast, and then jab the trident with all my strength into the back of Alyssa's neck, right through her oesophagus. I twist the three pronged weapon, severing sinew and circuitry, and detach her skull from her body. It causes a flurry of bloody debris to be released into the water and transforms it a gory crimson. She cries out, still alive, a mangled plea for life before I thrust upward, ending her existence.

It's over too quickly, and unlike the body of a mer, her body doesn't disappear into sand. Ew.

ORION

"Alyssa," the single word leaves my lips. Shock overtakes my body as hers falls, a tangle of dead unmoving tentacles. Callie is revealed behind her, a vision as seen through a bloody tinted hue. Cole removes his hand from my chest, letting me go. I don't move though, I just float, watching Callie wielding the trident in shock and awe.

"Is that Gideon's other half?" Cole asks Callie who nods. She looks flushed, panicked at the weapon in her grasp. She drops it to the floor like it's hot.

"Yes. She wasn't dead. Saturnus lied. She's been turning the young ones. Picking them off beaches near San Diego State," her voice is monotone, like she's on autopilot. Her blonde hair that falls over her shoulders is still. She is motionless. I feel something stir at my back. It's Azure.

"We've found some weapons. They're crude, but they're all we've got. The others are outside... they were too afraid to come in, bunch of freaking wimps." She notices we're not turned to her as she breathlessly exhales her words like she's bored of them. We continue to stare at Callie. "What are we looking at?" she asks, more enthused than I've heard her in a while. I know she's devastated at losing Starlet again, as am I, but she's enjoying being in charge and is, as ever, good at compartmentalising her emotions.

"Callie, she killed Alyssa." Callie is looking down at her hands as Cole's words reach her, her head snaps upwards and I can see tears are streaming down her face. She's just hanging in the water, hands outstretched. I move to go to her, but once again someone stops me. This time it's Azure.

"No. I'll go," she moves over my head, her long tailfin leaving bubbles that tickle my face in a burst of raw power.

I watch as Azure moves over to Callie. She puts her pale, long fingers into the palms of Callie's hands. Callie looks up at her and her eyes come back into focus. Azure doesn't say anything and they just hang together, the silence enveloping everything in an eerie calm. Callie gasps suddenly, inhaling in that shocked way she does, like a squalling infant taking its first cry, before collapsing to the floor next to Alyssa's mangled corpse. Azure bends her tail underneath herself and strokes Callie's hair, looking back over her shoulder at me and rolling her eyes. She shouldn't be so brash. I envy that soft touch.

CALLIE

Azure's vision overtakes me, it's one from the past I think, but it's just as disturbing as one from the future. I can see Alyssa, her body encased in red silk, luring in hundreds of boys, kissing them, seducing them, killing them, and transforming them. Turning them to the darkness. It's over quickly, kind of like a shot of adrenaline, which leaves me shaky and I fall, my tailfin no longer wanting to keep me suspended tucks beneath my body which feels of such weight that I crumble underneath it. Azure's arms fall around me, cradling my head and stroking my hair. Mothering me. I'd never thought of her as maternal, but right now it's what I need. She understands, she gets it. The darkness had infected me, but I'd never actually killed another before. I had felt Alyssa's life slip from my grasp and the moment it had I wanted to claw it back. In a world that seemed so fantastical, no death seemed real to me. Atlas had been old; he'd lived a long life and even my own death, I hadn't really thought would ever be so permanent. Luckily for me it hadn't been. It was a view to mortality I had forgotten. I had forgotten the thread that connected everyone to this plane was frailer than it appeared.

As I weep, Orion's words come back to me, from the time before the ritual. He had refused to train me; he hadn't wanted me to be burdened with killing another creature. He knew there was a price, but I hadn't listened, too proud to accept his wisdom. Maybe I should have listened.

"Callie..." Azure whispers in my ear. I continue to cry in her arms, feeling the weight of what I've done crush me into her body. "You know why I showed you that, don't you?"

"No," I sniffle, inhaling water and trying not to look at the dead body next to me.

"You've just saved all those people. Those are the people that Alyssa was *going* to kill. Hundreds. I know you feel like a monster, but it was for the greater good. Besides, better her than you. Don't forget she wouldn't have hesitated to end you." *Oh.* I suddenly think back to all those faces, the terror, the light lost from their eyes. Because of me that will never come to pass. However, I still feel a knot of guilt anchored solidly in my gut and I can't get away from it.

"I still killed her," I say the words bluntly and move back from Azure. The flow of my tears halts and I breathe in the water, still smelling blood.

"Callie..." Orion speaks up and I rise, looking him square in the eyes.

"No, I did. I killed her. I'm not shrugging this off as some act of heroism. It was instinctual. I wasn't thinking about the teens she's killed. I was thinking I wanted to save myself. That's it. I'm not dressing it up. I have to live with it," I speak the words, finding the truth freeing. A few months ago I would have sobbed, ran and lied about the fact I was okay. I'm not doing that anymore, I'm supposed to be a leader and I need to act like one.

"Okay," Orion looks taken aback, but Cole smiles at me. He must have killed hundreds in his time. Come to think of it, everyone here has blood on their hands. I guess that's kind of what you expect when you're drafted to be a warrior for eternity. If they can deal with their guilt so can I.

Azure rises from the floor, picking up the trident and examining it. Something catches her eye as she does and she shoves it into my arms, not looking at me. She passes me, and I turn to see what she's staring at. The mirror, the one so out of place.

"Azure, what is it?" I ask. Orion is beside me now, his presence sending my hairs rising along my spine. I ignore this.

"This mirror..." she traces her fingers along its edge. I move over to her;

I'm right at her back and Orion and Cole follow my lead. I look at the other mirrors on the wall, noticing how every other reflective surface is smashed in but this one.

"What about it?" Orion asks again, he looks like he knows something but isn't letting on.

"It's one of a pair, Star has the other."

"That's how Solustus and Saturnus have been communicating," Orion blurts.

"What?" Azure turns to us.

"Yeah, Saturnus said he was 'storing' the other in his office."

Azure turns and touches a fingertip to the surface again, closing her eyes. The mirror becomes foggy and then clears, revealing a window into the Occulta Mirum.

Well, I'll be damned.

"Nobody say anything," Azure warns, keeping her movements minimal. Suddenly, a familiar and angular face pops out of the corner. It's muttering... "Oh bloody hell keep your hair on woman, I'm going!" Vex moves into the centre of the mirror.

"Bloody hell, blondie is that you?" He looks through the mirror and taps on the glass. I wave sheepishly from behind Azure. "This is way better than high definition!" I roll my eyes at this. He's such a moron.

"Vexus. Where's Starlet, is she there? Can you tilt this thing?" Azure asks and he exhales, looking irritated.

"You know I don't enjoy getting bullied by twins... except..."

"VEX!" I yell at him and he rolls his eyes, looking annoyed again.

"Alright, love, stop with the yelling! Bloody women," he tilts the mirror on its stand so we can see into the study more clearly. Star is on the floor and Oscar is next to her. They're bound, but at least they're alive.

"Oscar!" I exhale, I can't wait to tell Sophia he's safe. Then I wonder if I should mention it or not.

"Star! I'm sorry! I tried to save you!" Azure yells and Starlet's eyes are wide. She looks like she might cry. Orion is silent at my back.

"What's going on there?" Cole asks him.

"Well, after you and I last saw each other I became best friends with Saturnus and Solustus, we had a nice tea party and they let me braid their hair!" His sarcasm makes me want to laugh, but somehow I manage to contain it. He continues, "How the hell should I know? They're not exactly good with the sharing their evil plan bit…From what I can tell they're clearing debris…" He finishes this and a question inside me surfaces.

"You don't suppose the Necrimad is underneath the city…" I look to Orion and he shrugs.

"I don't know…" He looks unsure. Vex suddenly turns his neck, looking at something behind him.

"They're coming back. I've got to scram!" He looks scared and it surprises me. Maybe he really is on our side after all.

"Tell Star I'll be watching. She knows what I mean," Azure blurts and he nods. The mirror turns back our reflections on us, cutting off the conversation.

"So he's on our side now?" Orion looks angry. I get ready to speak but Azure beats me to it.

"Yes. We need someone on the inside. Unless, of course, you want our sister to die?" He shuts up. Things get awkward between us and Cole takes it upon himself to break the silence.

"So what's with the trident?" He asks. Azure has an answer for that, too. I wonder when she got so helpful.

"It was Titus'… but he never used it. He thought it made him look cool more than anything. Bloody narcissus." I hear her turn of phrase and stare at her with a cocked eyebrow, she really can't pull it off without the British accent mixed in. "Yeah I heard it!" She snaps at me and I laugh.

"Should we try take that mirror with us? Could come in useful," Cole suggests, but Azure shakes her head.

"No, it's too big for a long journey. Besides, once it's cracked and the pieces are separated it useless. Eventually, Saturnus will smash the other one to pieces. He won't risk us looking in on him," she speaks with such certainty that no one questions her.

"We should go. I don't want to leave the others outside. Anything could come back and pick them off." Orion nods and we make a hasty exit from the throne room. I pass the trident to him as we make our way through the charred passages.

"Why you giving this to me?" He looks at me, suspicious.

"You're the best fighter here. You need a weapon more than me." I lie. The truth is I can't bare the feel of it in my hand, a reminder of the crunching and snapping of arteries and veins. He doesn't question me, but gives me a slight smile.

"Thanks."

Outside we're met by an alarming and yet slightly hysterical scene. The mermaids and Ghazi are staring down at something on the ground. Orion speaks first, sounding as authoritative as I've heard him in a while.

"What happened?" The girls all move to speak at once and Ghazi rolls his eyes. He's standing with his arms crossed. "One at a time!" Orion barks and they all jump at the volume of his voice. It reverberates off the walls of the city, ringing in our ears.

"We captured a Psiren!" Rose looks practically gleeful.

"I hit him over the head!" Skye states, pride radiating from her.

"I tied him up!" Emma is smiling. They move backward and reveal a Psiren, bound and unconscious on the floor. Sophia moves forward.

"Ghazi did most of the fighting part," she explains directly, I wonder if my expression is that obviously incredulous.

"Ah," I nod and give her a smile. I can't help myself, deciding then and there to tell her about Oscar. "Oscar, he's alive." I look into her eyes and watch them tear up.

"How? How do you know that?" She asks me.

"There was a mirror, we could see into the Occulta Mirum, just for a moment. I saw him. He's with Starlet." At this sentiment her face drops.

"She's been captured though, hasn't she?"

"Yes," I breathe out. "I didn't know whether to tell you, but if it was me, I'd want to know." I rub my left shoulder with my palm, feeling the tension in my muscles.

"Thank you," she sighs. It's not a happy sigh, but I don't think I can ask her to be happy. I hope I've given her at least a little relief. Our eyes break as I realise that Orion and Marina are causing somewhat of a scene.

"That thing needs to be killed. I won't risk it telling Solustus anything, or coming after us when it wakes up!" He barks at her, leaning forward. She's red in the face.

"I'm just saying! If I had to live in this place, I'd be homicidal too! Look at the décor! These creatures are in pain!" She is gesticulating wildly.

"They. Murdered. Christian." Orion spits. There's a gasp. The maidens recoil slightly and my eyes pop open a little. That was over the line. Even for him.

"Yes, and killing this creature won't bring him back," she spits, her Italian temper flaring. The group falls silent, suspended awkwardly in the water, nobody daring to move. A few moments pass, and Orion eventually shrugs.

"Fine. Leave it here. We need to go," he doesn't look anyone in the eye but rises high above, leaving us behind. I look at Azure with a confused expression and she shrugs too, mimicking her brother. So she doesn't know what's going on either.

Well, I think, *I hope he sorts himself out soon.*

We have never needed a Crowned Ruler more. With that thought, I realise things have changed forever. The city I had fallen in love with is gone and a new reign of darkness and terror has begun for everyone under the surface. Fear knots in my belly, melding together with the guilt that still hangs heavy in my soul. I have hope though; hope born from the instinctual gut feeling that journeying north will bring answers.

24
Sea of Voices
ORION

My steed shifts underneath me, his hooves galloping against invisible earth, treading water. His leathery wings extend outward as I sit side-saddle, my sister at my back. We're leading the pod, if that's what we are called now. We are divided. Azure and I are sitting on Philippe's back, riding ahead, and the mermaids and Callie are lagging behind us while Ghazi and Cole are keeping watch at the tail end of our fragmented processional.

"You're quiet," Azure notes and I nod, not saying anything. "You know, this is going to be a real long trip if you've decided to play mime." She rises from the Equinox's spine and moves to face him, keeping pace with the horse's continuing forward motion while caressing his nose. She looks up at me, her eyes the familial ice blue and sighs. "I thought you'd be happy. Callie isn't infected anymore."

We pass over coral reefs vibrant with colour but they do nothing to soothe my ragged temper. I'm not really in the mood to talk, but knowing my sister she won't shut up until I say at least something.

"I'm not happy. Callie... she's different somehow. She doesn't need me anymore," I feel my shoulders sag and my heart sink. The ocean has lost its thrill and as I look around all I can see is endless, darkening blue pressing in on all sides.

"Are you serious?" Azure's eyebrows pinch together.

"What?" I look at her as her expression becomes angry.

"You're seriously telling me you have a problem with her, the person you waited all that time for, because she doesn't *need* you like some pathetic

290

whiner?" Azure's fist is clenched, she's taking long strokes backward in the water, totally erect now as Philippe continues to canter onward, his leathery wings outstretched and beating a pulse. Suddenly I feel her gaze on me, burning into me and I shrink further.

"Yes?" I answer, unsure of how to respond. She's making me seem ridiculous. She moves forward, slapping me across the left side of the face.

"Have I taught you nothing? You think I *need* a man? No. Do I *want* a man? Well… also no. But if I did, I wouldn't be pussyfooting around."

"Azure, this really isn't any of your business," I sigh, running my hands through my hair. Cole comes into view, swinging his tail to the left and pivoting round in front of me. He looks suspiciously at Azure.

"Everything alright here?" He looks at my sister with a wary glance sideways.

"Everything is fine. I'm just slapping my dumbass brother for being… well, a dumbass."

"Fair enough," Cole says it with such a straight face that I almost don't register with what he's said. When I do, my head snaps back to the left, scorning him with my stare. He swims leisurely back to the rear of the group.

"Seriously, we're not in the position to take the fact the people we love are still here for granted, Orion. Just look at those women back there; half of them are widows. Are you and Callie really going to not be together out of stubbornness?" I'm sort of shocked to be hearing this from her at all, when I think about what a state she was in only a few weeks ago. She's starting to radiate Starlet's tone and attitude with each passing remark. She has a point, but that's exactly why I don't want to talk to her about it anymore.

"Butt out. It's over," those two words are out of my mouth quicker than I realise and I wonder if I still believe them. Everything that had pulled us apart is still an issue, isn't it? Callie has changed, so much so that I almost don't recognise her when she speaks. She's so authoritative. When we had first met she was so unsure of everything, except of course the fact that she didn't want to be looked after. She's certainly changed, hardened somehow.

"Do you think… that the darkness, made her, you know…"

"Screwed up in the head like me?" Azure finishes my trail of thought, but I give her an unsavoury look before turning to look back at Callie.

291

"Yeah," I sigh.

"Did you not see how she reacted to killing Alyssa? I'd say she's doing okay. She's strong," Azure comments and I'm surprised by her words.

"You really think that?" I exclaim and she rolls her eyes.

"Well, not that my opinion means anything, but yes. She lived down there and she's come back tougher. She's not so bratty as I remember anyway." I shoot her a stare and she pokes her tongue out, returning to stroking Philippe's mane. It's the calmest I have ever seen her and I think the open ocean is doing her good. I'd heard people say that the ocean could heal the most broken of hearts, and it looks like my sister is slowly piecing hers back together.

We're a long way from the city, travelling fast and making good pace and the natural world is all consuming as we wade through it. While I would usually be savouring its richness like honey, I can't help but find everything around me bland; that is until I clamp eyes on the one thing I can't bear to want. Callie.

She's among the mermaids, smiling and laughing. She's a good ruler, or so it seems. Despite her time with the Psirens the mermaids seem to like her. They trust her, even though she's young, inexperienced, and naïve. They can't help but listen when she speaks, respecting her. The new her is more compassionate to the pain of others than I've seen before. She's less impatient with the mermaids who I know she once considered shallow and is trying her best to get to know them better. I think back to the fire in her eyes as she turned, spinning to a halt before facing Alyssa. She had killed her, single-handedly. I wonder if I would have done as well with all those tentacles, which she had unbelievably outwitted without any help at all. I had known her death had affected me, but maybe something inside her had snapped at that moment too. Perhaps she felt as helpless as I had, and she knew the only thing that could keep her truly safe was knowledge, strength of will, and physique. Not me. Had I made her feel so terribly weak by locking her away, adorning her with jewels and love bites, staking my claim? Maybe I've sold her short all along. Maybe, just maybe, she's stronger than I thought. Maybe, after everything I've tried to do to keep her safe, I'm the weak one, for not being able to let her go.

CALLIE

The mermaids are really starting to get on my nerves. It's been a long, empty journey so far and it would seem that the demons we are all so afraid of are nowhere to be seen. I wonder if it's because the threat of the Necrimad rising into our dimension is pulling them elsewhere, or maybe we've just been lucky. The mermaids, despite the lack of a threat are all clutching onto their crude weaponry, as though their very lives are held within the rotting wood boards slammed through with fishing hooks, crude bone daggers and primitive spears.

"I'm tired..." Skye whines for the thirtieth time this hour. Even though I'm no longer fuelled with dark magic I can't help but think about gagging her.

"My tail hurts....." Alannah picks up where Skye leaves off, starting up the complaining brigade all over again.

"This is so boring..." Rose pouts.

"Are we there yet?" Emma joins in. I clench my fist and Sophia shoots me an irritated glance sideways. With that I lose it.

"Oh. My. God. Can you all just shut the hell up?!" I yell back at them. They stop swimming, recoiling backward from my pissed off expression.

"Well, sorry we aren't all into playing warrior princess!" Rose retorts.

"What the hell is that supposed to mean?!" I put my hand on my hip and sit back into an erect position in the water.

"Some of us actually did what we were supposed to, Callie. Some of us stayed at home, married a warrior, and took care of him like Atargatis intended! We didn't need to go getting ourselves into trouble for attention," she snarls the insult and the rest of the group back up slightly.

Wow girls, thanks for the support.

"Jeez, and here I was wondering why it took feminism so long to get anywhere. I guess now I know," I spit out. She looks confused. I can tell she has no idea what the hell I'm talking about.

"She's only saying what we're all thinking, Callie," Skye looks up at me, dark circles around her eyes.

"And what's that?" I ask them with a cocked eyebrow.

"Maybe if you'd have married Orion, we wouldn't be in this mess. Maybe if you had just said yes like you were supposed to, then Orion wouldn't have been off trying to win you back. Maybe he could have spent more time preparing the army," Alannah sighs and the three girls look at me, half-guilty, half-angry.

"Right," I don't want an argument. Instead I decide to move from the group. Their eyes follow me as I swim, tight lipped, past them and toward the rear of the travelling procession. I always did prefer the company of men anyway.

"What you doing back here then?" Cole asks me. The sun is beginning its descent toward the horizon and the water is turning a happy orange in its glow.

"Mutiny is afoot," I roll my eyes and he contorts his sculpted lip into a grimace. His onyx eye scales make his blue eyes pop. I look at his scales in more detail than I ever have before, it's true, they're black like a Psiren's, but they have this oily blue sheen coating them, making him utterly unique.

"That bad?" He asks and I shrug.

"They think it's my fault that we're here. They say if I'd have said yes to Orion when he proposed then we wouldn't be in this mess," I sigh and he looks serious, the orange light is making his black scales look like they're on fire.

"Do you believe that?" He takes another powerful stroke with his tailfin, surging forward.

"I don't think it matters what I believe. They've already made up their minds about me."

"Don't forget, Callie, that they're grieving. They're looking for someone to blame. Death does not come easily to those who have been lured with a promise of forever," his face is stony, each of the lines definite and harrowed. Suddenly I realise: Jack isn't here.

"I'm sorry. About Jack." It hurts me to think of Cole being alone. He had been one of the first people I'd met as a mer, he served around the clock and always put the needs of the Crowned Ruler before his own. He didn't deserve to be alone.

"Do not be sorry. Jack is alive," he replies, smiling sadly.

"How do you know?" I feel curiosity stir within me.

"I just do," he doesn't give any more information than this, but leaves his reply shrouded in mystery. I remain silent for a minute, giving myself space to breathe.

I look around at my surroundings; subtle changes are starting to catch my attention. The temperature has become slightly chilly and the ocean fauna is changing slowly too. I can see shoals of large salmon and porpoises becoming visible more frequently, and more green vegetation on the seafloor too.

"Hey, where are we?" I ask Cole, breaking the silence.

"We're nearing the Gulf of Alaska, I think. Those fish over there are Chinook Salmon, they're pretty popular around here."

"That's why it's so cold. I thought it was the mermaid's frosty attitudes starting to get to me," I laugh at my own joke and Cole gives a tired smile.

"You really need to unify them, to give them strength. They're all we've got now."

"What, shared hatred for me isn't enough unity for ya?" I crack a joke but this time Cole doesn't smile. His expression stays serious as the sun falls behind cloud and shadow is cast across his face.

"I'm serious. If we have to fight off a demon, Psirens... anything, we need a group that can work together effectively. They need someone to lead them."

"You think that's me?" I exclaim, half laughing.

"It could be. But you hanging back here with me and the mute isn't going to help your case," he laughs at this, his face breaking a smile once more as he shoots Ghazi a look out of the corner of his eye. I wish I had his faith. Somehow he is still as cheery as ever, somehow he knows Jack is still alive out there somewhere. I nod in reply, thinking about him and I marvel at his strength to keep going when everything is falling apart.

"Thanks for the advice, chief," I give a fake salute and he rolls his eyes, peering out into the sea as the movement of a nearby porpoise catches his attention.

I sigh, I guess he's right. I need to get a handle on the maidens before anything else can happen. We need to work together if we can ever hope of seeing Oscar and Starlet alive again.

I move forward towards the maidens, nervous after the revelation that they're blaming me for the fall of the Occulta Mirum.

"I'm sorry I snapped earlier," I say boldly, the chill of the water making hairs on my skin rise. Skye, Alannah, Rose, Emma, Fahima, and Marina all look up surprised. Sophia smiles slightly at me, giving me a knowing look.

"We're sorry, too. We didn't mean to gang up on you," Skye apologises and looks like she might cry.

"Hey, it's okay," I move forward and put my hand on her shoulder as the group stops once more. Azure and Orion move further away from us on Philippe, not noticing the halt in our momentum. I look into Skye's eyes and then up and into the faces of each of the maidens. The one thing I notice, that I hadn't seen behind all their bitching and moaning, is clear to me now. Fear. They're all scared out of their minds.

"It's not okay! Everything is ruined. Everyone is dead!" Skye begins to sob. I grab her and pull her into my scaly chest, her shoulders heaving in despair. The rest of the maidens start shedding tears too.

"Don't cry. You're all just in shock. A lot has happened. You haven't had time to grieve," I try to stay calm, stay logical.

"We haven't even had a funeral. Jason died and I haven't even said goodbye," Rose whispers this shocking truth and I watch it rattle through her like a storm.

"This is why we need to support each other," my arms are still clinging to Skye's shaking body.

"No more fighting," Sophia whispers, sniffling. I think back to Atlas' funeral, the amazing vocal tribute that had been given by these women. Their voices had seemed to collectively soothe everyone who watched their ruler turn to sand.

"We can't have a funeral right now. But... we could sing. You guys sang that amazing song for Atlas. It made me feel, I don't know, peaceful. I think we should do that now." The girls nod, smiling at me through their tears as I release Skye. I look down and see diamonds being moved from beneath us by a thick and cold current.

"Okay... on my count," Alannah as the head of their singing group wipes the oily tears from her cheeks. "One... two... three."

May your arms envelop us,
as you caress the ocean deep.
You are but a rolling wave,
You do not sleep.

May you mirror the stars,
as those you touched are weeping.
You are but a still reflection,
but I know you're not sleeping.

May your new life be bountiful,
as the secrets oceans keep.
You are but the song of whales,
You do not sleep.

May your soul be returned,
the sand of your body now sweeping.
You may be back by her side
But I know you're not sleeping...

The harmonising voices rise, reverberating through the water and pulling at me. I can feel their loss, their hurt and it's crippling to behold.

I feel something stir in the water and I turn. Philippe is at my spine, nudging me. I turn and caress his nose gently, enjoying his horsey noises.

"What's going on?" Orion looks at me, clueless.

"They're scared, Orion. I said that they should sing to make themselves feel better… They need to grieve," I whisper, not wanting to interrupt the melody, but the mermaids don't seem to notice. They continue to sing, trying perhaps a little harder now that the Crowned Ruler is present. They move, rising like their pitch towards the surface of the water, swimming in synchronised circles together.

"That's…" Orion starts, searching my face for something before he sighs and smiles at me, "A beautiful idea. Well done." I beam, feeling pride wash over me, a warmth that fights back the chill of the water. It makes me realise that I do really care what Orion thinks, whether I want to admit it or not.

The mermaids continue to sing and that's when I notice something that I'd never seen before. Sea life is starting to move toward them, encircling the group. The porpoises join in, clicking and popping in excited song, while fish swirl around them in shoals that flash silver in the darkening light, and sea lions playfully dance in intricate patterns that look like Celtic symbols from below. I'm looking up at the maiden's singing out their pain in belting, sweeping notes and that's when it happens. A voice… a voice inside my head.

Help.

I blink, shaking my head. I wasn't going to be victim to Titus' poisonous influences again.

Help.

There it is again. It doesn't seem malicious, it seems scared. I shake it off.

Help.

An insistence growing louder this time, coming closer.

"Whoa!" Azure cries as Philippe whinnies, bubbles flying from his nostrils in a flurry of terror. Orion swims upward, dismounting the animal immediately. That's when I see what he's spooked by. A humpback whale is heading for us, swimming at high speed. As it moves its hulking, crustacean covered mass toward us I hear the voice again, but this time it's so loud I cover my ears.

HELP.

As the whale passes over us it slows, turning.

"Callie's what's wrong?" Orion asks as Azure steadies the Equinox, whispering in its ear and patting its mane, attempting to keep it calm. The mermaids have stopped singing and the rest of the animals have darted into the blue shadows of the distance. The whale inches closer. I rise to look into it's dark, beautiful eye.

Help.

The voice whispers to me this time, velvety soft and I gasp, my eyes welling with the thought of a gift so precious it makes my heart stop just thinking about it.

"I think…" I whisper, not looking at Orion, transfixed by the majesty of the animal before me. "This whale needs help."

"What do you mean?" Azure asks, speaking softly toward me, trying not to spook Philippe as the mermaids gather around.

"It… it spoke to me," I exhale dreamily as the giant eye of the humpback blinks. Nothing in this sea of voices ever ceases to amaze.

25
Ballet

CALLIE

The whale is bigger than any marine mammal I've yet encountered as a mermaid. Now I think about it, I really haven't seen that much of the ocean since I turned. When I had first become a mermaid, Orion had wanted to keep me close and after the first Psiren invasion was unsuccessful nobody had wanted to venture far out of the city either. I'm astonished by how different it feels to swim, undulating next to such a massive animal, whose weight alone causes massive shifts in the water around it.

Come.

Its message is clear and I stroke the old grooves that run across its face underneath its giant, soulful eye.

"It's okay, we're not going anywhere," I whisper. Orion is next to me.

"How is this possible?" He looks at me curiously and I wonder what he's thinking. How he sees me now. Does he think this is some darkness left over that I'm concealing?

"I don't know," I say, feeling breathless. I hope he doesn't think this is some trick, after all he's so paranoid now since Saturnus' betrayal. I have a real connection with this animal and the second I looked into her eye I knew I had to help her. It wasn't a connection through words, despite the fact I'm hearing her in my head; it's something deeper. Something that stems from the fact we both have souls tied to the earth. An earth that we share.

"I might have an answer to that one," Azure's tones are serious. She's on the back of Philippe, who I can see now she has a past with. She's touching his mane in the way I know Orion often does.

"Huh... why?" I look at her confused. I hope she isn't about to tell me something that will turn Orion's opinions of me muddier than they already are. I really need us to get along right now.

"Titus could talk to animals, before he became a Psiren," she reminds me of a simple fact I'd forgotten. It makes sense, but I don't want to seem like I'm still under Titus' influence. I know now that I have to reveal how my darkness had disappeared so suddenly.

"So once the darkness that latched onto me got pulled out by Vex..." I begin and Orion's head snaps toward me like he's been slapped.

"Vex?" His face is stony and his jaw is hard set, the glacial surface of his eyes turn as cold as the colour they exude.

"Yes. He took the darkness from me," I sigh and he licks the front of his top teeth.

"What a hero," he shakes his head and I change the subject.

"So this is what's left behind? I can talk to animals now?" Azure nods at me.

"Titus, from what I recall of him back then anyway, said they came to him in fragments. Just single words, sometimes phrases." Azure replies, trying to be helpful in spite of her brother's issues. I nod and smile.

"That's what it's like with her!" I want to cry, feeling an overwhelming joy at something so wonderful coming from the darkness that I had never thought I would fall into so deeply.

The whale rises, taking a large exhalation of water and showering the surface with droplets of salty sea spray. It takes in the oxygen it needs, and I fall back along it's pectoral fin as it's body lurches back beneath the surface with a crash, obliterating the surface tension.

"So the darkness really is gone!" I smile, beaming wider than I have in a long time, since perhaps before the night Orion and I left our beach house after our long pre-coronation night of passion. I suddenly find myself tracing the area around my neck with my fingertips, feeling over the flesh that had once been bruised tender at his mouth's hot clutch.

"Callie," my name is but a short, sharp burst from Orion's unforgiving lips. I find my temporary nostalgia broken as I look at where Orion is pointing. It's a hole in the lush green sea floor, covered over with rocks from a landslide or some other accidental natural disaster. I hear a calling, the ethereal haunting song that can only belong to another humpback whale.

Skye and the other mermaids move effortlessly beneath the belly of the whale that has led us here, diving so they can get closer to the rocks covering whatever cave or hole is underneath. The whale stops, letting itself hover in the dark green waters. I plunge down, diving to join the pod of mer who all look rather horrified.

"Oh Callie, it's so awful!" Sophia is babbling, looking worried. With an abruptness that shows we are on a time limit, the other mer move backward and I see why they're so concerned. A baby humpback whale is trapped beneath the rock, crying out to be let free. A feeble voice echoes in my mind, faint.

Stuck.

The voice alarms me, because it sounds so pure, so guttural and innocent. I want to be sick and I feel my chest constrict as I realise that the baby humpback can't rise for air.

"It's drowning!" I exclaim, horrified.

Help.

The mother's voice echoes in my mind again and I cover my ears, not wanting to hear their pain anymore.

"We have to help him!" I exclaim again.

"Him?" Skye looks at me confused.

"Yes, it's a boy. Now come on, help me move some of these rocks, it's running out of time! Fahima, tell Ghazi to help too! We need all the muscle we can get!" I'm barking orders left, right, and centre, as though the infant beneath the rockslide isn't a whale, but my own baby sister crying out in need. It's ripping my heart apart from the inside, hearing their pain within my head. I need it to stop.

Moving the boulders causes my shoulders to ache and my back muscles to burn. It takes me back to the day I had first used my power as the vessel on an unsuspecting Ghazi. I look over at him, hauling rocks from the entrance to the cave trapping the baby whale. His arms are bulging, straining with the weight of the task at hand as well as the consequences should we fail. The mermaids have discarded their stolen weapons in a clumsy pile and are moving smaller rocks. Unfortunately, it's not cutting it.

"Guys, why don't you try working together to lift some of the bigger rocks?" I ask, feeling some algae come off the boulder I'm holding; it clings to me like cheese off a day old pizza, slimy and cold.

Ew.

"You think we could lift that one?" Skye asks me, cocking her eyebrow and tossing her caramel coloured hair over one shoulder.

"Why not? Come on, I'll help," I charge over to where they're moving pebble sized stones and spiral my body so I'm facing one of the largest rocks in the pile. Ghazi moves to help me, but I hold up a hand and point to one of the smaller boulders a few metres away. I want the girls and I to tackle this one by ourselves; they need a serious infusion of confidence. I smile to myself, hearing how I'm now referring to them as 'the girls', I hadn't given that title to anyone since becoming a mermaid, and the last group of girls who had been entitled to it had been Chloe, Mollie, and Manda. I think back to Chloe and Mollie at the frat party I had attended with Vex. They had looked so different, so *available*. Mollie was lucky Vex had stepped in when he did, otherwise she might be dead right now, or worse.

"Okay, on my count," Alannah says for the second time today. She seems to take to authority well; the other maidens listen to her at least. "One, two... three!" The strain begins as our tails motion together, out of time and unable to take the weight of the stone. It's slippery to touch, but I know that's not the problem. The mermaids stop straining and begin to float back to what they were doing.

"Hey, wait, where are you going?" I ask them, flipping my long blonde locks back over my left shoulder.

"We can't lift it, Callie. You saw. Get Ghazi to do it." Ghazi's ears prick up at this and I see him begin to swim back toward us.

"Hey! No! We can do it. We just have to swim *together*."

"We just did!" Rose looks at me like I'm stupid.

"That's not what I mean. We need to be synchronised." The mermaids roll their eyes. "Trust me," I say again and they let out what seems to be a collective sigh, moving back to their positions around the enormous boulder.

"Alannah. Count again if you would," I command her and she frowns slightly, I explain. "Once Alannah reaches three, each of us count in our heads... one... two. Each number is tied to a tail stroke. One is forward, two is back. Got it?" Suddenly they all look appeased and nod. Alannah clears her throat.

"One, two... three!" I begin counting in my head and I see that the rest of the girls are doing the same. The way they usually move is so effortless, almost ghostly, but right now they're going for pure strength and it's not pretty. Some are red in the face, others have hair floating into their eyes and Sophia in particular is breathing out, straining like a female body builder. If I weren't holding so much weight, I'd be laughing my ass off. Truth is, I probably don't look much better.

The boulder shifts, and we move upward, taking its enormous earthy mass with us. We somehow all know which direction to move to dump it, and release its weight with a collective deep breath, revelling in the loss of such weight. The removal of such a massive boulder has rendered the blockage of the cave exit unstable and suddenly, in a massive mushroom cloud of dust and sand, the rockslide pile collapses again. I hold my breath, terrified that I've put a catastrophe into motion. I can't move, can't even speak until in one giant exhalation of song the baby humpback rises from the seabed hollow in which it was trapped. It rises quickly, swimming with miniature, unpractised strokes of its fluke. Finally, it breaks the surface above, gasping for air and blowing a large amount of water from its blowhole. Its mother is relieved, surfacing with her calf in one powerful push through the murky green water. As she immerses herself back in the chill, clear waters she begins to sing and then something extraordinary happens.

"Callie... look," Sophia says, breathlessly. Out of the shadows come more humpbacks.

"It's her family," I say, in awe at the sheer number of whales in the pod. I see Orion looking stunned from the other size of the hole in the seabed. I smile slightly.

From the murky blue of the Alaskan waters, that are illuminated by the low hanging sun, they move toward us slowly and in a way that is more than graceful.

Thank.

The word reaches me and I notice the baby humpback coming toward me. It rests before me as the mother whale watches us from a caring proximity.

"You're welcome," I reach out as the rest of the mer watch me, moving forward to touch the baby's face.

"What's your name?" I ask him. I get one very simple reply.

We are blue.

I don't understand what that means. But I nod, guessing I'll call him Blue and his mom Big Blue.

The other whales are closing in on the mother and calf now, coming together in a crowd of giant hulking bodies that seem immovably beautiful. Big Blue's voice echoes in my head.

Dance.

I shake my head, not knowing what that means. I turn away from the whales and see that the mer have gathered at my back.

"I'm glad we could help, but we really need to keep moving," Orion reminds me as Philippe shuffles from foot to foot at his side. Fahima is stroking his mane and Ghazi is holding her hand lovingly. I wonder if they're talking in whispers only they can hear.

I nod at Orion acknowledging his request and trying not to hold his eye contact for too long as Sophia comes over to me.

"That was amazing. What did they say to you?"

"Dance," I repeat the word

"What?" She looks at me and I shrug, turning toward them.

Dance.

The whale is insistent this time, turning to look at me intensely and I watch as something magical happens. Something that I can only describe as a silent ballet.

ORION

I want to look away. I want to break the hypnotising effect she has on me. I don't want to stare upon her, but I can't help it.

The Kiss That Saved Me

Callie rises, moving among the whales with a kind of calm I haven't seen from her before. Her movements are exact, effortlessly planned, flowing into one another. She's usually so excitable in her movements, so careless and quick, but not any longer. Now she's graceful, at peace.

I catch a glimpse of her face as she moves closer to the surface and she's beaming. Her long blonde hair is twisting around her in a torrent of gold and the light of the sun, finally reaching her from behind a mass of clouds, bathes her in peach splendour. The whales begin to sing, calling out in low harrowing song, moving around her in thanks for saving their calf. She spins, laughing loudly among them. They touch their pectoral fins to her and she grabs on, moving around in concentric circles, dancing.

I turn to talk to the other mer, willing them to move on before my heart shatters, but Azure is eerily transfixed and beyond my reach somehow. I look around the rest of them, with their mouths hanging open and eyes wide as I turn away. I wouldn't break the spell she has over them for the world, it's the first time I've seen them overcome like this in the eternity I can remember knowing them. My eyes rest on the scene, and I feel something within me stir. Some epiphany that I'm yet to fully grasp.

The light shines down, like a tonic after all the darkness that has covered our lives and the whales continue to sing. They erect themselves, their long bodies almost reaching the sea floor as their tails brush against the tall sea grass. They begin to spin, pirouetting and Callie follows. I wonder if they're conversing with her, speaking in tongues that I can't hear and all of a sudden I wish I was the one whispering to her. I wish I was the one making her beam and freeing her spirit from whatever burden that has been weighing on her. She's so beautiful and her aquamarine eyes sparkle like precious stones as her scales shimmer.

She raises her arms and throws her head back, allowing the light from the surface to cover her face. She's laughing wildly, like nothing in the world could touch her. It's the most beautiful I've ever seen her look, more beautiful than the night we first met, more stunning than even her descent down the staircase at the Lunar Sanctum before I accepted my crown. I run my hand through my hair, unable to look away, and letting myself surrender not only to the awe-inspiring nature of the scene before me, but the truth. No matter what happens with this woman, to this woman, no matter how she hurts me or how much I want to escape her stubbornness, it still isn't over.

It will never be over.

The light hitting the ocean dissipates as the sun sinks below the horizon. The moment has passed.

The whales still and something sacred passes between them and her. She smiles to herself, quietly content and then comes over to us, unable to wipe the ecstasy off her face.

"They want to escort us," she breathes.

"Really?" Sophia bursts before I have a chance to respond.

"Yes," Callie replies, quickly glancing to Sophia, as though she's distracted her and then at me. "What? Is there something on my face?" She's suddenly removed from the pedestal of goddess like grace on which she'd danced, and is back to being a self-conscious teenager. I realise I'm staring in a most obvious manner and have to put myself in check. I feel embarrassed for the fact I can't take my eyes off of her. I must look like such a schmuck.

"No... uh. Sorry," I shake my head, trying to clear the stupid out.

"So we can go now?" Callie is waiting for my approval and I nod silently. She turns, looking to the pod of humpbacks and gesturing for them to follow. The mermaids pick up their weapons from the ground and Azure moves over to Philippe who is nibbling tentatively on sea grass nearby. The waters are dim now that the light of the day is almost gone and we travel in silence, our forms undulating together, surrounded by the massive shadows of the whales that aren't so close to be intruding, but close enough to make sure we're safe should any demons attack.

As the night drives forward, lost in the din of far off echoes and chatter, I find myself confronted with something I've only ever seen once, something I've wanted to revisit but I had never found the time to travel so far north.

"What is it?" Callie is curious, and her proximity, which I hadn't noticed, is suddenly startling.

"It's the place where two seas meet. The Baltic Sea begins here. But it's water doesn't mix with that of the Gulf of Alaska, something about too much iron I think," I explain, moving across the boundary and into the water deposited by glacial rivers. I shudder slightly, letting the cold wash over me. As a mer, it doesn't affect me like it would a human, but it still feels too chilly for my liking.

"You know everything," Callie smiles. I remember her saying something similar to me when I had taken her to the cave where I had counted my years alone, and my heart weeps nostalgia.

"Not even close. I promise you," I roll my eyes, thinking of all the things I wish that I did know. I wish I knew how to fix things with her. I wish I knew what she was thinking. Most of all I wish I knew how to be the kind of man and ruler she deserves. Sadly, on all of these I'm a blank slate.

She's silent, her eyes watching my face with intrigue. It's like any ounce of anger or fear that was driving her before has evaporated. "Back there... I mean... wow," I feel nervous. Like I'm talking to a stranger almost.

"Don't. There are no words. I don't want to ruin it with classification or poor attempts at description." Her face is an oxymoron of conflicted feeling. She breathes and a wave of calm engulfs her body.

"Okay," I exhale, not mad, just tired. I want to communicate, but it's like we're speaking two different languages.

"This is awkward," she whispers and I laugh.

"Yeah, why is that?" I reply, feeling my gut twist with anxiety.

"Maybe we're just like the two sea's that meet but don't mix." She has this inspired thought, spilling it in a moment of pure reckless abandon.

"Don't say that," I whisper back, aware that the voices around us have ceased. I feel like I might cry. "I'm sorry... I just, I missed you," I blurt the words without a second thought for my reputation, how weak I look by buckling under the weight of her absence.

"I missed you, too," she sighs. I start to respond, but she speaks again suddenly, not filtering what she's saying. "We need to talk. I know that. But we can't do it here. Everyone is staring," she's looking around, conscious of her actions as a ruler. It's the first time I've seen her care about spilling our personal life to the entire mer population and it once again cements the fact that she's matured.

"Okay. I can wait," I sigh and she looks crestfallen, her lips pressed hard in the darkness.

"Wait right here," she commands suddenly, and then she's gone into the murky distance. She returns, her swimming speed faster than I'd ever seen before.

"Come on," she says, grabbing my hand and pulling me with her. We slide into the foggy distance together, as she leads me toward the mother whale. "She's going to give us some privacy." She explains and my forehead creases, not understanding her meaning at all. She rolls her eyes, not wanting to explain and pulls me again, onto the whale's back, lying down on her stomach. I follow her and slowly the mother humpback rises.

We emerge from the surface on whale back, icy water falling from my skin and scales as the night sky opens up above us and the smell of pine hits my nostrils with a pungent and cool freshness.

"Wow," is all I can manage to utter as Callie smiles at me, her eyes shiny.

"Now," she sighs, "we can talk."

26
Amends

CALLIE

The sky is alight with a million stars, cold and crisp, contrasting against the utter blackness of the surrounding wilderness. Orion is on his back, lying with his hands behind his head, his abs cut and pectorals rising and falling lazily with his breath. It reminds me of the nights we spent on the beach in San Diego, when everything was so new and fresh. Lighter almost.

"So..." Orion starts and my heart begins to pound. This is the conversation I've been most dreading. I'm different now, and I know I trust him. I can't keep holding back or I'm never going to move forward. He suddenly exhales and stops talking.

"So..." I continue. It's awkward and the air between us isn't just chill; it's dense, dense with everything that hasn't been said.

"Nice night, right?" Orion cocks an eyebrow and I melt slightly, bursting out into a massive full-bellied laugh that I can't contain.

"Oh yeah, great. We're fleeing from a group of savage killers, freezing our balls off in the process, and I'm trying to whip a bunch of Barbies into G.I Jane," my sarcasm metre is exploding and Orion laughs too. He's actually almost crying because he's laughing so much he can't breathe.

"Some rulers we make!" He blurts and I start laughing all over again. It's absolutely insane. We're fleeing to the farthest reaches of the earth because the guy we trusted turned out to be a psychopath and Orion and I are in charge. Absolutely. Freaking. Hilarious.

"When did everything get so completely screwed up?" I ask him and he smiles coyly.

"I don't know," he sighs outward, giving a final chuckle. "Somewhere between when I started adorning my head with jewellery and trying to make you wear an engagement ring." That stops my laughing cold.

"So we agree then. Jewellery is to blame?" I ask, serious this time as I stare into his eyes. The whale shifts beneath us slightly and I watch as ocean passes us by.

"I guess what's happened makes our problems seem kind of ridiculous," he shakes his head, freeing several cool droplets from his tangled mahogany locks. I feel my breath catch in my throat as I gush my next statement.

"I just, I wish we'd talked more. You needed me. I know that. But I just couldn't talk to you." He sits up suddenly, his head coming close to mine. His icy blue eyes bear into me.

"Why?" He is curious and I wonder if perhaps I'd spoken to him sooner I could have prevented all this. Was a lack of communication really at the root of everything?

"You... you were so cut off. I tried to talk to you about everything... about that night I died. About your father. I couldn't reach you," I whisper, scared of my own words.

"I know. I don't deal with loss well. I guess that's a side effect of having everyone you love live forever," he blinks, looking at me.

Finally. He does understand.

"I should have done more. I should have been there for you better," I admit. It isn't all Orion's fault. I'm just as uncommunicative sometimes, if not worse.

"You were there for me."

"I swam away. You asked me to marry you and instead of talking to you about why I wasn't ready, I left. That's my fault." I'm feeling very earnest, like the silence encasing us is allowing me to finally open my heart all the way out.

"I shouldn't have listened to Saturnus, but I won't lie, it stung like a bitch when you said no. I let my pride get in the way. I should have listened to you, even though I was hurt," he confesses this truth.

"I just felt trapped. Like all control was being taken away from me. I'm just a teenager; I don't want a crown or a ring. I just wanted you," I make the

311

next confession and he smiles to himself.

"I shouldn't have trapped you in. You're so... different now. You're growing into this incredible woman. I didn't see it. You have the potential to be so much. So much more than a wife." I want to cry as he whispers these words to me, feeling every ounce of the darkness in my soul evaporate as I fall into his eyes, wrapping myself up in his words. "I wanted you to be what I wanted. It's only now that I see how stupid that is. You're far too beautiful and far too unique for me to even begin to put my finger on what you are, let alone what you should be." His eyes fall and I breathe outward. He finally sees that I'm best when I'm free. I need him to know that doesn't mean I'll leave. Not anymore, I'm not fleeing any longer.

"You should know no matter how far I go, I'll always come back to you," I whisper.

"I'm your anchor," he kisses my forehead and I want to weep. Be weak and crumble into him.

"Why didn't we ever talk like this before?" I ask him and he smiles.

"Because we're stupid."

"I was so mad at you... until..." I stop, blushing slightly.

"Until?" He asks, not letting the sentence drop.

"Until I saw you looking at me today. With the whales. I saw the look on your face and I *knew* I would never find anyone who adored me like that," I admit this to myself and a shrill terror runs through me.

He's the one.

It's like I'm feeling what that really means for the first time. It means I have to take care of him like he's the most precious thing in the world. Once he's gone, there'll never be anyone like him again.

"I like this honesty thing. I so often wish I knew what you are thinking," Orion admits.

"Why don't you just ask?" I cock an eyebrow.

"You're not forthcoming either," he laughs slightly and I hit him across the arm. It reminds me of something and suddenly my heart sinks like a stone.

"In the uh, spirit of honesty. There's something I have to confess. But you're not going to like it," I breathe out, exhaling and trying to calm myself.

"What's that?" He strokes the round of my shoulder.

"It's about Vex." His finger halts in its track and he looks up at me. "I...I slept with him," I admit, watching the colour drain from Orion's face. "I'm sorry... I was drunk and Titus' darkness was at its worst. We'd just had that fight near the shoreline and I..." Orion doesn't say anything. He just holds a finger up to my lips, shakes his head with a disappointed look and disappears beneath the still water's surface, leaving me alone on the top of Big Blue.

I sigh, *so close... and yet so far.*

AZURE

Whispers keep coming from behind; the maidens are talking about me. I'm ignoring them. I want to look in on what's happening with Star, check she's okay, but the fog won't roll in. I wonder if that's because I'm really scared of knowing what's going on. As long as I can't see her, I can imagine her at least alive from the two way looking glass.

I'm also pissed at Callie. It's irrational I know, but her darkness was taken from her, she doesn't have to bear it any longer. She's back in the Goddess' favour, being rewarded and bathed in the glory of the sea. I have no such relief, constantly keeping my temper in check, feeling uncomfortable in my own skin. Callie gets to go back, be a Queen, adored by all who lay eyes on her. While I'm stuck with black roots and eyes that unnerve even the bravest of warriors. I've always thought of my darkness as power, but right now I am an outsider to everyone, and the understanding that I would have gotten from Callie has disappeared along with her own dark roots. I'm not quite a mer, neither am I Psiren. I don't belong.

The whispers of the mermaids are riding on my last nerve and as I look around Orion and Callie are nowhere to be seen. I guess I'd better shut them up then. I turn Philippe, yanking the reins and lay eyes on them, the Equinox beneath me treading water. The maidens look startled and erect themselves from the position in which they're swimming.

"If you have something to say to me, I suggest you say it to my face. Your whispers are shockingly not all that discreet. You guys know you have to actually lower your voices right?" I cock an eyebrow and allow my lips to pull back over my teeth. Rose, the one with seemingly more backbone than the others, narrows her eyes.

"We were just saying about how we wish we could fight like you. Orion said you pulled him out of the rubble... you know, when the Psirens attacked." She shrugs and I'm taken aback for a second. What, they like me now?

"Uh, yeah. I did," I say, dumbfounded. They shift, uncomfortable.

"We're sorry. About your sister. None of us knew her that well, but she seemed nice," the one with the mint green scales adds.

"Don't give me that shit. You and I both know that Starlet is an acquired taste," I bite out.

"Anyway, we just wanted to say we're sorry about your father too. We don't want you to think we don't care. You were one of us once. We can see you're trying," Sophia pipes up and once again I'm surprised. My heart feels weird, like it's squeezing slightly in my chest. I shrug it off. Must be the change in temperature.

"Um... thanks."

"We also... we had questions," Rose blurts. Ghazi's wife is behind her, looking worried.

"What questions? I'm not the answer type." I look at her suspiciously as Philippe continues to keep us stationary with a steady beating of his scaled wings.

"Your eyes... why do they do that thing? Is it because of the visions, I never saw Starlet's eyes go like that," Skye is curious, too curious for my liking. I note Cole and Ghazi are almost with us now, we've been stationary for long enough for them to catch up from the rear of the group. I can only hope one of them will save me.

"The dark magic... that's how it presents itself. When I get angry or excited. It helps me see in the dark too. It's nothing to do with my visions," I give a blasé explanation, bored of the conversation and pull on the reigns so the Equinox moves away.

"How do the visions... how do they work?" Skye is still tentative, but the other mermaids are absorbed.

"Why didn't you ask Star all this?" I sigh, shrugging my shoulders.

"She wasn't around much," Alannah cuts in, interrupting Skye.

"My visions work two ways. I get them sent to me from upstairs and I can also look in through Starlet's eyes. It's how we kept an eye on each other when I was…" I trail off, not wanting to remember being with Titus again. The girls look fascinated. I don't know why I'm still talking to them. I guess I must like the attention.

"So you can see what's happening right now, you know, back in the Occulta Mirum?" The question comes from the back of the group. It's from Sophia and I know she's asking for her soulmate.

"Not really, it's not something you can pick and choose. It doesn't work all the time," I explain, still bored. I look at my nails. Damn, I need a manicure. All this saving the world stuff is really cutting into my personal time.

"Do you think you could teach us to fight?" A squeaky voice reaches me and my head snaps up. I dismount Philippe momentarily, letting him move ahead.

"What did you just ask me?" They back up.

"We want to know how to fight. We want you to teach us." The voice comes from the shy girl with blonde hair and baby blue fins. I'm kind of flattered and at the same time half offended that they think I'd so easily relinquish my secrets.

"Why don't you ask Callie or Orion? Or Ghazi?" I enquire, sure there must be some kind of catch here.

"We don't want a man to teach us. We've seen you fight, we watched from my apartment when you fought the lion-fish looking guy," Rose cocks her head and furrows her brow; clearly thinking is hard work for her.

"Caedes?" I look at them and they nod. Rose continues.

"Yes, we saw how you outwitted him. You're small like us, and you don't have big muscles like the men, but you still won."

"You know I had help with Caedes, right? That Psiren with the slingshot, he…" I begin.

"Yes. But you fought in the first Psiren attack too and survived. You've survived with the Psirens for longer than anyone. We'd like you to teach us.

If you want. If not, we could always ask Callie," Rose puts this to me as a challenge. I accept, my eyes turning a little darker as my temper flares.

"Okay. When we make it to where we're going I'll put aside some time. But it won't be easy and I don't want any whiners!" I scold them and they blanche a little, I smile. I like the fact that they're still ever so slightly afraid of me. They all look like they're holding their breaths. I goad them.

"Thank you, Azure," I harp with a high-pitched girly tone. They all suddenly gush forward with thanks and I roll my eyes. "Whatever." I turn on my tailfin's axis and whirl away from them, leaving them to eat my bubbles.

When I finally catch up to Philippe, he's not alone. Orion is slumped lengthways, lying along his spine.

"Hey," I mutter, feeling annoyed. He doesn't reply; he looks rather pissed actually. "I said hey!" I repeat, not enjoying being ignored one bit. "What the hell is wrong with you?" I poke him in the abs, moving upward and examining him the way a coroner examines a corpse.

"He had his hands on her. He touched her…" I can't quite make out what he's blithering on about and so I roll my eyes. I'll use my simple words.

"Orion. Use words," I motion for him to hurry the hell up. I don't have time for his drama.

"Vex and Callie…" He begins and my stomach flips in a horrible vomit inducing type somersault. I don't know why.

"Oh my God! You freaking serious? That's gross… I thought Callie had better taste… Then she did agree to be with you. Jesus," I try to perk him up, jibing him with faux insults that I'm so used to dishing out.

"Azure. Go away," he's seriously heartbroken. Or pissed, I can't tell. I still can't wrap my head around Callie and that tentacle sporting douchebag bumping uglies. Oh man that is so wrong. What the hell was she thinking? I knew something had gone on between them, that much was obvious. I mean he had pulled the darkness out of her according to Callie. But sex? Ew. Wrong. No.

I shake my head, trying to stop my wicked imagination from putting images into my mind that I somehow can't stomach.

I look up at Orion, unfocused and wallowing in his own misery.

"Hey, it could be worse," I remind him, I regret this immediately when I'm subject yet again to more whining, courtesy of the Callie and Orion relationship drama of the week.

"How? How could this be worse?!" He exclaims sitting upright on horseback, twisting his body so his long tailfin hangs down the side of the Equinox.

"OUR SISTER COULD BE DEAD!" I yell, finally having enough. I feel my voice reverberate, echoing back at me through the empty space of the water. Silence falls from the rear of the group. "How self-absorbed can you be? There are BIGGER problems here than your goddamn love life. Get a freaking grip on yourself!" I go to raise my hand, disgusted, to slap him across the face again, my eyes dilating and turning black with my rage. He grips my wrist, his eyes softening.

"Okay. You're right. I'm sorry," he whispers, stroking my cheek slightly with his index finger. I yield, letting the rage dissipate and lowering my hand. He lets it drop, suddenly looking crushed beyond compare. "Why did it have to be her?" He shakes his head, now I'm sure he's talking about Starlet.

"I've been thinking about that. Callie said about purity. I thought we were talking in purely sexual terms, but I'm pretty sure that Solustus has never gotten any either. So why not him?" I'm thinking aloud. "It's about her connection to the Goddess, and more than that, I think it's about the fact she's never killed."

"Never? Wait, that can't be right?" Orion looks confused.

"You're telling me father let her go out and fight? That doesn't seem like him," I mumble, wondering if I am in fact wrong. Maybe Starlet has killed before.

"No... I guess not. She's gone all this time never killing anyone."

"At least we know why she's so damn cranky now. No sex. No bloodshed. How awfully boring," I comment and Orion scowls. I shrug unapologetically.

"I think it's more to do with the fact that by the time she turned you were already gone. She's been alone a long time," Orion reminds me.

"You think that's an excuse? I wasn't exactly destined to be with Titus, but I still went there. It was that damn convent. They brainwashed her. I'm telling you," I babble on, finding my stride for the first time in a while, but still can't get out of the habit of clipping my sentences short with disdain.

"Convent?" He looks confused and I scowl at him, wondering why he's not up to speed. He spent more time with my sister than I did.

"Oh... she didn't tell you about that?" I cock an eyebrow, and he's still pulling the dumbfounded, stupid expression. Guess not.

"After Katriona married me off, Starlet started having visions in public. Katriona sent her to a religious convent, to prevent her getting herself put to death. You know how our people are about the devil." Orion suddenly looks startled at my candour, it's the first time I've used our mother's name in centuries.

"I should have known. I should have gone back for you two. I should have..."

"Shoulda, woulda, coulda. If you spend your life worrying about what you should've done, you'll be topping yourself before you know it. Don't worry about Starlet. If she didn't tell you, then there has to be a reason."

"Maybe she was ashamed," he muses.

"Maybe those nuns had a bigger impact than I thought. These rituals are so damn non-descript. Either way, we'll definitely never know if we don't get her out of there. We have to save her, Orion," I plead with him, for the only thing I really want. The safety of my sister.

"I know, we will," he comforts me, but something behind his eyes tells me he doesn't know whether it's possible. I wonder if it actually is possible, saving Starlet, or if it's too late.

After all, we are so very far away from home.

27
Ice

CALLIE

The chill has grown, morphing silently into an invisible enemy that is making a clutch, bone deep, for all the energy in my body. I should have brought a blanket or something... why didn't I think to do that?

"God... I'm f-f-f-f-rreeezing..." Skye complains, but I can't even scold her for whining, it's cold enough to send the devil ice skating.

"I know. It'll take time for your inner thermostats to adjust. Just remember, you can't be killed by the cold," Orion comforts the women, not making eye contact with me.

"I can still feel it though!" Alannah complains through chattering teeth.

"You will acclimatise. Stop being such a baby. Some of us lived here for YEARS before," Azure reminds them, rolling her eyes, unamused.

"How far to the city?" I ask, Orion turns away from me, not answering.
Great.

Cole comes to my aid, scowling slightly in disapproval of Orion's attitude, which makes our surroundings feel positively tropical by comparison.

"It moves. We'll need to track it down," Cole explains and I scowl, rubbing my hands against the skin of my arms.

"Moves? How can an entire city move?" I ask incredulously.

"You'll see. We need to keep moving. I don't like us being out in the open like this," Cole hurries the group forward, encouraging us to keep moving.

I can see what he means about being in the open. The humpbacks still

319

surround us, but the ocean floor has fallen away, leaving us hanging above a cold emptiness.

The waters are silent. You wouldn't think it, but I now realise that tropical waters are loud, the movement of tiny creatures, shifting rock, and blowing bubbles of air that rise steadily to the surface. The pacific has its own rhythm, its own heartbeat - like the most unique sound you've ever heard, but you hardly notice when you're among it so long. I know I'll always notice it now, because I have been here. In utter and completely deafening silence. The waters are barren, bare and empty. No life except us existing for miles. The pack ice on the surface of the water blocks out the sunlight, leaving frosty shadow to fall into the nothingness below. The sparseness here is eerie and quiet.

The arctic water's peace is broken suddenly, a flock of penguins diving from the ice above, searching for fish. They look so amazingly energetic for such a cold climate, leaving me awestruck. The humpbacks swim upward toward them, taking a gasp of air at the ice hole they're diving into.

"Wow. Look at that," Sophia sighs, smiling. I love her appreciation of the natural world, and I hope when I'm as old as she that I'm still awestruck by the raw power and elegance of the ocean.

"There!" Orion points to a hulking mass of shadow, far away. Cole nods and smiles slightly, but I wonder how they can be so sure.

"How can you tell from just a shadow?" I ask Cole as the blue sheen of his black facial scales reflect back at me coldly. He doesn't reply, but moves forward, pushing himself to the front of the group. Azure is riding Philippe at a steady canter and Orion is beside her, his back to me and the maidens. The trident is strapped to Orion's spine, and I immediately feel naked without a weapon. Almost as though eyes are watching me that I cannot see once again.

As we near the shadow I begin to understand what they mean about it being mobile. It's a giant iceberg and apparently the only one among the pack ice for miles.

"It's an iceberg," I say, confused slightly. A hand grasps mine.

The city is inside, Callie.

It's Ghazi's voice, travelling across my consciousness like a lone ship in a stormy sea.

Oh. Is all I can reply, slightly dumbstruck. A city inside an iceberg? It seems ridiculous, but then I remember that everything about my life seems somewhat ridiculous.

I catch up to Orion and he passively moves to the other side of his steed. Azure glances between us and rolls her eyes. I assume he's told her what happened between Vex and I.

I'm not going to apologise. I needed it. I don't know how to regret something that showed me so much. I feel my heart start to close, but I stop myself. I need to keep myself open if I ever hope to fix things with Orion. I can't run away from what I've done. I just have to work through things with him. When he finishes being angry that is.

I ignore the fact that Orion isn't talking to me. After all, there are bigger issues here. I am grateful that the journey is almost at an end, but more grateful of the fact that there have been no demons in the waters we have travelled. The mermaids clutch their weapons to their chests, holding them like stuffed animals for comfort. The mermen have them strapped to their waists or their backs, ready to be drawn at a moment's notice. I look between the men and the maidens and I wonder why I'm so different from the mermaids. I guess that must be pretty difficult for Orion, seeing all his male counterparts with women who are so very much damsels in distress. Then there's me, not quite a bulky, muscle clad man, but not a helpless maiden either. Is it any wonder he's confused? I just don't fit.

Rose breaks my internal monologue as she poses an interesting question. "How do we get inside?"

"There is a single entrance tunnel on one of the sides of the ice structure. It's good for defence that way if I recall - like a bottle neck effect," Orion answers her quickly, his tone clipped and clearly still angry. Rose looks annoyed at his briskness, frowning in distaste. I hear a call to me in the distance.

"Wait here," I make the order, not caring if anyone follows it or not, flexing my tailfin and gliding through the icy water, which is making my mind clear and sharply aware. I approach Big Blue, her giant eye following my path through the water toward her.

Go.

The single syllable is uttered between us and I nod slightly.

"Thank you so much. For everything," I whisper, placing a hand on the humpback's face and letting it gently slide across its skin. I would never forget this animal.

See you again.

I blink. Wondering if that really is true. The whale calls out a song to the rest of its pod and they turn to leave. I return to my own pod slightly sad.

"Let's go," I say, feeling my heart break at the animal's departure. I hope they won't forget me.

"I'm glad we have your approval," Orion snorts. Swimming off. God, he's being such a diva. He should really wiggle his hips more. I laugh slightly to myself and Rose is looking at me weird, staring at me like I'm insane. I poke my tongue out at her and then watch as her eyes follow Orion, glazing over in a dreamy haze. If I didn't know better, I'd say she was checking him out.

We rise through the too clear water, moving across the iceberg's massive surface vertically. The water, if it's possible, is even colder close to the ice, but I try to toughen up and ignore it, curious as to the city inside. We find the entrance quickly and journey into the heart of the iceberg in single file. I can see what Orion means about the bottle neck effect, and wonder if the Occulta Mirum would still be standing if such an entrance to the city had existed. I sigh, missing the warmth of my home, the glinting bottle tops and spires of sea glass.

Skye is right in front of me, and all I can see is her lemon scaled backside until suddenly the tunnel ends and the hollow of the iceberg implodes in a panoramic view that's enough to make me inhale.

The iceberg is massive in volume and the city itself is bathed in pale sunlight from a lake on the surface, enclosed on all sides by thick white ice. I shiver, letting the cold seep into my bones. The city itself is dead and silent.

Spiralling shards of ice rise from the basin of the construct, shimmering like fresh frost and cut through the water with the definitive sharpness of a knife-edge. I am astounded as always at the intricacy of the buildings, some of which are adorned with balconies and sweeping staircases, swirling around their exteriors. Others are made up of spherical structures; like someone's blown bubbles and they've frozen on top of icy pedestals. At the centre of the city is an ice palace. I don't know why I'm surprised, after all the mer built this, so it only makes sense that features of it remind me of the Occulta Mirum.

I'm so busy gawping I don't even realise what's going on until a pair of angry silver eyes rise into my field of vision and I feel someone at my back. I look around, suddenly confused. There's no noise, only silence and yet we are surrounded by strange and angry people.

"We're not enemies! We seek sanctuary!" I can hear Orion's suddenly urgent tone as the strange looking mer raise their harpoons and angle them in on us. We are surrounded from all sides.

"Drop the weapons," the woman with the angry silver eyes that interrupted my admiration of the icy city barks. Her teeth look razor sharp and I'm stunned at her pallor. *Who are these people?* Is all I can wonder as she inches closer to me, jabbing her harpoon under my chin and causing my head to turn. It's like she's examining me.

"What kind of demon can disguise themselves to look like one of us?" The woman barks this question to her left; I dare not peek to see who she is talking to.

"We're not demons! We're here to seek sanctuary!" I can hear Orion repeat. I can also hear Azure behind me muttering.

"They want to see a freaking demon, I'll show them..." I watch the silver eyes of my captor flick to her.

"Azure... shut up," I whisper urgently, feeling the cold of the harpoon's blade jerk against my skin.

"Azure? What kind of demon is-"

"We're not demons!" I repeat, trying to get her to lock eyes with me as I examine her face. They have odd half eye masks that climb to just under their pale eyebrows and frame eyes of pale irises and white eyelashes, but the skin under their eyes is bare of scale. She catches my gaze finally and something odd happens.

"You have the same eyes as…" She begins but is cut off by a man.

"If you're not dangerous then why do you have weapons?" His voice is deep and threatening.

"Drop your weapons!" I hear Cole call out to us. I hear a clatter of weaponry being handed over.

"And the horse! We want the horse!" I hear another male voice demand. I feel the water stir behind me, and assume Azure is handing over the Equinox. Poor Philippe.

"Take us to your ruler. I can straighten this out. We are no threat to you. We've given you all our weapons." I want to turn, to see what's going on behind me, but the only thing I can do is stare down the handle of the harpoon at my throat and into the increasingly curious silver eyes of a woman with jagged teeth and long silvery blue hair. I smile, trying to seem harmless, she loosens her grip slightly, but her expression remains the same. My heart hammers, fearful in my chest. I am at least grateful for the increased circulation, and find myself almost sweating with panic.

"We cannot take them to the chief. What if they plan to harm him?" The woman says to the man with the deep voice.

"The chief can handle himself. They have no weapons."

"But what of magic?" She says, whipping her hair sideways and hissing slightly. She is beautiful, so much so that her sharp features are bordering on cruel.

"The chief will decide what to do with these intruders, stand down Nika." The man's tone sounds bored, and I can tell there's some kind of rivalry between them. I gulp, feeling my gills open against the sharp edge of the harpoon at my throat. It's more than a little uncomfortable, and I feel myself relax as she pulls back on the long handle and gives me a cold stare.

"Well go on then! Move!" She demands, jabbing her harpoon my way. Orion overtakes me, looking sideways at me out of the corner of his eye. I want to mouth *what the hell is going on here?* But then I remember we're in a fight, so instead I press my lips into a cold hard line.

"Where are we going?" I hear Rose ask; brave I'll give her that. I bet she immediately regrets it as the one they call Nika turns, pivoting faster than any animal I've ever seen.

324

"We're taking you to see the chief. So you better respect him, and us. Or I'll have your pretty head as a flotation device," she snarls the words, curling her lips around them.

I look at Orion and notice he's not even paying attention; he's too busy staring over one of the other strange women leading us into the city. She's got long flowing lilac hair and a curvaceous physique, her breasts hang heavy as she swims, clad with ice blue scales and her tailfin is hypnotic in its motion, though not ethereal like our maiden's, it reeks of raw power, of strength; and he can't keep his eyes off of her. I want to pull back my teeth and snarl, feral and pissed, but I remember I have no power here and swallow my fury as I feel my heart shatter.

I look away, back to where Rose cowers before Nika, the cruelly beautiful temptress.

"I'm... I'm sorry...." Rose's resolve snaps like a twig under the scrutiny and Nika's top lip curls into a self-satisfied, sharp smile. She whips her tail in front of Rose's face, startling her and making her jump slightly, interrupting the stroke of her swim and moving back to the front of our pod to lead us.

We move through the streets of the city, and I can feel eyes on me. I look up, around at the buildings and realise now that it's not even slightly empty. The strange people are watching me from their frozen bubbles, from their icy glazed windows with pale, cruel eyes. I feel like I'm swimming to my death, being watched like some kind of criminal headed for public execution. I can hear the mermaids start to whisper behind me and I cringe internally as I watch Nika's ears prick.

"Quiet back there!" She barks like a drill sergeant as hush immediately falls.

We reach the staggering height of the ice palace and I see now that it is covered in staircases, twisting around each of the shard like towers and all likeness to the Alcazar Oceania at home is lost.

The strangers climb, herding us like cattle up the winding coolness of the staircase. I wince as my tail touches the icy hardness of a step, the cold sending a sharp jolt up my spine, almost like I've been burned. This place is so much more than frozen; it's practically glacial in temperature.

We reach the top of the staircase and icy double doors greet us. Nika and the man with the deep voice go inside and the other's turn on us, watching with narrow eyes. Orion is still staring at the lilac haired woman, his eyes wide and his pupils dilated. It's sickening how obvious it is that he finds her attractive, and I wonder if he ogles me like that and I just haven't noticed.

"What are we waiting for?" He asks her.

"You don't just go into a meeting with the chief unannounced. Nika and Cain will present the situation. He will decide if he wants to address you, or if he'd rather us just kill you."

"Oh, thank you for clearing that up..." Orion searches for her name and the woman with lilac hair looks like she might blush.

"Sirenia," she corrects him, actually blushing now. It's hideously obvious with her pale skin and I wonder what it must be like to touch someone who looks that pale, I bet her skin is like that of a cold fish.

A man behind her with an icy blue tailfin and mint green eyes looks like he might punch Orion.

"Best not talk to the prisoners, Sirenia," he says, pulling on her shoulder so she has to turn and stare at him.

"Cage, you realise they haven't actually *done* anything wrong..." She begins, but as she breathes in to say something else the double doors behind her swing open, revealing Nika and Cain.

"This way please." Nika's expression doesn't reveal anything and I exhale slightly, feeling weary after so much drama. We have come here for sanctuary, but at this rate I'd say we'll be lucky if we aren't beheaded.

I think of my father, of how I'd had some dream that I might find him here. That seems impossible now. If he hadn't been murdered by these pale savages then it seems likely he isn't here, and there's an awful lot of ocean to search. I close my eyes for a moment, slowing as the other mermaids overtake me. I feel weak. I feel tired. The mer no longer have a permanent place to call home, and the nomadic life that seemed so incredible a few months ago seems terrifying now. I miss having a home. I miss having a family too.

"Move," the stranger with mint green eyes shoves into me, his abs rock hard against my spine.

"Alright I'm going! Geez!" I exclaim, annoyed. He looks surprised. His expression starts to develop into an angry one, but I stop him. "Sorry. It's been a long trip," I sigh out and he looks taken aback once more. I wonder if he's shocked that I'm melancholy, that I'm perhaps a little more human than he had first thought. He shrugs and I hurry forward. The corridor is long behind the double doors and the architecture inside is elaborate, as icicles hang and the ice that makes up the walls sweeps in arching swirls and fleur-de-lis. My tail sweeps through the cold water, propelling me in quick time as I catch up to the crowd. They're gathered before another set of icy double doors, which I wonder how they can bear to touch.

"You're going before the chief. So no speaking unless you're spoken to. If one of you even so much as looks threatening, I'll..." Nika is rambling on and Cain rolls his eyes, thwarting her authority.

"Relax, Nika. The chief can handle himself. He hardly needs saving by the likes of you." He turns away from her silvery scorn and shoves the high arches of the doors open before us.

We enter into the room, following in single file, not wanting to rush all at once. I push myself forward and past some of the pod, wanting to get a good look at what's going on. I hear Orion inhale slightly. Rising slightly to get a better view of him I can see he's looking around for someone.

"Callie..." I hear him say my name and I'm suddenly confused. Why would he want to speak to me? After all, he's been acting like a constipated rhino since I told him about Vex.

I move toward him, my heart racing as his gaze burns with intensity as it find me, swimming through the crowd toward him. I don't recognise the look on his face, and I thought I'd seen them all.

I reach him and he doesn't say anything. I hear someone else calling my name, someone unfamiliar, but before I can turn, Orion has both his palms on my shoulder and is spinning me toward the centre of the room.

A man with a long silvery beard and a snowy white tailfin, massive and clad with more muscle than anyone I've ever seen is hovering, looking directly at me like I'm the sun and he's spent his life eclipsed in shadow. One word, instinctual as a child's very first, falls from my lips before I can stop it.

"Dad?"

The Kiss That Saved Me

28
The Man with the Frozen Heart

CALLIE

Aquamarine eyes are staring at me and there's a hush that's fallen, like the kind that comes after someone has died and there's nothing more to say.

Instead though, this silence is because there's too much to say, and I don't know where to begin. My heart is thudding, unable to slow and I'm frozen in the water, unable to move, statuesque and stuck in the moment I had laid eyes on him for the very first time.

"Well, this is sufficiently awkward," Azure acknowledges the atmosphere, rolling her eyes. Good old Azure, always there to make a snarky comment when you need her. Orion is staring at me, intensely. I turn to him, rather than addressing my father, automatically thinking of him as the one with answers.

"How... I... I don't understand," I look at him, into his wide eyes that are half-pity filled, half-shocked.

"I'm sure I can explain," the voice rings out, but it does not fall from Orion's lips. I turn again; facing the man I had been waiting to meet for so long and yet I can't quite figure out how to act around him now it's finally happening.

"What is this? What are these people?" It's not a personal question; it's not even anything to do with me. As a first question it is merely unimaginative, and yet I ask it.

"You're currently in the throne room of the Gelida Silentium, home of the Adaro. Children of Sedna." I look back to Orion again, unsure of what this means. He shrugs, equally confused.

"Sedna, what is that?" I ask as the mermaids behind me stir slightly.

329

"He is the God of these waters. The Adaro are his warriors. Just like you are the warriors of Atargatis."

"But I thought..." I begin, my voice seeming small in the vastness of the cavernous room.

"You thought that Atargatis was the only Goddess of the sea? Well, that is hardly surprising. Given circumstances." My father moves from the centre of the room, coming toward me. He's huge, bigger than Ghazi, Orion, or Regus. He's different now from the photo I had seen, of back when he and my mother were together. His hair is longer, whiter, but I don't think it's through age. It's something else. Something more magical. "You look just like her..." he whispers. I blush, feeling the eyes of so many on my back. I turn slightly and Gideon senses my unease.

"Nika, Cain! Take the others and find them somewhere to stay please. These people are guests, and I want them treated as such. Please explain to Orion anything he wishes to know. I need some time alone with my daughter." He's looking above me, past the top of my head and I feel people start to shift. They're moving, leaving me behind without them. Orion leaves too, giving me not so much as a parting gesture or word.

"So..." Gideon begins as the icy double doors behind us slam shut. His tailfin flexes and he moves in the water like it's nothing, effortless.

"I'm glad I finally found you. I wondered what happened. I mean why you weren't there when I turned, and then I got your letter," I blurt out this explanation, babbling on in the way I always do when I'm nervous.

"Your mother, she gave it to you?" He asks me, eyeing the necklace I'm wearing with a subtle flick of his gaze.

"Yeah. I mean, I turned, and then I went to say goodbye to her. She gave it to me then," he nods.

"I'm sorry I wasn't there when you woke up." The apology seems empty somehow, like words cannot possibly make up for the time that's passed. It's weird, I'm in the same room as my father, the person I'd been longing to meet, and I'm oddly numb inside. Kind of like I'm defending myself sub-consciously, paranoid as always.

330

"It's okay. You were exiled right?" My father's brow rises slightly, surprised that I'm aware of this fact.

"Not exactly. What precisely did Saturnus tell you?" He looks at me, his eyes scanning my face intensely.

"He told me you were exiled, to keep the peace with the other couples. You were exiled for falling in love with my mother. He didn't want the other mer knowing it was possible. Something like that," I shrug my shoulders, feeling my heart rate calm a little. My body feels the chill suddenly seeping into my flesh once more and I shudder.

"Sounds about what I'd expect from the likes of him," Gideon rolls his eyes and I narrow mine.

"You knew he was evil?" I ask him, more confused still.

"I know he's not right in the head."

"He killed everyone. The Occulta Mirum, it's gone dad," I use the term, seeing how it feels rolling from my tongue. It's kind of nice and I smile. Gideon smiles too.

"God, how long I've waited for today... but wait, the Occulta Mirum is..."

"Destroyed. Saturnus, he dropped the protective glimmer, the Psirens, they overtook everything."

"Atlas, he must have known...is that how you all got out?"

"Atlas is dead," I say sourly. It feels all too awful to have to break the news again. The death of such a wise, wonderful man still stings. Gideon sits back into a throne, draped with sodden furs. It towers with cascades of ice swirling upward, twisting and creating the seat itself. My father's eyes widen and then his shoulders sag slightly. His tail is still, it's snowy whiteness lost amongst all that is frozen.

"That's why we're here," I admit, my voice small.

"You... fled?" He bites his bottom lip, furrowing the brow of his thick skull. He's such a large man.

"Yes. We're all that's left."

"But the Psirens... how did such a small number manage to overtake a whole city?" He looks so confused. I breathe in, knowing I need to explain. I look around for a place to sit. This is going to be a long conversation and I'm so cold. "Allow me." Gideon flicks his wrist lazily and the water behind me transforms, manipulating itself into a delicate chair made of ice. "Here." He passes me the furs on which he's sitting, smiling.

I turn, draping them over the seat before placing my scaled behind down. Gideon goes back to sit in the now bare throne, I wonder how he's not frozen, sitting with his scales on the bare ice.

"Here's the thing. The Psirens, they started growing; turning others, humans to be like them. Alyssa… she would lure boys out and then kill them. Mixing her blood with theirs."

"Alyssa?" My father's eyes narrow slightly, and my breath catches in my throat. The woman I killed, my father's soulmate… how could I ever explain that to him? Will he hate me? I don't want to ruin our relationship before it's begun, but I worry I have no other choice.

"Yes, she was mixing her blood, making 'children'. That's what she called them anyway," I know I must sound nervous all of a sudden and I shift in the chair.

"We need to stop her," his face is stony, horrified. I hold up a palm, silencing his emerging rant.

"She's dead. I killed her," I whisper it, like it's the darkest secret I know.

"What?! What happened?" He looks horrified.

"She attacked me, we fought and I beheaded her with a trident," I whisper the answer again, like I'm a tiny child being scolded.

"What! Why wasn't Orion protecting you?!" My head rises and suddenly I meet my father's gaze, blasting him with intensity. He wasn't worried about the death of Alyssa at all; he was concerned about my safety. How utterly ridiculous.

"Orion doesn't protect me, I protect myself. Why aren't you sad about Alyssa. She's your soulmate!" I look at him, angry now.

"Whoa… okay. Sorry. I can see how this appears untoward. You have to understand, Callie, I never loved Alyssa. I was told she was my soulmate, by Saturnus, so I did my duty by her. I thought I was in love, but I discovered this was not the case. I never knew love until I met Patience."

"How can that be?" I ask him and he shrugs.

"I don't know. I've had years to look back, to try to figure it out. The only thing I can think of is that Alyssa was the soulmate of one of the Banished, who turned to the darkness before she became a mer. Who knows with Saturnus," he shrugs and I'm unsatisfied with the answer, but I know he is too. He gets a crease in his forehead just like mine. I frown. "Callie, please don't look so sad. It's okay. I'm just catching up. I want to know about you, everything. Everything I've missed. Is there anything important I should know?" I think about this hard, as I stare out at the pristinely white and twinkling buildings that lie beyond the palace.

"Orion is Crowned Ruler now. I was Queen. But..." I begin, but I don't know how to finish that sentence.

"But?" Gideon leans forward, enraptured.

"I don't think I'm Queen anymore. I left him. He wanted me to marry him... and well..." I begin, Gideon chuckles.

"Nice of him to ask for your father's permission!"

"He didn't even know you were my father until a few months ago." I laugh back at his overprotectiveness. When it comes to Orion I've always hated how he's so guarded of me. How he doesn't believe in me and my ability to take care of myself. With my dad it's different... it's probably awfully hypocritical of me, but I like the displays of aggression about my safety. I like that he cares so much. It proves to me that every time I thought I wasn't wanted, wasn't good enough to be someone's daughter, that I was wrong. I have a father, and he loves me and in this moment, I'm soaking up all the affection I can get.

"I didn't say yes. So it's not like it matters," I shrug and he looks perplexed.

"You don't love him?" I'm blown back by the personal nature of this question. I blink a few times. "It's okay if you don't want to answer. I know you don't know me that well. I'm just... trying to get to know you." He runs his hand back through his thick white hair and I can tell he's nervous. We're both teetering between pure joy and fear. I decide to try, knowing that a relationship with him isn't going to spring up out of nowhere. I need to make an effort.

"I do love him. More than anything. I know now what we have is real... I just can't get away from this pedestal he's put me on. He doesn't listen to what

I'm really saying... he just hears what he wants to. He waited so long, he was alone so long... I've got an impossible fantasy to live up to," I feel weary at the explanation, sick after having gone over and over the issues in my head.

"I don't know Orion that well, mainly because for the time I lived in the Occulta Mirum he wasn't around that much. He was a lone wolf... so to speak." Gideon looks at me and angles his head slightly to the left, examining me.

"That's part of the problem. He isn't used to sharing. Then Atlas died, he got all this responsibility thrown at him. It screwed everything up," I admit. Gideon nods his head, looking grim.

"I am sorry to hear about Atlas. He was a wise man, an excellent and well respected ruler too."

"Titus killed him. It was the night I died."

"When you turned?" He's truly caught up in the conversation. I feel probed, but I don't want to hold anything back. I've waited too long. I have too many questions to be picky about which one's I answer.

"No, the other time," I reply quickly, my dad begins to nod again, clearly a habit of his, but then stops and raises an eyebrow.

"Wait... you died twice?" He looks confused and I laugh.

"Yeah. I'm the vessel, whatever that means."

"What's that?" He looks slightly worried.

"Come here and I'll show you," I rise from the icy seat on which I'm perched and Gideon begins to move from his throne. We ebb through the water, rising. "Give me your hand," I request, he smiles.

"You do so remind me of your mother, she's bossy too," he places his giant hand in my smaller one. His palm feels like it's the size of a saucer.

"Yeah, but mom can't do this," I flick my wrist, just like I had seen him do. I feel the chill rush through me, an icy river that runs, unstoppable and rabid down my arm. I watch as the magic moves through the water, crystallising it and turning it to ice. I make an uncontrolled web, unable to stop. I let go of my dad's hand and feel the warmth of blood begin to thaw my palm. The ice I have created from water sinks to the floor with a thud.

"You... you took my power."

"Yep," I say, proud and smiling.

"That's incredible. Wow, and you're my daughter," he looks elated, happy.

"I've waited to meet you for so long. I can't believe you're actually here," I admit, shocked that after thinking I was going to be beheaded, I was actually headed to meet my dad. "It's a good job your... Adaro didn't behead me."

"They're harsh people. Everything is harsh here. This environment, the cold, it changes people." I can imagine what he's saying is true. I haven't been here long, but I'm already finding my mood flattened by the chill.

"I can see that. It's a shame they're not for hire. I'm sure we could use people like that against the Psirens," I speak the thought as though it's nothing, but then the idea comes to me, fully formed. My father's expression changes into something like a half-smile. It's odd because he's looking down on me, but it's an approving gaze.

"You're going to be a great Queen. There was a ruler before you who thought the very same." I raise my eyebrow and brush my hair back behind my shoulder.

"Oh... who?" I ask, curious.

"Come, there is much that must be explained," Gideon moves forward and beckons for me to follow him. I swim behind him, exiting the throne room. "Right before you were born, Saturnus learned of what was going on between your mother and I. It was Alyssa who ran to him for comfort when I told her I was leaving, that was how he discovered us." I nod, as his expression turns grave.

"So, I was exiled from the city, or rather that is what you have been told. I actually left of my own choice to begin with. It was my intention to be with your mother and you for as long as possible. I hung around the local tides, killing time between the night's when she would sneak down to a local cove, away from prying eyes to meet me. It lasted until Alyssa discovered I was still in the area. She ran to Saturnus, claiming I was risking the exposure of our world by flaunting my mer form with a human. It resulted in an argument, which Orion burst in on momentarily." I inhale; remembering the half memory Orion had given me as explanation.

"He showed me," I recall the horror I had felt, seeing my father sent away.

"Saturnus demanded he get out of the palace, claiming it private business, but Atlas was away at the time and I'm pretty sure it was because he didn't want Atlas knowing. I had spoken with Atlas at length you see, he knew my feelings for Patience, he knew about you too. He understood, still missing his human wife after all this time. Her name was Katriona," Gideon gives me this information, which I had not known before, Orion had never talked about his mother and I had never wanted to pry.

"So you left after that fight?"

"Yes. It was for the best. By this time, you were getting older, to the point where your first memories would be forming. I didn't want to confuse you. Your mother and I agreed it was best, as I explained in my letter."

"You did," I agree as we turn a corner and begin our journey down another long icy corridor; I have no idea where he's taking me.

"Before I left though, I bumped into Atlas, he was on his way back from a salvaging trip, or so we'd been told. He gave me a few things for my journey and told me where to go," he gesticulates to the halls of ice.

"He told you to come here. To the Adaro?" I feel the impact of this information. Atlas had never mentioned any other types of mer before.

"Yes. He also gave me a letter. He said I would know what it was for and who to give it to when the time came," he looks at me.

"You think it's for me?" I raise my eyebrows.

"No dear one, Atlas could not have known you were to become a mer this long ago. If Starlet had foreseen such a thing, Orion would have known too. At this time, he was still hopelessly angry at being alone, at waiting." We reach the end of the corridor and ascend up a spiral ramp, carved from sharp ice. It leads into one of the cylindrical frozen bubbles I had seen on my way in. The views are spectacular.

"But my mom said she knew I was destined for this. You must have known too." I say, looking at him.

"We knew, both of us, it's true. But we didn't want to risk your safety. Especially with the way Psirens seem to enjoy turning new mer. You were only a child; we had to protect you as well as the secret of the existence of the mer world. We kept Atlas and Orion in the dark. Our intention was to tell them about you once you had reached maturity, but you were my daughter, my family and my responsibility." He gazes across me, his eyes feral. I can tell how much he cares by this one look. It's clear he had my best interests at heart.

I wonder for a moment what life would have been like growing up with a merman for a father. Now I think about it, about the risks that come with this life, the demons and the Psirens, I'm glad I never had to find out. I think about Kayla for a moment, I know I would never want to put her at risk; it was why I had left too.

"So who do you think the letter is for?" I ask him, pressing my fingers to the ice of the bubble and reverting the subject back to business. The ice becomes sticky against my cold skin. I look out, through the blurring of the frozen liquid and onto the whiteness, perfect and untouched below.

"I think the letter is for Orion," Gideon replies, no falter in his response.

"That would make sense, but why wouldn't he just give it to Orion himself?" I turn my back on the city below and look into the study. All the furniture flows from the ice of the floor, as though the entire place has been carved from one solid piece. There's a large desk, a globe, chairs, and bookshelves all made from the cold, slick substance. The real things out of place here aren't the furniture though; it's the objects that aren't made from ice at all that stand out. There's a large wooden trunk in the corner, which my father is now rummaging through, his white and ice blue scales moving incrementally to keep him stationary.

"Atlas said he needed me to keep it safe from Saturnus," Gideon says, pulling it out and holding it up to the light.

"So did you know Saturnus was evil?" I enquire. Gideon puts down the letter, letting it rest on the ice of his desk. He moves over to me, meeting my gaze with intensity.

"I didn't know he was a Psiren, but Atlas gave me the impression when he gave me this letter that he had been corrupted. He said he was only trusting me with the truth because I was leaving. He didn't want anyone else in on Saturnus' little charade, in case someone made a mistake and let slip they knew his true intent. Not everyone was as careful with their words as Atlas. He was also worried about mutiny, as you can imagine." I nod.

"You can say that again. Did you know he could glimmer himself? The mer worshipped him, like they do Atargatis in some ways, because he looks like he's been blessed. It wouldn't have surprised me if they'd have sided with Saturnus over Atlas because of that fact alone." I'm curious now; I have a window into the past, someone who had seen things from the beginning. Orion was so withholding, my father on the other hand is not.

"Like he glimmers the city? That's a useful little skill."

"Tell me about it," I roll my eyes and he laughs. Suddenly I'm curious.

"How did you die? When were you born?" I ask the two questions in a tumult of curiosity that springs from nowhere.

"I died of old age. I was born in 1525. In Norway."

"Oh... I thought all of the mer came from an island off the coast of Cyprus..." I begin.

"Some, not all. I was buried at sea, and as you can imagine was quite surprised when I awoke in a wooden box at the bottom of the ocean, very much alive. A young woman, Azure, had a vision of my transformation and sent Atlas to find me." I shudder at the thought of such tight quarters. He looks at my face and places his large fingers under my chin.

"Do not shudder. It will be alright." Suddenly something within me that I didn't know had wound itself tightly unravels. I know he's not talking about the past any longer.

"How do you know that? Everyone is dead. Everything is gone," I feel a tear fall slowly, oily against my cheek.

"Because I have lived through much worse. You are so young. You haven't seen the strength of the mer like I have." His words aren't a lot, but they're enough. I find myself trusting them without having any reason to. "So, tell me more about yourself." Gideon demands, sitting down at the desk and placing his hands upon it, like I'm here for a job interview or something.

"Well, there's not much to tell." I sigh outward.

"I find that hard to believe." He smiles and I suddenly feel slightly embarrassed at his probing.

"Well, I was going to go to brown university... I really like biology. I got in, but then this happened." I gesture down at myself.

"That's wonderful! So you're clearly smart, what hobbies do you have?" He asks me the question again.

"Well... I used to like to hang out with my friends and stuff, I don't really know. I was just your average teenager and now..." I begin to answer but trail off, self-consciousness creeping in.

"Now?" He pushes me to finish my response, but I don't know how. I twist my mouth to the left, thinking of how to explain it.

"Now, I'm still trying to work out who I am. I became a mermaid, someone's soulmate and a Queen within six months. I guess part of the reason I wanted to meet you, to know you, was because I thought it would give me more of an insight into who I am now. Into the mer part of me." I breathe outward, finding relief at the truth. My father plays with his beard, rolling it backward between his finger and thumb, thoughtful.

"I suppose that's understandable. It seems like you haven't had much time to settle." He's giving me a kind stare.

"No, and for now that's going to continue." I shake my head, frustrated at how fast paced everything has become. I sit down on the chair, feeling like I need some support as I think of everything that has happened,

"Well, if I may say, you seem to be dealing with things a lot better than most would in your situation. You will find yourself, but it will be through learning and experiencing things that push you, challenge you and scare you. That's a part of what growing up is about. Knowing yourself won't come from knowing me, you are your own person after all, but what I can offer is support and to let you know that I am in awe of you. You're remarkable and I'm astounded, proud even, of the fact you've come so far from that tiny baby I held in my arms 18 years ago. You're also not alone. If I can help you in any way Callie, I'll move heaven and earth to do so. I promise. I want to be there for you now, it's long past due, and I want to be the father you deserve." He's serious in his expression and I feel my heart falter, it was the approval I had always sought, always wanted and I haven't begged for it. It's been given freely. I think on his words, on the fact that only time and life experience will show me my own mind, it's not the quick fix I'd been hoping for, but I suppose things rarely are.

"Thank you." I whisper, feeling shy. Gideon in a way reminds me of Atlas. You can't help but listen to his words and be filled with hope at their intent. I feel like a child again, not a Queen or a lover, not responsible for those around me. I feel like now, after everything, there's finally someone who will love me, look after me, and want for nothing in return. I can just be Callie and that's enough.

The Kiss That Saved Me

Gideon rises from behind the desk, placing a large, warm hand on my shoulder. I rise from the chair in which I'm perched too, moving toward Gideon and putting my arms around his waist, resting my head over his heart. His body is stony, surprised, but after a few moments he relaxes and wraps his arms around me. Together we are suspended in time, and I feel my heart start to thaw along with his. It's like this paternal love had been frozen, lost to time but ready to resume all along. Now we're back together, nothing can touch me, not even the cold.

29
Sedna

ORION

The double ice doors slam shut behind us, separating me from her once more. I know she needs to be alone with her father and I know I'm still reeling with the shock and wound of her betrayal, but it doesn't mean I don't still worry about her.

Damn it. Why can't I just stop? I need to sever this; it isn't good for me. I'm swimming around in circles over this woman. It's driving me insane.

I look at the Adaro called Sirenia, at her long lilac hair, at her pale smooth skin, her well-formed assets and smooth scaly behind. She's stunning and I want to take her. Make things simple… and yet the thought of touching her most certainly makes me want to wretch.

"Where are we going?" I hear Cole asking Cain. They're talking as we swim through the chill water and out of the palace. Away from Callie.

"I think you would agree you'll want to stay together. After all we did try to behead you," there's not an ounce of humour in Cain's tone. Cole looks back to me, always bound by honour and not wanting to step on my toes so to speak. It then occurs to me that he *should* be looking to me; I'm the Crowned Ruler. Not a very good one though, if I can't even remember my role here.

I inhale deeply, as though making pleasantries with these pale foreigners is the most painful thing I can imagine. I suppose I should be grateful I wasn't killed on the spot, but the thought of more niceties and small talk is more than I can bear. I don't want to perform a song and dance. I just want answers and sanctuary for my people. A place to rest, to heal. To shrink back from the light which has been shone on me as my father's shadow fades and the eclipse of his protection, of his wisdom, vanishes along with it.

"Yes. We'd like to stay together. I also have some questions," I breathe out my reply. It sounds rushed, but I cannot muster the energy to care. Azure looks at me, squinting slightly with distaste, but I ignore her. If she's so equipped for this job I wish she'd just goddamn take it.

"We don't owe you any explanation," Nika snaps, rounding on us.

"Nika! You heard what the chief said! They're guests. Now kindly retract your fangs," Cain retorts, defending us for which I'm grateful. I don't want to have to get into it with Nika. She seems tough. Azure laughs, not as discreet as she thinks she is.

"I like her. She's feisty," Nika turns and Azure winks at her cheekily. She's probably tempting some kind of violence, but to my surprise Nika actually smiles.

"I think they'll do well in the training centre," she suggests, her tone is softer now but I'm not fooled as to her true nature. I look at her arms; they're wired with veins and sinew. The arms of a killer.

We're descending down the spiral staircase as they decide where to take us. I can see Philippe down below and I instantly want to grab the steed from them. He's mine.

"So you don't mind bunking all together?" Nika asks me, her eyes connecting with mine in apology.

"No, we'd prefer it that way. We're all that's left of our race. We need to be together. Grief is still finding each of us in its own time," I say these words, and double take slightly at how much I sound like my father.

"It'll be like a sleepover. But a really cold one," Rose snaps slightly, her attitude as frosty as the water. I wish she'd stop moaning. The cold is bothering me too, but I have to be nice.

"You're the last? What happened?" Sirenia turns and begins swimming backward, her movements graceful as any ballet dancer.

"Where we're from, there's another kind of mer. One created by Poseidon, from his fury. Their magic is spread by blood, like a plague. They multiplied beyond what we thought possible and decimated our city. They want to raise a demon. They're called Psirens." Her eyes are kind as she

342

listens to my words. She really is stunning.

"A demon? Why on earth would anyone want to raise something so vile?" Sirenia tosses her hair over one shoulder. The lilac colour shimmers, looking cloudlike in its softness.

"I take it you have your own share of problems with demons?" I ask them as a group, looking between the four Adaro warriors leading us through streets, surrounded on all sides by cascading ice towers. Cage snorts.

"You could say that. We're here for the ice. To protect it."

"I see," I power forward, taking my place at the head of the group, falling in among the Adaro. They allow me to swim with them.

"The chief, he has power. He can create ice from water. Things have been better since he first found this place. Before then, the demons here, they radiate heat. They melted so much. The wildlife above, it suffers." Cage looks broken at the story and his mint green eyes spark with emotion.

"I understand. So is that why you were made? To protect the ice?" I ask them, curious. It had never occurred to me that there were other Gods and Goddesses besides Atargatis and Poseidon. I suppose that's pretty narrow-minded of me. I mean, there's no way such a small city could hold down protecting the entire world's oceans. Maybe I've been ignorant all along. Maybe I'm not as alone as I thought.

"Yes, Sedna took each of us from the Inuit. Most of us are Inuk anyway. We whaled to survive. This is us repaying our debt." A simple explanation. I nod, looking at them, each one so harsh.

"You're all so strong."

"We must be. This is no island paradise. We fight each other for practice. Strength is the only option," Nika states this as law. I can tell they take their practices and culture very seriously. I suppose that is just as well. Perhaps if I had been more serious about eliminating the threat of the Psirens when they were merely few, I could have saved us all this trouble.

"Yes and some of us lose, quite badly," Cain quips and I hear a growl emit from Nika. So that's why she's so aggravated.

"But you're so small," Skye comments, shy as she places one hand across her mouth.

"Size is not what is important. It is strength of will. The will to survive,

343

which truly matters."

"Do you have soulmates?" Alannah pipes up.

"What?" Sirenia looks confused.

"Well, our Goddess, she split the souls of mermen in half. Gifted them with mermaids." Azure laughs slightly as Rose explains the lore.

"No. Women of the Adaro aren't gifts. We are warriors," Nika spits the reply, clearly offended and I shoot the girls a glare.

"I assure you, our women are just as capable as any of yours," I laugh slightly, trying to lighten the mood. It makes me wonder, has my father, in his old-fashioned wisdom, overlooked a valuable resource in the women of our city. Callie has certainly proven herself. If she could do it, why can't they? I wonder if they haven't, in fact, been slightly coddled.

Our pod, the last of us, undulates through the icy streets. The silence within the hollow iceberg is peaceful. It allows for a type of clarity I haven't had in a long time. I think about Callie, about Vex touching her. I blanche slightly, but I force myself through it as I trace Sirenia's form with my gaze. I think about my hands on her, Vex's hands on Callie. I think about every time Callie had asked me about the rush of faceless, nameless women that had come before. Is this what she had felt like? This nausea, rushing like sickly sweet syrup across my tongue and down my gullet.

I ball my fist as we approach a structure that looks like the colosseum in Rome, but completely alabaster. We turn a sharp left and begin our ascent into one of the ice turrets. We reach the top and a porthole slides away, allowing us passage into the top of the structure. It's massive, a giant rounded ice bubble. Beds are carved from ice and slathered in furs, the hairs of which sway like tall grass in the minute movements of the otherwise still seeming water.

"This is where you'll be staying," Nika says unenthusiastically. There's a moment where everything is still and the pod takes in the room.

"There aren't enough beds," Rose comments. Trust her.

"Your ruler can bunk with me. I'm sure he has more questions," Sirenia's voice is sudden, rushed. It takes me a second to resonate with the fact she's talking about me.

"Oh, I uh…" I mumble and the girls behind me giggle. I brush through my hair, resting my hand on the back of my neck. I look down at the floor and then up at her. Her pupils dilate.

"No excuses hot shot. No-one wants to share with the boss man," she's quirky, and for a moment I find myself falling into the spell of her icy blue eyes. She's into me. I can tell. She thinks I'm a hot shot? Maybe I'm better at this ruler thing than I thought.

"Ok," I shrug to the girls and Rose gives me a snotty look. Azure snorts again. Cole raises an eyebrow. They're all judging me, but I know it would be rude to refuse the offer of our hosts.

"Are you all settled?" I ask the pod, watching them chatting, my mind slowing down after the constant state of anxiety had set my mind into overdrive on our travels.

"I think we'll be fine. Even if your giant Crowned Ruler-ness is all the way down the hall," Azure looks at me, sarcastic and swinging her scaly hips.

"You keep your wits about you," I whisper. She looks at me, for the first time in a while, seriously.

"I can take care of them. You don't need to worry. Don't go giving away all your secrets either," her black hair sways slightly as she drops to the bed she's suspended next to.

"I'm just sharing her quarters. It's necessary," I make the excuse. I know it sounds feeble.

"You keep telling yourself that," she shoots a glance sideways at Sirenia and exhales. "Just don't do anything stupid."

"Yes ma'am," I do a mock salute and she rolls her eyes.

"Ready?" Sirenia comes over to me.

"Almost. Ghazi, Cole, you'll come and fetch me if anyone should need anything?" Ghazi nods and Cole looks between me and Sirenia. The maidens are too busy fluttering between one another's beds and rearranging furs to notice. "I want the weapons back that you took from us." I look to Nika. She sighs.

"Fine. I'll return them in a while. When I find time."

"Much appreciated," I bow my head to her, out of respect. "Let's go." I turn to Sirenia. She smiles, her teeth a brilliant white.

"Come on then. Let me show you my place."

We reach the outside of the training centre and suddenly something reminds me of my other charge. Nika and Cain disappear.

"I need my horse. Philippe." She looks surprised.

"How awfully sweet. I don't know many rulers so attentive to their steeds," she smiles, trying to be sweet, fluttering her eyelashes. She's definitely not one for subtlety; I'll give her that.

"He's special. I need him nearby," I command, not leaving her any option but to do as I ask.

"Okay, well, Cage took him to the paddocks. Let's go see where he's at." She's instantly moving, flurrying in trail of bubbles ahead. Damn she's fast. She's at the end of the street before I can blink. She's calling me, continuing in her feminine laughter, "Orion, come on!" I follow her, moving down countless nameless streets. The chill bites at my skin and I shudder against all voluntary response.

"Alright. I'm coming," I mutter. She's so enthusiastic. So happy despite the fact she's living in a wasteland. I clench my tail muscles together, resisting the urge to collapse against fighting the cold. Eventually I catch up, and as I do she halts. We're near a stable I think. I'm not sure because it's not like any stable I've ever seen. The stalls are too small for horses, as is demonstrated by the fact my steed can be seen tied to an icy bollard at the end of the stout building. I swim over to him, giving him the once over. I run my fingers through his mane, calming myself. Sirenia touches my back.

"He's beautiful. Such a unique animal." Her eyes are alight with excitement. She's enthralled by me. I think back to Callie, have I ever seen her so intrigued? I don't think so. When I first introduced her to Philippe she was afraid. Sirenia doesn't seem afraid of much. She reaches out to touch him with a delicate palm.

"Thank you. We call him Equinox," I explain.

"You must be quite the warrior with a horse like this," she compliments

346

me, pressing her shoulder against mine, not hiding her intention of proximity.

"I have been around a long time. I've seen my fair share of battles," I don't hold back. I'm not afraid she'll run.

"I have too. I mean all the Adaro are fighters."

"What are the stables for?" I ask her.

"Narwhal," she smiles.

"Seriously?" I laugh.

"Yes. Would you like to ride?" She suggests, moving past me in an ethereal rush of cold.

"Are you kidding! That would be great." I watch her unbuckle the paddock, revealing a narwhal that sits within the stable. The structure is a fusion of thick ice and wood. I peer inside, examining the mammal, It's an odd looking creature to say the least, with a greyish purple body and a long unicorn looking horn protruding from its bulbous face.

"Don't they mind being tied up like this?"

"This pod in particular prefer the enclosed space. We rescued them. They were being picked off by a demon," Sirenia explains.

The Narwhal moves from the paddock slowly and I place a hand gingerly on its face, smiling. It doesn't frighten or falter, not afraid of my touch. It reminds me of when Callie had looked at the whale, heard it speaking with her. That kind of joy comes only from looking into the soul of another and finding innocence and grace.

"He's beautiful," I try to be complimentary, despite the creature's strange appearance.

"She," Sirenia corrects me. She places an odd looking saddle over the creature's spine and invites me to hop on. "This is Leia. Treat her well." She strokes the narwhals face and then makes an acute whistle by bringing her forefinger and thumb up to her white lips.

The narwhal jerks, with more speed and less weight than my Equinox, launching herself forward and taking me high above the city. I can hear Sirenia laughing, probably at my startled expression. The narwhal beneath me is a nippy little thing; more manoeuvrable and streamlined than Philippe. I let Leia take me where she wills, urging her on, the cold water rushing past my ears and making me laugh with a wildness I thought I had lost. I haven't felt this free in a long time, and by the time she returns me back to Sirenia and the paddock, I'm grinning from ear to ear.

"That was fun!" I exclaim.

"Jeez, it's just a little narwhal ride. You clearly don't get out much," Sirenia laughs at me and I realise that she's right. It's been a long time since I just enjoyed myself.

She backs the narwhal into its stall, talking about how she trained Leia. It's a fascinating process, but for some reason I'm not listening. My blood is still rushing around my body, energising me from my narwhal flight. I turn and look up at the city, no longer cold. When you forget it's made of ice, that everything is so cold and barren, it really is beautiful.

"This is my place," Sirenia swings open a porthole and we emerge into yet another icy sphere of an apartment. It's close to the stables and it's taken us all of one minute to arrive within its chill interior. If one can call it that.

It's minimalistic, with a giant four poster bed draped in lilac velvet and snowy white furs. There are bookshelves, a weapons rack, and several punch bags strung from the curved dome ceiling. There's a chandelier formed from ice that glints throwing light across the domed ceiling and walls. In each of the places where a lightbulb or candle would usually reside, is a jar full of bioluminescent algae. This method of lighting reminds me of home. Or what had been home. There's a sofa too, lined with furs and more velvet.

"Where do you get all the furs?" I ask. I remember showing Callie around our apartment once before. How many questions she'd had. I know now I was harsh in treating them as interruption. I had wanted our first week together to be a romantic fantasy, but instead she'd been so unsure. Now I think about it my expectations were completely unrealistic.

"The Inuit make deliveries via sled and dog. We catch them fish in return. It's all about balance here. They bring weapons too," she explains it, bored.

"I see."

"Gideon carves each of us the furniture we desire. He's been busy," sighing she waves her hand through the water, as though brushing the subject

348

aside. "You know, you're asking me all these questions and all I really want to know about is you. I've been waiting for someone like you. A mysterious stranger from a far off sea. I want to know everything," she's moving in, fluttering those white eyelashes like the feathers on a peacock's behind. She's so gorgeous; I inhale slightly, feeling my heart start to pound.

"Well, the pacific is beautiful." I say, thinking of the warm waters wistfully.

"And you're King?" She floats, gracefully landing on top of the bed on her stomach. Her tail flicks from left to right, distracting me.

"Yes. I was crowned recently." I say, remembering the ceremony and how nervous I'd been, how quickly those nerves had shifted into boredom as I sat in my throne, facing the ballroom of the Lunar Sanctum, giving in to the fact I could no longer escape the ball and chain of regality.

"But you're so good at it!" She makes a faux gasp of surprise. I laugh.

"So the mer, we can go on land beneath the full moon..." I begin to ask but she answers before I can finish.

"We are aurora bound," she whispers slightly.

"The northern lights." I sit down on the couch, making sure to keep distance between us.

"Yes, when Sedna is visible, his aura lights up the northern sky and we may walk again among the humans. We rarely venture outside the ice castle above. It's nice. There's a party." She's lacklustre, sweeping my questions away with explanations that are lacking in detail. Almost like I'm boring her with my personality and yet she's imagining me to be someone else in her mind's eye.

"I see; you don't sound so sure," I enquire, flicking my tail once for good measure as I stretch out along the icy three seater.

"Everyone here is... they're all so harsh. I'd never admit this in public.... But sometimes I just want to be taken care of. You know?" She cups her chin in palm, and sighs dramatically. She shakes out her lilac hair and looks at me, content.

"I'm the Crowned Ruler. You'd think that would mean I'm taken care of. It's true, I have a soft bed to lie in, but I also have the responsibility of keeping a lot of people safe." I admit, looking up at the ceiling and observing the fissures in the thin icy dome above.

"That must be so stressful," Sirenia is looking at me, I'm wondering if she's for real.

"It is," I am slightly snappy. I'm beginning to think she's just telling me what I want to hear.

"I'm sure you're amazing at it," she sighs.

"I got hundreds of people killed," I reply, she blanches slightly. The fantasy of my being a stranger, a King no less, from a foreign land shattered.

"I'm sure it wasn't your fault," she purrs, trying to slick over the jagged edges of my shortcomings.

"How would you know? You weren't there," I close my eyes, remembering the death. Remembering the slaughter. Sirenia rises from the bed and drops to the floor, bending her long tailfin beneath her.

"Handsome, it's okay. You're just too hard on yourself," she's saying everything I know I want to hear. She's absolving me, this gorgeous woman. Then I'm brought back to what I know is true. It's what I want to hear, but she barely knows me. To her, I'm a fantasy. It shocks me, something which I had thought was no longer possible after everything that has passed. I've known this woman barely an hour, she's supposedly perfect in every way, gorgeous, adoring, happy to listen to my pain... and yet...

Sirenia is down on the floor, her fin bent underneath her, looking at me like I'm the sun, but I'm not and I never will be. She's not attracted to me. She's attracted to the fantasy I fulfil. The mysterious ruler from a far off land, lonely and longing for a queen.

"I'm sorry..." I look at her and she does something entirely unexpected reaching up and trying to kiss me. I grab her by the arms and push her away from me, furrowing my brow at the distasteful state of her desperation. "I'm sorry, Sirenia. The position of Queen has been filled."

"By whom?" She's upright with a single flick of her tailfin and looking extremely angry.

"By a real Queen," I rise and leave the tower, leaving Sirenia behind, to find her. To find what's real, and appreciate it when I do.

I reach the outskirts of the city, hoping Callie has headed back to the training centre to be with the others. I think she's probably done with her father by now, knowing her she probably fled his company. I know she struggles to trust, and with someone who she thought had abandoned her, that would be twice as difficult. I wonder how I'll ever live with the fact that Vex has touched her, tasted her, but I can't dwell on it. I know now that I have to make things right. There is no other option.

As I round the corner I almost collide with Cole. He looks worried as he speaks, slightly out of breath.

"Orion! I've been sent for you… it's Azure."

30
Pure Of Heart

SOLUSTUS

The city is dark, no longer a shining edifice of hope, but a mere reminder that nothing can stand against my power. The Necrimad will rise. Tonight.

"Solustus. We're ready. Bring her," Saturnus pokes his head around the door, commanding me as if I'm nothing more than his dog. Well, fuck him.

"No. Make Vexus do it. I'm not your slave," I bite out, irritated.

"Very well. VEXUS!" He yells. The pale, tentacled Psiren startles in the corner. We both laugh at the fear in his eyes as they open.

"Bring the girl. It's time. If I catch you slacking off again, you'll wake up with less tentacles than you started with." He snarls, the malice in his eyes immense.

Saturnus leaves the room with a flourish of one of his hands. His yellow eyes are unnerving even me in the dark. There's something about cat's eyes that I can't help but find unnatural.

"Bloody prick... I'll show you what one less tentacle looks like when I cut off your..."

"Vexus! Do shut up," I bark. I've had enough of his bad attitude. I haven't slaved for centuries only to have my shot at being one with such a beast ruined by his insolence. Vex shoots me a look, like he's debating whether or not he should say something more. I retort, flashing him a warning glance. Starlet is in the corner asleep, or so it would seem. Vex shakes her awake. She moans, opening her eyes. The horror in her pupils grows as they dilate and the octoman pulls her upright. She looks around, startled. She's mumbling.

352

"Vex, ungag her. I want to know what she's moaning about," I command. Vex rolls his eyes and pulls away the seaweed that's balled up and planted firmly between her jaws.

"Where's Oscar? What did you do to him?" She cries out, instantly annoying me.

"Gag her again. My mistake. I thought she might have something useful to say." I order him to resume the silence I had been enjoying.

"Where is the merman?" Vexus looks to me, curious. We hadn't returned him after we'd first commissioned the giant order for chains and manacles to hold the beast.

"None of your concern. You'll be seeing him soon enough. Now move," I draw Scarlette, having had the scythe removed from my possession by Saturnus the second we'd reunited. He hasn't let the damn thing out of his sight. Pushing the rapier to Vex's spine, he inches forward, pulsating in motion out of the room. He's got Starlet by the back of the neck, nice and uncomfortable. She's squirming in front of him. As we leave the tower which has been the captor's place of containment, I can see what Saturnus has done with the city in such a short space of time is miraculous. Even to someone like me who is not easily impressed. I had made him, I was his elder, his maker. Why should he impress me after all? Anything he can do, I can do better.

The city is in ruin, and the Psirens are gathered, encircling the space where the seal has been uncovered by weeks of toiling over broken glass, rubble, and bone. Each Psiren holds a candle with magnesium flame, they burn in the water, releasing light that is almost too bright. These candles bring a kind of candidness to what is about to happen, and as I approach the seal I notice the fountain, which had once held a golden statue of the Goddess with palms outstretched, now lies defaced. The statue has been torn from its place and severed in two, eyes scratched out with arrows and flesh scoured with careless blades. I smile.

We reach the seal and the crowds of Psirens are radiating out from the space, cleared from the rubble of our victory, that displays the seal. It's a wicked looking piece of architecture, as one would expect from a God with such a wicked temper. The black metal of its massive crest twists, creating a cyclical symbol containing four crescent moons. Three chains trail across the design, one from the left, one from the right, and one from below, meeting in the middle where the one who is pure of heart must bleed.

"Vexus. Restrain her," I use my hand to make a grand motion, putting on a little show for the crowds. This is not just a ritual. It is a spectacle.

Vexus looks to me and cocks an eyebrow. I stare at him, deadening my expression. I am not amused.

"Do it. Or I'll do it for you," Saturnus' voice shoots over my shoulder, the scent of blood mingling in with the water. Vex moves, forcing the blonde downward and crushing her body flat into the hard metal of the seal. He removes her bindings and places her wrists into the manacles we have forged for her sacrifice.

Finally, he catches her tail within the manacle attached to the single shortest chain, making her lie still, horizontal, looking up at the stars for which she is so named. I take my place next to my brother. This is it, my moment. I am given the scythe from Saturnus and I sweep a large circle around the outside of the seal, before diving in and making the first slit. I cut it clean across her belly. Blood plumes into the water like a mushroom cloud, red and sweet. It heals quickly, as to be expected. The exsanguination of such a creature might take a while. But it's alright. Anticipation is so often the best part of a murder. After all, we've got all night.

AZURE

The fog rolls in like an unstoppable tsunami of gloom. I cannot stop it, even if I want to. I've held it back too long, that was my mistake. I'm overtaken, transported and translated into her head like ancient code. I'm trying to work out what the heck is going on. I was bitching to the mermaids about their obsession with perfect hair and then bam. I'm smashing my head into the ground. Which is really cold by the way. Just my luck.

I have collapsed, I think. All I know is I'm not awake now and instead I'm staring through her eyes at the sky. The ocean surface ripples high above. She's chained down to the earth, suffering the wrath of Saturnus and

Solustus. Helpless and screaming. I can feel her pain, it transfigures into my mind, tearing through everything. I take a moment, breathe. I need to keep a clear mind if I'm to understand what I'm supposed to see. If I'm to save her. I will save her.

Caedes is hovering above. That psychopath. He's giddy and that's never good. He's got blood all up his arms, on his face. Oh my God there's so much blood. Starlet looks down at her body and I can see it's cut to shreds. Her scales are missing. Torn from her tail and scattered across the black metal beneath her like confetti. Jesus. This must be the ritual. Starlet is chained to the seal. Above her Saturnus and Solustus are watching, with joined hands and moving mouths. Chanting. Waiting. Oh my God, we're too late. She's going to die. I'm going to watch. I struggle a little, but then I hear a tiny voice, echoing to me through the dark.

Azure. Sister? Is that you?

"Yes it's me!" I reply, startled at her presence. We had never been able to talk to one another like this before. So that's new.

It hurts so much. I'm so tired.

"Don't give up. Don't let them win!"

So tired... She breathes, like she's next to me whispering in my ear.

"Please, please don't leave me, Star. I need you. I can't fight it without you."

The darkness... She muses the word slightly, she sounds so different, almost like a ghost. *It's who you are.* She whispers again. I feel my heart break inside her chest.

"No! No it isn't! I can be good again! I can be good! Just don't leave me okay, don't let go!" I'm screaming at her, inside her own head. This is so fucked up.

You're in my head. Right? She starts to sound a little more like herself.

"Yes. I'm right here," I reply, making the vow not to leave. I have to stay, for her.

Don't leave. Stay. It's important. You need to see... I don't understand what she's talking about.

"What? What do I need to see?"

I'm going to die. But you need to see... it's important.

"YOU'RE NOT GOING TO DIE!" I yell out. Her body visibly flinches as she lies there, bleeding.

I have to die. It has to be this way.

"Why? Because some Goddess said so?" I cry out, wondering when she got so goddamn stupid.

No. Because it's meant to be.

"Starlet! WHAT DID YOU SEE?!" I'm screaming, not caring that I'm completely encased in her skin. In her body.

Death. Extinction. The Psirens will overrun the earth. The blood. There's so much blood.

"Show me," I command her. She closes her eyes, playing back the memory of the only vision she has ever kept from me.

The Psirens swarm like angry hornets, screaming and cussing. Bloodlust over-taking them. They're unhinged. Solustus and Saturnus are surrounding the seal, no Starlet in sight. A different future, it must be. They sacrifice one of their own instead... Vex. He bleeds, gritting his teeth and baring the agony with a distorted and twisted smile. Solustus is desperate, his face concerned. He swings the scythe, severing skull from shoulder. The octoman is destroyed. Silence falls. They wait. Nothing...

The Psiren army become enraged... uncontrollable under the white glare from a thousand magnesium lit candles. They disperse, but not before tearing Saturnus and Solustus limb from limb, leaving them in a cloud of organs and skin. Nothing more than pink mist in the ocean's clearness.

Flashes, images of their faces. The hundred nameless human beings being bitten and drained dry. The Psirens are a cancer, spreading their malignancy across the globe. Black eyes open under blood red skies. The end is Nigh.

The vision brings with it a strange realisation. It's not about the Necrimad at all… this is about what happens if that beast doesn't come. If we don't have a chance to stop it. If we don't have a chance to defeat Solustus and Saturnus, the Psirens will kill everyone. Regardless of whether the demon rises or not, their numbers are too dangerous. They need to be destroyed. "So you're saying that this ritual, the Necrimad, it's distracting them from going on a killing spree?" I ask her this question and she responds immediately, her voice is so tiny, like when we were little girls.

Yes. If Saturnus and Solustus fail to bring forth the beast. The Psirens will revolt. They will be set free on this earth from Solustus' command. Everything will fall.

"So the Necrimad needs to come?"

You need a chance to get them in one place, unite them with a cause, a leader, and make a final stand.

"I don't understand."

Without the Necrimad, they will lose faith in Solustus. He may be strong, but they outnumber him now. They need to believe. They need to be contained.

"Starlet! NO! You can't let this happen."

She showed me. All will be well.

"You're speaking like a goddamn martyr. Now snap out of it. You will not be pulling a Callie Pierce on me today! NO."

I'm sorry. It's too late. I watch as Saturnus comes forward, as he slits her wrists with the scythe. It's not my body but the blood-letting is painful to watch. I can feel her writhe, trying to stop the agony, the draining of her life force with each new cut on white flesh.

"I feed you this blood, from the pure of heart. So that you may be birthed from the earth. In flesh," Saturnus' voice reaches me through Starlet's ears. She's bleeding out, faster than her skin can heal. He opens up more wounds and she screams.

"Oh, I'm so glad I let him ungag you. Hearing you scream makes this all the more rewarding," Saturnus, the sick fuck, licks his lips. God I want to kill him, shred his oesophagus into dust and stab him with his own ribs after I pull them from his worthless skin sack. But I can't. I'm trapped in her body. A prisoner to watch this sick spectacle. Why would the Goddess do this to me? After everything, I guess I'm still irredeemable.

The pain lasts longer than anything should. Blood lost, litres, gallons. From thick like syrup to thin like water. What doesn't change though is the colour. Scarlet plumes like an explosion.

Suddenly, a rumbling from deep within the earth. It's here. It's too late. It's coming. Caedes unchains Starlet. Taking the body from which I watch and dumping it on top of broken shards of sea glass. I feel pain from the thousands of cuts scream out through her nervous system and I cringe. I want to cover my eyes, close my ears. But they aren't my senses to extinguish.

She lies staring up at the sky as something is born from the earth. The glass shifts and she tumbles, rolling and finding herself impaled on more of the broken shards. I hear a roar, a roar that's beyond terrifying and beyond primal.

The Necrimad has risen.

A few minutes later I wonder why I'm still entrapped within her. I can't leave, and yet there is nothing left for me to see. She is bleeding out, lying on sharp shards and unable to move from exhaustion. Suddenly, out of the bloody tinge of her vision, someone is rolling her over. Lilac eyes blaze.

"Starlet... Hey, Love... still with me?" Vexus is with her. He's found her.

Thank god.

"Kill me." The words come from Starlet's lips. Hoarse and calm.

Don't you dare.

"No Love..."

Good boy.

"I've had enough. Please."

No, Star. We're not done here... don't you dare. I swear to God if you...

She grabs the back of his neck, shifting on top of the wreckage, I feel

358

glass shred the skin around her spine. I watch as she takes Vex to her and looks deeply into his irises. He doesn't move, stunned.

She places her lips to his and he gasps, like he's run out of air. It's her very first kiss, and I feel her heart leap at his closeness, though why she's chosen him of all people to share this with I can't understand. Vex's eyes widen.

Suddenly something shifts and my perspective changes. I'm watching through another pair of eyes as Starlet leans back and exhales her final breath, turning to sand and being swept away.

I'm still screaming bloody murder as I return to myself and open my eyes. Head thudding.

The first thing I see is my brother's face as I awake.

The next thing I know, I'm lunging for his throat.

31
Atlas' Burden
ORION

I'm not having a good day. One moment I'm watching Azure scream her lungs hoarse with closed eyes and the next thing I'm on the floor and her hands are wrapped around my throat. Her eyes are diluted black and her face is mapped once more by darkness.

What on earth has gotten into her?

"Azure...." I gasp, reaching up. I don't want to use my power over air, but I think she's too far gone to be reached. I feel my mental processes beginning to slow and I realise I'm running out of time. Choking, gasping for breath, I turn my head only to see Cole and Ghazi are stationary, shocked to my left. So much for the royal guard.

I summon my strength and push outward with my free hands blowing Azure backward into the wall. She hits her head hard and yet still remains conscious.

"WELL, RESTRAIN HER!" I bark at the two stunned guards. Cole and Ghazi bound forward, grasping onto an elbow each, and fighting against her increased dark strength.

A shocked voice from behind me speaks out. Making me turn.

"What's going on here?" Callie asks, her father at her side. She looks horrified.

"I have no idea. She passed out and then she just went crazy!" I blurt. Callie looks concerned. Gideon moves forward quickly.

"Turn her around," he demands. The guard revolve the hissing Azure and Gideon ices her hands, creating a pair of makeshift handcuffs. "That should keep her from getting loose." He nods at Cole and Ghazi, "Good job."

Callie comes forward and lays two palms on the side of Azure's skull. Azure struggles a few moments. Suddenly they both gasp. A few moments pass before Callie speaks once more.

"We need to contain her," she says nodding. Everything is moving so fast.

"Wait, I don't understand!" I bark out. Callie looks suddenly miserable.

"Starlet… they sacrificed her. The Necrimad is loose. She's dead," she moves to me laying a soft hand on my shoulder. I don't pull away as reality comes in a torrent. No.

"Gideon, can you put her somewhere she can't get out? I don't want her grief to make her do something she'll regret," Callie requests. Any words I might say are lost.

"Yes. I'll ice her into the top tower of the palace," Gideon suggests.

"That should work. Make sure the walls are thick," Callie reminds him and he nods with a worried expression.

"Come on," she whispers to me. I think I'm in shock. I can't take in where she's leading me. I just keep blinking.

We move through the ice city in silence, each moment passing as an eternity. I can't process what's going on. So I turn to her, hoping her face will guide me as to how I should feel. She keeps looking at me out of the corner of her eye, an expression that's pitied coming across her angelic face.

We enter the ice palace together as a set of guards move aside, more at her presence than mine. I suppose the news of Gideon's daughter has travelled quickly. "Nearly there," she coaxes, leading me in a left turn into a long corridor. Eventually we reach what I assume is the room Gideon has given her. She moves me over to the bed and sits me down. My scales brush against furs.

"Okay. Here we go," she says. I can't look her in the eyes. If I do. I'm afraid I might crumble. "It's okay. Everything will get sorted. You'll see. I'll take care of it." I feel my heart shrivel at her words. I can't have her taking care of me… it's supposed to be the other way around. I'm supposed to be the strong one. "Orion, please look at me. Starlet just died. It's okay to be devastated. If you didn't feel that way then you're not the man I know you are." I look up. Surprised. Her eyes are welling and glassy, tearing up. They're reaching out for me, seeking to comfort.

"I'm so sorry." She reaches upward, placing a palm on the side of my face. With this kind touch I am bereft. I can't hold it back, no matter how hard I try.

Tears start to fall. She wraps her arms around me and holds me as I weep. I weep for Starlet. I weep for my father. I weep for the Occulta Mirum. Most of all though, I weep for her. I weep because I almost lost her. I almost lost her because of my pride. I weep because I can. Because she's here. Holding me up with incredible strength I have been blind to. She's all I have left. She's not something fragile. She's a crux.

I lean on her as I have never allowed myself with anyone else.

The walls within, built over hundreds of years, fall to dust, just like the city I had so loved.

I awaken, having sobbed myself to exhaustion and lacking the discipline to stay conscious, I had chosen sleep as a sanctuary for my broken heart. I realise now this is my mistake, because waking up and realising that Starlet is dead all over again, with memories now crystalline in their perfection, is perhaps worse than the first time I heard the words fall from Callie's lips. I look to my right seeking her. Needing her to hold me again. She is gone. I hear something open and see her re-appear around the door.

"Azure has been contained," she informs me with a sigh. She runs one hand through her long blonde hair. Her eyes are bright, like a weight has been lifted. I dislike consciousness, despite her presence. My heart becomes heavy as my mind begins to work overtime.

"Where did you go?" Is all I can think to ask. Callie swims over to the bed in her normal raw stroke, placing an envelope on the delicately crafted bedside table. I lie amongst the furs, which are littered with diamonds from my grief.

"I was just getting an update from my dad about Azure. He said she kicked and screamed and howled all the way there. He's iced her into the top tower like we discussed, but she's bloodied herself up something nasty trying to get herself out," Callie sighs again, twisting her mouth into a tilted pucker and scrunching up her nose.

"Can't we restrain her? Knock her out?" I ask with a cringe. I don't want any more blood spilled. Especially not hers.

"To be honest, I think it's better if we let her go at it. She's angry. She has a right to be. Her soulmate just died," Callie speaks with wisdom.

"You sound like my father," I say absently.

"Yes. That's the other thing... I have a letter for you. It's from him." I look up at her, my eyes wide.

"Where on earth did you get a letter from my father?" I must sound suspicious, but I can't help myself.

"He gave it to Gideon," she explains, leaning back over one shoulder and grabbing the envelope she had placed on the bedside table. I look down at it.

"I don't think I want to open it," I shrug.

"Oh... why not?" Callie doesn't have an expression, she remains impassive, waiting to hear what I have to say before she reacts.

"He'd be so disappointed of me... so ashamed," I look down at the dull blue of my tailfin. Ashamed of myself. I can't bear to look at her.

"Oh, Orion, that's not true!" She puts her hands on my face, cupping my chin and looking at me deeply. Her aquamarine pupils dilate and shine, looking upon me with more kindness than I deserve.

"I let you take the crown and I wasn't man enough to let you rule with me. I got everyone killed... even my own sister," I gulp at the last part, fighting back tears.

"Orion, those things would have happened even if you weren't Crowned Ruler. They might have been worse! You don't know." She's trying so hard to make me see myself through her eyes, but I can't. They're tainted with her emotion, distorting my image by kaleidoscopic proportions.

"I pushed you away," I feel the truth sting.

"You did," she nods. I turn slightly and she looks at me, frowning. "I let the darkness take all my anxiety, all my unhappiness, and turn it into hate... I slept with Vex... I thought I was finally free. Then I realised that being free was just my way of wanting to escape the consequences of my actions. Of not having to deal with my choices." She looks now like she might cry.

"Why did you go to him?" I ask her, a shudder.

"Because I didn't want to be alone. I was scared of more people dying. I'm still scared," she admits this and I'm taken aback, looking at her like she's a different person than I've ever known.

"Sirenia tried to kiss me," I admit, fingering the paper of my father's letter. I expect Callie to go off on an angry rant, but she doesn't, she just sighs.

"Tried?" She cocks an eyebrow and then lets a slight giggle escape her lips. She covers her mouth shyly, as though she's aware she shouldn't be laughing after the loss of Starlet.

"Yes. I told her the position of Queen was taken. By someone real."

"Real?" I can see her questioning my choice of phrase.

"That's the thing… You were right. I was in love with a fantasy…" the minute the words leave my lips I regret them, she drops her gaze and looks uncomfortable.

"I'm sorry I can't be what you waited for," she whispers.

"It took Sirenia making me into a fantasy of her own to make me realise something I'd been missing," I continue quickly, wanting to get to my point before she flees.

"Bigger… assets?" She asks and I burst out laughing against my better judgement.

"No. It made me realise your flaws. You're passionate and you're stubborn. You have this tiny little dimple that comes up here when you smile, and a tiny wrinkle in your forehead when you cry. You're not graceful like the others, you're raw, un-practiced, and brash. You're completely hilarious in all the wrong ways. Your hair is never perfect and you *always* put yourself in harm's way…" I keep going and her eyes glaze. She gets up to leave, to bolt, but I grab her arm. She turns to me, eyes burning deep, about to say something she'll regret. I push my finger to her lips, silencing her as I rise slightly from the bed. "And that's… why I love you. You're passionate because you love with everything and if you love you do it properly. You're stubborn because you have self-respect and you know your own mind. You get that dimple when you're eating and there's barbeque sauce all over your face because you appreciate the small things. You get a wrinkle in your forehead when you cry, because you care so deeply about everyone, you're empathetic. You're not graceful, because you're too excitable and busy loving life to care about appearance. You're hilarious in all the wrong ways because you're so honest and you never hide from what's real. Your hair is never perfect because you don't care how you look, as long as I'm kissing you. And... lastly... you *always* put yourself in harm's way... because Callie, you're a strong woman. I love you. All of you. Even the flaws. Because that's what makes you special. It's what makes you mine," I'm out of breath by the end of this declaration.

She's not fighting to get out of my grip anymore. She's just looking at me, her eyes wide and her mouth slightly open. I feel grief surge forward as we hang in the moment, as we savour the small things, as we care, as we love with everything we have. I need her. Now.

I move forward and bring her mouth to mine. The kiss reminds me of the one we had shared before she transformed. Except this time there's no eclipse, no blade. Only us. Real and together. No magic. Only love... if they are not in fact one and the same.

"I think we need to stop kissing. I want to know what Atlas' letter says," Callie reminds me of the letter. I don't pout, not wanting to ruin the mood.

"Really. I've missed you... I could do this forever."

"I know... I'm just..." She bites her lip. I realise I'm not getting them back until I've done as she's asked.

"Okay. Okay," I mutter, rolling my eyes. She's so stubborn. Damn woman. I turn on the bed, propping myself up and finding the paper wedged between our intertwined tailfins. I slip my finger under the seal and pry the letter from inside. It's on thick white parchment and my heart begins to palpitate as I see my father's handwriting. Callie watches me as I read...

Son,

365

The Kiss That Saved Me

If you're reading this letter, then I have failed. I have been waiting for so long, for the moment Saturnus will expose his true nature, but if you're reading this, then it is up to you to finish what I could not. To explain, I never wanted you to be burdened with this fate, but I, as rulers so often are, have been put in an impossible position. You're probably startled at the fact I'm reaching out to you at all, considering that if you're reading this, then I haven't been able to tell you myself and am long gone from this world, but it is beyond imperative that you read this letter, and take with you what I have to say. As usual, the fate of the world lies on our shoulders.

Saturnus, as you know, turned six months after I did. He was murdered by his father, a man who had two other sons. Their names were Solustus and Caedes. Their father was a brute, and it is therefore not surprising that the youngest among them is riddled with insanity, as he was left at the mercy of that man for years. Not everyone on our island was good, and it is probably my fault. I knew of the abuse within their family and yet I did not step in. I was too fearful of bringing the wrath of such a man down on your mother and your sisters, too. Saturnus loved a woman before his death, a woman who he planned to marry. His father didn't want him to leave with her, and so he murdered him in cold blood, his own son. Saturnus was a sweet boy, an innocent who had been left at the hands of cruelty for longer than anyone should have to bear. When the Goddess opened her arms to him, he fell more deeply in love than anyone I have ever known. He was desperate for love, so desperate that merely being chosen was not enough. He wanted to have been her first pick, but that of course, was not his destiny, but mine. Saturnus stayed loyal to Atargatis for some fifteen years, pledging more hours to her worship than anyone I have ever seen.

Then one day, as our growing pod was travelling the Atlantic something changed. I did not know it at the time, but Solustus, newly made with the full power of Poseidon behind him, opened Saturnus' eyes to power the likes of which he could not imagine. He told me of this man, of the brute strength and unimaginable power he possessed, born out of the rage of Poseidon, and I reminded him that Atargatis had given us all the power we needed. He agreed and we went on with our duties to the Goddess.

366

Over the next year I found him restless, an envy growing against my connection with Atargatis, she came to me in dreams and when I shared these things with you and the others, I could feel his anger stir. The dreams informed me of something called the conduit, which I will get to shortly. We parted ways for a while, each deciding to go and serve the Goddess on our own terms, but when he returned he was a different man. His aura was the only way I could be certain, it was the colour of coal, and corrupted. I knew he had given into the power of his brother. Solustus also tracked down his youngest brother after his madness drove him from our midst. Caedes began his underwater existence a mer, but soon Solustus infected him too. This making of two new Psirens was what I believe led Poseidon to strip Solustus of the majority of his power and create the Necrimad. Saturnus left our midst, and as our numbers grew, as you will remember, we became vulnerable, as moving in large numbers was less than discreet. Then, in 1725, after decades without being seen, Saturnus returned, bathed in what seemed to be glory of the Goddess. He told us he had a vision, of a city that was to be built in her honour at a very specific location in the pacific. This was to become the Occulta Mirum. It is my belief that during the years Saturnus was absent from our people, he was searching with his brother for the power Solustus had lost and believed rightfully belonged to him. That is why the city was placed where it was. It was built as a hold over the place where the Necrimad had been created, and banished to its dimensional prison. I knew Saturnus' motives were corrupt but I could not call him out without looking as though I was power hungry or concerned of him taking my crown. I needed my people's respect and trust if I was going to ever have the power to defeat such a beast as they want to raise. So I kept Saturnus close, made him my right hand and watched him closely as I could, waiting for him to reveal himself to our people as a Psiren. I protected you and your sisters as best I could and tried to outwit him at every turn. You must remember, Saturnus has been pulling strings from deep within the Occulta Mirum, so for every single move he made, I had to make two to diffuse whatever he was trying to set up. It worked well, but with the imminence of your soulmate's arrival at this point, I sense change is coming upon us too quickly for me to act.

The Kiss That Saved Me

There is something else.

I am not giving you this information for information's sake. I have kept many secrets, but perhaps the greatest is the existence of others like us all over the world. We are not alone. Nor have we ever been. While Saturnus and Solustus were off chasing down the Necrimad's location, I was meeting with these clans and making alliances, guided by Atargatis to their places of origin. It's now up to you to activate something called 'the conduit'. The Goddess is not alone either. She belongs to a society of oceanic Gods and Goddesses. They call themselves the circle of eight and besides herself and her beloved there are three other couplets with forces dotted around the globe. You must find them to create the conduit, the failsafe that can decimate the Necrimad and the power within it. You must remember that Poseidon never intended to release such power into the world after seeing its destructive nature, and only the vilest of acts such as the sacrifice of innocence and the shedding of blood will prove the human race is in need of eradication and release it from its prison. I am hopeful that by the time this letter reaches you I will have sacrificed my life in order to stop its re-birth, but should it be among us, you will be in need of a failsafe. The conduit is that failsafe. It was put into place by the circle of eight, and is made up by eight vessels and their 'pieces of eight'. I have been searching for the exact meanings for these terms for years, and have come up empty.

I am sorry I could not be of more use and I am sorry I am not there with you, but this is the most important thing I have ever asked of you. Without the conduit, without the help of others like us, this world, which we have both given so much to protect, will fall into ruin and darkness. We must now, more than ever, believe in the higher power that has kept us together for so long and hope that it will give you what you need to succeed.

I know you, son. I know you believe that you cannot rule. But I will tell you something, I once felt the very same, and it is not wanting the power of leadership that makes you so very qualified to wear the crown. Remember, I do not have, nor have ever had, all the answers. As a ruler all you can do is make choices and stand by them.

368

The brave may not live forever, but the cautious do not live at all.

All my love,
Your Father.

I look up from the paper and hand it over to Callie, my mouth still hanging open. He knew. The whole time. He knew about Saturnus. Oh my Goddess what has he gotten me into?

"You are not alone..." Callie reads aloud, half a mumble, half a gasp.

"What?"

"You are not alone. That's what Atargatis said to me. When I died!" She squeaks.

"Seriously?" I ask her and she nods, her pupils move to the upper left hand corner of her eye, like she's physically trying to look back into her memory.

"Wait... she also said... oh God what was it. Something about corruption... Wait, yes. She said, 'Even those most directly in the light of my love can be corrupted'... I think," she looks at me with wide eyes.

"Saturnus," I say his name like a curse.

"She was warning me all along," she gasps. "We have to do this, Orion. We have to find the others... the others like me."

"More vessels..." I say it, unable to conceive how large my world just became. There are others. We aren't alone.

"Yes. I think I know..." She suddenly looks shy.

"You know what?"

"I don't want to... we only just made up," she looks away.

"Oh for Goddess' sake, Callie. This is the fate of the world," I remind her and she rolls her eyes.

"Fine, but you're not going to like it," she sighs. "When I saw Starlet's sacrifice, before she died... well, she kissed Vex. I saw it through Azure's vision. The funny thing was, the end of the vision switched perspective. And... well, I also kissed Vex...we sort of blew each other backwards, like magnets of the same polarity or something..." I narrow my eyes.

"If you're about to tell me he's a vessel then the world is doomed," I warn her.

"I think he's a vessel," she confirms my fears. It would make sense. "He took away my darkness." She reiterates, as though she needs to convince me.

"I don't care if he's Poseidon himself, I want him dead," I growl.

"It's not his fault I slept with him. It was my choice. It's not like he tricked me into it."

"Show me," I demand. Irritated.

"What?"

"We can share memories. Show me!" She lets out a laugh. I don't get what's so funny.

"Oh my God, do you not see the irony here? I begged you to show me the other women you'd slept with before, you said you didn't want to hurt me! What makes you think I want to cause you anymore pain than I already have?" She asks me. She does have a point.

"Okay… if I show you the other women I've slept with, will you show me what happened with you and Vex?"

"Like pulling off a band-aid or something?"

"Yes. I guess you could put it like that. I want us to start fresh. Things are so different now. I don't want us to spend any more time apart. Life's too short." I laugh as Callie rolls her eyes at this.

"It's true, being immortal doesn't make you as un-killable as I'd thought," she admits with a sad smile. I stroke down her shoulder. I know she and Starlet didn't really get on, but Starlet had believed in her. She knew she'd make a great ruler. I guess it's time I start putting in the effort to make things work. Even if it's against my better judgement. I need to know what she had with Vex.

"Okay. Here," I place my hands on either sides of her skull and she inhales slightly. Her mouth goes slack, and I close my eyes, concentrating on the past I had long since forgotten. Once I'm done. She opens her eyes.

"Oh my God… you were so lonely," she looks like she might cry.

"Hey no tears, you said you could handle it." She nods, biting down on her lip. I cup her cheek and she holds onto my hand. Hers are so tiny in comparison.

"I know, it's just not what I expected. I thought I'd feel jealousy... but it's nothing like what we have. It's not even close. You were so... lonely." I nod, this is most certainly true.

"I know. It's over now, so no use getting upset. Now it's your turn." She sighs, almost as though she's unsatisfied. I wonder if she had expected to see me loving someone else, married with children. How wrong she was. It was just skin. Just bodies. For me, my soul, there would only ever be one other.

"Okay. Don't flip out?" She looks at me sternly.

"Okay," I vow, not sure how I'll remain calm, but hoping I can manage it.

"Promise?" She isn't satisfied.

"I promise," I vow once more, rolling my eyes. She frowns, twisting her mouth into that cute pucker again, but before I can laugh she's got her fingers on my temples.

Once the memories have passed between us I want to scream. Not because I'm jealous, or hurt. But because I'm angry. He left her. He left her naked and vulnerable. He treated her body with vile disposure, like it was nothing more than something to be tried on and discarded. He hadn't given pleasure willingly; it wasn't about her. It was about him. His needs. His pleasure. He'd had her on her goddamn knees for Goddess' sake. Red mist creeps across my field of vision, mingling in with grief. Suddenly I feel her hand on the back of my neck.

"Orion, you're shaking. Breathe," she reminds me. I exhale, letting the rage simmer lightly beneath the surface.

"I'm sorry. I don't care if he is the vessel. I'm going to kill that bastard for what he did to you. He's no better than Daryl!" Callie hushes me.

"No. You won't. I've already had it out with him. I broke his nose." I turn to her, stunned. I sort of love her a little bit more in this moment.

"I'll still be murdering him. But it's nice to know he has a crooked snout," I joke, relaxing my shoulders.

"I feel better," she smiles, leaning over and kissing me on the cheek. I can still feel the murderous tendencies crawling within my muscles, longing them to smash and crush. But they can wait. For now.

"Me too. I think we need to go and talk to Gideon about this. He'll want to know. We also need to go about finding the vessel for Sedna. I'm assuming it'll be one of the Adaro. I guess that makes as much sense as any of this does," I exhale. She smiles.

"How are we ever going to convince them to fight for us?" Callie asks me the question, it's a good one, I'll give her that. However, I think I have the answer.

"Azure. The vessel will be able to absorb her visions. I think that should do the trick," I reveal.

"But we can't get near her," she reminds me. I sigh.

"I know. I have a little family reunion to attend beforehand." I don't want to go near her, but I know I'm responsible for her. After everything, she's the only family I have left.

32
Whirl

AZURE

My internals are cold, slimy, and red. I can feel them squirming beneath my skin like worms, trying to get out. I feel nauseous. Like spewing my guts up will bring her back. Or at least end my suffering.

I slam my fist against the ice wall, watching my knuckles shatter, blood spattering in archaic fireworks, exploding onto white. It's no use. No matter how many layers I punch through, Gideon just keeps making more. I've been watching him pace, swimming lengths and adding layers where I've thinned my prison. That is until his martyr extraordinaire of a daughter shows up and starts talking in her high-pitched harpy tones again. I bang my skull against the hardness of the frozen walls, smashing bone against ice. It doesn't knock me out. The darkness has come and I can't rein it in. I can't even knock myself out, I'm too strong, strengthened by the hate, the loss... the grief. I scream out again, deafening myself with echoes of my own agony. I want to rip it all to pieces, shred and tear and bite and cut until there's nothing left of me. Muffled voices spike the adrenaline within my veins. I push my ear to the thick ice, listening in as my breath comes quick and shallow. It's him.

"Let me in. I need to see her."

"What if she tries to kill you again, Your Highness?"

"Well, I'm assuming you two will actually do your jobs this time. Am I correct in that assumption?" He's talking to Ghazi and Cole. Weaklings.

"Yes, Sir."

"Drop the wall," he commands. Like he has any actual authority? Such a pathetic excuse for a ruler, for a brother. He deserves to be the one flayed and exsanguinated.

I hear Gideon let out a sigh. Cracking... like the breaking of bones reaches inward toward me. I move backward, readying myself. Chunks of ice fall away slowly. I wait... biding my time. Orion takes a long tailfin stroke backward.

"Get ready, Sire."

"I got it." I hear them talking at me, like I'm an animal that needs to be contained... well, right they are. I clench my fists, tensing each individual muscle in my body, winding it tighter and tighter, ready to release my rage like a spinning top. Whirling around like a wicked edge, ripping them all limb from limb. I am about to move as the ice clears, the last of it falling away. I clench my teeth and just as I'm about to launch forward Orion catches me off guard. Never one to use his powers unless he absolutely has to, he's actually pre-emptive of my assault. He uses the water surrounding my body and his power over air to catch me in a new prison. But this time it's not one I can hit. The ball of water continues to spin, swirl. I can see him, his familial blue eyes blinking in through the blur of the moving water. He looks too much like her. No.

"LET ME OUT!" I scream.

"No, not until I've said my piece."

I let out an ear-piercing screech, wailing, trying to get him to drop his guard for just a second.

"Azure. You can scream and punch and wail all you like. I'm not leaving this place without you. I'm your only family. I'm the only one left who cares about you. I know you; I know you self-destruct when you're hurting. It is my fault. I know that. I know it's my fault Starlet is dead..." he pauses, I wonder if he's crying, so human. Ugh.

"I will never forgive myself for what has happened to her. I don't expect you to forgive me either. But I also won't ever forgive myself if I don't save you from yourself. You're the strongest person I've ever known. I know you can beat the darkness."

"I don't want to fight it. It's who I am. Starlet knew that. She was so much smarter than you. She wouldn't have gotten everybody slaughtered," I hit him where it hurts. Expecting him to give up. To leave me for dead.

"I'm not leaving. You can try and beat me down all you like. I love you Azure…" He says it so calmly; I feel something within me slip… something for just a second, recedes.

"No…"

"Yes."

"NO!" I bellow. No more love. No more compassion. Nothing matters but pain. That's the only thing you can count on.

I muster all the strength in my tailfin and break free of the air binding in which I'm trapped. I find his flesh, soft and flawless beneath my fingers. The darkness overtakes me and I lose all sense of myself. It is just me, my fists, and the rage inside. I'm rolling like a wave, crashing into everything in my path and decimating it.

My stupid brother just lays back and takes it.

CALLIE

My muscles tense. This has gone far enough. I power forward to aid Orion, but find myself flung backward through the water. Gideon catches me within his large arms, as though I were no more than a baby. Ghazi and Cole look at me.

"He doesn't want anyone's help," I comment, feeling my heart hammer against my ribs. What the hell is he playing at?

"How the hell are we supposed to do our jobs if he won't let us?" Cole barks. I shrug.

"Just let them go at it," I sigh. Gideon almost laughs to begin with, but as time moves on, silent horror falls over us. I watch as Azure pummels Orion, biting and scratching. He lets her, only making sure not to contaminate his blood with hers. I watch as she bloodies his face. All I can hear is him taking the punches, letting her project her grief onto his physical form. It goes on…

"I still love you," he whispers, spitting water tainted red.

"NO!" She screams. She moves her assault, banging her fists onto his chest, pounding his heart over and over again. Smashing his ribs. I wince.

"I'll always love you. You're my sister." I watch as something shifts. Azure collapses.

Just like that, it's over. She's done.

She lies on his chest and begins to sob. It all seems so wrong. He brings up bruised and beaten limbs and holds her. Letting the air field around them drop.

The sound that emits from her lungs is unholy. It's the most tortured sound I've ever heard, almost as though her soul has been fractured, left torn and bleeding, losing vital fluid. She continues to sob as I cock my head and watch her, pity filling my eyes. Orion continues to keep his arms around her form.

Finally, he props himself up and leans against the back wall of the tower. It's then that I get the first proper glimpse of his face. Oh my Goddess. His nose looks broken. His forehead is split open where her finger nails have scoured him. His lip is split open, and both his eyes are swelled under his scales to the point where he can barely open them. They're bruising already, because of his accelerated healing. His chest is covered in scratches where her nails have gauged skin from muscle. He looks exhausted, but he still manages to smile sadly at me. I can't grasp how beautiful he looks, even bloodied and bruised.

I'm aware someone is at my back.

"Chief. There's something you need to see." It's Cage.

"Can't it wait?" My father and I turn together, meeting the mint green eyes with impatience.

"You really need to see this." He looks concerned, and my stomach flips. What could be so serious?

"I'll come too," I suggest, looking back over my shoulder to look at Orion. He's now crying too, holding Azure and mourning the loss of his sister. Just as he should be.

"We'll stay here. Just in case," Cole suggests this before I even have to ask. He's in tune with what needs to be done for Orion. I had never really appreciated it before, but he's so selfless, always putting his King's needs before his own.

"Okay. Let's go." My father places a hand around the back of my shoulders and squeezes. He smiles at me and I feel my heart swell in spite of everything that's happening around me. I'm glad I hadn't given up on finding him, now more than ever.

I can see what Cage is so concerned about when we finally reach the outside of the hollow iceberg. In the open arctic sea, a whirlpool has appeared.

"What the hell is that?" I ask, slightly shocked.

"I would say that's your ride," Gideon says with a sly smile. I had filled him in on Atlas' letter already and in the few minutes I had to discuss it with him, he'd agreed following in Atlas' mission to create the conduit is the only lead we have on how to defeat the Necrimad.

"What?" I look at him.

"A long time ago... I remember reading somewhere that whirlpools can be kind of like portals."

"Sedna's codex," Cage nods, saying the words as though they mean something to me. They clearly mean something to Gideon, his eyes widen.

"Ah... yes." My dad clicks his fingers, as though the memory has just fit into the puzzle of his psyche.

"So you're saying I have to go in that thing?" My tail muscles throb as I imagine the water taking control over my body, like it had when I'd been lost to Orion in the storm.

"You all do. When you're ready. If you think finding these vessels is the right thing to do?" We hang in the cold chill of the open water, looking into the terrifying speed of the whirlpools spinning depths.

"What do you think?" I look at him, feeling unsure of myself. I wonder if I'm really qualified to be making these decisions. Orion seems to think so, but he loves me.

"I think that Atlas was a wise man. But he's no longer here. It has to be your choice to undertake such a mammoth task. It's not going to be easy. You may very well die in the course of such a quest." I swallow hard as my dad's words reach me. He looks morose, devastated. I think on them. I might very well die, so could Orion.

"I don't want to die." I whisper. I look up at the surface of the water, it wasn't a few months ago I was ready for death, I had wanted to martyr myself for the mer, but somewhere inside myself I'd known that everything was going to be okay. That it was the right thing to do. I don't know that about this situation. What if we're slaughtered? What if in recruiting all the other mer pods we wipe out the world's defences in one flail swoop. I'm scared, I don't know if I can lead an army, I don't know if I can beat Saturnus and Solustus. They're so much older than I; have so much more power and wisdom. I feel tiny and insignificant, fragile and vulnerable. I then feel an anger begin to stir, something irrational coming to the surface.

Why do they have to do this? Why can't they just leave us and the world in peace? Why is this happening to me? Why can't it be someone else's problem? I sigh as the torrent of questions come forth in a tormenting cascade. My dad looks at me and frowns.

"I don't want you to either, you're my daughter, but you're also a queen, and if a queen won't fight for her cause who will? It is not my place to stand in the way of this world's safety for selfish reasons." He passes this wisdom but I can tell he's forcing it out, like it's duty bound. I know he really wants my safety above all else deep down.

I think on this, looking into the swirling waters of the whirlpool. I wonder once more why it is me who has to make this sacrifice, why everything fell on the shoulders of the few of us who became mer to begin with.

Then, something Orion said once comes back to me.

We're not made. We're chosen.

I was chosen. I was chosen by Atargatis to be her vessel. If that isn't a sign for the undertaking of such a journey, then I don't know what is. I realise that being among the mer has shown me how to believe. I never would have trusted in the plan of a Goddess six months ago. But how can I deny that she knows what she's doing? I have proof in the very man who I would never have chosen for myself, who was born five hundred years before my time, and yet suits me so perfectly.

"I want to do it," I decide aloud, sure of myself for the first time in a while.

"Very well then. But before you do, I want to have a celebration. Just one night. I feel we must honour Starlet and Atlas. I have waited so very long to meet you. I also want a dance with my daughter before she leaves again," Gideon sighs, looking at me with hopeful eyes, as though he's wishing for my safety in the days ahead.

"Sure, why not? After all, we could all be dead tomorrow," I reply carelessly, looking over at Cage. He's watching me with bright eyes.

"We still need to find the vessel among you. You got that from what I said before?" I ask my father.

"Yes. I know. You said about wanting to use Azure's visions."

"I know. But I don't think she's really in the place for socialising right now," I sigh.

Goddess, this is such a complete and utter mess. I realise suddenly that my heart is heavy in my chest; it's been that way for a while I think, but I've stopped noticing. I breathe outward, keeping focus on the whirlpool that continues to spin, trying to calm myself.

"There's another way," I remember, thinking back to the Necrocazar.

"Oh?"

"Well, actually there are two. We can either use Ghazi. That's how I first found out. Or, we can have me kiss every Adaro in the land..." I joke but my dad frowns.

"Yeah, Orion might not be too happy about the kissing idea. Also, I'm not ready to see you kissing random strangers quite yet. How about we try seeing if someone can absorb my powers?" Gideon suggests.

"We could do that... but when I first used my powers to absorb things, I only managed it because I was frightened. I was fighting," I admit this.

"Well, we have a colosseum inside. Nothing the Adaro like more than a test of strength. Why don't we set up a tournament?"

"Sure... I guess. Just no more killing okay?" I request with a faux frown, he laughs.

"Of course not. I'll announce it. Come on." Cage turns at my father's final sentiment, leading us back inside the city. I watch Gideon swim next to me, his white tailfin stark in the clear water. He catches me staring out of the corner of his eye and smiles.

I find it hard to believe how quickly everything happens once my father announces the tournament. Adaro come from all over, rising from their frozen homes and flocking to the colosseum . My father blows out of a conch, which I know he must have brought from warmer waters, calling attention over his people. While he does this, I head back up to the tallest tower of the ice palace, seeking my other half. I'm worried. Azure was calm and sobbing when we'd left, but I know that she could turn back to a violent frenzy just as easily. I also need to find Ghazi and Cole. I'll need them as fighters in the colosseum if I'm going to make this thing work.

I reach the top of the spiralling ramp that leads to the tallest room of the highest tower, take a deep breath and open the doors, swimming forward into the room.

Ghazi and Cole are still inside, so is Orion, right where I left him; slumped against the wall, battered and bruised. Azure is still in his lap, her long onyx locks covering her face like a shroud of mourning. I shut the doors behind me softly.

"Hi. I need you two. We're gonna hold a tournament to find the Adaro vessel," I explain. Ghazi looks concerned.

"Don't worry, it'll be a controlled situation. I won't let anyone get hurt. Besides, Gideon is refereeing," I explain, trying to reassure him. Ghazi twists his mouth in a frown, looking concerned still. Slowly he nods. Cole looks back to Orion and Azure. A familial heap of melancholia.

"Can we leave them?" He asks me.

"I don't think she can do anything worse to Orion than she already has," I shrug.

"Well, she could kill him," Cole suggests and I cock my head, scowling. Suddenly a cracked voice reaches us.

"I can hear you. I'm grieving, not deaf," Azure looks around to us, her hair falling from her cheek and back down her back. Her pupils are icy blue. Her skin pale. She looks different. I smile at her. "What are you staring at?" She barks at me. I blanche slightly and she laughs. Orion rises from beneath her, his tailfin sliding out, stiff. He looks broken. His body is a sick masterpiece of coloured bruises. He moves over to me and I place my hand on his chest. He winces.

"Oh God. Sorry," I apologise and he goes to smile, but then winces. Even his cheeks look swollen.

"It's okay… I'll be okay," he says but I don't believe him. "I'm going to take Azure back to the room with me. You go. Go find the vessel." I twist my mouth, not liking the idea of leaving him alone. He senses my reserve. "If she was going to kill me, she'd have done it by now. We're family. It's going to be okay." He places a hand on my cheek, whispering. I watch him wince again, the patch of ribs beneath his arm are exposed, showing purple and red blotches appearing beneath the skin.

"Okay. I'll come and find you later. Hopefully I'll have an answer by then." He doesn't acknowledge that he's heard what I've said. I'm glad, because every minute movement seems to give him agony. Instead, he turns and takes Azure by the hand and leads her past us. Her eyes drop, and it's the first time I've ever realised how she feels about herself. She's ashamed.

Once they're gone, I feel myself exhale a breath I hadn't known I'd been holding. Ghazi and Cole do the same. I turn to them.

"Let's go," I command. "We've got a vessel to find."

Sitting in the chief's box on the balcony surrounding the pit of the colosseum had been exciting at first. The Adaro were extraordinary warriors, there is no denying that. I have been watching them now for hours though and it is wearing thin. There has been no sign of the vessel, not anywhere. No matter how closely I look at the fighting, I'm not getting even a glimmer of anything vessel-like about any of them.

Gideon approaches me, rising up from his refereeing duties down in the snow-covered arena, now speckled with tiny spatters of red from minor injuries and scrapes.

"You look bored," he frowns. I'm draped across the chair that is slathered in thick white furs; my tail cocked over one armrest, and my spine pressing against the other. I exhale.

"How can you tell," I roll my eyes. This has been going on for hours and we still have nothing. Nika and Cage are sitting next to me, looking at me with disapproving stares. I know as queen I should probably pretend to be interested, maybe *oooh* and *aaahh* at regular intervals, but with Orion pulverised, Azure falling apart, and the mermaids being ridiculously over-excitable at the announcement of a celebratory ball, people are exhausting me beyond the point where I give a damn.

"I have brought you some light reading," my dad gestures over to Cage, he swims toward us holding something large and brown in his hands. Gideon takes it from him as he stills, reaching us, and passes me what turns out to be a book.

"What it is? It's huge!" I exclaim and he laughs.

"Sedna's codex. I wondered if it might help us narrow down the search. You flick through it while I start the next match." He turns from me and I watch him leave. I can't believe he respects me so much. I've never had such trust from a parent before. I've not known that a relationship with a parent could be so much like a friendship, but better. I smile to myself, content momentarily.

The moment passes too quickly, but I look down, distracting myself, as I trace my fingers across the cover of the old leather bound book. It's thick and the pages are aged and heavy, preserved in wax as usual. I open the book and the language inside is, thankfully, English. Diagrams of icebergs, text about ice formation and maintenance run on for chapters and chapters. Fighting techniques and indexes of several different types of heat radiating demons catch my attention with terrifying pictures. I flick through them absent-mindedly, not stopping until something catches my eye.

I sit up, and flick back a few pages, enjoying the crinkle of old paper beneath my touch. There it is. A symbol I had seen before. A circle filled in with four intertwining crescent moons. I look down at it, trying to remember where I had seen it. Then I realise I'd seen it twice. Once in Azure's vision, the seal had been carved with the very same design. I know I've seen it somewhere else, somewhere before Azure... I stop, replaying my crystalline memories. The location comes back to me, the epiphany cresting like a wave.

The temple of Atargatis.

The symbol had been crafted into the wall of the temple. The temple where I'd found my scythe. The scythe that had been used to cause so much blood shed. The passage isn't like the others. It's been written in. Not printed. How strange. I read it to myself a few times. It doesn't make sense. It just seems like a lot of crazy ramblings.

The vessel is a container. The vessel is a container. The vessel is a container, a container with bars.

I look at that handwriting. It seems familiar.

The conch blows a hollow sound, demonstrating that the latest match has come to an end. I see that Ghazi has smashed Sirenia's face into the snow. Good.

"Next up... we have another challenger for Ghazi. Cage!" My father's voice booms deep, reverberating through the water and making the particles within it vibrate. His last word hits me and I drop the codex.

"A container with bars... WAIT!" I call out but it's too late. The fight has already started. It doesn't take long for me to witness what I already know to be true. Cage absorbs Ghazi's strength and slams him into the furthest wall with a massively overcharged outward push of both hands. He looks down at himself, clearly confused. The codex forgotten, I swim down into the arena. Ghazi looks at me as if to say *happy now?*

"It's him! He's the vessel!" I point at Cage. I hear gasps above.

"It can't be him. Why on earth would Sedna choose him? He's not even the best fighter!" Cain yells from the stands. I turn to look up at him and shrug. If I knew the answer to his question I wouldn't be fumbling around in the dark for answers myself.

"How did you know? You knew before he even touched Ghazi," Gideon swims over to me, his tailfin barely moving but creating an immense speed.

"The Codex... there was a handwritten piece. It said the vessel was a container, a container with bars..." I begin. Gideon's eyes widen.

"A cage!" He stares at Cage, his eyes wide with surprise. Cage himself looks like he might be sick.

"The lines. They were handwritten," I whisper, feeling confused.

"The lines next to the symbol? The one with the moon?" My father cocks an eyebrow. He smiles knowingly, finally able to remember now I've pointed out the exact location of the information.

"What?" I ask him and he smiles

"That Codex was in the backpack Atlas gave to me. Before I came up here," he laughs. Suddenly I understand.

"That wasn't Atlas' handwriting though…" I say. I've seen Atlas' handwriting recently on the letter he gave to Orion. The scripture doesn't match.

I think hard, trying to remember where I've seen the script before, where I've seen the long swirling lines.

Suddenly it comes to me in a wave of grief. It comes to me that long before I was ever a part of this world, visions of dark things yet to pass had plagued another. We had never seen eye to eye, we had never even been friends, and yet I miss her. I utter her name. Vowing never to forget her sacrifice.

"Starlet."

33
Aurora
CALLIE

It has been three days since we discovered that Cage was Sedna's chosen vessel. Everything is moving so quickly, kind of like the rushing waters of the whirlpool that still holds steady, a rumbling tumult. The full moon is high over the farthest northern peak of the world, melding in with the aquamarine aura of the Aurora overhead. It casts a fresh, mint light across the ice as my head breaks the surface of the water, making me shudder and inhale suddenly, coughing slightly as the frozen night air stings the back of my throat. The fusion of mer and Adaro surface, following my lead as Orion comes up next to me, looking just as shocked as I feel at the cold.

"Oh my God... they can't expect us to walk from here. I'll freeze to death!" He exclaims, grumpy as the temperature saps the last remaining ounces of his attempt to appear manly and strong.

Suddenly, I hear a loud high-pitched whistle. My father surfaces in front of me, his aquamarine eyes sparkling and refracting back the green light of the night directly upon my face.

"Our ride should be coming, fear not." As his last word falls, I hear a barking pierce the night air; a group of men travelling by sled and husky dog are approaching from the Aurora Sanctum. It stands, towering behind them, piercing the sky with its glistening icy turrets that are fused in with stone and other strong looking materials.

"Sled and dog?" I look to Orion surprised and he shrugs.

"We have help here, some Inuk run the Aurora Sanctum when we cannot and ensure everything is ready for our arrival and departures. The Lunar

385

Sanctums are much the same way. I don't know if you are aware of this or not?" Gideon is directing his question to me and I shiver slightly, feeling my face burn under the cold breeze.

"Yes, I knew that. I'm sorry, it's just… I can't imagine why anyone would want to give up their days to live on top of an iceberg," I'm honest, Gideon laughs.

"They have been compensated, I assure you," he smiles, but doesn't elaborate on this fact as the sled and dog teams approach the lake's edge. They quickly turn the sleds, dismount, and place pairs of fur boots on the edge of the water. Each one hurries as they move back to their dogs and grab a mass from the bundle atop their sleds. They stand, an army of devoted individuals, holding open a dozen fur coats. I look up to the moon and feel the change take me, tingles running down my spine, which if I didn't know any better, I'd put down to the chilly waters. I feel myself fall slightly as my legs return, my chin getting coated in the icy cold of the water.

As I'm falling, Orion and Gideon grab hold of me, pushing my body upwards and onto the edge of the lake.

Holy crap, I don't ever think I've been this cold. I groan internally as I place my feet into the indicated pair of fur boots and a man comes forward, enveloping me in a giant fur coat.

If I were anyone else, or anywhere else, I'd be terribly timid, but with the frozen temperatures and the fact I seem to spend all my time naked, I've lost the ability to care about modesty.

"Come," the Inuk man who has smothered me in fur demands, gentle in his tone, pulling me forward with his rough calloused palm. I hear more individuals behind me shivering, their teeth chattering as I stumble across the ice, my legs betraying me with their lack of ability to manoeuvre its slick surface. I slip, beginning to fall backwards but the Inuk man catches me with a kind smile.

"Only you could trip with snow treads on your shoes. Yes?" He laughs and I scowl slightly. Making fun of me really isn't fair in this situation, I'm sopping wet, freezing cold, and naked except for boots and a long coat. Not an ideal situation for anyone. "Sit," my attendee commands, gesturing to the sled. It's hooked up with some kind of white furry sleeping bag. I sigh, well, it's better than walking I suppose. I move forward, sliding into the sleeping bag. Suddenly, I hear someone complaining behind me.

"It's fine. You take Gideon, I'll ride with her," with this sentiment, I feel someone come up behind me. I'm pushed forward, further down into the fur cocoon, as someone sits down at my back, sliding their fur clad feet in beside my thighs and wedging my body between their muscular legs.

"Sorry, it's a bit tight, but there aren't enough sleds," Orion murmurs against the shell of my ear. I breathe him in as I lean backward, feeling the warmth radiating from his chest.

"You just can't deny that you love a woman dripping wet in nothing but snow boots," I purr, laughing slightly as I hear his breathing spike. Suddenly he winces.

"That is true, can you lean forward a bit... I'm still, sort of bruised."

"Oh, sorry. I forgot," I apologise, leaning forward a little and feeling the furs of the inner sleeping bag brush soft against the back of my legs.

"Hike!" I hear a voice call out and suddenly the dogs lurch forward and we begin to move. I fall forward slightly, afraid to move backward and hurt Orion, but he pulls my body back to him, afraid I'll fall, grunting with the pain as my spine collides with his pectorals.

"Ow," I hear him complain. I cringe. He looks so beaten up and broken. I don't want to cause him any more pain than I already have.

"Wow, look at that," I gasp as we round a corner marked with sharp icicles protruding from the iceberg's surface. In front of us is the Aurora Sanctum, it's such an odd looking place. The accents which make the building so very beautiful are all constructed from glistening layers of ice, but I can see that the majority of the building is constructed from stone, sturdy against the Arctic winds and storms that rage so frequently here. It stands, enormous, beneath the night sky, it's size even more evident as we approach and I can't help but stare. It is definitely far more obvious and much larger than the single Lunar Sanctum I've visited, but I suppose around here there's not much need for discretion. As we pull in through an archway of grey cobblestone and flint, held together with ice instead of mortar, I feel a warmth flow over me. The dogs slow and we come to a halt as Orion rises to his feet, offering me a hand and helping me to stand. As the rest of the sleds pull in behind us, the others rise from their fur travelling cocoons as well, taking in the building. The journey here had been over quickly and I watch as the dogs turn around, moving back out of the double doors and into the night to retrieve more guests for tonight's ball. The double doors to the foyer close behind them as the last sled passes through the archway, emitting a dull thud as the two ice constructs meet. The second the doors close, I stop shivering quite so much.

I'm dripping a little, but I'm warmer than I had been out in the open. I pull my coat around myself, worried about indecent exposure.

"Welcome to Aurora Sanctum!" My father bellows to us, his voice reverberating back in a parrot-like echo. The crowd of new arrivals turn to him.

"Please, feel free to take a room. I know you'll all want to dry off and warm up. Clothing and anything else you should need for tonight will be delivered to your rooms shortly. Don't hesitate to ask should you need anything at all. The Ball shall commence in around three hours, as the full moon reaches its peak and the Aurora is at its most vivid. I look forward to seeing you all there," he takes a slight bow, catching my gaze. He's in a white coat, not like mine, which is a dark brown colour. He's such a huge man, he sort of looks like a human-polar bear hybrid at this point. He smiles and gestures up the grand staircase, which is covered in a white silk runner. Orion grabs my hand and I wave slightly to my dad as we pass. He turns and exits the foyer quickly, probably eager to wring out his long white beard.

"Come on, we've got a little while before you have to help Azure..."

"Help Azure with what exactly?" I cut him off. It was news to me that I was helping Azure with anything. I didn't even think she liked me that much.

"I told her you'd help her get ready. She doesn't belong yet, or at least she doesn't feel like it. She's having a hard time. I thought it would do her good. I'm sorry, did I overstep?" His face is so battered as I look up into it, so bruised and pained that I can't say no.

"Of course. No problem. I'm just surprised," I sigh.

"You didn't think she'd come to the party?" He raises an eyebrow and I nod.

We begin to move, walking up the staircase together, our long coats trailing behind us. The rest of the mermaids are arriving on the second round of sleds. I pull Orion along behind me as I speed ahead, not wanting to get caught up in any more chaperoning. I just want to have a moment where I can breathe, slow down, and make sure Orion is okay. We speed along the corridor, picking the furthest door away from the landing of the grand entrance hall, needing to be alone.

"This okay?" Orion asks me, opening the door and standing aside. The room isn't massive, but it's got plush blue carpet and a ceiling made of almost transparent ice, so we can look up at the stars from beneath. The far end of the room has a set of white double doors frozen into their frame.

I step forward, passing Orion as he holds the door open for me. Inside the room is a large circular bed, covered in white furs and plump cushions. There's also a stand-alone roll top bathtub at one end with silver taps that gleam in front of the balcony doors, elevated on a cobble stone platform. I would relish a warm bath right now.

"I don't care. I just want everything to slow down. Here is fine," I turn my neck slightly, eyes frozen on the tub. I hear Orion shutting the thick door and locking it behind us.

"Oh, do you think they have hot water?" I ask, turning to Orion, desperate. He nods.

"I imagine so… though I don't know how."

"I don't even care at this point. I'm so cold," I move forward toward the tub, twisting the cold silver tap that's marked as being for hot water. The water pours, gushing in a steady stream into the tub, steam billowing from it in heady waves upward.

"I never thought I'd be so happy to see a bath," I murmur and Orion chuckles.

"The cold is slowing my healing down too, I think. My body is just getting drained by the cold. It's no wonder the Adaro are so pissed off up front," he laughs and I turn away from the bath to face him.

Orion has dropped his coat to the floor and taken off his boots. Standing in front of a floor-length mirror with an ice-constructed frame and stand in the corner of the room, Orion is examining himself. I can see why immediately, because he's still covered in bruises. We've been through some battles together, I've seen him hurt before, but I've never seen him *let* someone beat the crap out of him. Azure's nails have left his body gouged in places, her tiny fists leaving blue and black marks in others. He looks so pale, so vulnerable. Like he's, for the first time, wearing his pain on the outside, rather than holding it in.

"Do you want to take a bath? Might help," I suggest, looking away, not able to bear the colour marring his skin any longer.

"Sure, that's why..." he turns and smiles, his mouth creasing at the edges. I giggle, trying to remain upbeat in spite of his injuries.

I look down into the tub and turn the taps off, it's nearly full, but I want to be totally covered in the hot water, desperate to feel warm for the first time in what seems like forever. After undressing quickly, I step in, gasping slightly as the heat prickles my skin, burning as it washes away the cold.

A few seconds and a deep pleasurable groan later, I'm neck deep.

Orion walks over with a bottle in hand, which he seems to have magically procured, and pours its contents into the water. The smell of it blooms from the rising steam and gives away its identity as jasmine bath oil.

"That smells amazing," I hum, allowing my body to sink and my muscles to unfurl in the heat.

"Make way for my 'Crowned Ruler-ness'," Orion laughs and I tuck my knees up so their caps rise above the water, resting my chin on them, sighing at the satisfaction of being alone with him. Orion lowers himself into the water and whimpers slightly. As he lays back I stretch out my legs, he takes one of my feet in his hands and begins to rub my soles.

"Oh my God... don't start that or I'll make you do it forever," I moan laying back. It's like now that I've got a moment to myself, I realise how tense I've actually been and how much weight I've been carrying around on my shoulders. He smiles slightly but doesn't say anything. I scan his bruises once more as my gaze falls across him. "I should be doing this for you, look at you," I comment, needing suddenly to take care of him.

"Really?" He cocks an eyebrow.

"Of course," I say, surprised. What? Does he think he's the only one who wants to look after his soulmate?

"Okay," he turns around and moves backward so he's between my

390

thighs, with his back to my head. I put my cheek against his spine, wrapping my arms gently around his waist in the water. I kiss, gently across the flesh of his back, tracing my lips across his skin. Next, I bring my hands up, leaving feather light touches across his shoulders and lulling him into a state of calm. I feel him relax, his form slumping as he exhales deeply. Bringing my fingers up to caress the back of his neck, I watch as goose pimples run rampant across his skin and kiss where I have touched, gently relaxing him, letting my fingertips soothe his battered muscles.

I lose track of time, cupping water in my hands, reaching forward and letting it fall, sprinkling droplets of heat across his pectorals. After a while we just sit, silent as I hold him. My fingers flutter across his temples as he leans back against me, closing his eyes as I tease my hands through his hair, adoring every inch of him. After everything we've been through, I see now how very precious he is, how fragile and vulnerable, just like me. He is completely and utterly one of a kind and he is mine.

We stand, our bodies intertwined, nude and eclipsed by the full moon, shining through the window. My arms twist up like vines, sweeping across the back of his neck and up into his hair, pulling him down to me, my mouth seeking his. There is no more desperation; there is no more anger. I am at peace, taking my time and enjoying him, as I have always wanted to, on my terms. He's not insistent; he's been broken in too many ways over recent days. Instead, I am the insistent one now, showing him where to touch, how to hold. His eyes are full of so many emotions, so many that I realise now just how many he's kept at bay. I place my hand on the side of his face, putting my lips to his and tease him with my tongue. I take his hand and lead him to the bed, lowering him on top of me, not wanting to hurt him. We are strong, in a state of weightlessness above anything real, sensory abandon, and knowing each other so completely that we take each other away from everything that has fallen from beneath us. I love him, for perhaps the first time, with a wholeness I had not known had been missing before. It's not just touch, it's not just wanting.

It is *more*.

It's looking into his eyes and knowing he is feeling the same way I do, knowing he's taking solace in me and experiencing him burying himself in the sanctuary of my arms. It's a freedom I've been seeking for so long, that now I'm practically soaring with him above the pain of this life, I know I was right.

Love is not smothering, though he is wrapped up in me, love is not caging, though I'm caught eternally in his gaze.

Love is freedom. Freedom to grow into the most beautiful version of yourself, upward toward the light of the stars you wish upon, the moon you admire, and like untamed night blooming jasmine.

I'm standing behind Azure, looking over her shoulder at her face in the mirror.

I'm stood in the room she had chosen when she'd arrived via sled and dog, shortly after Orion and I had made our arrival. The room I'm standing in now is constructed of a fusion of ice, stone and crystal, adorned with rugs and sparkling chandeliers, of crystal vanities and wardrobes. Everything sparkles. The double glass doors lead out onto an icy balcony, the rails of which twizzle and swirl, reeking of feminine delicacy. The room is much larger than that Orion and I had found ourselves occupying, but it didn't bother me how large it was as long as it was warm and I was sharing it with him. I glance around again, finding it hard to believe my father created all of this, but then again, maybe that's where I get my sense of style. I look around the room, relaxed after my time with Orion, content. I wonder how long this will last, specifically because I'm about to unveil the dress the Adaro have provided for Azure. I turn, moving toward the garment back, feeling like I'm walking on eggshells.

"I am NOT wearing that!" She scowls after I unzip the garment bag, it's hanging on a curtain rod that has been frozen into the walls of the room, the ice keeping it set in place.

"I know it's not exactly your colour... but..." I begin. Azure rounds on me, twizzling on the vanity stool.

"No. It's pink. Absolutely not. When have I ever worn pink? Do I look like a freaking Princess to you?" She snarls, her eyes diluting black like someone's injected ink into them. I sigh. She definitely isn't a Princess. I'll give her that one.

"These were provided by the Adaro, Azure. They're our hosts. Can you at least *try* to seem grateful?" I plead with her and she rolls her eyes. In a way I'm glad, it's the first time I've seen her acting like her usual sarcastic self in days.

"I'm not going to thank someone for making me look like a shrimp puff," she turns away, bratty as usual. I roll my eyes and laugh, shaking my head, at a loss for what to do next.

There's a quick knock at the door. I walk over to it briskly, knowing I soon need to be ready myself. When I'd offered to do Azure's hair and makeup I hadn't realised it was going to be this traumatic. My hand stings against the cold of the door handle as I heave it open. It's Orion. I breathe out, relieved at his proximity.

"Oh my God... you're healed!" I burst out in a smile at his blemish free appearance. He rolls his eyes.

"Um... no. The mermaids... they made me put make-up on," he looks like he might cry, his manly beauty marred by the mermaid's shallow obsession with perfection and vanity. I can't stop myself from almost choking as I try to suppress my building laughter.

"He's wearing what!?" I hear Azure move from the glass stool on which she's perched, darting behind me to get a view. "Well what do you know, they make even his ugly face look pretty. Damn, I might have to start listening when they're going on about pore shrinkage!" Azure is beside herself, giggling and laughing. Orion cocks his head but a sly smile slips across his lips, unable to ignore the long awaited return of his sister's eccentricity.

"Fine, fine, laugh it up. I was only being nice, coming up here to bring you something to wear that isn't salmon!" He moves to walk away and I grab his arm, noticing the sheen of black silk draped across the sleeve of his tux.

"Don't you dare. I'm not listening to her moan about that dress for hours," I yank the dress from over his arm and dart in, kissing him on the cheek. My lips come away powdery and he winces. "I'll see you when we're ready." I wink at him and close the door.

For a moment, just a moment, I forget that tomorrow we're leaving this place. Leaving the Adaro and heading somewhere new and unknown. The reality that this is all temporary silliness before the harshness of real life comes back in and kicks us all in the stomachs once more. I sigh.

Azure looks at me impatiently as she sits back down at the mirror.

"Well, what are you waiting for? Beautify me!"

If I'd thought the Lunar Sanctum was large I'd been wrong. The ballroom of the Aurora Sanctum is tall, spiralling upward in an icy shard that pierces the night sky with its acuteness. The room is huge, with windows lining every wall so that it's almost as though we're floating. I can look out into the night and see the bluish, green hues swirl and dance. The night is drawing on and the Adaro are dancing, talking with members of the mer pod, trying to learn about our customs, our ways. Gideon and I have spoken about them fighting with us before, but as I look around at all the happy faces and then back up into the face I had most wished to see for so long, I can't help but wonder if I want to be responsible for putting yet more lives at risk.

"What are you thinking about?" My father asks me. A jazz band is playing. As it turns out, a few of the Adaro are righteous on the saxophone. Marina has offered to sing and is belting out Unforgettable by Nat King Cole.

"Everyone is so happy. I wish I didn't have to leave," I sigh.

"Well, once this is all over you can come back whenever you like. You know my doors are always open to you," he promises me this, kissing me on the forehead and pulling me in close to his hard body.

"If I'm still alive." I murmur, fearful.

"You will be." He replies, so sure.

"How do you know?" I ask him, biting my bottom lip.

"Because I haven't had time to know you yet. You can't go anywhere, because I need more time with you. I love you so much already and I barely even know you." It's exactly what I need to hear, but a lump forms in my throat as we dance, wondering if this will be the last time. Then I realise if this is the last time, I better savour it.

"I love you, dad," I whisper. My dad's forehead is creased, his eyes watering slightly.

"Thank you for finding me," he whispers back.

I feel eyes on me all of a sudden and hairs rise on the back of my spine. I know what it means immediately. Orion is watching.

"Thank you for giving us your army. Your people. The Adaro are incredible," I say it, knowing it's a lot to ask.

"No matter what happens, we'll be there. The question... is when," Gideon frowns. Suddenly Orion is behind me. Gideon stops dancing.

"I might have an answer to that. Azure just had a vision. The blood moon." He runs his fingers through his hair, his black tux slimming his figure and making him look taller.

"But that's not long away..." I think, starting to panic. My heart picks up the pace, thumping a frantic rhythm.

"Calm down, Callie. It's okay. We have time. I've been speaking with Cage and with Nika. We're going to be prepared. If Saturnus and Solustus want a war, we're sure as hell going to give them one." He's animated, perhaps more animated than I've ever seen him in his role as ruler. It feels like at the death of Starlet something within him has snapped, allowing him to heal, come back stronger, and ready to rule.

"You've got that right." Gideon nods, removing his arm from around my waist and letting my hand drop.

"We still have five more vessels to find though, and these 'pieces of eight', whatever the hell they are. This is *if* Vex is in fact the vessel for Poseidon!" I try to express my anxiety as I turn to Orion. His eyes meet mine and comfort me instantly.

"I know. We can do this. I know we can," Orion startles me with his confidence.

"Well look at you all confident," I hear Azure's dull tone travel over his shoulder. I look back to her, appreciating the work I'd done. She's in a black strapless floor-length gown. She looks so pretty, and then she pulls the top of her bustier up under her arms, reigning in her assets. The picture is ruined. So much for ladylike. "What? Don't look at me with that horrified expression. It's all fun and games until they pop out of the top and I blind someone!" She says this with a deadpan, serious expression. Orion snorts and I smack my hand to my face. Oh dear God...

"Azure... why don't we just sit you down over here... so you don't injure yourself," Gideon takes her by the hand and she looks stunned at his forwardness. Orion can't help but laugh and I nearly choke on air.

"My sister everybody..." Orion makes a faux announcement. I purse my lips together trying to reign in my laughter. I must be ladylike... I must be ladylike... I am a queen, I remind myself of this, inhaling deep. My father waves to me as he takes Azure to a nearby table and sits down with her, they begin to talk about something and suddenly she starts to laugh.

"Well, I'm glad to see she's finally back to her old self... sort of." I roll my eyes.

"Rather unkempt and crude than beating me senseless I suppose," Orion sighs. Suddenly we both realise we're standing awkwardly in the middle of a dancefloor, Adaro couples swirling around us, some of them on ice skates, twirling and spinning together in antiquated rhythm. I had also been offered a pair, but I'm not even confident on two feet half of the time, so the thought of blades attached to them makes me even more nervous about falling on my face in front of these new people than normal.

I look down at myself and fold my gloved hands over one another. I'm wearing a white fur wrap over the top of my shoulders and an ice blue A-line gown that had been chosen by my father. My hair is up in a messy bun and curls fall around my face. I catch Orion looking at me as I gaze out upon the northern lights.

"Do you want to go out onto the balcony? The air is refreshing. It might help you feel calmer," he suggests. I nod, giving him my gloved hand. He takes it and we sweep across the floor of the icy ballroom floor, careful not to slip, especially because I'm in heels. We reach the large glass doors and Orion opens them before me. I hear a sigh and look back; the mermaids are watching us. I poke my tongue out at them and they all look at me, mock offended looks plastered onto their heavily made faces.

Outside on the balcony, the chill of the Arctic rustles my fur wrap, making the hairs move in a gentle sway.

"Wow!" I say, looking up at the Aurora Borealis, I run to the edge of the balcony, reaching the railing and leaning over, looking up into the diamond scattered deep blue of its velvet. The lights flicker, shimmering in and out. It's incredible. Every shade of green from aqua to jade undulates.

I feel my eyes widen. "It's so beautiful!" I gasp, propping my head into my hands, resting my elbows on the icy sheen of the guardrail.

"Yes. You are," Orion announces, his eyes connecting with mine as my head snaps sideways in response to his compliment. His hands are hidden in the pockets of his pants and he's staring at me, leaning back against the edge of the balcony. I turn my body to him, blushing.

"Thanks," I reply, bringing my hand up to cover my mouth shyly. I walk over to him, keeping his gaze tenderly. I wrap my arms around him, resting my head over his heart.

"I can't believe tomorrow we could be on the other side of the world," I admit.

"I know. We could be anywhere," Orion puts his arms around my spine and I look up at him. "I said I'd show you the world, remember?" He smiles at me and I narrow my eyes coyly.

"Ah… because of course you knew this was going to happen…" I jibe and he laughs.

"Yes, of course. I purposefully allowed for the destruction of an ancient city just so we could go on a 'jolly holiday'." He cocks his head, widening his eyes in distaste.

"Well, now that you mention it I thought that was suspicious." I laugh and he rolls his eyes.

"You are extraordinarily unfunny… you know that?" He says with a deadpan expression.

"Well compared to you with a face full of make-up I'd say that's true, you do make quite the Miss Teen Mermaid 2016." I contort my mouth into a pucker and wiggle my eyebrows.

"I have the crown… got a sash stowed somewhere?" He jokes back and this surprises me.

"The man who doesn't know what In 'N' Out burger is, knows about the ins and outs of beauty pageants? Well that's nothing short of suspicious. Something you aren't telling me?" I prod him in the chest with a gloved finger and I immediately regret it as he winces.

"Starlet loved to watch them. She thought they were fascinating... she used to love to yell out how fat they all looked in their bathing suits. She was always a huge spoil sport too, because she always knew who was going to win..." Orion starts to laugh but then trails off and looks out into the night in deep thought. "I miss her." He sighs, pulling me closer to him and resting his chin on the top of my head.

"I know. I'm so sorry. She was so brave, in the end. Your father would have been so proud of her." I try to comfort him but there are no words to fill the hole Starlet has left behind.

"It makes me feel better to think that they're together right now." He smiles a little, melancholy, but at peace. The anger I had known to rage inside him before has been extinguished by the cold of this place. "There's a fight coming though, I can feel it. It's unavoidable and people are going to die. More people..." He looks out across the empty, snow covered waste land of the night covered arctic, his face looking stormy and determined. "Starlet would have made a better ruler than I ever will." I don't know how to reply to this, I don't know what kind of ruler Starlet would have made, nor what he saw in her that sparked such a claim. Their relationship was so different from any I'd seen between siblings. I breathe out, needing to lighten the mood.

"It will be okay though, right?" I ask him.

"I don't know... I could lie to you and say yes. But that's not real," he sighs.

"No more fantasies," I whisper.

"No. Our lives are filled with enough fantasy for anybody," Orion laughs and I nod my head against his lapels. "I know one thing though," he continues as I listen to his breathing. "You're strong enough to handle whatever comes next." He bends down and kisses me, his lips gracing mine. My heart rests beneath the stars as I kiss him. It had been at war for too long. For now, it would be my sanctuary, just like Orion.

"You really believe in me?" I say to him as he breaks the kiss. We stand beneath the aurora's heady magic, its glow illuminating our faces.

Orion looks down at me, his eyes sparkling, reflecting back at me all the magic of the Northern Lights.

"Always."

34
Sacrifice

SOLUSTUS

The Necrimad sits back on its haunches, the colossal size of it boggling even my mind. It breathes in, its scales flaring and parting, revealing a white-hot orange glow from beneath. Its eyes burn with the same intensity and every time it moves, the very earth beneath its talons rumbles, shifting. I watch as the Psiren army struggle, idiots that they are, to contain it. To place the chains forged by the metal master around the beast's neck, around it's legs. It moves once more, swatting them away with its skull, which is covered in spiny protrusions. It impales one or two of them, and I watch as they flail, laughing at their misfortune. I'm watching from far away, mainly because the beast can exhale gallons of boiling water into the surrounding ocean in mere seconds. It is magnificent. I see more of Alyssa's children coming back from the place where it rests, their skin boiling, falling from bone like it were no more than pork from a spit-roasted pig. I look around, realising I haven't seen Alyssa lately. Where the hell is she? Do I really care?

"Solustus. Brother. Isn't it magnificent?" I hear the slithering tones of Saturnus creep toward me. His face is maniacally happy. In this moment I can see the family resemblance between him and Caedes certainly.

"Yes. It is. And yet…. It is still in flesh." I'm impatient now, for the first time that I can remember. It has always been so very illusive, the premise of power, and yet to see it in flesh, in a form that causes the very men made from its power to tremble, it makes me hungry for the power I know is mine. It makes me wanton. It makes me desire.

"Yes. Now all we need to do is wait. Wait for the return of those with light magic running in their veins. Destroy it... and we shall be victorious."

"And you're certain? Absolutely certain, that there are only a few mer who survived?"

"Of course I'm certain! I'm not incompetent! They'll come back here and we'll pick them off one by one. We will succeed!" My brother is ranting, raving even. "Then that bitch... she'll know what she was missing when she chose Atlas... and Poseidon...."

"What was that?!" I demand, cutting him off, suddenly feeling uneasy. Saturnus has never spoken of Poseidon in such an angry tone before. I feel my suspicions grow. Wondering if he has motives I don't know about.

"Oh... he'll have to return the power to its rightful place. Of course."

"Yes. Right you are, brother," I say, looking down my nose at him.

"Have you seen Alyssa around here?" Saturnus asks me, as though he'd read my previous thought. I laugh at his intrigue.

"Oh Saturnus you think you're so sly... don't tell me you're softening to something as ridiculous as your soulmate now?" I laugh, knowing full well that my brother, after his death, could never stand the love of anything beneath the rank of Goddess.

"Would you desist in being so goddamn vile? The thought you'd even suggest I would look at such a revolting creature... just ugh. You know full well that's why I stuck her with that stupid merman Gideon, Solustus. Though of course you can't deny her devotion did become incredibly useful in the end, him breaking her heart and unlocking her true potential as Psiren, it was genius if I do say so myself. I couldn't have orchestrated it any better if I'd tried. That's the only reason I asked. I thought a little more recruiting to the cause couldn't hurt. Besides, Alyssa is too stupid to work out that I was her soulmate, hidden in plain sight. However, *somebody* didn't find me soon enough to stop my soul being split in half by that...bitch. So I'd watch your tongue. It's your fault." He goes on and on like this for a few minutes and I zone out, thinking back to the night his soul had been split. It had been only a few days before I had tainted his blood with Poseidon's fury, a shame, but not entirely useless as he's suggesting. Alyssa was stupid and naïve when she had turned, being a prostitute in her mortal life, she wasn't exactly clear on what the difference between love and sex was. Besides, by the time Saturnus had met her, his heart was blackened and love was impossible, but confusing her and manipulating her for his own agenda had been easy. I remember speaking the truth of the matter aloud to Vex, a generous piece of wisdom that I hope he'll remember and cherish...

Psirens don't love. It's not who we are.

"I haven't seen her." I say lazily, bored of the conversation. Saturnus halts and cocks his head, dismissing the thought of Alyssa altogether before continuing on with business as usual.

"Oh... another thing before I go, Solustus. Regus caught Vexus having a vision. He's torturing him as we speak."

"What!? That should have been the first thing out of your mouth!" I bark. Coming up close to Saturnus, my grey eyes burn into his yellow pupils. I push my rapier into his stomach ever so lightly. Letting him know I'm not playing around.

"Apologies, but I thought I'd take the issue in hand. I'm sure you'd agree it needed to be handled swiftly."

"I should have been informed!"

"It's done now, Solustus. Calm yourself," Saturnus cocks an eyebrow and I want to slash his abdominals open and watch his guts fall out.

"I'll calm myself when you stop taking goddamn liberties! This is my army, my destiny! You're just... my sidekick," I spit. Saturnus looks at me and blinks. A mask of cool composure rolls in across his features.

"Very well, brother, I apologise. You are, of course, in charge," his expression remains still.

"Yes. That's right... Now go and get that beast handled. The Psirens are failing miserably."

"Of course..." Saturnus smiles.

"Of course... what?" I demand, feeling myself inflate at my defeat of his attempt to take my power away from me.

"Of course... sir," Saturnus cocks an eyebrow once more, surprised. Then turning away, he swims over the top of the ruined city into the distance to do my bidding.

Something stirs within my psyche as I watch him go. A memory, something that would have troubled me once. For now, I am too impatient to care. I want my power. I want the death of the mer. I want what is rightfully mine. The wrath of Poseidon behind me; and mine for all eternity.

Epilogue

CALLIE

The water of the whirlpool thunders around in cyclical motion, like a race car speeding around a track. It's unstoppable, the momentum too great for me to even think I'll be able to survive going in, let alone coming out the other side somewhere totally random. The pod is at my back and I can hear their anxiety.

I turn to my father, his large aquamarine eyes full of concern for me.

"Goodbye," I whisper, trying not to cry in front of the other mer. I don't want to leave him though. It feels like I only just found him.

"Don't cry. I'll see you again before you know it."

"I know. It just feels like I only just got here," I explain my frustration at having to move on. He nods.

"I know, but be strong now. I have to prepare the army for war. We'll see each other again, I promise." He lets me go, letting his lips fall on me gently, kissing my scalp. I'm covered in armour provided by the Adaro, so it's uncomfortable, but I'm not about to leave without a hug. I back away and Orion moves forward taking my place. He holds out a hand. Gideon looks down at it, before taking it and shaking a few times vigorously. "You take care of my daughter! If not there'll be hell to pay," he tries to seem stern, to put on a frown, but there's no mistaking the fondness in his eyes for the young ruler.

"Of course, sir, I wouldn't have it any other way Orion turns away from him.

"Come on everyone," Cole calls back to the mermaids. They're in armour too, but they've covered it in glittering diamonds and strings of pearls. I have no idea where they got them, but they look ridiculous.

Orion and I approach the whirlpool. I grab his hand, turning and looking

405

at him, drinking in his face before we take the plunge. He's plated and sporting bracers as usual. The trident I took from the Cryptopolis is pressing flat against his spine. Our bracers clang together as I knot my fingers through his, feeling my pulse heighten.

I turn back. The Adaro are watching us intensely and I know there's no backing down now. We need to show them we're not afraid of anything. Even if it is huge and spinning and terrifying.

"Okay. On three…" I say to Orion. He breathes in, moving us still closer to the whirlpool.

"One…" he kisses my hand.

"Two," I smile back at him.

"Three!" We're ripped apart as we meet with the force of the spinning water, finally getting close enough to be swept up in its devastating wake.

It's not the most uncomfortable I've ever been, I mean, I have died twice, but it isn't far off. I feel my joints pulling from their sockets and my skull rattling around, the water pounding it. I can't see anything, can't hear anything except the rush of the cold icy water. I try to pull it into my lungs, to breathe, but even that hurts. I try to look for Orion, but all I can see is a melding of colours and faces, one running into another. I would scream but the rush of the water, the pushing and pulling of the spinning currents, takes my breath and all noise with it, chucking us into what feels like a vacuum outside of time and space.

Suddenly the spinning stops. Everything rights itself in the blink of an eye and I'm hurtling toward something. A hand grabs me and I feel hard muscle against my back as I'm pulled to a stationary upright position. I sigh, relieved. Orion must have caught me.

I look as the whirlpool dissipates before me in the new and murky waters. Orion comes into view. I inhale, shocked as a blade finds itself shoved beneath my throat, threatening to slit my carotid and leave me for dead. My captor speaks.

"And what, in the name of Loch Ness, is a pretty wee lass like you, doing in a place like this?"

END OF BOOK 2

Acknowledgements

Another chapter finished, another book done. This one has gone so incredibly fast and I'd like to thank my nanny in particular for supporting me and my dreams as you have done throughout my life, I couldn't have done it without you. A big thanks to my parents and my wonderful partner Mark, who listen to me rant and rave whenever I doubt myself, or the quality of my ideas. This book is very much about growing up, the fact that age is just a number and that there is always more to learn. Thanks to my content and copy editors the wonderful Jaimie Cordall and Kristine Schwartz, who constantly remind me that I have not, nor probably ever will, fully master the complexities of the English language. You keep me grounded and sane, so thank you! Also I'd like to give a special shout out to my soul sisters and partners in crime, to whom this book was dedicated, Authors Ali Winters and Juanita Gracian, who have watched me flounder (pun intended!) and struggle in the run up to release and who never left me or stopped believing I could do it.

For my readers, please remember this novel isn't like book one, it's not flowers and rainbows and equinox floating on a cloud of fantastical perfection. Instead it's about the real. That which, for me, must be treasured most of all, because even when our lives become that which is close to fantasy, we must not forget that they will never last forever. It is this that makes them that much more precious.

Want more Tidal Kiss Trilogy magic?

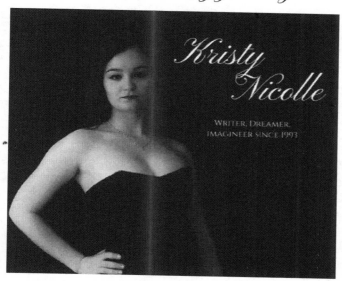

Want to know what's next for Callie and Orion?
Follow the Trilogy @
Website: www.kristynicolle.com
Facebook: https://www.facebook.com/TheTidalKissTrilogy
Twitter: Nicolle_Kristy
Instagram: authorkristynicolle
Goodreads: Search The Tidal Kiss Trilogy

Photographs by the fabulously talented Trish Thompson

QUEENS OF *Fantasy*
Trilogy One - Book Two

ABOUT THE QUEENS OF FANTASY SAGA

Kristy Nicolle's Queens of Fantasy Saga is a collection of 3 trilogies, following the lives of three extraordinary women and their journeys, both personal and fantastical, into three unique but interconnected fantasy worlds. The first trilogy in the saga, 'The Tidal Kiss Trilogy', captures the fantastical underwater world of the Occulta Mirum and its scaly tailed residents as their world, which seemed stable for so long, begins to shift.

The following two trilogies in the series are yet to be announced.
Stay tuned for more information.

Made in the USA
Charleston, SC
24 June 2016